A shot rang out, cruiser.

"Get down!" Jackson shouted and laid a hand across her back to push her down.

Rhea's heart thumped loudly as she struggled with her seat belt. Another shot sounded. She finally got her belt free and sank even lower, hoping the dashboard would provide cover.

Jackson had thrown his door open and knelt behind it for protection as he scoured the area. Another shot rang out, coming straight at them, and Jackson grabbed his radio.

"Shots fired. Aspen Ridge Road."

Another bullet pinged against the door by Rhea.

"Identify yourself," the dispatcher asked.

"Detective Whitaker. Regina PD. We're pinned down. Shots fired."

"Sending backup," the dispatcher said.

Jackson reached for his own weapon and shouted out to their assailant. "Police! Backup's on the way!"

The response was the roar of a car engine starting up and the squeal of tires...

COLORADO RESCUE

New York Times Bestselling Author

CARIDAD PIÑEIRO

&

CINDI MYERS

Previously published as *Cold Case Reopened*
and *Ice Cold Killer*

 **HARLEQUIN®**

ISBN-13: 978-1-335-42696-3

Recycling programs for this product may not exist in your area.

Colorado Rescue

Copyright © 2022 by Harlequin Enterprises ULC

Cold Case Reopened
First published in 2021. This edition published in 2022.
Copyright © 2021 by Caridad Piñeiro Scordato

Cold Case Reopened deals with topics some readers might find difficult, such as sexual assault and domestic violence. If you or someone you love is the subject of domestic violence, please consider contacting the National Domestic Violence Hotline at 1-800-799-7233.

Ice Cold Killer
First published in 2019. This edition published in 2022.
Copyright © 2019 by Cynthia Myers

For questions and comments about the quality of this book, please contact us at CustomerService@Harlequin.com.

Harlequin Enterprises ULC
22 Adelaide St. West, 41st Floor
Toronto, Ontario M5H 4E3, Canada
www.Harlequin.com

Printed in U.S.A.

CONTENTS

New York Times and *USA TODAY* bestselling author **Caridad Piñeiro** is a Jersey girl who just wants to write and is the author of nearly fifty novels and novellas. She loves romance novels, superheroes, TV and cooking. For more information on Caridad and her dark, sexy romantic suspense and paranormal romances, please visit caridad.com.

Books by Caridad Piñeiro

Harlequin Intrigue

Trapping a Terrorist
Cold Case Reopened

Visit the Author Profile page
at Harlequin.com for more titles.

COLD CASE REOPENED

Caridad Piñeiro

To my absolutely fabulous and amazing agent Michelle Grajkowski. Thank you for believing in me. Thank you for being such a beautiful person who can always bring a smile to my face and make me laugh. May we share many, many more slices of cheesecake together in the future!

Chapter 1

It was hard to believe that such beauty possibly held unspeakable evil.

Rhea Reilly stood on the shore of the mountain lake where six months earlier her twin sister, Selene, had disappeared on a cold fall night.

Rhea's artist's eye took in the scene before her. The waters of the lake sparkled like diamonds beneath a sunny cerulean sky. At the farthest end of the lake, the waters tumbled over a spillway for the dam that held back a rush of water during a spring thaw or heavy rain. In the distance, ragged mountains leaped into the sky, still frosted with the remnants of winter snow at the highest elevations.

Normally she would have savored painting such a lovely sight, but not today, when it might be her sister's watery tomb.

Rhea hugged her arms tight around herself, closed her eyes and listened to the soft lap of the water against the rocky shores of the lake. Imagined Selene standing there that fateful night, tapping out the message she'd sent to Rhea.

I can't take it anymore. I can't. I'm finally going to do something about it.

The police had taken that text to mean that Selene had decided to end her life that night, right there on the shores of those stunningly beautiful mountain waters. But Rhea wasn't convinced.

Although her sister had been troubled the last few months, Rhea was certain that Selene would never take her life. If anything, it was more likely that Selene's husband had killed her, but the police in Selene's hometown had been unable to find enough evidence to charge him. No-body homicides were apparently very difficult to prosecute.

The police here in Regina, Colorado, where Selene's car had been found by the lake, were convinced that her sister had committed suicide, even though they also hadn't been able to find Selene's body.

But Rhea was sure her sister wasn't dead. There was something inside her, that special twin connection they had always shared, that had been saying from the very beginning that Selene was alive and hurting.

That was why she'd undertaken her own investigation once her sister's case had become inactive because the police had run out of leads.

Rhea dashed away the tears that had leaked from beneath eyes screwed shut.

Her sister was alive and, if she wasn't, her husband was responsible. She intended for the police to do something about it based on the information she had collected over the last six months. But for the truth to come out, she needed more corroborating evidence and only the police could provide the resources to accomplish that.

She whirled, stumbled a bit on the rough rocks beneath her feet. Righting herself, she marched to her car, which she had parked on the street near where Selene's sedan had been found. The street would have been deserted when Selene had texted her that night.

Rhea stopped to look around, examining the scene. Along the edges of the lake, a marina spread out across the shore. Dozens of boats were parked at the docks behind a large building that held a restaurant, a marina office and a shop that sold supplies for boaters, as well as tourists, partaking in the lake's many summer activities.

Across the way were a few homes and in one of those homes was a witness who had seen Selene park and walk toward the lake. The older woman hadn't thought much of it because people often stopped, even at night, to take in the splendor of the lake.

Rhea intended to speak to her, but hopefully with the police to back her up and add their own expertise to the interrogation.

The police.

It all kept circling around to needing their assistance, so it was time she got going and spoke to them about Selene's case.

She got in her car and headed to Main Street and the Regina Police Station. As she cruised down Main

Street, she was once again struck by the loveliness of the town. It was postcard-perfect, with its charming downtown filled with an eclectic mix of shops that catered to locals as well as the tourists who would visit for skiing and water sports.

Rhea found a spot just a block shy of the police station, parked and grabbed the thick folder bulging with the information she had gathered over the many months. With it tucked under her arm, cradled as securely as a newborn baby, she walked to the police station and paused at the base of the steps.

Like everything else about this town, the police station looked like something off a movie set. The building blended harmoniously with the other structures along Main Street. On either side of the wide steps leading to the door, spring flowers in a riot of colors cascaded over the edges of the terraced garden. Bright pink, purple and blue blossoms waved at her in welcome as a slight breeze swept across the street, still a bit cold despite it being early spring.

The chill settled in her bones as if warning her that she might not be happy with what she found inside.

She dragged in air through her nostrils and then expelled it with a harsh breath.

Time to get going. She stomped up the stairs and to the reception desk.

The sergeant at the desk did a little double take, as if seeing a ghost, and Rhea understood. She and Selene were identical twins and Selene's case had caused quite a stir in the normally placid town. It was unlikely that the police officer hadn't seen a photo of Selene in the station or on the news.

"I'm Rhea Reilly. Selene's sister. I was hoping to

speak to the chief if he had a moment," she said. She hadn't made an appointment because she wasn't sure of the welcome she'd get. Especially considering how poorly the meeting with the Avalon police chief had gone. What with rumors about the Blue Code, she hadn't wanted to take any chances; the Regina police chief might not see her if word of her mission had traveled to him.

"I'll see if he's available," the officer said and gestured for her to take a seat in the reception area, but Rhea had too much nervous energy to sit. She paced as the young woman called the chief. Heard the murmurs as the officer spoke to him before rising to say, "The chief will see you, but he has only a few minutes before another meeting."

The young woman gestured toward the back of the building where the police chief stood at the door to his office. He was dressed in a bright blue shirt the color of the lake waters and dark blue pants. The shirt strained against a bull chest and broad midsection. A shiny gold badge pinned to the right breast of his shirt identified him as the chief while on the left breast the town's emblem was embroidered on a patch. White, blue and gold colors on the badge-shaped patch showed the mountains in the background, skiers on a slope to the left and a swimmer in waves to the right. *Tourists. The town's lifeblood*, Rhea thought. Because of that, a murder in their town was the last thing the police and town officials would want. Easier just to call it a suicide.

The chief did a "come here" wave with his hand, but his weathered face was set in stern lines, his mouth a harsh slash that was clearly at odds with his gesture.

Despite his less than friendly demeanor, she pushed

through the barrier the desk sergeant buzzed open and marched to the chief's office, her folder tucked tight against her.

As she did so, she passed one man who sat hand-cuffed on a bench by an officer's desk. Rough-looking with a heavily bearded face, he jumped, almost startled as she neared, and the color drained from his face. His hard eyes, dark and brooding, widened in surprise much like the desk sergeant's before he schooled the reaction.

Something about him sent a shiver of apprehension through her, but she tamped it down and proceeded to the chief's office.

"Miss Reilly," the chief said with a dip of his head and sweep of his hand to welcome her.

She sat in the chair across from him as he took a spot behind his desk. Like everything else about the town, the desktop and nearby bookcase were neat as a pin. So neat they almost looked staged, but then again, she remembered this chief being quite orderly and controlled. Compassionate even in the days after Selene's disappearance.

"What can I do for you today?" he said, as he laced his fingers together and leaned his thick forearms on the edge of his desk in a slightly friendlier posture.

The folder sat in her lap, heavy against her thighs. She shifted her hands across the smooth surface of it and said, "I really appreciate all that you've done for my family, Chief Robinson."

He dipped his head and his attitude softened a bit more. "Thank you. I know it was a difficult time for you. Rhea, right?"

She nodded. "Yes, Rhea. It was a difficult time and,

again, I appreciate all that you did. What I'm hoping is that you'll reopen the case. I have new information—"

Chief Robinson held up his hands to stop her. "Miss Reilly, this isn't *Murder, She Wrote*. I'm sure you think you've unearthed some 'new evidence,'" he said, using air quotes for emphasis. "But we did a thorough investigation."

Anger built inside her at his dismissiveness, but she battled it back, certain it wouldn't help. "I know you did, but I've gotten more information—"

"Let me guess. From social media," he said with a rough laugh and wag of his buzz-cut head of salt-and-pepper hair.

She couldn't deny it. "Some of it. All I'm asking is that you let me show you what I've collected. Let me explain why I think…" She hesitated. The chief would never believe that Selene was still alive, but at a minimum she hoped that he would reopen the investigation and either find Selene or her killer.

At her silence, Chief Robinson leaned toward her again, compassion replacing his earlier disbelief. "Look, Miss Reilly. Rhea. I know this must still be difficult for you, but we have limited resources to… expend on this case."

She was certain he had really wanted to say "waste on this case" but she pressed on.

"Please, Chief Robinson. All I'm asking is that you look at this," she said and held up the bloated folder for him to see.

The chief stood. "I'm sorry. I have another meeting in a few minutes and have to prepare for it."

She'd been dismissed. Again, just like at the Avalon

Police Department in her sister's hometown. But she didn't intend to give up.

"I'll be staying at the Regina Inn for a few days. Just in case you change your mind. And if not, rest assured I'll be reaching out to people in town to complete my investigation."

With that she shot out of her chair and escaped his office, her veiled threat hanging in the air. She was sure the chief would be less than pleased with her playing detective on his home turf. It would draw too much attention to the fact that not all was as perfect as it seemed.

She rushed through the pen of police officers and clerks, past the reception area and out the door, nearly running into an officer as he walked up the steps to the station.

"So sorry, miss," the officer said and caught her as she stumbled and dropped the folder. The rubber band around the folder snapped, and papers spilled out. She bent to collect them before the breeze swept them away.

Detective Jackson Whitaker kneeled to pick up the thick folder the young woman had dropped and round up loose papers. But, as he handed them to her and met her gaze, he felt gobsmacked.

Selene Davis. Her beautiful face was indelibly etched into his brain since he had been the one to find Selene's abandoned car by the lake.

Only Selene was dead, which meant this had to be her twin sister.

But before he could say anything, Selene's sister snatched the folder and papers from his hands and stomped off.

Whoa, so not happy, he thought and walked into the office, wondering what had set off the young woman. As he entered, he said to the desk sergeant, "That was—"

"Rhea Reilly. She wanted to speak to the chief," Desk Sergeant Millie Rodriguez answered and jerked her head in the direction of the chief's office.

Speaking of the chief, he stood at the door to his office, his features a picture of upset. His lips were set in a tight line, and his beefy arms crossed against his thick chest. With a sharp wave of his hand, the chief summoned Jackson to come over.

Certain that he knew just what this meeting would be about, Jackson hurried to the chief's office but didn't take a seat. He stood before the desk, hands jammed into his pockets, rocking back and forth on his heels as he waited for the older man to sit. Once he had, the chief looked up at him and said, "That was Rhea Reilly."

Jackson nodded. "I gathered as much. She's a dead ringer for her sister. Twins if I remember correctly."

"You do. Rhea has been doing her own investigating and wants us to reopen her sister's case," Chief Robinson said and laid his muscled forearms on the edge of his desk.

Jackson considered the request, but only for a second. "It's hard for people to accept that someone they knew and loved would kill themselves. I imagine it's even harder for a twin."

The chief's eyebrows drew together in puzzlement, creating a deep furrow across his broad forehead, and Jackson quickly explained, "That twin connection some people claim they have."

"You believe that?" the chief asked, leaned back in

his chair and steepled his fingers before his lips, scrutinizing Jackson as if he was a bug under a microscope.

Considering what he had seen of Selene's sister and her anger, she clearly believed something contrary to what their report had said. Because of that, Jackson shrugged. "Stranger things have been known to happen."

The chief continued to stare at him, as if sizing him up. "You know you're my choice to replace me when I retire next year."

Jackson nodded. "I do, and I appreciate your confidence in me. I promise that you'll be leaving the department in good hands."

"I think so. Maybe it's time I turn over some of the more difficult tasks to you, so that you acclimate to that position."

Jackson wasn't above hard work. His years in the military and on the police force had been filled with long days. Tough days, like the day he'd finally had to close Selene's case as a suicide. It had bothered him then because, much like Rhea, it had been hard for him to understand how a beautiful and vibrant woman with so much to live for could just walk into the lake and end her life.

"Whatever you need me to do, Chief," he said with a dip of his head to confirm his acceptance of any task his boss assigned to him.

"I want you to look at Rhea Reilly's information and then tell her she's barking up the wrong tree."

Chapter 2

Rhea had barely finished unpacking her things when the knock came at the door.

She hurried there and threw it open, expecting to find room service with the extra blanket she'd requested. That earlier chill hadn't left her, not that a blanket would end it, but it had been worth a try.

It wasn't room service. It was six-plus feet of lethal male, dressed in police blues, with a white Stetson held in hands that he shifted uneasily on the brim. He had shortly cropped sandy-brown hair that screamed former military and eyes the gray of lake waters on a dreary day. He clenched and unclenched his chiseled jaw as he stood there, obviously hesitant, before he finally said, "You should be more careful and check to see who it is before you open the door."

Anger ignited instantly at his chastisement. "I was expecting room service. Not the police."

He tipped his head, seemingly sorry, but he didn't strike her as the type to apologize. Not willingly anyway. And it occurred to her then that he was the officer she'd run into outside the police station. The one who'd helped her pick up her papers and whom she hadn't thanked.

"Rhea Reilly," she said and held out her hand. "I'm sorry I was so rude before. I was upset."

"I understand. Detective Jackson Whitaker. Jax to my friends." A ghost of a smile danced across full lips, and he enveloped her hand with his big calloused one.

His touch roused a mix of emotions. Surprising comfort. Unwelcome electricity and heat.

"We're not friends…yet," she said as he continued holding her hand, longer than expected. Longer than necessary. She withdrew her hand from his and wrapped her arms around herself. "And I doubt that you can possibly understand."

That slight dip of his head came again, as if accepting her statement, and he motioned inside her room with his Stetson. "Do you mind if I come in?"

She both did and didn't mind. Something about his presence was unnerving, but if he was here, maybe it meant that the chief had reconsidered her request.

"Please," she said and waved him in.

He entered and, as he did so, his gaze swept the room, assessing. Observant. A cop's eyes taking in the scene and immediately focusing on the thick folder sitting on a small bistro table beside French doors to a balcony facing the lake. The lake was a constant reminder of why she was here.

"May I?" he said and pointed toward the folder.

"Is that why you're here? Did Chief Robinson change his mind?"

Jax hated to burst her bubble so quickly, but he also didn't believe in lying. "The chief asked that I review your information."

Rhea narrowed her eyes, a bright almost electric blue that popped against creamy-white skin and dark, almost seal-black hair. "He just wants to shut me up, doesn't he?"

"Whatever he may want, I promise you that I'll be objective when I look at your information," he said and meant it.

Rhea focused her eyes even more pointedly and then suddenly popped them open, as if surprised. "Detective Whitaker. You were the officer who found Selene's car."

He nodded. "I was. I also secured the scene and took part in the investigation afterward."

"And you agreed with the conclusion that Selene killed herself," Rhea pressed and laced her fingers together before her. An assortment of silver and gold rings decorated her slender fingers while a mix of bracelets danced on her delicate wrist.

With a quick, negligent lift of his shoulders, he said, "The evidence we had available indicated that, Rhea. I know that's a hard thing to accept—"

"Selene would not do that. She was too full of life to just throw it away," she said and shook her head, sending the shoulder-length locks of that dark hair shifting against the fine line of her jaw.

Jackson couldn't argue that it had seemed unlikely at first to him, as well. That her disappearance was likely foul play at her home prompted him to ask, "Why didn't you go to the Avalon police with your information?"

Rhea looked away and worried her lower lip and in that instant he knew. "You went to them and they didn't believe you, did they?"

She shook her head again, a softer almost defeated motion, and as she glanced his way, her gaze held the sheen of tears. Damn, but he couldn't handle tears. They were his kryptonite. He held his hands up and said, "I'm sorry, Rhea. But you have to understand that we're both small towns with limited resources."

"And what's one missing woman, right? Do you have any idea how many women go missing every year? How many women deal with domestic abuse every day? End up dead because no one believes them?" she said, her voice husky with suppressed tears and anger.

He nodded and juggled his Stetson in his hands. "I do. My sister…" He hesitated, the reality all too real for him still. "She was lucky. She got out."

"I'm sorry, Detective," she said and walked over to stand hardly a foot from him. She was so close he could smell her fragrance, something flowery and clean, like the scent of a spring day. The top of her head barely came to his chin. She was fine-boned beneath the gauzy floral fabric of her blouse. So slight, and he imagined Selene must have been built much the same. It bothered him to think any man would beat on her.

"We had no indication of domestic abuse when we investigated," he said as Rhea removed some papers from her folder and laid them out for him on the smooth mahogany table.

With a shrug of her slight shoulders, she said, "She never told me, but I had sometimes seen bruises on her

arms. She always had an excuse for them. After she…
disappeared, I found out that Selene had gone to a domestic violence support group. Just once. Only once…"

Her voice trailed off, and she fixed her gaze on the
papers, avoiding his.

Jackson placed his thumb under her chin and applied gentle pressure to urge her to face him. "It's hard
for people to admit they're being abused."

"And it's even harder to admit that someone you
love killed themselves," she shot back, clearly anticipating what he would say, but Jackson didn't want to
fight with her right now. You had to pick your battles,
and he intended to save his ammunition for what would
happen after he looked at her evidence. For when he
might have to tell her that she was "barking up the
wrong tree."

"May I take this information? Take a look at it?"
he asked, intending to review the materials later that
night after he had finished his shift.

Rhea hesitated, almost like she'd be trusting a
stranger with her only child. It bothered him, but he
tried not to show it. "I'm the one shot you have to reopen this case, Rhea. You've got to trust that I'll look
at this objectively."

She laughed harshly and twisted away from him.
Her loose blouse swirled around her slim midsection
and then she faced him again with a heavy sigh. "I bet
the chief told you to bury this. Am I right about that,
Jax?" she said, emphasizing his name in a way that
said they were anything but friends.

Since he believed honesty was the best policy, he
said, "He did, but I'm not the chief. If I give you my

word that I'll look at this with an open mind, you can bank your money on it."

"The Code of the West? Or the Blue Code? Which will it be?" she challenged, one dark brow flying up like a crow taking wing.

Exasperated, he blew out a heavy sigh and jammed his hat on his head. "I gave you my word. So what will it be?"

She settled her gaze on him, assessing him again. Then in a flurry of motion, she gathered all the papers and stuffed them into the folder. Grabbed it and handed it to him. "Don't disappoint me, Detective."

He cradled the binder to his side like a fullback cradling a football, put a finger to the brim of his Stetson and nodded. "Like I said, I give you my word."

He pivoted on his cowboy-booted heel and marched out of the room, intending to make good on his promise no matter what the chief had said.

The little voice in his head pestered him with, *What will you do if Rhea is right?*

I'll fight that battle when I get to it, he responded.

Rhea was too wired to finish unpacking after the detective's visit. So she did the one thing she always did when she needed peace. She drew.

She grabbed her knapsack, which always held a sketch pad, pencils, erasers and a blanket she could spread out to make herself comfortable while she worked. She snatched a jacket against the spring breeze, slung her knapsack over her shoulders and hurried out of the inn and onto Main Street.

The inn was at the farthest end of the street, away from the nearby highway that ran all the way from where her sister lived in Avalon to Denver, where Rhea had her home and art gallery. Her pace was hurried at first since she was in a rush to sketch, but there was a peacefulness about the town that was impossible to ignore. It seeped into her body, replacing the earlier chill she'd experienced. Slowing her headlong flight, she took the time to window-shop, appreciating the eclectic mix of shops.

By the time she reached the end of Main Street, her itchiness to draw because she was upset had been replaced by a desire to capture the charm of the quaint town nestled beneath a cloudless sky and the jagged snow-frosted peaks of the mountains in the distance.

A low stone wall with a wide granite ledge ran across the end of the block, marking the entrance to downtown. She opened her knapsack, pulled out the blanket and her materials and began to sketch. With swift determined strokes, an image of the town took shape on the paper. The trim and neat shops with their wooden signs and shiny windows. The many pots of flowers and shrubs before the shops. The wooden posts with streetlights that looked like old-time gas lanterns.

Beyond that, the slopes leading up to the nearby mountains, thick with evergreens in shades ranging from deep green to the bluish-gray of the spruces. Here and there big clumps of spring green identified groves of aspen that in the fall would turn golden, making for a spectacular display against the darker evergreens.

It popped into her brain that dozens, sometimes even hundreds, of aspens were often joined underground by a single root network, making them a massive living organism.

It made her wonder if the loss of one of those intertwined trees caused pain to the others. If they felt the connection the way she did with Selene. A connection that hadn't diminished despite Selene's disappearance. It was the reason she believed with all her heart that her sister was still alive, not that she would tell the detective that. He would dismiss it without question, so she had kept it secret to avoid dissuading him from reopening the case.

But she knew that eventually she would have to tell him, because if they couldn't confirm that Selene's husband, Matt, had killed her or that Selene had killed herself…

She shut her sketch pad abruptly. She'd finish the sketch later, when her mind wasn't as distracted. Packing everything away, she put on her knapsack and marched to the side of the street she hadn't visited yet.

Little by little peace filtered in, but it was tempered by the reality that her sister's last steps might have been down these streets. That these were the last images she might have seen.

Or that maybe they were the images she still saw if she was alive.

As she neared the spot opposite the inn where she was staying, she paused and turned, feeling as if someone had been following her. But there wasn't anyone there who seemed to have any interest in her. Shoppers went from store to store, or just strolled up and down the quaint downtown streets.

She rolled her shoulders, driving away the uneasiness, and did a quick look around to once again confirm she was just imagining the sensation. Satisfied, she returned to the inn to drop off her knapsack and relax before going in search of dinner.

Not that she could really relax with Detective Whitaker's decision hanging over her head. A decision that would make all the difference to her sister's case and maybe even help find Selene if she was still alive.

She hung on to that thought and the hope that Detective Whitaker would keep his promise. That he would keep an open mind to look at the evidence she had diligently gathered over the last six months.

An open mind that would help her find her missing sister.

Chapter 3

It had been a tiring day, filled with the kinds of routine things Jackson had come to expect in Regina.

A fender bender when someone had pulled out of a parking spot without looking.

A couple of tickets for speeding or running a red light. Another for someone failing to leash their dog in one of the public parks.

At a pub located close to the highway, which sometimes hosted a rougher crowd, he had been forced to issue a warning about a minor public disturbance.

Mundane things. Some might even say boring, but Jackson relished it after the many years he'd spent in the military. He'd seen too much death and destruction in Afghanistan, which was why he'd turned down jobs in other areas for the peace and tranquility of his hometown of Regina.

Selene's disappearance six months earlier had upset

that serenity. From the moment the BOLO had come in and Jackson had discovered her car by the lake, it had been days of nonstop action. Securing and scrutinizing a possible crime scene. Coordinating with the Avalon Police Department and, after, searching the lake for Selene's body. A body that had never been found and maybe never would be if the spillway had been open, allowing her body to go over the dam and down the river.

It had taken a few weeks for things to die down. For the press to stop pestering the police and people in town about Selene's disappearance.

Things had gone back to normal, but now Rhea was here and determined to ask questions, possibly upsetting that peace.

But Jackson had never refused any mission in the military, no matter how scary or dangerous. He'd led his team on assignment after assignment and was proud to say he'd kept them safe with a level head and preparation.

He would do that with Rhea's request.

Much like he had prepared for a mission, knowing all he could about the terrain and the enemy, he intended to do the same with Rhea and find out more about her.

He put up a fresh pot of coffee, poured himself a big mug and sat down at his hand-hewn cedar kitchen table. Grabbing his laptop, he logged on to his police department account and searched through their resources for any information on Rhea Reilly. No criminal record of any kind. Not even a speeding ticket.

Hitting that dead end, he shifted his focus to a search of public information on the internet and quickly had

hundreds of hits. Rhea Reilly was apparently a criti-
cally acclaimed artist who worked in several different
disciplines. Oils, watercolors and mixed media. She
owned the building where she lived and had a number
of tenants who rented apartments, and a shop, from her.

The building was located on the 16th Street mall
in Denver, a popular location for both locals and tourists. She also had an art gallery at the location, and he
surfed to the gallery's website. From the portfolio on
the site, it was clear that Rhea sold not only her work,
but that of local artists, and not just paintings. Photographs, jewelry, pottery and other art pieces were
proudly displayed on the site.

He scrolled through the images but was pulled back
to Rhea's work time and time again. He understood
why Rhea was so successful. There was so much...
life in her work. Passion. The images jumped off the
screen with their vibrancy, much like the woman he
had met earlier that day.

Filled with life. Filled with passion for finding out
what had happened to her sister. Stubborn, too. He
had to throw that one in, as well, and he suspected
that she wouldn't back down even if he refused to reopen the case.

The case, he thought as he set aside his laptop and
pulled over the bulging folder with Rhea's evidence.

Opening it, he found it as neat and organized as
any case file he'd ever prepared. The pages held timelines of Selene's husband's possible movements from
Avalon to Regina and back, and then up to his client's
building location in the mountains just outside Avalon.

The timelines she had documented, if true, deviated

from the account Selene's husband, Matt, had provided in the days after his wife's disappearance.

Matt's testimony about the bonfire in his backyard was also contradicted by Rhea's evidence. According to the neighbors she had spoken to, Matt had kept the bonfire going almost overnight and not just for a short time to dispose of some leaves and branches.

Had he done it to dispose of Selene's body? Jackson wondered. *Was it even possible to cremate someone so completely in a home bonfire?*

Rhea had also reviewed the state of Matt's SUV the morning after Selene's disappearance. She had combined photos of his newly detailed SUV with those of his client's building location and the road leading to it, graveled and in relatively good condition. Not a dirt road that would have muddied his SUV, as Matt had claimed.

Not to mention the nighttime trip to a building location. It had hit him as implausible when he had heard that detail from the Avalon police, but they had investigated and found that the alibi held water.

But as Jackson went through all of Rhea's detailed notes, photos, maps and more, it was impossible for him to ignore the discrepancies that were piling up, deeper and deeper, like the winter snows when they came.

He leaned back in his chair, cradled the now almost-empty coffee cup and scrutinized the materials. Sucking in a breath, he shot to his feet and poured himself another cup. He searched through the junk drawer for a pen and pad and sat down once again, taking notes as he went through the papers a second time. He added his own questions to those that Rhea had raised until he had filled a few pages in his pad.

An ache blossomed in his back, and he tossed his pen onto the paper. He rose slowly, unfolding his large frame vertebrae by vertebrae into a stretch until the ache died down. Pacing around his kitchen, he ran his hand through his hair as he considered all the questions jumping around in his brain. Once the ache had been relieved, he returned to the table, leaned his hands on the top rung of the chair and examined all the materials again. Stared at his own pad of growing notes and questions.

With a sharp shift of his shoulders and a jagged exhale, he realized that there was only one thing he could do.

The hamburger she'd eaten hours earlier sat heavily in her stomach, keeping her awake.

It had been a large burger and quite tasty. Since she hadn't eaten all day, she'd scarfed down the burger and fries, but was paying the price for it now.

She was about to give up on sleep when the thump against the French door frame drew her attention.

Is someone trying to open it? she thought and held her breath, listening intently for any other sounds.

A rattle and another slight thump came again, louder. As if someone was jerking the door handle, trying to enter.

Her heartbeat raced in her chest as she carefully reached for the smartphone beside her bed, telling herself she was mistaken about what she was hearing. But the rattle came again and was followed by a scratching sound against the frame of the door.

She had no doubt now that someone was trying to break into her room.

She leaped from the bed, her phone in her hand and held it up, shouting as she did so.

"I'm calling 911! You hear me! I'm calling 911!" she shouted, while also engaging the camera and snapping off a burst of shots of the French door, hoping to capture an image of whoever was on the other side of the glass. For good measure, she raced toward the fireplace and grabbed a poker from the andirons. She held it up and said, "I'm armed! I'll use this!"

Heavy footsteps pounded across the balcony and down the fire escape, confirming that she hadn't been wrong. Someone had been out there.

Her own heart pounding as loudly as the footsteps, she raced back to the night table and snapped on the light. She pulled out Detective Whitaker's business card and dialed his number, hands shaking as she did so.

He answered immediately, almost as if he had already been awake. "Detective Whitaker."

"It's Rhea. Someone just tried to break into my room."

Jackson raced over to the Regina Inn, where a police car sat in front, watching the building.

He pulled up behind the cruiser, got out and approached the officer behind the wheel.

"Good evening, Officer Daly. Have you seen anything since I called?" he said.

The young man shook his head. "Nothing except the innkeeper coming out to ask what was happening. She's upset that someone might have tried to break in, but also that we're drawing too much attention."

Jackson understood. "Do me a favor and pull around the corner where you're not as visible. That might help if someone was here and decides to come back. They won't spot you on the side street."

He pulled his flashlight from his belt and walked the grounds around the inn. At the fire escape there were clear signs of footprints on ground softened by yesterday's rain.

To avoid any further upset, he dialed Rhea to advise her that he was coming up and also dialed the innkeeper.

The innkeeper met him at the door in a bathrobe she had tossed on, her face filled with worry. Lines of tension bracketed her mouth and her hair was in disarray, as if she had repeatedly run her fingers through it.

"Mrs. Avery. I'm so sorry to drag you out of bed at this late hour," he said with a tip of his head and swept his Stetson off as he entered.

"Is everything okay? Do we need to worry?" she asked, clutching the lapels of her robe with age-spotted hands.

He hated to cause upset but had no choice. "There's evidence someone was in the area of the fire escape. I need to check Rhea's room and balcony just to confirm and will let you know once I finish my investigation."

"Investigation?" she hissed and glanced up the stairs to the guest rooms.

"If something happened, I don't think you have to worry about the other guests, and we'll try to keep things quiet," he said, understanding the older woman's concern.

Jackson went up the stairs, careful not to make noise

so as to not wake the other guests. He tapped softly on her door, and it flew open.

Like the innkeeper, Rhea had a robe wrapped tightly around herself, dark hair tousled. Her face was pale and she worried her lower lip for a second before she said, "Thank you for coming so late at night."

"Just doing my job," he said, although he had already started thinking of Rhea as something other than just a job. "May I check the door?"

She nodded, and he hurried over. He opened the French door and looked out. Muddy areas on the balcony appeared to be footprints. He slipped onto the balcony, avoiding the footprints, and noted that some paint had been scratched off the frame close to the latching mechanism. Someone had clearly been trying to pry it open.

He slipped back in, closed the French door and locked it shut. For good measure, he engaged the security bolts at the edges of both doors that would prevent it from sliding open even if someone broke the lock.

When he faced her, she stood hugging herself, obviously fearful. "Please tell me I was imagining it."

He shook his head. "You weren't. Someone tried to get in. When you called you said you snapped off some photos. May I see them?"

She nodded, slipped her hand into the pocket of the robe and removed her smartphone. She unlocked it and handed it to him.

The blurry shots of the doors didn't show much. If you looked closely, there was a shadow on the balcony, but the photos were too dark to reveal much about whoever had been out there.

He handed her the phone. "I'm sorry. There's not

much to work with, but someone was there. Did the person look familiar?"

She quickly shook her head. "I couldn't see much. I was too scared. I'm sorry."

Jackson walked over and laid a comforting hand on her forearm. "No need to apologize, Rhea. You were understandably frightened. If you had to guess who—"

"Matt. Selene's husband. He's angry that I'm pushing for Selene's case to be reopened," she immediately said.

Her response was possibly a little too quick. "How do you know?"

She swiped her screen again and held it up for Jackson to read Matt's message.

I've had enough of your lies and the trouble you're making for me. Leave me alone.

"You think he knows that you want to reopen the case?" Jackson asked.

Her answer came quickly again. "Yes. I think he has a connection on the force. Someone who works for Matt when he's not on duty."

Since it wasn't unusual for officers to have second jobs for when they had multiple days off on their shift, it didn't seem unlikely that there was some overlap between the police force and a local contractor. But it was something he'd have to check out, if his chief agreed to let him proceed with the investigation.

"I'll speak to the Avalon Police Department and have them see if Matt's at home. In the meantime, I can stay—"

"I'm okay. There's no need for you to stay," Rhea

said, thinking that while the detective's presence would be comforting in one way, it would be disturbing in another. He called to her too strongly in a physical way. Even with tonight's upset, he was hard to ignore.

Jackson narrowed his gaze, considering her, but then he heaved his shoulders up in a shrug. "If you're sure, but I'll arrange for an officer to stay outside and keep an eye until the morning."

Only until the morning, Rhea thought. "What happens after that?"

Jackson hesitated, but finally said, "After that, we'll decide what to do."

"With an open mind?" she reminded him, still worried about what he thought about the evidence she had gathered.

"With an open mind," he confirmed and then gestured to her front door. "I have to get going. If you need anything, don't hesitate to call."

She dragged a hand through her hair and blew out a harsh breath. "I won't. Thank you for coming tonight."

He tipped his head. "Just doing my job, Rhea."

But as his gaze met hers, Rhea suspected that he was thinking of her as more than just a job. Her heart sped up at the thought, but she tamped it down.

Her one-and-only involvement with the handsome detective had to be finding out the truth about Selene's disappearance.

Anything else was out of the question.

Chapter 4

"You want to do what?" Chief Robinson said, eyes wide in disbelief.

"I want to reopen the Selene Davis case, Chief." He sat in front of the older man's desk, leaned toward him and argued his case before his boss totally shut him down.

"I looked at all the materials Rhea gathered."

"It's Rhea now, is it?" the chief muttered.

"It is because I was trying to establish a rapport with her in order to determine if she was a crackpot or genuine," he said and plowed on. "She's genuine, Bill."

His chief sniggered and shook his head. "Never figured you'd let a pretty face sway you."

The heat of anger burned through his gut, but he tempered the flame. "If that's what you really believe, then maybe I shouldn't be your choice for police chief when you retire."

His boss's big body shuddered with a rough laugh and he wagged his head again. "I'm sorry, Jax. You know I trust you—"

"Then trust me on this, Bill. I looked through all her materials. Did a thorough review just like you asked. There are major discrepancies in Selene's husband's alibi and his actions the night she disappeared. And neither us nor the Avalon Police Department were aware of the fact that there might have been domestic violence going on," he said, arguing his case the way a lawyer might before a jury.

Chief Robinson laced his fingers together and placed his hands behind his head. He leaned back and his chair creaked from his weight. "I know that's a hot-button topic with you on account of Sara."

"It is, but you have to admit that if we'd had that info we would have looked at Matt Davis much more closely since—"

"Most murdered women have previously been victims of domestic violence," his chief finished for him.

With a chop of his hand against his palm for each item, he said, "There's evidence he abused her. His business was in trouble. The life insurance payout would keep that business afloat. He had a bonfire going almost all night. Who keeps a bonfire unattended for that long and takes a trip up a mountain at night to look at a building site?"

The chief swung back toward his desk and laid his forearms on the edge, steepled hands held before him. "What about a body, Jax? Hard to charge someone without a body."

With a dip of his head, Jackson agreed. "True, but

we didn't find a body in the lake and were still prepared to label it a suicide."

When his boss didn't respond, he forged ahead. "I
know it's all circumstantial, but we may be able to
make a case. Maybe that's why someone tried to break
into Rhea's room last night. Either to silence her or to
get their hands on the evidence she collected."

Chief Robinson scrubbed his face with his hands.
"This could be embarrassing for both departments,
Jax. And if it is, you can forget ever becoming police
chief here or anywhere for that matter."

"I know that, Bill. But again, none of us were aware
of the abuse. If we had known we would have handled
the investigations differently."

With a sweep of his hand, the older man said, "Go
ahead, Jax. But if this all goes south—"

"I'll take responsibility for it, Bill. Count on that. I
won't dishonor the department no matter what."

Rhea hadn't been able to sleep after what had happened. She'd snapped on the television and snuggled
on a couch with a clear view of the French doors and
windows, the heavy brass poker resting by her side. In
the early morning hours she'd dozed off, but woke as
the sun rose and bathed her room with light.

She'd made a cup of coffee and sat impatiently, waiting for the detective's call, even if only to arrange for
the return of her folder. She was surprised when he
suggested that they meet for lunch to discuss her materials and last night's intruder.

She tried to tell herself not to be too optimistic. Not
to believe that the detective might actually be reopening her sister's case. She didn't want to have her hopes

dashed, as they had been when she'd gone to the Avalon Police Department.

But then again, that police department hadn't even taken a moment to review her evidence. The Regina Police Department had.

Or at least she hoped the detective had done as promised.

At the restaurant, Detective Whitaker had already taken a seat at a table by a window. As she entered and met him, he straightened his long, lean form and wagged his head in greeting.

"Miss Reilly."

"Detective Whitaker. Thank you for meeting with me, and thank you again for last night."

"I wish I could say it's my pleasure, but we both know this meeting isn't about pleasure." He pulled out a chair for her.

She sat and clutched her hands together tightly in her lap. "Have you made a decision?"

A momentary flicker of some emotion, indecision maybe, flashed across his face. "I have, but first, I'd like to know more about Selene. About you."

It was her turn to hesitate. With a quick shrug, she said, "We were very close as you can imagine. Inseparable until Selene got married."

"What happened then?" He angled his big body toward her as if to hear her better. His gray gaze, steely with determination, fixed on her face. Slightly unnerving professionally and personally. Her body responded to him in a way it never had to any other man, maybe because she wasn't used to being around such physically powerful and lethally potent men.

She shifted her chair back a little. "We grew up in

Boulder but moved to Denver for school. Roomed together during college and after. My career took off like a rocket while Selene was getting her master's."

"She was a teacher?"

"She's a music teacher, but also a very talented pianist and singer. She often performs in Denver when she visits," she said and her voice grew husky with emotion.

He stroked a hand down her arm to offer comfort. "Take your time, Rhea."

She nodded, dragged in a breath and released it with a rush of words. "She got a teaching job in Avalon and moved there. Met Matt and they married. After that we would have regular girls' weekends, mostly in Denver. Matt didn't like having me around."

"Maybe because you saw more than you should," Jackson said, sympathy alive in his tone.

With a shrug, she continued. "Maybe. When I first saw the bruises, I asked Selene how she'd gotten them. She told me she had fallen while on a hike. I forced myself to believe it, but then it happened again. A few times, but Selene had an excuse each and every time."

"You can't blame yourself, Rhea."

"But I do. I tell myself that if Selene's dead…" She stopped short, well aware of the slip and that the detective had caught it. For a long moment she sat there, trying to decide whether to be honest, but if she was anything, she was honest.

"Something was off that night after the text. I knew Selene was in trouble. I still feel her—" she tapped her chest "—in here. I know she's still alive."

Long moments passed, but as she peered at the detective's face, she had no clue what he was thinking.

His face was as stern and stony as the summits of the mountains in the distance.

The waitress approached at that moment, but sensing the tension between them, and at Jackson's raised hand, she walked away.

As he had before, the detective leaned toward her and, in a low voice, he said, "Selene is gone, Rhea. We both wish it was different—"

"She's alive. I know it," she insisted, and his features softened as he sat back. She worried that she'd blown whatever chance she had of his reopening the case. But then he said, "Promise me one thing, Rhea."

Relief speared through her. "Whatever you want."

He arched a brow. "I know you're not normally that agreeable. If you were, we wouldn't be sitting here discussing this."

She couldn't argue with him. When it came to finding out what happened to her sister, she'd fight him tooth and nail if she had to. "You're right. What is it you want so that you'll reopen the case?"

"Promise me that you'll accept Selene's gone if that's what all the evidence says."

Accept that her sister was gone. Forever. That they'd never have another girls' weekend. Never share another laugh. Or cry. Never see that face that was like looking in a mirror. Something that anyone who wasn't a twin could never understand.

"That's some promise," she said and swiped away the tears that spilled down her cheeks.

The detective looked away and muttered something under his breath. *Kryptonite*, she thought he said before locking his gaze on her again. "Well? Rhea?"

"I promise."

* * *

Jackson sucked in a deep breath, held it and in a rush said, "I spoke to the chief, and we're reopening the case. Especially after last night."

Rhea's face paled, and she leaned away from the table. "It was Matt, wasn't it?"

He looked away for a moment, but then focused his gaze on her. "The Avalon police went by his house. It doesn't seem as if he was home."

"And if he wasn't, he was here," she said as she dragged a hand through her hair, making the thick locks dance around her face.

"Possibly. It's something I'll have to investigate."

She gestured between the two of them. "We'll investigate. I want to be a part of this investigation."

Jackson shook his head vehemently. "No way, Rhea. This is a police investigation."

Rhea shifted toward him, the blue of her eyes icy cold. "There wouldn't even be an investigation without me." She tapped a finger to her chest. "*I'm* the one who got all this evidence. *I'm* the one who knows the information inside and out."

"And *you're* the one who is too close to this. Too close because it's your twin, your mirror image. The person who is a part of your soul," he shot back.

A pregnant silence hung in the air, heavy with emotion, but then Rhea broke that silence in words barely above a whisper, as her gaze sheened with tears yet again.

"You made me a promise and you kept it," she said, voice husky with feeling.

He nodded. "I did."

"I made you a promise, as well. But the only way

I can keep it, that I can know Selene is gone, is if you let me be a part of this investigation."

Silence reigned again as Jackson considered her request. As he skipped his gaze over her features, taking in her pain and her determination. She wouldn't rest until she had an answer. And she would never believe that answer unless she was certain that he had turned over every stone, even the tiniest pebble. Because of that, there was only one thing he could think to say.

Chapter 5

"Okay."

She jumped, startled by that one-word answer. "You mean that? You'll let me help you?"

He nodded. "I hope I don't live to regret this, Rhea."

"You won't, Detective. You won't regret it," she said.

Jackson had no doubt that she meant every word. But his gut told him that this investigation was going to test him. He hoped he didn't fail the test.

The waitress slowly approached once again and, at Jackson's nod, she came over to take their orders, even though they'd been so busy they hadn't really looked at the menu.

"The soup and salad combo here is really good. My favorite is the grilled cheese and tomato soup. But if you're hungrier, the French Dip is good, as well," Jackson said.

Rhea nodded. "I'll have the grilled cheese and to-mato soup combo. A little comfort food is always good."

"I agree. I'll have the same, but the full version, Sheila. Some pop also," Jackson said.

"Diet pop for me, thank you," Rhea added, which earned a long look from the detective and a raised eye-brow. The look sent butterflies into flight in her stom-ach and ignited warmth at her core.

"I've been missing my regular workouts," she of-fered in explanation.

"What kind of workouts?"

"Is this some kind of interrogation?" she parried, eyes narrowed as she considered him.

He shrugged those broad shoulders. "I just like to know more about the people I'm working with, Part-ner."

Partner. Rhea liked the sound of that but, other than Selene and a few, very few, close friends, she wasn't used to sharing details of her personal life. But as her gaze locked with his, it occurred to her that the de-tective wouldn't be satisfied if she didn't answer his questions.

"I normally do a yoga class or two each week, plus some strength training. I also like to take really long walks or hikes when I can."

"In between painting and running the gallery?"

The waitress brought over the sodas at that moment, but once she'd gone again, Rhea answered, "I paint in the early morning and late afternoon when my stu-dio has the best light. I have a full-time manager for the gallery, although I'm the one who decides what to show there."

"I've seen some of your paintings on the website. They're beautiful. Did you always like to paint?"

Rhea nodded and with a laugh said, "My mother said I used to paint myself and Selene with our baby food."

"Is your mom—"

Rhea shook her head. "She and my dad passed a few years ago in an automobile accident. I'm glad, because the worry over what happened to Selene would have killed them."

But Rhea didn't want to revisit Selene's disappearance right now and luckily the waitress arrived with their meals at that moment.

Hunger for the food replaced his hunger for information for the next few minutes, but then he began again.

"I understand. My parents always worried when I was deployed," Jackson said in between bites of the grilled cheese.

"Where did you serve?" she asked and murmured in appreciation of the sandwich, "Delicious."

Jackson smiled and it transformed his face from that of the stern-and-stoic police officer into an almost boyish dimpled grin that made him look much younger.

"I'm glad you like it," he said, but didn't answer her question.

She pressed. "So where was it? Iraq? Afghanistan?"

"Afghanistan. Marine just like my dad."

"Are your parents still alive?" she asked, wondering about her "partner" and his life.

He spooned up some soup, ate it and nodded. "They live in Florida now, close to some of my cousins. Got tired of the Colorado cold, but they come back in the summer to visit."

"Must be nice," she said, thinking of her parents and how much Selene and she had loved to spend time with them.

He nodded and polished off the last of his meal. "It is. I miss them."

"You're lucky to have family," Rhea said wistfully, and Jackson quickly picked up on it.

He raised his glass of soda and peered at her over the rim. "Is it just you and Selene?"

"It is. My parents were both only children, and my grandparents are all gone. It's why it's so important to find her," she said, and Jackson winced as she said it. He didn't believe Selene was alive and didn't want her to get her hopes up, but she'd keep hope alive as long as she could. Because of that, she said, "So, Partner. When do we start this investigation?"

After they'd finished lunch, Jackson had suggested that they go to his office at the police station, where he'd taken all the materials Rhea had gathered and locked them in his desk for safekeeping. Especially after what had happened at the inn the night before.

If Matt had been the perpetrator, he might have not only intended to do harm to Rhea, but to also destroy the materials so that the police would not use that information against him.

In the police station, Jackson got Rhea settled in one of their conference rooms so they could discuss her evidence. Normally he would set up a board with all the pertinent information, but since Rhea and he would have to move from Avalon and back, he had created a notebook in the cloud to hold the info, questions and any answers they gathered.

He grabbed his laptop and her evidence and joined her in the room, where he displayed the digital information on a large monitor. As he laid out the hard copies, he said, "I locked these up to keep them safe, but I also plan on scanning everything and adding it to my notes."

"Thank you. I appreciate all your hard work," she said. She splayed her long, elegant fingers, with their teasing rings of gold and silver, against the tabletop, almost as if to still any nervous motion.

As he would with any board he made for an investigation, he talked through the info in the digital notebook, filling in Rhea as he worked.

"There are three possible scenarios. The first is that Matt Davis murdered your sister. The second is that Selene killed herself. The third is that an unknown suspect murdered your sister."

"And another scenario is that Selene is still alive, and we need to find her," Rhea added. Even though Jackson had only known her for a couple of days, he knew not to argue with her. At least not yet. In time the evidence would eventually rule out that possibility, but he wasn't going to press the issue at that moment.

Pick your battles, he reminded himself.

He went through Rhea's evidence, entering the information into his notes. As he did so, she jumped in with her thoughts to add to the materials. When they finished, it added up to a lot of questions and doubts about the story Selene's husband had provided to officials, making him Number One on Jackson's list of suspects. Which he should have been from the very beginning since the spouse was generally the prime suspect.

But there were also questions about the other scenarios and overlaps. "If there was an SUV by Selene's car that night, and if it wasn't Matt, it's possible that the owner of that vehicle may have something to do with Selene's...disappearance," he said, biting back the murder reference in respect of Rhea's beliefs.

"It *is* possible that SUV is tied to Selene's...disappearance," Rhea agreed, likewise holding back. "What do we do now?"

Jackson rifled through the papers and pulled out her notes on the insurance policies that had been issued barely weeks before Selene's disappearance. Holding up the papers, he said, "How was it that you found out about the policies?"

"I got a call from an investigator from the insurance company. They were doing their own review about Selene's disappearance since the policies were so new," she said and gestured to the bottom of the page. "That's his name and number."

Jackson thought about it for a moment. "Normally most policies are paid out very quickly. At the most, maybe sixty days after the death, but since they had questions, maybe we'll get lucky." He pulled over the conference room phone and dialed the investigator.

"Winston Summers," he answered after a couple of rings.

"Good afternoon, Mr. Summers. This is Detective Jackson Whitaker with the Regina Police Department. You're on speaker and I have Rhea Reilly with me, as well."

"Good afternoon, Detective. Ms. Reilly. How can I help you today?"

Jackson shared a look with Rhea and plowed on. "I

understand you were investigating the insurance policies issued to Matt and Selene Davis."

"I was, but we're getting ready to close our case and
pay out the policy on Mrs. Davis," the investigator said.

Jackson detected something in the other man's tone.
"You don't sound too happy about that, Winston."

A rough laugh came across the line. "I'm not. I can't
prove a thing, but this just doesn't smell right to me."

With a quick sidewise glance at Rhea, whose face
had paled with those words, Jackson said, "It doesn't
feel right to us, either. That's why we've reopened the
case here in Regina."

"Well, you've made my day, Detective. No offense
meant, Ms. Reilly. Now that you've done that, I'll tell
my superiors to hold off on the payout," Winston said.

Jackson laid his hand over Rhea's and squeezed reassuringly. "I'd appreciate that. If you don't mind, I'd
like to tell Matt Davis myself about that decision."

Summers chuckled. "I understand, Detective. I'm
sure he won't be happy. I hope that helps your case."

Jackson provided Summers with his contact info
and hung up.

Rhea was confused by the investigator's statements.
She shook her head and said, "Why will it help the
case?"

"It'll make Matt angry and angry people act rashly.
They make mistakes, and those mistakes may help us
find out what really happened to Selene."

Rhea blew out a breath. "Matt will be pissed, especially if his business is still having problems."

Jackson flipped through her papers again. "You say
Matt was having financial issues at the time Selene
disappeared?"

She nodded. "Selene had told me business had fallen off and his bills were mounting. That was creating a lot of tension in their marriage." She hesitated, remembering how upset her sister had been, as well as something troubling. "I think that's when I first spotted the bruises on Selene."

"The pressure blew off his lid. Revealed his true nature. Hopefully our visit, and the news about the insurance policy, will do the same. Are you up to going to Avalon?"

Am I up to it? she thought, but then an image of Matt's smug face flashed through her brain. He hadn't even tried to deny the abuse when she'd confronted him shortly after her sister's disappearance.

"I am *so* up for it. If Selene is dead, I'm sure Matt did it, and I want to prove that," she said, her throat tightening as she said the words.

Jackson's touch came against her hand again, comforting and secure. His palm rough, but soothing. "We'll go in the morning."

Which meant she had to spend another night at the inn. Another sleepless night, watching the doors and windows for signs of an intruder.

"You'll stay with me tonight," he said, almost as if he'd read her mind.

She peered at him, weighing the risk he presented to her in a very different way, but if they were going to see Matt tomorrow, she had to be sharp.

"Thank you, Detective. That's very kind of you."

He raised a hand to stop her, like a cop directing traffic. "Just part of the job," he said, but she doubted that it was standard procedure to take partners home.

When he rose, he grimaced, grabbed his back and

stretched, as if to work out a knot. She realized then that they'd been sitting for hours reviewing the case. A second later, his stomach emitted a loud rumble that he tried to hide by covering his lean midsection with his big hand.

"Sorry," he said with a chagrined smile.

"No, *I'm* sorry. I didn't realize how late it was. How about I treat you to dinner?"

He did another stretch of that long lean body and grimaced again. "Actually, I have a nice big steak I was going to cook tonight. How about we pick up your things and we throw the steak on the grill? It's enough for two."

Since she felt like she was already imposing on him, she deferred to his request. "That sounds nice. Thank you."

"Don't thank me just yet. My cooking skills leave a lot to be desired."

She doubted that. Detective Whitaker struck her as someone who was likely quite capable in many ways, which brought a rush of unwanted heat as her mind drifted where it shouldn't. To hide her reaction, she turned her attention to organizing the papers scattered around the table while Jackson scooped up his laptop.

She handed him her notes, and he stood before her uncertainly, his gaze traveling over her face, examining her. But surprisingly, he seemed to misunderstand what she was feeling. "It'll be okay, Rhea. Everything is going to work out."

She went with it, not wanting to clue him in to how uneasy he made her on a personal level. "I know it will," she said and tilted her head in the direction of the door. "I guess it's time for us to go."

Chapter 6

It *was* time to go, and Jackson hoped he wasn't making a big mistake by taking Rhea home with him. But he'd barely gotten any sleep the night before thanks to the intruder at the inn. He needed a clear head tomorrow when they spoke to Matt Davis, which meant he needed to get some rest.

But as he caught sight of Rhea's slim but enticing figure as she walked out the door, his gut tightened with desire, and he wondered just how much sleep he was actually going to get.

In no time they had checked Rhea out of the inn and were at Jackson's home on the outskirts of town. The log cabin home was on a large wooded lot that provided gorgeous views of the lake below and the dam's spillway in the distance.

"This is lovely," she said as she set down her suitcase, walked through his home and out to the large deck that faced the lake.

He shrugged. "Thanks. My dad and I built the place when I got back from Afghanistan."

"You did an amazing job," she said, leaning against the railing and glancing back toward his home.

"Let me show you to the guest room," he said, walked back in and snared her suitcase. He took her upstairs to a room a few doors down from his and set her things by a queen-size bed. With a flip of his hand, he said, "The bathroom is across the way if you need it. I'm going to get started on dinner."

"Let me help," she said, and they returned to the ground floor where the open-concept space held the kitchen, dining room and living room with a wall of glass that opened to the deck and offered views of the lake, mountains and Regina.

They prepped a salad and sliced up some potatoes and onions to cook on the grill beside a large steak. Since it was still nice outside, they decided to eat out on the deck.

Rhea stood by Jackson as he laid the potatoes, onions and steak on the grill. Contrary to what he'd said earlier, he was quite a capable cook and the meal they ate was simple, but delicious.

Unlike lunch, dinner was a quieter affair, maybe because they had already done a lot of talking during the day. Although Jackson offered an after-dinner coffee, Rhea was eager for some time alone to think about all that had happened the last few days and what would happen in the days to come.

She helped Jackson clean up, but when she offered

to help him wash, he demurred. "It's okay. I can handle this."

He could. He seemed to be able to handle a lot, from cooking to building a house. She told herself to have faith that he would handle the investigation of her sister's disappearance as capably.

"Thank you for everything," she said as she inched up on her tiptoes and brushed a kiss across his cheek before making her escape. She noticed his home was almost spartan, but had fabulous bones and stunning views. There were a few bedrooms upstairs, hinting at the fact that the detective hadn't planned on living there alone.

Which made her wonder if he'd built the home with someone special in mind.

She forced that thought away and went to her room. Although it was early, she was tired and wanted to be at her best when they confronted Matt. Closing her door, she changed quickly and got into bed, hoping to make it an early night.

Jackson stood at the sink, listening for the familiar creak of the floorboards just inches away from the landing and in front of the first bedroom. More than once he'd thought about fixing it, but it served as a very reliable alarm system.

The creak came as Rhea went across the hall to the bathroom and then back, telling him it was safe to head up once he finished the dishes. He took his time, thinking about the materials they'd reviewed earlier, as well as planning an approach to Matt Davis tomorrow.

If Davis was as Rhea had said, he'd be less than pleased about their reopening the case and holding up the insurance payout. He'd push the other man in the hopes of either eliminating Matt from that prime suspect spot or collecting enough evidence to be able to charge him for Selene's murder.

Selene's murder.

Rhea wouldn't handle it well if that's what the evidence proved, but it would at least bring closure. Even if that closure brought pain.

He finished the dishes and went upstairs, careful to step around the creaky floorboards to not wake Rhea. Once he was in bed, he returned to his earlier thoughts, planning tomorrow's mission. The approach and what would follow if Matt's alibis failed to satisfy the many questions he had.

He was just starting to drift off, the plan running through his brain, when he heard the warning squeak that someone was in the hall. A second later, a soft footfall, someone barefoot, alerted him that Rhea was coming down the hall.

His door was open, and he rose up on one elbow as the shadow of her petite figure came into view. She leaned her hand on the doorjamb and, in barely a whisper, she said, "I can't sleep."

Jackson sat up, revealing a broad bare chest with a smattering of chest hair angling down...

Rhea wouldn't think about where that happy trail led, and was reconsidering her visit when he said, "Bed is plenty big, and I've got lots of pillows." He grabbed a couple and laid them down the center of the king-size bed, creating an effective bundling board.

"Thank you. I promise not to be a bother." She hurried to the side of the bed where he wasn't, slipping beneath the sheets. They were smooth, but slightly warm from where he'd been lying earlier.

The bed dipped a little as he settled down again. "Good night, Rhea," he said, his voice husky.

"Good night… Jax."

Rhea woke to an empty bed and the smell of coffee and bacon.

Hurrying, she washed, dressed and met Jackson in the kitchen, where he was forking perfectly crisp bacon slices onto a plate.

"How do you like your eggs?" he said.

She didn't have the heart to tell him she normally didn't eat breakfast. "Whatever is easiest."

In no time, he was cracking eggs one-handedly and scrambling them like a pro.

She poured cups of coffee and asked, "Milk and sugar?"

"Cream and two sugars, please," he said, and she smiled.

"Just like me," she said, earning her a heated look and a laugh.

"Light for sure. A good wind could blow you away, but sweet?" he teased.

She laughed and shook her head. "I can be difficult at times," she admitted.

He lifted an eyebrow in challenge, but she ignored him easily, especially when he laid a plate of eggs, bacon and toast before her and the smells awakened her hunger. She dug into the meal with gusto.

In truth, she was much lighter than she had been six months ago because she hadn't been sleeping or eating well, worrying about what had happened to Selene. Hoping against hope that the feeling inside her that Selene was still alive wasn't wrong.

She was so famished, she finished her plate well before Jackson had finished his, prompting his laughter. "Girl, you sure can put it away."

"And you can sure cook. Thank you."

"You're welcome, but we should get going. Avalon isn't all that far away, but we've got a lot to do."

In a rush, they cleaned up and were on their way to Selene's hometown, which was only about forty-five minutes away from Regina and two hours from Rhea's home and gallery in Denver.

Rhea had done the drive many times before tensions between her and Matt had cropped up and the trips had become one-sided, with Selene only visiting Denver for their girls' weekends.

As they drove, Rhea went over the discrepancies in Matt's alibi. "He said he was gone for only about an hour to check out his client's building location, but I spoke to the neighbors and they said that he was gone for a lot longer. At least three hours if not more."

Jackson shot her a quick glance as he drove. "That gives him more than enough time to do the round trip to Regina."

"And still supposedly 'check out his client's location,'" she said, emphasizing his explanation with air quotes.

Jackson shook his head. "Who goes to a building site at night? I didn't believe it then, but the Avalon officers confirmed the alibi."

"They did, but how much of that was influenced by the officer who works with Matt?" she asked, questioning it the way she had from the very beginning.

Jackson clenched his jaw, clearly not liking her assertion. "I'd rather not think that an officer let a murderer go free on account of a personal relationship."

Rhea scoffed. "You think that's never happened? That it's possible it didn't happen this time?"

Jackson sucked in a deep breath and held it, recalling his chief's words about embarrassing either of the two police departments. But if losing the police chief's job was the price to be paid for the truth, he was willing to pay that price. "Let's not go there until we've run out of options. First thing I'd like to do is talk to Matt and hear what he has to say. After, we'll take a run to the building site. See how long it takes us to get there and then back to Avalon."

"And we can check out the road there also. Matt said he detailed his Jeep the morning after Selene disappeared because it was muddy and he was meeting a client."

Jackson mentally reviewed the evidence Rhea had gathered. "You said the road was paved with gravel."

"It is," she insisted.

"Maybe it wasn't paved six months ago," he offered in explanation, and she shrugged her slim shoulders.

"I'm no expert, but it didn't look like a new road to me. You saw the photos, right," she reminded.

"I did. If things don't add up... I have a friend in the area who has trained dogs," he said, omitting that they were cadaver dogs in deference to Rhea's emotions. But, as he peered at her out of the corner of his eye, it was obvious she'd guessed exactly what kinds of dogs. She worried that full lower lip and glanced away, her gaze shimmering with tears.

"And what then? What if we get nothing from it?"

"We keep on looking, Rhea. I made you a promise and I intend to keep it. We'll go over every fact and every discrepancy. We'll talk to the Avalon police. I called to let them know we were reopening the case," he said.

She shot him a quick look, eyes wide with surprise. "How did that go?"

"They weren't happy. Felt like I was interfering in their jurisdiction, but I reminded them that the Regina Police Department had been involved in the investigation, as well." He reached over and laid his hand on hers as it rested on her thigh. "We have an appointment to talk to them this afternoon."

A deep furrow raked into her brow as she considered what he'd said. Long moments passed until she said, "I appreciate all that you're doing."

He brushed his hand across her cheek and said, "No need for thanks. It's my job." A more difficult one thanks to what he was starting to feel for Rhea.

Returning his attention to the road, he continued the drive to Avalon and the discussion about the case. "Matt started a bonfire that night. It was one thing that struck me as really odd back then. Who starts a fire and then leaves it unattended for any length of time?"

"And he kept it going almost all night, according to the neighbors," Rhea added.

Jackson nodded, wondering what that might mean. "Matt may have been trying to dispose of..." He hesitated again, sensitive to Rhea's feelings, but that was only making things harder and not easier, so he plowed on. "I'm not sure you can fully cremate a body in a bonfire, but it's something we'll have to check out."

A tired sigh, as if Rhea was carrying the weight of

the world on her shoulders, escaped her. "And what if it doesn't prove Matt killed my sister?"

"If it doesn't, we have other scenarios to consider and resolve," he said without hesitation.

"The turn's just in a few miles," Rhea said and gestured toward the highway exit. "Is Matt expecting us? Did you call him?"

Jackson smiled and shook his head. "Matt is in for a surprise. We've got to rattle him, remember?"

Rhea blew out a breath and wagged her head. "Get him angry. Get him to make mistakes."

He jabbed his finger in her direction to confirm it. "You got it. If he's guilty, we will unravel that supposed alibi and get enough evidence to build our case."

Matt Davis's Jeep Wrangler sat in the driveway, hinting that he was likely at home.

Jackson parked his police cruiser directly in front of the Davis home in a clear line of sight to a big bay window. He cut the engine and shifted in his seat to peer at Rhea. "Are you ready?"

Face a sickly pale, lips pressed tight, she nodded.

"Let's roll," he said as he sprang from the car and around to open the door for her.

Her hand was ice cold as she slipped it into his and they walked to the front door.

He scrutinized the home as they did so, taking in the recently mowed spring green grass. The landscaping was well-kept, and the home spoke of someone who took care of it.

He had barely raised his hand to knock when the front door flew open and Matt Davis stood there, his face mottled with angry red blotches that grew larger as his gaze settled on Rhea. "What are you doing here?" he said, his voice trembling from the force of his rage.

"Matt Davis?" Jackson said and angled himself so that Rhea was partially behind him.

Matt jerked his head up in challenge. "Yes, and who are you? You're not with the Avalon Police Department."

Jackson reached into his jacket pocket, removed his business card and handed it over to Matt, who snatched it away with a swipe of his hand.

Matt shot it only a quick look and said, "What do you want?"

"Detective Whitaker, Regina PD. We've reopened the Selene Davis case," he said calmly, sensing that the more controlled he remained, the more upset Davis would become.

Matt glared at Rhea. "Why won't you leave this alone? I told you I had nothing to do with Selene's disappearance."

"Just like you had nothing to do with those bruises she had?" Rhea challenged, her voice steady even though Jackson felt her trembling beside him.

Matt angrily jabbed a finger in her direction. "I never touched her. If Selene told you that, she lied."

"She never told me, Matt. I saw for myself. I saw the way you treated her. That's why you didn't want me around," Rhea challenged.

Matt made a move toward her, fists clenched, but Jackson swept up his arm, blocking his access to Rhea. Calmly, Jackson said, "Seems to me you've got an anger problem, Davis."

Matt whipped his head around to nail Jackson with

his gaze. "You'd be angry, too, if you were being accused of something you didn't do."

There was a sincerity in the man's response that was unexpected. But sociopaths could be quite convincing, Jackson reminded himself. "If you didn't do it, I assume you'll be willing to answer a few questions."

Davis deflated before his eyes, his shoulders lowering as he took a step back. But then he looked toward Rhea again and jabbed his finger in her direction. "If it means I never have to see her face again, I'll answer any questions you want."

"Where were you two nights ago?" Jackson said.

"Home. Asleep," he said with a nonchalant shrug.

"The Avalon police came by and said no one answered," Jackson pressed.

He shrugged, but met Jackson's gaze head-on. "I sleep with earplugs, and I'm a heavy sleeper. I probably didn't hear them."

The Avalon Police hadn't seen Matt's SUV, unlike today, where it sat in the driveway. He gestured to the Jeep. "Do you normally park in the driveway?"

Matt shook his head. "I normally pull it into the garage, but I'm custom-building something in the garage. I started the project yesterday afternoon."

"Mind showing it to me?"

With a harrumph, Matt pushed past him and to the garage, where he entered a code and opened the door to reveal a number of sawhorses covered with plywood and pieces of a woodworking project.

"Thanks," Jackson said, but pressed on. "Let's talk about the trip to your client's location. You say you went the night Selene disappeared? At night, Matt?"

The other man shrugged and looked away this time,

a telltale sign that someone was lying. "I had been at a site all day and, when I came home, Selene and I had a fight. I needed to blow off some steam and went outside to do some yard work."

"You had lots of scratches and cuts on your hands. You told the officers you got them doing the yard work," Jackson said.

Matt nodded. "There were lots of brambles, but I was so mad, I didn't pay attention and got cut up while I piled them in the firepit."

"And then you started the bonfire?" Rhea asked.

Matt glared at her again, but nodded. "I did. I like to keep things looking neat, and it was the easiest way to get rid of them."

Jackson peered all around the house once more and said, "I see that you care, which makes me wonder why you left a live fire to drive up a mountain."

Matt dragged his fingers through unruly waves of blond hair. "Stupid, I know, but I was still too wired after doing that and decided it was as good a time as any to check out my prospective client's building site."

"Up a mountain? In the dark?" Rhea pressed. She had never believed Matt's alibi from the very beginning and nothing had happened that would change her opinion.

Matt glared at her, and spittle flew from his lips as he said, "Maybe if Selene had earned more at that stupid school I wouldn't have had to bust my ass just to keep a roof over our heads."

Rhea was barely controlling her anger. Her body shook with the force of it, but Jackson laid a hand on her shoulder. Gave a reassuring squeeze.

"I understand you were having some financial difficulties," Jackson said.

Matt's gaze narrowed to almost slits and settled on her. More bright splotches of red erupted on his cheeks and down his neck as he said, "I was working out of it. That's why I drove up the mountain. It was a big job and really helped me get things back on track."

Me *and not* us. *It had always been about Matt*, Rhea thought, but kept quiet to let Jackson continue the interrogation. But he surprised her with his next statement.

"That's good to hear, Matt. Especially since I told the insurance company we had reopened the case. They're holding up the payout on Selene's policy until we close the case."

Matt's barely leashed anger turned toward Jackson. "You had no right to do that. No right," he shouted and leaned toward Jackson, his pose threatening. But he was no physical match for Jackson, who had several inches on him in height and width.

Jackson met him dead-on, his nose barely an inch from Matt's. "I had every right, Davis. A woman is missing. Likely dead and, from what I can see, you had a hand in it."

As he had before, Matt backed down. Bullies couldn't handle being challenged, and it made Rhea realize why Matt hadn't wanted her around. Unlike Selene who hated confrontation, Rhea wouldn't have put up with the way that Matt treated Selene.

"I didn't kill Selene. I don't know what happened to her after she left here that night," Matt said, a defeated tone in his voice.

"If that's true, you'll have no issues with helping us prove that," Jackson said.

Matt gazed away again and nodded. "Whatever you need. I just want to get on with my life."

"Great. We'll be back," Jackson said and exerted gentle pressure on her shoulder to guide her toward his cruiser.

"He just wants to get that insurance money," Rhea said under her breath, not believing a word of Matt's explanation.

"For sure, but he won't get it if he doesn't cooperate to clear his name," Jackson said.

Rhea stopped dead and glanced at Jackson. "You think that's possible? That he didn't do it? That she killed herself?"

"Or that she's still alive, like you hope." His gaze was a dark gray, like a troubled sky, when it settled on her. With a harsh breath, he said, "Anything's possible right now. But, fact by fact, we'll determine what really happened."

Although he had voiced her hope as a possibility, Rhea was certain he didn't believe it likely. But she'd take it for now.

"What's the plan?" Rhea asked, impatient to continue their investigation.

"A trip up a mountain."

Chapter 7

Rhea had visited Matt's client's site barely a week after Selene's disappearance. She directed Jackson down the highway for several minutes until the turn-off for a narrow gravel-paved road.

Jackson pulled the cruiser off the smooth highway and onto the rougher gravel. The car dipped deeply before beginning the rise to the building site on the ridge.

"This road had gravel when you came up," Jackson said as he drove, navigating past a rut here and there on their journey up the mountain.

Jackson had given her a link to the digital notebook they had created the day before. She pulled her tablet out of her bag and, in no time, she had opened the notebook and navigated to the pages that held the photos she had taken shortly after Selene's disappearance. She held the tablet up so Jackson could see it.

He stopped the car to take a better look at the photos. "Definitely gravel, but not as deep as right now. Do you remember how deep it was?"

Rhea shook her head. "I wasn't thinking about that at the time," she admitted, wishing she had been more observant.

Jackson ran the back of his hand across her cheek. "Don't blame yourself. What you've put together is amazing."

She appreciated his words and braved a smile. She scrolled to other photos of what the site looked like before any construction had taken place. "There was a lot of land cleared along the ridge. Plenty of places and time for him to..."

She couldn't say it and left it at that.

Jackson clearly got it. "Let's go see what's up there now."

They bumped their way up the road to the wide hilltop ridge where Matt was building his client's custom home. A truck was parked before the home's double garage doors. One of the garage doors was open, and a large stack of siding sat there, waiting to be installed.

"Looks like they're almost done with the build," Jackson said.

The home was a large contemporary structure, situated to provide views of the valley below, the town of Avalon and the mountains in the distance.

As they got out of the car, one of the laborers walked over, a puzzled look on his face. "Can I help you?"

"Detective Whitaker with the Regina PD. We're just here to take a look at the site. Is that a problem?"

Obviously uneasy, the man held his hands up in a stop gesture. "Above my pay grade, Detective. I'll have to check with the contractor." Without waiting, he walked away, whipping out his cell phone as he did so. A short, clearly upsetting conversation ensued, but the man returned and said, "Matt says look away, but don't bother the workers."

Jackson dipped his head and touched the brim of his hat. "Thank you. We appreciate your cooperation."

The man said nothing, only pivoted and returned to work, shouting out instructions to his people who were busy installing the siding.

Rhea brought up the photos again to show Jackson how the ridge had looked before the construction had begun in earnest, since there had already been some digging going on.

Jackson looked around, comparing the site to the photos. With a shake of his head, he said, "The home takes up most of the flat land at this point."

He walked toward the home and backyard, Rhea following. With a sweep of one hand, he held up the tablet with the other and said, "This was all woods. They cleared a good bit to make this open space for the house, the deck and the grass area beyond that."

Rhea nodded. "It was. I remember wondering how big a house they could build without taking down some of the aspens." The thought stormed through her brain again about the aspens being one and feeling the loss.

Jackson tightened his lips and tipped his hat back. "It didn't take that long to get here. When Matt made this round trip, he had plenty of time at this location, but... I can't imagine him burying Selene anywhere on this ridge. Most of the land here would be touched during construction. It's too risky."

A numbing chill erupted inside Rhea at the thought

of her sister buried here or somewhere else, and she wrapped her arms around herself. Rubbed her hands up and down her arms to chase away the chill.

Jackson immediately noticed and hugged her. "I want to check out the ridge," he said, and they walked, joined together, to the edge of the property where the land dropped off sharply to thick woods at least a hundred feet below.

"It's more likely he would have dropped her over this edge. The woods down there are dense and probably not well traveled."

Jackson paused and whipped off his hat. He dragged a hand through his hair in frustration. "I don't remember anyone searching that area."

Rhea nodded. "As far as I know, they didn't. They searched all along the ridge up here, but not below."

"Well, that's where we start tomorrow," he said with a quick nod and urged her in the direction of his cruiser. He paused by the edge of the build site.

Bending, he ran his hands across the gravel. "It's pretty thick. Enough to keep an SUV from getting too dirty," he said as he rose and brushed the dirt off his hand.

She was satisfied by that assessment, but not about any possible delay. "Why tomorrow?" she asked, eager to do the search as soon as possible.

Jackson pulled her door open and she sat, but he didn't join her right away. He leaned his arms across the top of the door and peered away from her as he said, "Today we see Matt again—"

"Why?" she asked, wondering at the reason for another visit.

Jackson met her gaze. "We press on why he spent

so much time up here and why he says his car was dirty. Maybe even push him to let us examine his SUV again."

"They found Selene's blood in the house. On the sofa in the living room. Matt claimed it was from a nosebleed," Rhea said and tried not to picture Matt hitting Selene. Hurting her.

"I know it's hard but try not to think about that. We have to stay objective," Jackson urged.

Rhea expelled a sigh. "Objective. She's my sister. A part of me I still feel in here." She laid a hand over her heart.

"I get it. When my sister finally told me about what was happening to her, I wanted to rip the guy apart, but that wouldn't have helped her," Jackson said. "We can help Selene by keeping calm and following all our leads."

He was right, but it didn't make it any easier. However, she would do as Jackson said. Well, for now. She wasn't about to roll over if she didn't agree with what he planned.

"So Matt first. Then Avalon PD. And tomorrow?"

"I arrange for my friend with the dogs to help us scope out the base of the ridge."

He shut the door, walked around and slipped into the driver's seat. Executing a K-turn, he started the drive back down the road. They had only gone about halfway when a shot rang out and pinged against the metal of the cruiser.

"Get down!" Jackson shouted and pushed her down with his hand.

Rhea's heart thumped loudly as she struggled with her seat belt. Another shot and ping rang out. She finally got her belt free and sank even lower, burrowing against the dash and hoping it would provide cover.

Jackson had thrown his door open and knelt behind it for protection as he scoured the area for signs of the shooter. Another shot rang out, coming straight at them. Jackson grabbed his cellphone and called 911.

"Shots fired! Shots Fired! Aspen Ridge Road."

"Say again," the dispatcher responded.

"Shots fired. Aspen Ridge Road."

Another bullet pinged against the door by Rhea.

"Identify yourself," the dispatcher asked.

"Detective Whitaker. Regina PD. I'm on Aspen Ridge Road. We're pinned down. Shots fired."

"Sending backup," the dispatcher said.

Jackson reached for his own weapon and shouted out to their assailant. "Police! Backup's on the way!"

The response was the roar of a car engine starting up and the squeal of tires as they took off.

Jackson peered at her. "You okay?"

She nodded, unable to say a word, throat tight with fear. Heart pounding so loudly it was almost all she could hear.

Jackson rose, and she screamed out, "Jax, no! He could still be there."

"He's gone, Rhea. It's okay." He held his hand out to help her up.

Jackson swallowed up her delicate hand with his, and it was impossible to miss the violent trembling of her body. She was shaking so hard her teeth were chattering and he yanked off his jacket, leaned in and covered her with it. "It's okay, Rhea," he said again and tucked the jacket around her.

"Thank you," she said, teeth knocking together.

The screeching sound of a siren approached, followed by the crunch of gravel as a cruiser shot up the road until they were in sight of his car.

He held his hands up in the air and walked into plain sight. "Detective Whitaker. I think the shooter took off down the highway."

One of the Avalon police officers exited the car and called out, "Did you see what they were driving?"

Jackson shook his head. He'd been too busy making sure Rhea was safe and taking cover himself to see the vehicle. "Sorry. I didn't."

The officer said something to his partner, who also got out of the car. The duo approached and Jackson greeted them. "Detective Whitaker. Regina PD."

"Officers Watson and Hughes," Officer Watson said, and the other officer added, "You're a long way from home, Detective."

Cops could be territorial, and he got it. No one liked someone else stepping on their toes. "I am. I'm meeting with your chief later about the Davis case. I've got her sister with me," he said and gestured to his cruiser.

The two officers shared a look, and then Watson took a small notebook from his jacket pocket. "How many shots fired?"

"Four. They all hit the cruiser. I was just going to check it out," he said with a toss of his hand toward the vehicle.

They walked to Rhea's side of the car where two shots had hit the passenger door. The road angled at that point, exposing Rhea's section of the vehicle.

"He had a clear shot at your passenger," Officer Hughes said as he knelt by the bullet dings in the door. "Low caliber, as well," he added.

Jackson examined the damage and couldn't disagree. He glanced at the impressions on the door and imagined where the bullets may have ricocheted. He walked to his side of the car and noticed a mark along the dirt wall on his side of the road. He went there as the two officers examined the opposite area and a stand of trees.

He smiled at the glint of metal in the dirt wall. "I've got a bullet here," he called out to the officers.

"We have some damage to the bark but finding anything will be tough. Lots of duff in this area," Officer Hughes said while Watson came over. He took a small evidence bag from his pocket, and Jackson gestured to the bullet.

Watson dug out the slug with a pen knife. Deposited it into the evidence bag. He held it up for Jackson to see. "Definitely a .22. Small caliber, but it could have gone through the doors."

Jackson nodded. "He would have hit Rhea if that had happened. I wonder why he didn't go through the window or the windshield."

"You think she was the target?" Watson asked, one eyebrow raised in emphasis.

Jackson had no doubt about it. Between the intruder at the inn and now this, someone clearly wanted to scare Rhea off the investigation. Or worse.

He nodded. "She is, but they're going to be sorely surprised. Rhea isn't going to give up until we figure out what happened to her sister."

"We cleared Davis," the officer said, but there was something in the other man's tone that hinted at more.

"Seems like you're not buying the official story," Jackson said.

The officer looked toward his partner, who gave him a "Go ahead" jerk of his head.

"We both always thought the story stunk, but we just couldn't get enough evidence. If you've got it, we're all for you putting that bastard behind bars," Watson said.

Jackson tipped his hat in thanks. "Appreciate it. Right now I think we're going to see that bastard, ask where's he's been the last hour and if he owns a rifle."

"We'll meet you there for backup," Watson said.

Chapter 8

It had been well over an hour since they'd gone up to the site and returned. Davis wasn't at home when they first arrived but got there within a few minutes.

He appeared confused at the sight of the two police cruisers, but then immediately grew defensive as Officer Watson called out, "Hands on the wheel, Davis."

"I haven't done—"

"Hands on the wheel!" Officer Watson repeated and laid his hand on his holstered weapon.

Matt's gaze skipped across all their faces quickly and then he complied. He looked straight ahead as he said, "What is this about?"

"Do you have a firearm in the car?" Officer Hughes asked.

"No. I'm coming from one of my job sites," Matt explained, his jaw tight and mottled spots of color on his cheeks. His hands clenched and unclenched on the wheel.

"But you own a rifle," Rhea jumped in, and Matt whipped his head around to nail her with a cold stare. Filled with hate, it sent a shiver down her spine.

"Owned. I had to sell it to pay off some bills."

"I'm sure you did all the appropriate paperwork," Jackson said, and at that, the color on Matt's cheeks deepened and a nervous tic erupted along his jaw. He turned away from Jackson and faced forward again.

"Davis? You got the paperwork?" Officer Watson pressed.

Jaw muscles jumping nervously, Matt said, "No. It was a client, and I didn't want to hassle them."

"I guess you won't mind us checking with him," Jackson said.

Matt's head whipped around again and said, "Her. I'd rather you not bother her. I can't afford to lose a good client."

"Where were you the last hour?" Officer Watson said.

"Like I said before. At one of my job sites. You can ask any of the guys there," Matt advised.

"Trust us, we will. How about you give us the info so we can confirm your story," Officer Watson said, while Hughes jerked his head toward their cruiser to indicate he wanted to talk to them alone.

Rhea walked beside Jax to the car, where the three huddled together as Hughes asked, "Is there anything else you need right now?"

Jackson glanced at Rhea, who said, "If we can, a look in his trunk would be great."

"You want to look for the rifle?" Hughes asked,

but Jackson quickly said, "Blood. I know your office checked earlier, but I'd like to see the trunk for myself."

Hughes shot a look toward his partner and gestured to the back of the Jeep. "Ask him if he minds opening up the trunk."

Watson leaned in toward Matt, who shook his head, but a second later the glass went up and the hatch unlocked with a *kerthunk*. Watson stepped away to let Davis exit the SUV and open the back so they could inspect it.

"I'm going to lodge a complaint. This is harassment," Matt said as Rhea, Jackson and Officer Watson approached.

"This is an ongoing investigation, Davis, and you are the prime suspect," Jackson explained.

Rhea was so thankful for the presence of the officers. She could never have accomplished any of what had happened so far without them.

Matt shot her another withering look, but she refused to let him cow her. She met his stare head-on and raised her chin a defiant inch. Seeing that they weren't going to back down even with his threat, he swept his hand across his open trunk.

"Look away," he said.

Matt and Rhea walked over, and Rhea immediately noticed the difference. "You used to have a liner in here."

A belligerent shrug was his answer until Jackson said, "Where's the liner?"

"Tossed it about a month ago. It got damaged at a job site," Matt said.

Jackson shook his head. "Convenient. Mind if we take a look anyway?"

"Look away," Matt said facetiously.

Rhea watched as Jackson did, using a blue light to check for blood, she assumed. He did it thoroughly, examining every inch of the trunk area and then the ceiling, as well. But nothing showed up.

As Jackson stepped away from the trunk, Matt smiled smugly and crossed his arms. "Satisfied, Detective?"

Jackson tipped his hat back in a relaxed way, but Rhea couldn't fail to notice the tightness along his jaw and the way he clenched his other fist, as if he was barely restraining himself.

"I wouldn't be so smug, Davis. I'm like a dog with a bone and, right now, you're that bone. I'm going to chew you up and spit you out in pieces to get to the truth about Selene's disappearance," Jackson said, voice calm. Maybe too calm.

Matt clearly understood. "I didn't do anything to Selene. She ran away to her," he said and flipped his hand toward Rhea, but didn't stop there. Spittle flew off his lips as he said, "You were always in the way. Always putting foolish ideas in her head. Making her think she was something special. That she was too good for me."

The heat of anger burst into flame in her gut. She stepped toward Matt and eyeballed him, barely inches away. She sensed Jackson and the two officers behind her, ready to move if Matt did, but if anything, she suspected it was Matt they'd have to protect if she lost her control.

In a deceptively neutral tone, she said, "Selene is something special. Something way too good for the likes of you. You never appreciated just how unique and wonderful she is, and I'm glad she finally realized that. And if you think Jax is determined—"

"Jax, is it? Did you charm him into doing this or did you do something else?" Matt said with a snigger.

Jackson stepped toward him, fists clenched, but Rhea laid a hand on his chest to stop him. "We will get to the truth, Matt. And when we do, you'd better hope that you have been telling the truth all along, otherwise…"

She couldn't finish, because she couldn't imagine what she might do to him. She'd never pictured herself as a violent person, but…she wanted to hurt him the way he'd hurt Selene. She wanted him to pay for everything he'd done to her sister.

Afraid she would lose control, she whirled, grabbed Jackson's hand and dragged him back toward his cruiser. At the passenger door, Jackson opened it and then leaned on it, a hint of a smile on his face.

"You got…spunk, Rhea. I kind of like it," he said, surprising her and, before she could respond, he walked to his side of the cruiser, got in and started the car.

"Are we going to see the Avalon Police Chief?" Rhea asked.

"We are. I'm sure by the time we get there he'll know someone shot at us and have heard from Matt," Jackson said. With a strangled laugh he added, "I'm not sure he'll be happy to see us."

For once, Rhea couldn't argue with him.

"That went well," Jackson said and blew out a sharp breath.

"Not," Rhea added with a roll of her eyes.

Jackson leaned against the bumper of his cruiser,

tucked his arms across his chest and peered at the Avalon Police Station. With a shake of his head, he said, "At least he promised to check out Matt's story about the rifle."

"Convenient, right?" Rhea asked and likewise took a spot against the vehicle, her gaze also on the stationhouse.

"Especially since it was a .22. The same caliber as whoever was shooting at…us," Jackson said, careful of his words since he didn't want to worry Rhea that someone was targeting her.

Rhea shifted her gaze to him. Her blue eyes were dark, clearly reflecting her concern. "You mean me, don't you? Someone was shooting at me."

With a slight dip of his head, he acknowledged it. "I can't deny that it seems like someone wants you to drop this."

Rhea's gaze skipped over his face, questioning. Almost challenging before she said, "Do you think I should drop this?"

His answer was immediate. "No. The fact that someone wants to shut you up confirms that they're trying to hide something."

She looked away and sucked in a deep breath. In a voice tight with emotion she said, "I'm not afraid of pushing for the truth, Jax."

He ran his hand up and down her back, trying to soothe her upset. "I'm not, either. And to get to you, they're going to have to come through me. I won't let that happen."

She surprised him then by turning into his side, her head tucked against his chest, the gesture so trusting his heart constricted. He splayed his hands against her back and he almost spanned the width of it with one hand, reminding him of how petite she was. How vulnerable.

"I won't let that happen," he repeated and brushed a kiss across her temple.

That action propelled her into moving away from him. She tucked her hands under her arms and shook her head. "This is confusing, Jax."

He had no doubt she wasn't referring to Selene's case. He held his hands up in surrender. "It is, and I'm sorry. It's time we got back to Regina. I've got some calls to make and some more research to do before we return to search beneath the ridge."

"I've got some things I want to go over, as well," Rhea said.

With a nod, he opened the door and waited until she was sitting. "It'll be dinnertime by the time we get back to Regina. How about we get some take-out barbecue?"

"I'd love that. Thanks."

Jackson's dining room table was covered with a mix of spareribs, brisket burnt ends, cornbread, beans, coleslaw, and the photos and papers from Rhea.

Rhea sat at one end with a plate piled with food she had barely picked at, not because it wasn't tasty, but because she was too focused on reviewing materials she had already seen dozens of times in the last six months.

Jackson was at the other side of the table, a nearly clean plate sitting there while he read the papers. As Jackson set the materials down, he took note of her watching him, and of her virtually untouched dinner.

"You need to eat something. We didn't eat all day,

and you're going to need the fuel tomorrow for that hike beneath the ridge."

With a quick lift of her shoulders, she said, "I'm not really hungry."

He shot to his feet then, wincing as he straightened. Grabbing his back with one hand, he stretched before coming to her side of the table.

"You okay?" She'd seen him suffer with his back more than once in the last couple of days and wondered if it was from an old injury.

"I am." He gathered the materials at her side of the table and shifted her plate of food directly in front of her. "Eat. Once you do, we can go over this. Again."

Rhea stared at the food and then shot a quick glance up at Jackson. The hard set of his jaw and steel gray of his gaze said he wouldn't budge.

She dug it into the brisket and ate the perfectly cooked meat. It was tender with a delicious barbecue sauce. The taste awakened hunger, as did Jax's promise...or maybe it was better to say his threat that they wouldn't look at anything until she had eaten.

She forked up more meat and, after, beans and coleslaw. Before she knew it, she had cleaned her plate and, as promised, Jackson spread out the materials he had taken away earlier.

Jackson gestured to the police photos of Matt's SUV the afternoon after Selene's disappearance. The Jeep was pristine.

"It rained that afternoon," Jackson said, prompting her for a response.

"It did, but you saw that the road was paved with gravel. There was no reason for Matt to clean it. And why did he get rid of that liner? Because he was afraid someone would find evidence the Avalon Police missed?" she pressed.

Jackson hesitated, obviously uneasy, forcing Rhea to push on. "I'm not afraid of the evidence, Jax. It makes me sick in here," she said and tapped her chest. "It makes me sick to think of Selene dead. Of *how* she died, but we need to be able to talk about it openly."

Jackson pursed his lips and inclined his head, scrutinizing her as if to judge her sincerity. Apparently convinced, he said, "If Matt had Selene in the back of the Jeep, on that trunk liner, it would be hard to get rid of blood evidence."

"Unless she was wrapped in something. A tarp maybe."

He nodded. "Maybe. Or unless he put her in that bonfire instead and didn't take her up the mountain."

"But there were no bones there."

Another slow nod. "And we don't know if it's possible to do that in a bonfire. I'm researching that in addition to the timeline of Selene's trip from Avalon to Regina." Jackson grabbed a map where Rhea had written in the approximate time Selene had left and been seen by the lake and the exact time that Selene had texted her sister that night.

Rhea ran her finger along a route on the map and said, "Selene had to have stopped somewhere. Maybe more than one place. I did the route a few times to time it, but I'd like to do it again and see what's along the highway."

"First, we search the ridge. And then, depending on what we find, we investigate what's possible with the bonfire. Hopefully by then we'll have something from the Avalon PD about Matt's rifle and the cell phone location information I requested from both Matt's and Selene's provider."

Puzzled, Rhea narrowed her gaze. "Don't you need a subpoena for the cell phone data?"

"Not under ECPA," he began, but paused at her continued puzzlement.

"The Electronic Communications Privacy Act. I don't need probable cause, just sufficient facts to support making the request, and I think you gave me what I needed," Jackson explained.

"Thank you," she said, appreciative of his recognition of all that she'd done.

"We should be thanking you. I feel guilty that I didn't do more at the time, only… Once the Avalon PD cleared Davis, the most plausible explanation was that Selene committed suicide," Jackson said, real apology in his tone.

She laid her hand over his as it rested on the map she had marked up. "I get it, but Selene wouldn't do that. She just wouldn't."

Jackson had had his doubts in the weeks after they'd closed the case and was ashamed that he hadn't done more. But he'd been told to leave it alone and, by then, the winter crush of tourists had kept him busy with an assortment of problems and crimes. Mostly minor incidents, but enough of them that he'd been too busy to give any time to a case his department had closed.

"I understand," he said and turned his hand to take hers into his. He squeezed it tenderly and offered her a compassionate smile. "We will get to the bottom of this. I won't stop this time."

He cupped her cheek with his free hand and ran

his thumb across the dark smudges beneath her eyes. "We're both tired. It's time we got some shut-eye."

"Let me clean up." She started to round up the plates, but Jackson stopped her by laying a hand on her forearm.

"I'll get this put away. Go get some rest," he said, intending to not only clean up their dinner, but do a quick walk around his property to make sure all was well.

Rhea was too smart not to realize there was more to his request, but she complied, and he was grateful for that. He was too tired for another argument, although in the last couple of days they'd seemed to agree more than disagree.

He quickly loaded the dishwasher and went to the sofa, where he'd laid his service belt. Grabbing his flashlight and Glock, he exited his home, careful to lock the door as he did so. Aiming the flashlight, he first searched the woods close to the front door and then did his walk-around, vigilant for signs of any intruders.

Nothing.

Relieved, he went back inside. He turned on a small lamp on the first floor and softly tread up the stairs, careful to avoid the squeaky floor at the landing.

Rhea's door was closed. Jackson hesitated there, wondering if she was okay, but then he hurried to his own bedroom. After showering and slipping on a pair of pajamas, he got into bed and grabbed his tablet. He had reached out to some experts on body cremation and luckily he'd gotten a response. Rhea would not be happy with what the expert had to say.

He added the expert's response to his digital notebook and then skimmed through the remaining emails.

His friend with the cadaver dogs had answered that he could assist them the next day. Confirming that the time his friend had proposed was acceptable, he finally set the tablet away for the night.

Time to get some rest because the hike along the base of the ridge would not be easy, both physically and emotionally.

No matter what they found tomorrow, it was going to upset Rhea. He was certain of that. He only wished he could be as certain of what had happened to Selene that night.

Nothing they'd found so far had eliminated her husband in her disappearance. If anything, he remained the prime suspect in Jackson's book.

But with no body, a circumstantial case would be hard to prove. Based on what they had so far, no district attorney would bring the case before a grand jury.

If they couldn't find anything more on Davis, they'd have to push on with the other scenarios.

He just hoped Rhea would be satisfied by whatever they discovered.

Chapter 9

The sounds and smells of breakfast dragged Jackson from bed. He'd already been up, mentally reviewing last night's response from the forensics experts, as well as what they'd need for today's hike. But whatever Rhea was whipping up smelled just too good.

He threw on clothes and hurried down to find Rhea at the stove, already dressed for the day. He hadn't known what to expect given what she'd worn over the last few days. Loose and very feminine blouses and hip-hugging capri pants.

This morning she was wearing faded jeans and a light sweater that hugged those curves he'd noticed more than he should. Well-used hiking boots, and he recalled that she'd mentioned that she and Selene had regularly gone for hikes. A different side to the talented artist, and one that was more in his wheelhouse.

One that was more dangerous for sure, because it was too easy to picture the two of them taking long walks through the woods together.

"Good morning," he said and headed straight to the coffee maker to pour himself a cup. She already had a mug on the counter beside her as she worked at the stove.

"Good morning. I hope I didn't wake you by making too much noise," Rhea said and peered at him over her shoulder.

"I was awake, but those amazing smells forced me to move my butt," he said and ambled to her side to see what she was making.

"I just pulled some things from the fridge. Do you like Mexican food?" she said and, once again, glanced at him, a little apprehensive.

"Love it," he said and passed a hand down her back to comfort her. "It smells amazing."

"Thanks. I figured we'd need something substantial for today's hike." She opened the oven and removed a pan holding corn tortillas filled with eggs and chorizo.

"Take a seat and I'll finish these up." She tilted her head in the direction of the table she'd already set.

He did as she asked and, in a few minutes, she served him a plate with the corn tortillas topped with a red sauce. His stomach rumbled in anticipation, and he barely waited until she was seated to dig in. The flavors exploded in his mouth, and he murmured an appreciative sound. "Delicious. Thank you."

Rhea smiled, her blue eyes alight with pleasure at his compliment. "You're welcome. It's my small way of showing how much I appreciate what you're doing."

"It's my job, Rhea. But I wish we'd done more at

first. Known more, like about the domestic abuse," he admitted.

She did the tiniest shrug that barely moved her shoulders. "You couldn't have known. Even I didn't really know, and Selene and I were like this," she said and crossed her middle and index fingers in emphasis.

Despite her all-action clothes for hiking, her elegant fingers and wrists still bore her rings and bracelets. Those feminine touches tightened his gut and had him imagining things best left alone. Especially considering why Rhea was in his home.

"That won't happen this time. We will not leave any stone unturned, but even with that, we may not have enough to charge Matt. You realize that, right?"

The blue of her eyes darkened, and she paused with her fork halfway up to her mouth. "I do, Jax. Trust me, I do."

"Good," he said, hating that he'd dimmed her earlier joy and possibly caused her pain, but he didn't want to set her up for even greater pain by not being realistic.

The exchange created a pall over their meal, and they finished it in silence. Since she was already dressed, Rhea offered to clean up, and Jackson hurried to dress. In no time, he was ready and headed out to his shed to grab a machete. They might need it to clear their way through the underbrush at the base of the ridge. But as he neared, he noticed that the shed door was open.

He reached for his weapon and called out, "Police! Come out with your hands up!"

No sound came from the shed. He approached warily, ready for action as he pulled the door open. He immediately noticed that several items had been moved around, but other than that, everything was as it should be.

He wanted to believe that he'd merely forgotten to shut the shed, but he was the kind of person who had a place for everything, and things were clearly not in the place he'd left them.

Someone had been in the shed.

Matt Davis? he wondered. *Had he followed them back from Avalon to see where Rhea was staying? Had he also been the one at the inn?*

He grabbed his machete, but didn't touch the tools that had been moved. With a quick call to the station, he arranged for his colleagues to dust the tools for prints.

When he returned to the house, Rhea was standing on the back deck, arms tucked tight across her chest against the slight nip in the morning air. "Everything okay?"

"Fine," he lied, not wanting to worry her.

She seemed to see through his ruse, but didn't challenge him.

It took only a few minutes for them to grab some water bottles and their jackets for the hike and hit the road.

Rhea sat in silence beside Jackson, wondering what he wasn't telling her. She'd seen the look of concern on his face as he'd returned from his shed. Had he seen something unusual, or was he just worried about what would happen on their hike today much like she was?

She'd been up half the night imagining Selene out in the woods beneath the ridge. Trying to hold on to that belief that her sister was still alive, but even that vision brought despair. If Selene was still out there, what was happening to her? Was she being abused? Was she losing hope that she'd be found?

Rhea would never lose hope, but in that way Selene was the weaker of the two of them. Her mother had often used a Shakespeare quote to describe Selene's spirit. *Swear not by the moon, the inconstant moon, that monthly changes in her circle orb, Lest that thy love prove likewise variable.*

Selene's love had never been inconstant, but she'd been easily swayed at times. Rhea was convinced that was why Matt had deluded Selene about his real character. A character that had convinced Selene to abandon her dreams of being a singer for a more stable profession as a music teacher.

When they found Selene, Rhea would do her utmost to make sure Selene was able to follow those dreams and escape her abusive husband. In a way, Rhea was a lot like the goddess after whom she'd been named. She'd always been a mother figure for Selene and others and would do anything to protect her, much like the goddess Rhea had hidden away Zeus to keep him safe.

She'd been so lost in her musings, she didn't realize they were already close to Aspen Ridge Road until Jackson pulled over just past the turnoff for that street. Parked ahead of them on the shoulder was a pickup with a dog box in the bed. As they stopped, the pickup door popped open and a man in hunting gear stepped out. A second later, two dogs also leaped from the vehicle and followed him to Jackson's door.

The two men shook hands, and Jackson's friend leaned down to peer through the window. He was a handsome Latino with a dimpled smile and eyes the color of hot cocoa. "Good morning, Miss Reilly."

Jackson said, "Rhea, this is Diego. We served together in Afghanistan."

"Good morning, Diego. Please call me Rhea," she said.

"Rhea," he said with a deferential dip of his head. He glanced toward the woods by the turnoff. "Am I in the right place?"

Jackson nodded. "Our suspect claims he went up to a building site at the top of the ridge. Too easy to find a buried body with all the construction, so we think he did the next easiest thing."

"Tossed her over the edge," Diego said and straightened to scrutinize the area. After he did so, he said, "Let's get going. It may take some time to hike to the spot beneath that ridge."

"I agree," Jackson said and looked at her, his gaze sympathetic. "You ready, Rhea?"

Am I ready for what might lie ahead?

"I'm ready."

They hiked beneath the rising wall of the ridge for close to an hour, Jackson ahead of her, hacking through vines and thick underbrush. Yards behind her, his friend Diego gave the dogs free rein to check the area for signs of any decomposition. For signs of Selene. They didn't hit on anything, which was both a disappointment and a relief.

Sweat dripped down the middle of her back and her temples from the heat and humidity in the forest. Sweat lines were visible down Jackson's back and armpits as he cut their way through the forest. In another half an hour, they finally reached a spot directly beneath the building location.

Jackson stopped, sucked in a deep breath and wiped away sweat with a muscled forearm. He shot a quick look at her. "You okay?"

Her legs were trembling, she was a little out of breath and a lot hot, but she shook her head and said, "I'm okay."

Jackson peered over her shoulder at Diego. "How about you, *amigo*?"

Diego smiled. "A walk in the park," he teased. With a hand signal, he set the dogs into action. They scurried into the nearby woods, sniffing here and there, jumping over fallen logs and beneath tangled vines. As time passed, it was clear they weren't hitting on anything.

With a low whistle, Diego summoned the dogs back. "*Nada* here. Maybe we should press on a little more."

Jackson sighed and looked at her. "You okay with that?"

"I'm ready to do anything we need to do." She was determined not to waste this opportunity.

They pushed on, and then in an even wider circle in the area closest to the custom home's location up on the ridge.

But despite all their hard work in clearing the underbrush and hiking through the rough terrain, the dogs failed to locate anything.

It was impossible for Jackson not to see the mixed emotions spiraling through Rhea. Despair. Relief. Disappointment. Hope.

He laid an arm around her shoulders and drew her near. Brushing a kiss on her temple and ignoring Diego's surprised look, he said, "Don't let this get you down. We'll find her."

She turned into him and murmured, "It's just... I don't know. I'm upset, but also relieved, you know."

He knew, boy, did he know. "Let's go grab a bite and regroup. Decide what else we have to do in Avalon before heading home."

Home. His cabin had always felt like home, but with Rhea there now it felt more...complete, worrying him.

It was too much, too soon and, as Diego shot him another questioning look, he realized his friend was likewise wondering what was up.

Rhea nodded, and he released her so they could trudge back through the path they had blazed earlier. By the time they reached their cars, his entire body was bathed in sweat, and his arm was beginning to ache from swinging the machete to cut through the underbrush.

At his cruiser, Rhea stopped and offered a smile to Diego. "Thank you so much for doing this. We really appreciate your help."

"Anything for an old friend," Diego said and clapped Jackson on the back. *Maybe a little too hard*, Jackson thought and grimaced as pain swept across his lower back.

"We do appreciate it, *amigo*," Jackson said, but sensed his friend wanted a private moment. Especially when Diego jerked his head in the direction of his pickup.

He got Rhea settled in the cruiser. "I'll be back in a second."

She nodded, and he joined his friend as Diego rewarded his dogs and then loaded them into their boxes.

With a quick glance in Rhea's direction, Diego said in a low whisper, "Do you know what you're doing?"

Jackson didn't dare look toward Rhea, afraid he'd reveal too much. He also wasn't sure what to tell his friend. "I know we're trying to investigate her sister's disappearance."

"But that's not all, Jax. It's obvious you have feelings for her," Diego said and finished securing the latches on the dog boxes. He leaned on the tailgate. "Is that going to compromise your investigation?"

"No. I won't let whatever is happening between us change what I have to do."

Diego arched a brow. "Which is?"

"Find out what really happened to Selene Davis."

Chapter 10

After grabbing a quick bite at an outdoor café, they decided it was worth a go at the building location. They also wanted to look around Matt's home, but Matt refused to allow any inspection without a warrant.

Matt's client was not as reluctant. In fact, he welcomed it.

"I want this all behind me, and would feel better knowing there's nothing going on at my home," he said on the phone.

With that approval, Jackson, Rhea and Diego went to the ridge and allowed the cadaver dogs to roam the property. They were just about finished when Matt pulled up in his SUV and jerked to an angry stop in front of the home.

He jumped from the SUV and came at them, jabbing his finger in their direction. "You have no right. No right," he shouted.

Jackson tucked Rhea behind him protectively and braced for Matt's attack, but at his glare, Matt stopped dead in his tracks. But apparently Rhea wasn't about to hide behind him.

With the spunk he'd come to love, she shifted from behind him and said, "We have every right. We have the owner's permission, because he has nothing to hide."

"I have nothing to hide," Matt said and jabbed his chest angrily.

"Seems to me that if you had nothing to hide you'd let us search your yard," Jackson said and gestured to the dogs who had returned to Diego's side.

"You're six months too late. I'm done with this. I'm done with being harassed. You can bet I'm going to file a formal complaint."

Without waiting for a response, Matt whirled and stomped back to his SUV. Gravel spewed from beneath the tires as he whipped around and raced away.

"Someone's got anger issues," Diego said as he watched the SUV bounce down the road.

"It hurts to think of Selene suffering from that anger," Rhea said, the sheen of tears brightening her gaze. "What do we do if he files a complaint?"

While Jackson liked that it was a "we," he didn't want Rhea to worry. "Let him file a complaint. It won't go far. We'll put together all our evidence for the Avalon PD and see if they can't get a warrant to search the property with the dogs. Especially the bonfire area."

Rhea peered at the animals. "They can identify remains if there's been a fire?"

Diego nodded. "Their sense of smell is strong enough to detect human remains in ashes. Especially if they have a scent to pick up on. Do you have anything with Selene's smell on it?"

With a quick nod, she said, "I do, but back in Denver. Do you want me to get it?"

It was nearly a two-hour trip to Denver, but totally worth the time if Diego's dogs could rely on the scent. "Are you sure about the ashes?" he asked his friend.

Diego nodded. "It's possible, Jax. I can come back once you get the warrant."

With a nod, he looked at Rhea. "I guess we're going to Denver."

It was dark by the time they started the trip back to Regina from Denver. Rhea had picked a number of items that Selene had left behind in her apartment, and then they stopped for dinner since it was getting late.

It has been an emotional day, Rhea thought as she sat in silence beside Jackson. She'd been filled with dread as they'd hiked through the woods. Not finding Selene's body had been a mixed blessing.

When they were almost on the outskirts of Regina, Rhea said, "Thank you for arranging for Diego to help us today."

Jackson shot her a quick look, then immediately glanced in the rearview mirror. "He's a stand-up guy. I knew he'd come if I asked him."

"He served with you?" she asked and, as Jackson again checked the rearview mirror, Rhea likewise looked over her shoulder and saw something way behind them. The lights on the vehicle were off, making it difficult to see it on the dark roadway.

"What is that?" she asked, eyes narrowed as she

examined Jackson's face to gauge just how worried he was.

"Nothing good," he said and swept his arm out to press her back against the seat. "Hold on."

He increased his speed, trying to put distance between them and the vehicle that was racing toward them. In front of them, a slow-moving lumber truck blocked the road, and they were on a section of highway that made it difficult to pass.

Jackson muttered a curse beneath his breath and slowed. He shot another look in the rearview mirror, and she did the same. The unknown vehicle was advancing on them. Too quickly.

Inching into the lane for opposing traffic, Jackson whipped back behind the truck at the sight of lights coming toward them.

He splayed his hand across her upper chest and said, "Brace yourself."

The first hit against the back of the car sent her reeling forward and back, while Jackson battled to maintain control, working the steering wheel to stay on the road. Hitting the brakes to stay away from the back of the lumber truck and the logs that would break through the windshield and kill them.

A second jolt had the cruiser swerving, fighting against the momentum sending them toward the truck and a fatal collision.

Jackson swung the wheel into opposing traffic, searching for an escape, but the threat of lights coming toward them drove him back behind the truck again.

He shifted to the open shoulder and hit the gas. Gravel pinged against the underside of the cruiser. Another ram almost sent them off the shoulder and into the woods beside the road.

As soon as Jackson cleared the truck, he swung in front of it, earning a loud blare of the truck's horn as he cut if off. He used the truck as a shield for their rear, but the vehicle that had been chasing them switched tactics.

While riding on the shoulder, the vehicle smashed into the side of their car, sending them into the opposing traffic. It swung into the lane, blocking their way back onto the right side of the road, leaving Jackson little choice but to race onto the far shoulder. It was much narrower and, as he did so, the cruiser sideswiped a number of trees until he jerked to a rough stop.

Their attacker sped away, any view of them blocked by the slow-moving lumber truck.

"You okay?"

Am I? she wondered, finally taking a deep breath. Her heart pounded so powerfully in her chest it echoed in her ears.

"I'm okay," she said, forcing calm into her voice even though she was anything but.

The lumber truck had stopped, and the driver exited the cab and came racing over. Jackson lowered the windows on the cruiser to speak to him.

"You folks okay?" he asked, leaning in through Rhea's window.

"We're okay. Did you get a plate number on the vehicle that hit us?" Jackson asked.

The trucker shook his head. "No, sorry. I was too busy trying to control the truck. All I can tell you is that it was a Jeep Wrangler. Red, I think."

Jackson and Rhea shared a look. "How about the driver?" Rhea asked.

The trucker tossed his hands up in apology. "No, sorry. Didn't see him."

"Mind if I get your contact info before you go?" Jackson asked and, without hesitation, the trucker pulled out his wallet and handed Jackson his license. Jackson snapped a photo and handed it back to the man, who ambled to his truck and took off.

Jackson grabbed his radio to call in the incident, but they were in a dead zone. Same for their cell phones.

Grumbling, Jackson said, "We'll have to drive closer to town to get a signal. Are you sure you're okay?"

Rhea blew out a rough laugh. "As okay as you can be when someone tries to kill you."

Jackson brushed the back of his hand across her cheek. "Davis is obviously angry that you're not letting this alone."

"I won't let it alone until we know what happened to my sister," Rhea said, no doubt in her voice despite the fear that had filled her barely moments earlier.

Jackson smiled. "That's my girl."

She wanted to say she wasn't his girl or anyone else's, but in truth, it felt good. She felt good. Protected despite all that had happened in the last few days. Jackson would keep her safe, but she was no damsel in distress. She'd keep him safe, as well.

The cruiser, damaged and worse for wear, could be driven, and Jackson pulled back onto the road.

In less than fifteen minutes they had arrived at the Regina Police Station where Jackson had to file various reports regarding the attack. While he did so, Rhea sat beside his desk, sipping on a coffee someone had been nice enough to bring over. Despite the heat of the liquid, a chill had settled into her center as she considered that someone had tried to kill them.

Matt? she wondered again, despite the call to the Avalon police who had confirmed that Matt's Jeep was sitting in his driveway with a cold engine and nary a scratch on the vehicle.

A gentle hand on her knee pulled her from her thoughts. "I'll only be a little longer," Jackson said.

She nodded. "It's not a problem. Take whatever time you need." She didn't think she could sleep anyway once they got home. Cradling the coffee mug in her hands, she let it warm her cold fingers and still the slight tremble.

Less than five minutes later, Jackson shuffled all the papers he'd been working on into a neat stack, shot to his feet and held his hand out to her.

Without hesitation, she slipped her hand into his and rose unsteadily from the chair. He grabbed hold of the coffee mug from her other hand and set it on his desktop.

A gentle tug on her hand urged her close, and he wrapped an arm around her. Hips bumping as they walked, they left the station and walked to a different cruiser. The first one was now evidence.

Once she was seated, she wrapped her arms around herself, shock still filling her center with cold. "We're going to find out who did this," Jackson said and rubbed a hand across her shoulders.

"I know," she said, confident that Jackson would keep his promise.

Jackson started the cruiser, turning up the heat and, little by little, the cold left her thanks to a combination of the warmth blasting from the vents and Jackson's presence.

Another police cruiser sat in the driveway of his home.

Jackson waved at the young officer behind the wheel and the officer waved back, confirming he had their attention.

"He'll be there all night," Jackson advised, and it offered some comfort.

"Thank you for all that you're doing. I know it wasn't easy for you to buck your chief."

Jackson cupped her cheek. "It wasn't easy, but everything that's happened just confirms there's more to Selene's disappearance."

Rhea wouldn't read more into his use of *disappearance* instead of *murder* or *suicide*. There still wasn't enough to substantiate her belief that Selene was alive. But there was certainly enough to prove that whatever both police departments had believed might be wrong.

"Do you think Matt had anything to do with what happened tonight?" she asked, certain that her sister's husband had to have been the one who'd driven them off the road.

Jackson blew out a breath and swiped his thumb across her cheek. "He's my prime suspect, but if he did it, it was with another SUV. If he does own another one, we'll find it."

With another gentle caress, he said, "Let's get some rest."

She nodded and met Jackson at the front bumper. She tucked herself against him, wanting to not only draw comfort from his presence, but to offer it, as well.

When they entered, she had no doubt where she'd be sleeping that night.

Beside Jackson.

Upstairs they separated only long enough to change, but she went straight to his room and slipped into bed beside him. Turning, she laid a hand on his chest. His skin was hot beneath her palm, and she cuddled close, laying her head against him. But despite that, she felt restless with too many thoughts racing through her brain.

He eased his arm around her and splayed a hand across her back to hold her close. He soothed it up and down and said, "You need to shut it down and get some rest. Tomorrow is going to be a long day."

She raised her head to peer at him. At the strong, straight line of his jaw, stubbled with his evening beard. "I can't stop thinking about all that's happened. All we still have to do."

He shifted until they were almost eye-to-eye. Until his nose bumped hers and his breath warmed her lips. His body was hard beside hers. Strong. The body of a warrior with the scars to prove it, she realized, noticing the shine of old scars along his shoulder and upper arm.

She raised her hand and ran the tips of her fingers along it, her gaze on those injuries before skipping up to meet his.

"Shrapnel from an IED. Kandahar province."

He said it matter-of-factly, but there was no missing the tension that crept into his body.

"Did you lose anyone?" she said and stroked her hand across the scars, wanting to soothe him the way he had her so often in the last few days.

"We avoided the worst of the blast and didn't lose

anyone. Didn't lose anyone on my tours of duty and brought everyone home," he said, pride evident in his tone.

She had no doubt his leadership was part of the reason. That kind of leadership would have been coveted anywhere, which made her wonder why he had chosen Regina.

"Was Regina home for you?" she asked, wanting to know more about the man who was unexpectedly becoming a part of her life. A man who was tempting her at a time when she needed to be focused on only one thing: finding her sister.

He nodded. "I grew up in Regina, and my parents lived here until they moved to Florida. It's a safe place that I want to keep safe so I can raise my kids here."

Kids. She wondered if there had ever been anyone he'd wanted to have his children and the question escaped her before common sense could silence her.

"No one special," he said. "Before now," he quickly added and locked his steely gray gaze on her. He cradled her cheek and traced the outline of her lips with his thumb.

Her heart skipped a beat, and her breath trapped in her chest. The rough pad of his finger was a powerful caress and jolted her core alive.

"Jax," she eked out past the knot in her throat.

"Relax, Rhea. It's too soon, and we have too much to do," he said and tempered his touch, releasing her gaze and shifting his hand to the back of her skull to draw her close. He massaged her head tenderly, easing past the charged moment. Bringing some peace as her mind traveled from thoughts of the past and Selene to those of a happier future. One possibly spent exploring whatever was going on with Jackson. Maybe kids. Maybe a little shop along the quaint street in Regina. A Matt-free Selene finally doing what she loved.

Rhea's light snore and the softness of her body along his confirmed she had fallen asleep. It brought a smile and relief to Jackson.

It had been a difficult day and night with all that had happened. Tomorrow would be no less stressful.

Even though they had picked up clothing from Rhea's apartment that hopefully had enough of Selene's scent to examine the bonfire ashes, unless Matt consented they'd have to wait for a search warrant. Regardless of that, he'd done enough research to recreate the bonfire Matt had kept going all night.

Hopefully that recreation would provide the information they could use to either charge Matt or get the search warrant they needed.

And if not...

Jackson refused to consider that possibility. One way or another, he'd find out what had happened to Selene that fateful fall night.

Chapter 11

Jackson examined the circle of pavers that his friend Declan had recreated from the crime scene photos. A large pile of wood sat a few feet away, ready for a fire.

"What do you think?" Declan said, arms crossed as he also scoped out his work and shot a quick look at Rhea.

"It looks like Matt's firepit," Rhea said and strolled around the circle, likewise scrutinizing Declan's work. "Thank you so much."

"Anything for my friend Jax," Declan said and clapped Jackson on the back, making him wince from the force of the blow.

"Easy, dude," Jackson warned and eyeballed Rhea, hoping she hadn't caught his pain, but she had.

"Sorry, dude. I forgot," Declan said. He gestured toward the back of his restaurant. "I'm going to go get the hog, okay?"

Jackson forced a smile. "That would be great, and thanks again for helping us with this. Let me know what I owe you—"

"No way, dude. I owe you big time," Declan said, raising his hands to stop Jackson from insisting on his request.

"Well, thanks," he said and watched as his friend returned to his building to fetch the pig carcass they were going to cremate.

"You okay?" she asked. Laying a hand on his shoulder, she gently skimmed her hand from his upper arm to the middle of his back, as if trying to soothe his pain.

He nodded, his lips tight against both the slight sting that lingered from his friend's exuberance and admitting weakness to Rhea. "I'm okay. I still have pain sometimes from the shrapnel damage."

Turning into him, she surrounded him with her arms and hugged him, providing comfort and peace he hadn't felt in quite some time. Not since before Afghanistan.

The moment was shattered as Declan and one of his workers returned, arms wrapped around a large hog that roughly weighed the same as Selene. They wrestled the carcass to the center of the firepit and dropped it. It landed with a thud, kicking up dirt. Making Rhea jump with the sound.

He returned her embrace, hugging her close. Peering at her, he said, "Are you ready to do this?"

She shook her head. "No, but there's no choice is there? Not if we want to know if Matt did this to Selene."

Before he could warn Rhea not to get her hopes up, she was in action, making a pile of brush and kindling above the hog. As she started to expertly stack the logs, he joined her and said, "I see you've built campfires before."

"Selene and I were Girl Scouts. We started a lot of campfires in our day," she said, adding more wood to the tipi atop the hog.

He helped her, adding logs and tinder until the body of the pig was almost completely covered.

Jackson stepped back, hands on his hips as he scrutinized their prospective campfire. Rhea joined him, staring at the pile and then up at him. "What do you think?"

"I think it's ready." He reached into his pocket for the box of matches and, once the match was lit, tossed it into the tinder material. The first hint of flame quickly flared into more. Smoke came from the pile along with the crackle and snap of wood igniting. The fire had taken.

Satisfied, he headed to the trunk of the police cruiser where he'd stowed two portable camping chairs. Rhea and he set them up several feet away from the campfire. The heat quickly built from the intensity of the flames, but they still had to keep it going for several hours, much like Matt had done the night of Selene's disappearance.

Rhea was silent as they sat there, staring into the flames as they consumed the pig. The smell of the meat roasting was awkward. While there was no denying it was pork, it made her wonder…

No, better not to wonder, she told herself.

Jackson shifted from his chair to add more logs and keep the fire going. It had barely been an hour, but the greedy flames were quickly eating up the wood on the pile, as well as the carcass beneath the ash and embers. Because of that, Jackson walked over to an area with wood waiting to be split, grabbed an ax and went to work.

He swung the heavy ax with ease the same way he had chopped with the machete the day before. He was clearly a man used to physical labor, despite the injuries that still seemed to bother him. Over and over he swung the ax, the thunk of it hitting the log loud in the quiet of late morning.

Feeling guilty, she rose and went over to collect the split wood and add it to the pile by the fire. Tossing more logs into the firepit as well to keep the flames going.

The physical labor helped to keep her mind off what was happening in the firepit, but it also whet her hunger. Especially as Declan's restaurant opened for lunch service and the smokers that they'd loaded up that morning were opened, spewing the tasty smells of barbecued meats into the air.

Almost as if he'd read her mind, Declan exited from the back of the restaurant with a large tray loaded with food and drinks. He brought it over and placed it on a stump by their chairs. "I thought you might be hungry by now."

"Thank you. That was very thoughtful," she replied.

Declan did a side glance at the firepit as Jackson approached. "I know this is a tough thing for you."

She nodded. "It is, but your help has really made it easier."

Declan shrugged. "Like I said before. Anything for Jax…and for you since…well, you and Jax." He stopped, clearly uncertain and possibly uneasy as Jackson returned from splitting logs.

With a laugh, Jackson wagged his head. "Deck, you always manage to talk too much."

"And before I stick my foot in my mouth even deeper, I'm going," he said as he jerked a thumb in the direction of the restaurant and backed away.

Rhea smiled at the friendly and jovial exchange between the two. "I guess you've known each other a long time."

Jackson chuckled, sat and reached for one of the plates that Declan had brought out. "You might say that. We grew up together, but then I went off to college and Deck stayed to help his family with the restaurant."

"Have they had it for long?" The building was well-kept and had that look of age that hinted at permanence.

"A few generations." Jackson took a big bite of the brisket sandwich Declan had provided.

"Where did you go to college?" she asked, wanting to know more about the man who was intriguing her on so many levels.

"Annapolis," was his one-word answer around a mouthful of pulled pork.

She picked up her own sandwich, grateful it was beef and not pork. She nibbled the burnt ends, murmuring her approval. "Delicious."

With a nod, Jackson took another big bite. After swallowing, he said, "His pops taught him well, and Deck really upped his game. He's won quite a number of competitions over the years."

Rhea admired the pride that Jackson had in his friend, as well as the fact that they had been friends for so long. Much like the permanence of the restaurant, it spoke to Jackson's character and the fact that he was a man you could count on. But then again, he'd more than proved that over the last few days.

"You were a Marine?" she said, resuming her earlier quest for information.

"I *am* a Marine. Once a Marine always a Marine," he said with a smile.

Yet more proof of his ability to commit. "And then you came home and became a cop?"

With a small shrug, he swallowed the last of his sandwich. "I wanted to serve, and it seemed like the best place to do it."

In a town the size of Regina, she imagined crime was usually limited to minor incidents, which was why Selene's case had been such a big deal at the time. "It must be pretty quiet in Regina for the most part."

He placed his plate back on the tray and did another shift of his shoulders. "It is. Problems with people partying too much. Noise complaints. Shoplifting. Occasionally a burglary or assault."

"Cat up a tree," she teased, imagining him dealing with a dowager and her felonious feline.

Jackson laughed as she'd intended. "More like bear up a tree. Those suckers can really climb," he said, but then he grew a little more serious. "I like it. I like dealing with people. Solving problems. If I become chief…"

There was something in the way his voice trailed off that warned there was an issue there.

"Are you next in line?" she asked, wondering about his hesitation.

"I was…am," he said with a little more confidence, but she sensed his concern. When he shot her a hurried, almost furtive glance, she realized she was the cause of that worry.

"Your chief was going to blow me off, wasn't he?"

"Let's just say he wasn't sure there was enough evidence to reopen the case." Jackson rose and tossed more wood on the bonfire before returning to his chair.

He was in major avoidance-mode, but she wasn't going to give up until she had her answer. "But you decided differently, and he didn't like that."

Heaving a sigh, he nailed her with his gray gaze, now almost charcoal with his upset. "You know you would have made a great interrogator."

She met his gaze. "I suspect you think I'm more like a Grand Inquisitor. But I don't give up, which is why we're sitting here, trying to cremate a hog."

"It is," he admitted with a slight dip of his head.

"But that put you in hot water. Maybe even enough to affect you becoming chief?" She hated that she might be the reason Jackson's career was at risk.

His demeanor was deadly serious as he said, "If it gets to the truth of what happened to Selene, it's worth it, isn't it?"

She nodded. "It is."

"And you remember your promise, right?" he pressed, turning the tables on her.

She remembered, as much as she might not like accepting that Selene was truly gone. "I do, Jax. I remember it every time we hit another brick wall."

Jackson nodded and worried that today's experiment would turn into another disappointment for Rhea. With that in mind, he said, "I reached out to people who might know more about cremating bodies."

She tilted her head and focused on him, her gaze both questioning and challenging. "Does that mean you don't think this is going to prove anything?"

He hesitated, but had to be truthful. Especially since he'd already kept his problems with the chief secret. "It may prove something you don't want."

"Which is?" she urged and gripped the arms of the seat with hands white with pressure.

Gesturing with his hands, he mimicked the path of the flames in the bonfire. "With those low paver walls, we're getting a lot of flames, but the energy of the fire is being expended upward."

A deep furrow marred her brow. "What does that change?"

He once again used his hands to illustrate what he'd learned. "If the fire was contained, like in a barrel or a pit with higher sides, you'd get more heat in a concentrated area."

Her eyes opened wider and she nodded, getting what he was saying. "We may not have enough heat to cremate…"

She couldn't finish, and he didn't push on that point. "Bingo." He reached into his pocket and pulled out his smartphone. He opened up his digital notebook with the crime scene photos of Matt's bonfire. Leaning close to Rhea, he held the phone so she could see, although he suspected they were tattooed on her brain.

"There's a lot of ash here, but nothing else."

"He could have taken away anything that was left."

He couldn't deny that. "He could possible remove larger bits of bones, but getting rid of other—"

"What other?" she countered.

"Body residues. Teeth," he said, but she held a hand up to stop him, the sheen of tears glistening in her gaze.

"I don't want to upset you—"

She cut him off again with a quick wave of her hand. "I get it, Jax."

He had no doubt she did, but just in case, he reviewed what Matt had done that night. "He started a bonfire and went up to the ridge location."

"Supposedly. He could have also followed Selene to Regina."

Jackson drilled back to the pages in his digital notebook on the timelines Rhea had worked out. Analyzing them, he said, "He could have. It's only about forty-five minutes to Regina, and the neighbors say he was gone for a few hours."

Losing some of her earlier upset, Rhea jumped right into helping him work through the materials. "We have two witnesses who place an SUV near Selene's car."

With a nod, he ran a finger across his screen, scrolling through the notes and then thought out loud. "Let's say he and Selene did fight. She storms off. He's pissed and needs to literally burn off his anger. He starts the bonfire. But he's still really pissed at Selene and needs to do something about that."

Rhea joined in. "He goes after her to give her a piece of his mind. There's really only one way to Denver, and it runs right through Regina. He finds her. They fight again and something happens."

Jackson wagged his head. "But it's possible Selene took longer to get to the lake than everyone originally thought. We'll have to investigate that. But let's assume he ran into Selene right away. Why not just toss her body in the lake?"

"We'd find Selene right away in the lake, wouldn't we?"

Jackson immediately knew where she was going. "Which is why you think she may still be alive. Because otherwise we'd have found her body in the lake." He paused for a moment and then quickly added, "Unless the spillway was open to keep the lake levels in check."

She whipped out her phone, and her elegant fingers danced over the smartphone screen. With a satisfied dip of her head, she held it up for him to see a report she'd obtained.

He'd only done a quick glance at it before, but now he took her phone, used his thumb and forefinger to zoom the image. Rhea had filed a Freedom of Information Act request to obtain information on spillway activity from the department that managed it.

"Spillway was closed that night and for days after. If Matt put Selene in the lake—"

"Or if she killed herself—which she didn't—we would have found her body," Rhea finished.

The crackle and thump of logs collapsing in the fire drew his attention. Embers shot up and danced in the air as more wood fell in the center of the pit. "Time for more logs."

Together they piled on even more wood and, as they did so, it was obvious to Rhea that there was a little less of the pig carcass beneath the ash and embers.

She snuck a peak at her watch. "It's been about four hours since we started."

Jackson likewise did a quick look at his phone to confirm the time. "About. We'll need to keep it going a while longer to match what Matt did."

"Which means more time to get to know each other," Rhea said, wanting to find out all she could about Jackson.

"First, more firewood," he said and walked over to split more wood.

She recognized avoidance when she saw it, but she refused to let him avoid that talk. He was becoming too special to her in just the few days they'd spent together. Too hard to resist, even though becoming involved with a man was low on her priority list. Both before and after college she'd been focused on establishing her career. Once it had taken off, her emphasis had shifted to her gallery. In the years since then, she'd made a number of friends and spent time with Selene, but a relationship...nonexistent.

That she was giving the "relationship" label to what she was feeling for Jackson was a scary proposition. He was connected to too much hurt. He was also nothing like the artsy men who inhabited her life. But maybe that was why she found him so interesting. He was the epitome of the strong, silent hero type, but beneath that hard surface was a powerful and compassionate man.

Instead of sitting, she walked to where he was working and, as he split the logs, she picked them up and carried them close to the firepit. They had just finished making a nice pile when Declan came out of the restaurant with another tray, this time loaded with what looked like slices of pie and tall glasses of lemonade.

"Dude, if you're in the mood to keep on chopping, I

could use some hickory for the smokers," Declan called out and motioned to a far pile of wood with the tray.

Jackson nodded. "Sure thing. Least I could do to thank you for all your help and the food."

And to avoid talking to me, Rhea thought, but bit her tongue. He could run, but he couldn't hide.

When Jackson moved to the pile of hickory logs, she tagged along, picking up the pieces he'd split to add them to the neat pile Declan had beside the uncut logs.

"You've known Declan forever," she said, hoping to start the discussion on what was hopefully a safe topic.

Jackson raised the ax and sent it flying down onto the log, splitting it in half. "We grew up in the same neighborhood. Went to school together."

"I bet you were a jock," she said, picturing him on a football field.

Jackson grinned and shook his head. She thought she heard him murmur, "Grand Inquisitor," but then he said, "I was. Baseball, not football."

It was too easy to imagine that powerful and lean body in a tight baseball uniform, igniting heat at her core. But he was more than just a pretty face.

As she picked up a pile of cut hickory logs, she asked, "Why does a landlocked Colorado boy decide to go to Annapolis?"

Jackson set the ax on the ground and stretched, arching his back and wincing slightly. But before she could offer to help, he picked up the ax and went back to work.

She pressed him for an answer. "Why Annapolis?"

He finished quartering the log and set the ax aside, obviously in pain. But he finally answered her. "I didn't want my parents to have to pay for college since they still had my sister and brother to worry about. Dad is a Marine and I wanted to follow in his footsteps. Annapolis made sense."

She stacked the last of the logs he'd split and followed him back to the fire. Together they tossed on more wood, then sat to eat the slices of pie Declan had brought out. But that wasn't going to keep her from her goal.

"Are you always so sensible and responsible?"

Chapter 12

He paused with a forkful of apple pie halfway to his mouth and glanced at her. His steely gray gaze glittered with a heat she hadn't thought possible. "Not always."

The warmth that had kindled in her core earlier grew ever higher, like the flames in the fire a few feet away. It was so intense, she had to cool off with a few sips of icy lemonade.

"What about you, Rhea? I know you're talented. Determined," he said, the latter word followed by a playful chuckle.

She considered him over the lip of the glass, thinking about how to answer. After a pause, she said, "I know some people think artists can be temperamental and flighty. You probably did."

He smiled as he scraped the last of his pie from the plate and then licked the fork clean. "I plead the fifth," he joked, but then quickly added, "But you probably thought I was uptight and by-the-book."

She felt the urge to shake him up a little. "I still do, but I look forward to you proving me wrong."

His glass rattled against the tray as he set it down and, when he fixed his gaze on her, it seared her with its fire. "I look forward to that also."

She gulped down the rest of her lemonade to cool the blaze he'd ignited and turned her attention to her pie. Another collapse of the logs in the bonfire had them both bolting from their chairs to the wood pile. They almost collided there, forcing Jackson to reach for her to keep her from falling over.

Electricity sparked between them, and Rhea rushed back to her seat.

Jackson took his time feeding the fire, needing to control what he was feeling for Rhea. Banking the flames burning inside because he worried that if he released them, it might consume him. He was unused to such feelings, being, as Rhea had said, normally uptight and by-the-book.

But Rhea had loosed those bounds he'd lived with all his life, first as an athlete, then as a Marine and finally as a cop.

It couldn't have happened at a worse time, he thought. Rhea's emotions were too fragile, and he had to stay focused because so much was at stake, including his career. But more importantly, he had to keep Rhea safe.

His Crime Scene Unit was working on the cruiser, trying to get paint and metal samples in the hopes of identifying the vehicle that had attacked them. They were also trying to locate any CCTVs along the route that might also yield more information. The Avalon police were determining if Matt owned any other SUVs that fit the bill and still trying to get a warrant to search his property.

With a cruiser parked in front of his own home, he hoped that would be enough to safeguard Rhea.

The vibration of the cell phone in his pocket warned that they'd hit the time limit for their bonfire.

"Is it time?" Rhea asked.

He nodded. "We need to let it die down and see what we have."

"I'm ready, Jax. No matter what happens, I'm ready," she said and met his gaze, hers unwavering and filled with the kind of determination he'd come to expect from her.

"We'll be ready, Rhea. And if this doesn't work out, we'll move on," he said, wanting to reassure her.

"I know." She reached across the short distance separating their chairs, holding her hand out to him.

He grasped her hand and twined his fingers with hers. The comfort he offered her with that touch rebounding to bring him peace, as well.

It took another hour for the fire to die down enough for them to check out what had happened.

Jackson grabbed a shovel that Declan kept for feeding and controlling his smoker fires. Carefully, he shifted the still red-hot embers in the firepit, moving them away from the center to try to expose what, if anything, was left of the pig carcass. It was hot work, and sweat bathed his body from the heat.

As he moved the embers toward the edges, he had to take a step back to cool off.

Rhea was immediately there with another tall glass of lemonade.

"Thank you," he said. He swiped his forearm across his brow to wipe away the sweat and chugged down the drink.

After a few deep breaths, he resumed shoveling the embers until he had revealed a large portion of the carcass. Or at least what remained.

He stood beside Rhea, hands on his hips, staring at the pile of bones in the center of the pit. A dark residue, probably from the animal's fat, stained the area around bones that were relatively intact. Some spots near the edges, where the fire hadn't been as hot, still had minute remnants of flesh. Ashes and embers circled the pig remains close to the pavers.

Maybe if they allowed more time for it to cool down, the central section with the bones might be closer to the crime scene photos that the Avalon Police Department had taken in the days after Selene's disappearance. *But is it close enough?* Jackson wondered.

"It's not similar, is it?" Rhea said, dejection obvious in every line of her body. Her shoulders drooped, and deep frown lines were etched beside her lips. The blue of her gaze was dark, like the lake waters during a storm.

He eased his arm around her shoulders and tucked her close. "Let me get the embers back in place, add another pile of logs and then let the fire die out naturally. We'll come back later to check it out and, if that doesn't do it, we move on, right?"

She nodded and, in a tiny, hardly audible voice, she said, "We move on. I'll get you another drink."

Rushing away, he watched her go, aware she was

barely holding it together. He quickly returned to work, piling the glowing embers back into the center of the pit. He added another mound of logs and hoped that by doing so the end result might support continuing their investigation of Matt because the other alternative…

Rhea didn't want to believe that Selene had killed herself. He found it hard to believe, as well, but no one knew why someone would choose such an end. Why they didn't ask for help and kept it bottled up until the emotions were just too much to handle.

The sound of a footfall drew his attention, but it wasn't Rhea. It was Declan, with another tall glass of icy lemonade and deep furrows across his brow.

"Your…friend is… Maybe it's time you guys went home. Took a break. I can finish up here," he said with a flip of his hand in the direction of the fire.

Jackson hated to leave their experiment unfinished. But as he looked at Declan's face, his friend was obviously as worried about Rhea as he was. "Do you mind us leaving it here until later?"

"Until tomorrow, Jax. You need to take a break. A long one," he said and clapped him on the back, gently this time.

In truth, whether later or tomorrow it wouldn't matter. Not to mention that the ache he'd been feeling off and on in his back all day was blossoming into major pain. "Tomorrow," he said and followed his friend into the restaurant where Rhea was sitting in one of the booths.

The lunchtime crowd had died down, and Declan's staff was getting ready for the dinner rush.

He eased into the booth across from her and their knees bumped beneath the table. He laid a hand on her knee. Squeezed reassuringly. "How about we head home?"

She nodded, but remained silent, her face flat. Shoulders still fallen.

Declan hurried over and laid a pizza box on the table. At Jackson's questioning look, his friend shrugged and said, "Figured you might not want to cook dinner."

Jackson rose and bro-hugged his friend hard. "Thanks for everything, Deck."

His friend dipped his head in Rhea's direction, urging Jackson into action.

Jackson held his hand out, and she slipped her hand into his, but peeled away for a moment to hug Declan. "Thank you. We really appreciate all that you've done."

"Anything for friends," Declan said as he embraced her.

"Let's go," Jackson said, and Rhea seemed only too eager to leave. He understood. Their experiment was leading them on a path to other scenarios.

One of which included Selene's suicide.

Normally he'd be relieved when he eliminated one scenario during an investigation and moved closer to solving a case.

He felt no such relief today.

The short ride to his home was quiet, but Rhea's disappointment was almost palpable. In just two short days, they'd eliminated the idea that Matt had disposed of Selene's body at his client's location and probably the possibility that he'd cremated her in his firepit.

But that didn't eliminate Matt or their other scenarios, including the one where Selene was still alive.

"Matt could still be a suspect," he said, but as they

pulled past the police cruiser stationed in his driveway, instinct said something was wrong.

"Stay here," he said and opened his door while un-clipping the thumb strap on his holster. As he did so, the smell of smoke drew his immediate attention. A slight breeze carried smoke from beyond his home.

He leaned down and drew his backup Glock from his ankle holster. Bending, he held it out to Rhea and said, "Do you know how to use this?"

Rhea took the gun from him and pushed the button to remove the magazine and check it before slipping it back in. "I've got it."

"Good. Stay put."

Rhea eased the safety off the Glock and watched as Jackson walked toward the police cruiser. When he got there, he immediately acted, reaching in for the radio and calling for an ambulance.

The hackles rose on the back of her neck, and she hoped the officer wasn't badly injured.

She searched the area in front of the home, but the fading light of dusk and the tree line around the home created too many shadows. But her gaze caught on a brighter swirl of white above the home. Smoke.

No, not Jax's home, she thought and opened the door. The smell of smoke was impossible to miss now and, as Jackson rushed around the edge of his home, gun drawn, Rhea couldn't just sit there doing nothing.

Ignoring Jackson's instructions, she dashed from the cruiser, gun in hand. Following the path Jackson had taken, she ran into him as he stood on his deck, pull-ing a garden hose from a reel. He ran with it toward the shed. Licks of flame were just beginning to escape from a broken window at the front of the structure.

Jackson turned the hose on the shed, trying to keep the fire tamed. He had holstered his gun and was radioing with his free hand. She walked over and took the hose from him, and he mouthed a "Thank you." With his hands free, he drew his weapon again and finished calling for the fire department since the garden hose was barely keeping the flames at bay. If they spread to the deck or to the pines behind…

She didn't want to think about the fire destroying Jackson's home because of her. *Because of me.*

Keeping the hose aimed on the flames, she also kept her eyes and ears open for signs of anything out of the ordinary. Like the scream of sirens approaching and the lights flashing through nearby woods. Reds and blues escaped through the underbrush and tree branches as police cars, an ambulance and a fire truck raced up the road.

The crunch of gravel and pounding footsteps signaled that help was on the way. Jackson joined her a second later and said, "Whoever did this is long gone."

"I'm sorry, Jax. How is the officer?"

"Awake. He thought he heard a noise, opened his window to investigate and got cold-cocked. EMT is with him, and it seems like he'll be okay," Jackson explained and held his hand out for his backup weapon.

She returned it, and he strapped it back into his ankle holster. As he did so, he asked, "How did you know how to use the Glock?"

"Dad was a cop. He taught us how to safely handle a weapon," she explained and began to hose down the edges of his deck as the heat of the shed fire warned it was in danger.

Luckily, a crew of firefighters dragged a fire hose

from the front of the house and turned a burst of water on the shed, beating back the flames. But the fire had done major damage to the structure, and it collapsed with a loud crash, sending embers flying all around.

The firefighters moved closer to douse the burning remnants, as well as the area all around, to avoid the spread of the fire.

Rhea stood there, more worried about Jackson losing his home than the likelihood the fire had been set because of her. Jackson came up behind her, wrapped an arm around her upper body and drew her against his chest. She went willingly, the comfort and security of his arms welcome.

The firefighters shut off the water and walked over to inspect the remnants of the shed. One of them shook his head, tipped his hat back and walked to where they stood. He glanced at Jackson and said, "Can't say for certain yet, but I think an accelerant was used."

"I kept gasoline in there for the chain saw and mower," Jackson advised.

The firefighter took a look back toward the shed and nodded. "Probably used that, since it was handy. We'll know more once the arson investigator has his look at it."

"Thanks, Max. You guys did an amazing job," Jackson said and leaned over to shake the man's hand.

"Appreciate it, Jax. Sorry this happened to you," he said and shot a look at Rhea, as if wondering if she was the cause. Rousing her guilt again about what had happened.

Jackson and she followed them to the driveway, where the EMTs were pulling away and Jackson's colleague was standing by his car, chatting to the police chief.

"Stay here and, this time, do it," Jackson said and reinforced his instruction with a slash of his hand.

Since the chief shot her a look that was both annoyed and concerned, she decided to stay put as Jackson had instructed.

Jackson spoke to his injured colleague and the police chief in hushed tones, making it impossible for her to overhear what was being said. The chief waved to officers standing by another cruiser, who joined them as discussion resumed.

Not long after, the injured officer got into his car and pulled away, and the police chief did the same, leaving the one cruiser with the duo of officers. Jackson spoke to them for another few minutes. With a series of handshakes and some backslapping, the conversation ended, and Jackson returned to her side.

"Are we good?" she asked, wondering at what they'd planned.

"We're good. They'll stay all night and run hourly checks on the grounds," Jackson advised and opened the door on his cruiser to remove the pizza Declan had given them.

At her questioning gaze, he said, "Dinner. A man's got to eat."

Despite his comment, he handed her the pizza box at the front door and said, "First, a quick check through the house, although I doubt whoever did it is in here."

"Why?" she wondered aloud.

"If they really wanted to do damage they'd have torched the house. The shed was intended to be a warning," he said and, once again, drew his weapon.

He didn't need to say the words. His warning glance rooted her to a spot by the door, pizza box in hand.

She waited, patiently, as Jackson did a sweep of his living room, dining room and kitchen, and then went up the stairs. Long anxious moments later he came bounding down the stairs, his gun holstered once more.

"All clear," he said and took the pizza from her. But as they entered the house, the smell of smoke on them was powerful.

She wrinkled her nose and said, "I think I'd like to shower and change."

Jackson sniffed the air, as well, and said, "Me, too. I'll get this in the oven while we shower."

"Thanks," she said and rushed up the stairs and through her shower.

She beat Jackson to the kitchen, scrounged through his refrigerator to make a salad and set place mats and cutlery on the breakfast bar, trying to stay busy. Keeping busy was definitely a way to keep from thinking about the fact that someone was trying to stop their investigation.

Was Matt that desperate? she wondered, but didn't have time to dwell on it too much as Jackson came into the kitchen in a T-shirt and sweats. The T-shirt hugged hard muscle, and the sweats hung loose on his lean hips. Her brain went somewhere dangerous, especially as he came by to snag a piece of lettuce from the salad and brushed against her.

He smelled of soap and man. All man, but she had to contain that awareness of him. It was just too dangerous, too distracting, considering all that was happening. But try as she might, it was impossible to ignore his presence. Powerful. Comforting. Tempting in a way that no man had ever tempted before.

And surprisingly, despite all that had happened that day, hunger awoke as Jackson pulled the pizza from the oven. He cut the slices with a big knife, his movements competent. Almost elegant, which made her itch to sketch him. She'd been so crazed in the last couple of days she hadn't even touched her sketch pad, but maybe she'd try tonight.

If Jackson would model for her, that was.

Working together as if they were an old married couple used to routines, she served the salad and he brought over the pizza and sodas. A glass of wine might have been nice, but they had to stay alert, not to mention that a little wine might make him even more dangerous to her control.

The pizza was delicious and unusual. "I've never had grilled pizza with barbecued chicken before."

"It's one of Deck's specialties. People love that he turns things on their heads," Jackson said and stuffed the last bit of crust into his mouth.

"He's been great. Please thank him for me," she said, grateful for all that Declan had done.

Jackson leaned back in his chair and focused his gaze on her, his eyes locked on her face. "Your dad was a police officer?"

She nodded and nibbled at the pizza crust. "He was. My mother was a music teacher, like Selene."

Jackson dished out the last two slices onto their plates and said, "I guess that explains the information you gave me. It was as neat and complete as any case file I've ever read."

"Dad was a stickler for being orderly and for doing the right thing," she said with a lift of her shoulders.

"That also explains why you're so determined to make things right for Selene," he said, grabbed his slice and took a big bite.

Although she picked up her own slice, she held it before her, unsure how to answer without having him worry. But he'd been nothing but honest with her, even admitting that assisting her might cost him the position as chief. So she charged on. "The only thing that would make things right is to have Selene home again, Jax. That's what I want more than anything."

Jackson set down his slice and this time when he gazed at her, the gray of his eyes was almost charcoal with worry. "I know you want that—"

She raised her hand in pleading. "Let's just leave it at that. Please."

He did as she asked, finishing the rest of his slice in silence while she nibbled at hers.

They washed dishes much the same way, standing side by side in silence, Jackson washing and Rhea drying. When they were done, Jackson leaned against the counter. "It's not that late. What would you like to do?"

It came out of her mouth before she could stop it. "I'd like to sketch you."

Chapter 13

Jackson lifted a brow. "Sketch me?"

She mimicked drawing on paper with her hands. "It helps me relax."

It might help her relax, but being the object of her attention would do little for his peace of mind. Still, it had been a challenging day for her, far more than for him, so if it would help her, he'd suffer it.

"If it'll help." He pointed toward his living room. "Mind if I start a fire?" he said, even though between the bonfire and the shed destruction he'd almost had enough of flames and wood smoke. But, as night had fallen, a chill had settled in the air and in him.

One of her dark brows flew upward, as if questioning his sanity, but seeing that he was serious, she acquiesced with a tilt of her head. "I'll get my sketch pad and pencils."

She rushed out and, if Jackson was reading her right,

she was anything but relaxed. Despite that, he intended to go along with her request, no matter how dangerous it might be to his self-control.

He marched to the living room, determined to get this over with as quickly as possible. Since he always kept the fireplace ready, it took little time for the tinder to catch and spread flames to the logs neatly stacked above it. Much like Rhea's dad, he was also a stickler for being orderly and doing the right thing. Which meant, no matter how tempting Rhea might be, he had to control himself.

At the wall of windows facing the deck, he hit a switch to engage the privacy blinds built into the panels. He didn't normally use them, preferring to see the woods and stars beyond, but the last thing he wanted was for a colleague doing his rounds to see him modeling for Rhea. He'd never live it down with his friends at the station.

She returned to the living room with her sketch pad and pencils, and took a spot in a chair directly opposite his big leather couch. "Would you mind stretching out there?" she asked, peering at the couch.

He stretched out there often after a hard day at work, the fireplace lit and the television turned on to one of the fix it channels or a baseball game. But doing so for her...

Sucking in a breath, he lay down and spread out on the couch, his toes touching one arm while he tucked a pillow against the other arm and set his head down on it.

Half-facing her, he tried to inject comfort into his voice as he said, "Here I am. Draw away."

A half smile, the smile of a siren luring men, graced

her lips while she flipped open the pad and grabbed a pencil. "Would you mind…?" She didn't finish, only did a little wiggle of her finger that communicated her wishes.

Despite being filled with trepidation, he pulled off his T-shirt. She rose and shut off the light on the table beside him, leaving only the firelight for illumination. It created intimacy in the room. Maybe too intimate since desire seemed to catch and flare like the tinder and logs in his fireplace.

Instead of returning to her chair, she sat on the edge of the coffee table and skimmed her hand over his shoulder to adjust the position of his body. But her touch changed as she ran her hand along the muscles on his arm and down his side, getting lighter. Even hesitant, but it did nothing to quell the passion rising within him.

He grabbed her hand to stop her, but found himself twining his fingers with hers and drawing her close. "I thought you wanted to sketch me?"

With a big swallow, she said, "I did. I do."

"The wisest thing would be for you to sit back in that chair and draw," he said, his voice husky to his ears from the strain of not pulling her close.

A light huff escaped her before that siren's smile drifted across her lips again. "That would be the right thing to do. So would this."

She leaned down and covered his mouth with hers, her lips mobile against him. Wet. Warm, so warm.

He cradled the back of her head to keep her near as they kissed over and over until they were both breathless. And while he wanted to urge her down beside him on the couch, he mustered his last bit of self-control.

Sweeping his hand around to cradle her jaw, he applied gentle pressure to shift her away. He locked his gaze on hers, a turbulent navy blue with desire. "I want this... I want you."

She nodded, clearly understanding where he was going. "You do the right thing. *We* do the right thing."

Clapping her hands on her thighs, she shot to her feet and sat across from him. She snatched her sketch pad from where she'd laid it earlier, picked up her pencils, crossed her legs and leaned the pad on her knee.

Rhea worked furiously at first, pencil scratching against the paper as the initial lines of the drawing took shape. The rough shape of the sofa. The long lines of his strong body, lying there with tension in every muscle. The power nestled in the shadows between his thighs...

"Relax," she said and inhaled deeply to do the same, slowing the stroke and pressure of her pencil to add dimension to the drawing. She normally did landscapes and still lifes, rarely portraits, but she was pleased by the image slowly coming alive on paper.

"You look...pleased," he said, a sexy huskiness in his tone.

She was and flipped the pad so he could view the drawing.

He raised an eyebrow. "Is that how you see me?"

She turned the pad around and examined her work. The man in her sketch was passion personified, his gaze heavy-lidded. A sexy smile on his lips that promised the pleasure she had experienced barely minutes earlier.

"Yes," she answered without hesitation.

He shifted to sit, fingers laced together, forearms

leaning on his muscled thighs. His features were troubled, his brow furrowed and his gaze nearly black. "I think it's time for me to do another walk around the property and check in with my colleagues."

Without waiting for her response, he grabbed his T-shirt and jerked it on. Pushed to his feet and marched off. After the snick of the front door opening and closing, Rhea leaned back in her chair and sighed.

What am I doing? It was crazy to get involved with Jackson, and not just now, when all their focus and attention had to be on the case. She had her life in Denver that she loved. The gallery, her apartment and the vibrant city life. But she couldn't deny that despite Selene's disappearance in Regina, the town called to her with its beautiful downtown, homes and the surrounding countryside. And, of course, Jackson. She wanted to explore what she was feeling for Jackson, both emotionally and physically.

And he clearly felt the same.

He wanted her and she him, but it would have to wait.

She collected her drawing supplies, determined to avoid Jackson. Determined not to crawl into bed with him. This time it wouldn't be because she was afraid or needed comfort. When she did join him the next time...

Driving that image from her brain, she bounded up the stairs and to her room. As she did so, she heard the front door open and close again, as well as the grate of the lock. Glancing toward the stairs, she caught sight of Jackson and closed her door. It was the coward's way out, but she didn't trust herself not to give in to what she wanted.

Jackson.

Leaning against the door, she took a bracing breath and listened for his footsteps as they came near and stopped by her room. A long pregnant pause followed, but then the footsteps moved away, down the hall to Jackson's bedroom.

The breath rushed out of her. Arms wrapped around her sketch pad, she walked to the bed and quickly changed into her pajamas. As she slipped into bed, she took hold of her sketch pad and opened it to the drawing of Jackson. Ran her fingers over it, imagining it was his skin beneath her hand, but not tonight.

Closing the pad, she grabbed her tablet, too wired to go to sleep.

With a few quick strokes, she was in Jackson's digital notebook. As she did, the program notified her that Jackson was likewise reviewing the information, and she shook her head.

In some ways, we're too alike, she thought and gave herself over to considering the evidence. Again.

The little icon at the top of the menu indicated that Rhea was likewise logged on to the notebook with the case file.

It seemed almost silly that they were both working on the materials separately, yards apart, but Jackson understood. Being together right now was too dangerous.

With the evidence they'd gathered in the last few days, it pointed to the possibility that Selene's death may have happened in Regina and not Avalon. He opened the file with the information that detailed the witness accounts of Selene's visit to the lake and the possible presence of a second vehicle.

First, he reviewed the approximate times against the spillway activity logs Rhea had obtained. The spillway had opened for a short stretch of time early that night, but even with adjustments for possible witness error as to the time Selene had been at the lake, the spillway had likely been closed when Selene had been killed.

If she'd been killed, the little voice in his head challenged.

Despite that being one of the possible scenarios, it just didn't seem plausible. If she had run away from Matt, Jackson had no doubt she would have run to her sister.

And then there was the text she'd sent.

I can't take it anymore. I can't. I'm finally going to do something about it.

What had that "something" been? he wondered. Had it been ending her life? If it had, the timing of that text would put her by the lake. Wouldn't she just have walked into the lake to take her life? Especially since her purse and cell phone had been sitting in her car, supporting that supposition. And if so, they were back to the fact that her body should have been found in the days after her disappearance.

He and his colleagues had searched the lake and surrounding shores with a fine-tooth comb and had not found her nor any evidence of her.

Blowing out a frustrated sigh, he opened his nightstand and pulled out the pad and pen he kept there because he often got ideas about cases at the oddest times.

He switched to the page in the notebook with information on the timeline for Selene's trip from Avalon to Regina. Setting aside the laptop, he took the notes and transferred them to his pad of paper, confirming what they had discussed before, namely, that Selene had spent way more time on the road between leaving Avalon and arriving at the lake in Regina.

Since he was well familiar with the route, he listed a few places Selene might have stopped that night. Since Selene had rushed off according to Matt, she might not have been prepared for a trip to Denver. That possibly meant a stop for gas.

There were two different gas stations near Regina to check in the morning.

She might have also been hungry or thirsty. Maybe tired and needing a pick-me-up, like a cup of coffee. There was a general store and coffee shop right off the highway, as well as two different restaurants on the street leading to the lake.

He jotted down those names and, for good measure, grabbed his laptop and searched the route using one of the online mapping services. That had him adding a chain pharmacy location, as well as a local pub. It was the kind of place a single woman might go for a quick hookup, but Selene would not have known that. She also would not have known that on occasion a rougher crowd frequented the location.

A chirp on his phone alerted him to a message.

She had to have stopped somewhere along the route to the lake. Maybe the coffee shop. She's a caffeine fiend.

He texted back, I agree. I made a list of spots we can check in the morning.

A long pause followed before she texted, Thank you. I appreciate all that you're doing.

He wanted to say that it was his job, but it had become more than that to him. *She* had become more to him.

Fingers over his phone screen, he hesitated, but then finally wrote, We will find out what happened. Together.

Breath held, he waited for her response and smiled when it came.

Together. Good night, Jax.

Good night, Rhea.

Chapter 14

Morning came way too quickly.

Jackson woke just as the first rose-and-purple fingers of dawn were clawing their way into the sky. He dressed in his uniform, strapped on his service belt and chatted with the two officers in the cruiser.

"Nothing happening, Detective," said the one young officer.

"Thanks, Officer Troutman. I'm going to take a walk around the property, just in case."

He reconnoitered the grounds, but everything was in order, except of course for the burned shed, including the charred remains of his favorite chain saw and ax.

When he went back inside, Rhea was also dressed and putting up a pot of coffee.

"Good morning, Jax," she said, glancing over her shoulder at him.

He walked to her and laid a hand at her waist, urging her around. "Everything okay with us?"

She peered up at him, her blue gaze skimming over his face, as powerful as a caress. "We're...okay." With a flip of her hand in the direction of the stove, she said, "I was just going to make breakfast before we checked out some of those stops."

"One of the places, the general store, has a 24-hour cafeteria. Since you're up, how about we get breakfast there? The food is really good."

"That sounds great. We could also poke around. See if anyone remembers seeing Selene," she said and went to leave, but he tightened his hold at her waist to keep her close.

"Don't get your hopes up. Luckily, we'll have that cell phone information I requested later today. That should help us pinpoint Selene's and Matt's whereabouts on that night."

"I get it, Jax. Don't get disappointed that nothing we've done so far has helped us know more about what happened to my sister. I get it," she said, the threat of tears obvious in her voice and eyes, which shimmered with angry tears.

He wasn't going to push anymore. "I'll wait for you outside." He eased his grip, and she raced away to get her purse.

He went out to his cruiser to wait for her. When she approached, he held the door open and waited until she was settled to get behind the wheel for the drive to the general store.

Rhea tried to stay patient as Jackson drove, even though her insides were as turbulent as water boiling for tea. She hadn't meant to sound condemning but knew it had come out that way. But it wasn't Jackson's fault that they hadn't made any progress on the case. Well, not unless you counted ruling out scenarios as making progress.

But she was sure of one thing: If Matt had killed Selene, he hadn't taken her back to Avalon. Everything at the ridge construction site and the bonfire seemed to point to that. But everything inside of her continued to say that Selene was still alive. Rhea still felt her presence strongly and maybe in the next few days they would get the evidence needed to prove that.

The general store was on the road immediately adjacent to the highway. If Selene had taken the exit for Regina, she would have driven down that road on her way to the lake.

Much like everything else in Regina, the general store was a quaint throwback to earlier times. Way earlier times, like the 1800s. It had that old Western feel to it with a retail area where you could buy an assortment of items. Right beside the retail section was the restaurant area, complete with waitresses in neat candy-striped aprons that screamed 1950s instead of 1850s. Both areas were neat, clean and busier than she had expected at such an early hour.

As soon as they walked into the restaurant, one of the waitresses, a pretty twentysomething with dark brown hair, doe eyes and a brilliant smile hurried over to greet them. Well, greet Jackson.

"Nice to see you again, Jackson," she said and literally batted her eyelash extensions at him while barely flicking a glance in Rhea's direction.

"Nice to see you, too, Melissa. Table for two please,"

he said and smiled at Rhea. For good measure, he laid a possessive arm around her waist.

Melissa's smile immediately faded as she stared at Rhea and at Jackson's gesture.

"Right this way," Melissa said and, with jerky motions, pulled menus from a nearby holder.

They followed the young woman to a booth. After handing them the menus, Melissa rushed off with a muttered, "I'll get you some coffees."

Rhea stared after the waitress and raised an eyebrow. "Old flame?"

"Unwanted crush," he answered without hesitation and buried his head in the menu.

As handsome as Jackson was, she suspected he was the object of quite a lot of crushes, including her she had to admit. Although it was well past the crush phase and into the "What do we call this now?" point in a relationship.

To distract herself from where those thoughts would go, she perused the menu, which reminded her of one from a diner she had visited during a trip to New York City. There were dozens of menu choices, from a variety of omelets, pancakes and waffles to assorted breakfast wraps. Maybe too many choices, but Jackson had said the food was good here.

The noisy clatter of china and cutlery heralded Melissa's return as she set their cutlery and coffees down before them. She whipped out a pad and pen. "What can I get you?"

"Cream. Sugar. Huevos Rancheros, please," Rhea said and handed the menu to the waitress.

"Rocky Mountain wrap for me. Thanks, Melissa," Jackson said and likewise returned the menu. Before she could walk away, Jackson said, "Do you ever work the nighttime shift?"

She shook her head. "Going to night school, so I'm always on either the morning or afternoon shift." She jerked her head in the direction of another of the waitresses. "Judy over there sometimes works late night."

"Would you mind asking her to come over?" Jackson said and offered up a smile that seemed to restore some friendliness to the waitress.

"Sure thing, Jax. Anything for you," she said, stevia-sweet, but with a frown in Rhea's direction.

She sped away to place their orders and talk to another waitress, who was just hanging up her apron behind the counter. The older woman glanced in their direction, but seeing that it was Jackson, smiled and waddled over. She was at least six or seven months pregnant.

When she approached, Jackson popped up from his seat and offered it to her, but she waved him off. "If I sit down, I may never get up again," she said with a tired laugh, laid a hand at her waist and stretched.

Jackson chuckled and slipped back into the booth. He reached into his shirt pocket and pulled out a photo of Selene, which jerked a puzzled look to Judy's face. The pregnant waitress looked from the photo to Rhea and back to the photo. Rhea explained.

"She's my twin sister. She disappeared six months ago."

Judy nodded. "I remember. Her photo was all over the papers and on the news."

"Were you working that night?" Jackson asked.

Judy nodded. "I normally work those late shifts.

Lets me be home for the kids during the day. She wasn't in any night that I was working."

"You sure?" Jackson pressed and slipped the photo back into his shirt pocket.

Judy tightened her lips and wagged her head. "Very sure. We don't get that many people late at night during the fall months. More in the summer and winter. If I'd seen her, I would have contacted you back then."

"Thanks, Judy," he said.

Rhea parroted his words. "Thank you. We appreciate it, and good luck with the new baby."

"Thank you, and hang in there. You're in good hands," Judy said with an incline of her head in Jackson's direction.

"I know," she said as Judy waddled out of the restaurant.

At that moment, Melissa returned with their orders, and Rhea understood why Jackson's dish had been called the Rocky Mountain wrap. The wrap was huge and piled high with french fries, gravy and cheese. Not that her eggs were much smaller. A big pile of scrambled eggs were topped with fresh salsa and cotija cheese, and the smells...

Her stomach rumbled from the aromas of spice, fresh cilantro and the earthiness of the coffee.

"These are gut busters," she said, but dug into her eggs.

"Perfect," Jackson said with a wink and likewise forked up some of his wrap because it was way too big to eat with his hands.

Hunger tamped down any discussion for several minutes, but Rhea realized she'd never be able to finish. There was way too much food, no matter how tasty it was.

Jackson seemed to have no such problem as he continued chowing down. She hated to interrupt his enjoyment of the meal, but after Judy's comments, she'd been wondering where else Selene might have stopped the night she disappeared.

"My sister loves her coffee. If she was in a hurry, but tired, she might have stopped for a shot of caffeine to keep her going."

Jackson nodded. "It is another hour and a half to Denver, so that makes sense. We'll try the coffee shop next while we wait for the cell phone location information."

Rhea leaned back into the booth cushion and rubbed her belly, which she was sure was at least an inch bigger thanks to the delicious breakfast. "I feel like I need a nap and we just woke up," she said with a laugh.

Jackson grinned and chuckled. "I know what you mean, but I can't say no to the Rocky Mountain wrap," he said and kept on eating while she sat there, watching him and thinking about where else her sister may have stopped.

If Matt had attacked Selene, had she had fought back? If she had done that, had she been hurt? Had she stopped at an urgent care facility or a pharmacy for some supplies? Rhea wondered. All places for them to check, and she knew Jackson had placed the big chain pharmacy on his list. She felt confident that Jackson had things under control. That she was in good hands, as Judy had said.

And such nice hands, she thought, as he laid down his knife and fork when he finished his meal. She was a sucker for hands, and she had to admit that his touch, so comforting and strong, stirred intense emotions within her.

He raised his hand and signaled for Melissa to bring over the check.

"Let me," Rhea said, and Jackson was about to argue with her, but apparently seeing her determination, he demurred.

"Thanks, Rhea," he said and laid his hand over hers.

Comforting and strong, she thought again and took hold of his hand. "I should be thanking you for offering your time. Your home. Your protection."

Jackson wanted to say again that it was his job, but that would be a massive lie. It had become so much more than that. But he had to maintain his objectivity, which had slipped more than once in the last few days. Because of that, he tried to adopt a neutral and professional tone as he said, "It's what I had to do to help solve this case."

Her hand jerked in his, obviously stung by his words and tone. She awkwardly drew her hand away and hid it beneath the tabletop. When Melissa brought over the check, Rhea barely glanced at it before placing her credit card on the plastic tray. Melissa swept by and snatched it off the table, clearly still in a huff.

Great, two women pissed at me, he thought. His cell phone vibrated and chirped in his pants pocket, and he drew it out to see a message from the desk sergeant.

Just emailed you info from cell phone company.

He texted back, Great. Thanks.

He swiped to open his email and smiled at the data

the cell phone company had provided. Not only was there a spreadsheet for the week Selene had disappeared, the company had assigned one of their engineers to interpret the data.

Rhea was tucking her credit card back in her wallet when he said, "We have the info. I suggest we head to the police station to review it."

"That's good news," she said and slipped out of the booth.

He followed Rhea to his cruiser. It took only a few minutes to reach the police station and settle themselves in the conference room. With a few commands, Jackson had the spreadsheet and analysis on a large monitor.

His police chief strolled by the room, then backtracked to enter. The older man gestured to the information. "Is that the cell phone data?"

Jackson nodded. "It is, and we also have a report that pinpoints where Selene and Matt were that week."

With the laser pointer and mouse, Jackson reviewed the data and maps with Rhea and his boss. The information confirmed exactly when Selene had left Avalon, but more importantly, where she had stopped that night. The tracking continued after Selene's message to Rhea, but since the cell phone had been left behind in the car, it told them little about what had happened after the text.

Still, the data showed that there had certainly been enough time for Matt to follow Selene and then return to Avalon.

"The Avalon police didn't ask for Matt's cell phone info because he supposedly forgot it at home that night," he said, recalling the information they'd provided from their case file. He pulled up the report on Matt, which confirmed that his phone had been in Avalon the entire night.

"Too convenient," Rhea said, and the police chief echoed her comment.

"The kind of thing someone does if they don't want to be tracked," he said.

"But his Jeep has a navigation system," Rhea reminded them, only Jackson shook his head.

"Most NAV systems use a positioning system that's only a one-way stream of data. But if he has something with a cellular connection, that provider might have that info. It's something we'll have to investigate further if this info doesn't pan out," he said and went back to the data on the screen.

"It looks like Selene stopped for gas right before she got to Regina," he said.

"Just like we thought, since she left her house in a rush," Rhea said, recalling their conversation of the day before.

"That's our next stop. We'll see who was working that night and reach out to them." Jackson moved on to the next stop that the cell phone company engineer had identified.

"She was at the pub for a good half an hour. Probably to get dinner," Jackson said and frowned. "Not the best place for a woman alone."

"Not unless she's looking for a hookup. That is what you call it now, right?" the police chief said and glanced toward Rhea. "Sorry, ma'am. No offense intended."

"None taken, but Selene isn't that kind of woman. It makes me wonder why she would have stopped there."

The police chief snapped his fingers and screwed

his eyes upward, as if searching for something at the tip of his memory. "Isn't the guy who owns that gas station buddies with the pub owners?"

Jackson searched his memory. "I think you're right, Bill. They may even be related. Cousins, I think."

"If the cousin was working he might suggest the pub if someone asks for a recommendation," Rhea added to the discussion.

"Or he may tell his employees to suggest the pub," the chief said. With a smile and a point of his finger at Jackson, he added, "Good work, Jax. Just remember what we discussed."

With that, the chief pivoted and marched out of the room, leaving Rhea with a puzzled look on her face. Her eyes narrowed and settled on him, clearly expecting an explanation.

He hesitated, but Rhea deserved to know. "Nothing that embarrasses us or the Avalon PD."

"And what if it does that? Are you willing to bury the investigation—"

"Have I done anything that would make you think that?" he challenged, a wildfire of anger rushing through him.

Demurely, seemingly chastised, she said in a soft tone, "No. You haven't."

"I made you a promise and I intend to keep it, Rhea. If you don't trust me—"

"I do, Jax. I'm sorry that I suggested otherwise. It's just…emotional for me, and I can't be as objective as I should."

"Neither can I, Rhea. You make me feel…" He jammed his hands on his hips and sucked in a breath. "We've finally got a solid lead and we need to keep our focus on this." He circled the pub on the map with the laser pointer and then moved it to a location by the lake, the last spot on Selene's journey.

Subdued, head slightly bowed, Rhea said, "I guess we hit the road to talk to some people."

"We do. Are you ready?" The words seemed simple enough, but they were filled with many more questions. Was she ready to learn more about that night? Ready for possibly more disappointment?

So many questions, but at least now they had the data to continue to ask those questions. *Thanks to Rhea*, he thought.

She met his gaze directly, her chin tilted defiantly. A tight smile on her face. "I'm ready."

Chapter 15

The gas station was a no-frills no-name location that survived due to a lack of competition. For anyone who had underestimated the distance to either Denver or any of the ski resorts to the west, the gas station was a last resort.

Jackson parked in front of the tiny market the station boasted. *A patron can pick up some sodas or snacks, in addition to the gasoline,* Rhea thought. The far side of the station housed several mechanic's bays. As they stepped out of the car, a large mountain of a man clothed in grease-stained overalls ambled out of one of the bays. He wiped his hands with a cloth that wasn't much cleaner and frowned as he saw Jackson.

"Detective," he said when he approached, but didn't hold his hand out. Instead, he held them up to show they were just too dirty for a handshake.

"Hannibal. Good to see you. How's it going?" Jackson asked, totally at ease despite the hostile vibes she was sensing from the man.

"Got work and customers, but I don't think you're here to talk about that," the man said. His voice was deep and with his longish brown hair and beard and large size, he reminded her of a bear, but not the cuddly type. The kind with sharp claws and teeth to tear you apart.

Jackson held his hands up as if in surrender. "Not here to create any problems. Just to ask a few questions."

Hannibal shrugged. "Ask away. I've got nothing to hide."

Which was just what she would expect someone to say if they did have something to hide.

"This is Rhea. Her twin sister, Selene, disappeared about six months ago, and we've got info that says she stopped here for gas," Jackson said.

A careless shrug of Hannibal's wide, thick shoulders was followed by, "I get lots of people stopping here for gas. I'd have remembered a looker like that." His stare in her direction, very much a leer, left Rhea feeling dirty.

"Watch it, Hannibal," Jackson warned. "Do you work the night shift?"

Hannibal shook his head. "Too old for that. Couple of local kids work the late shifts."

Jackson nodded. "What about the pub? Doesn't your brother own it?" he asked, puzzling Rhea, since she thought Jackson had said it was a cousin.

With another shake of his head and wipe of his hands with the dirty cloth, Hannibal said, "My cousin Drew, but he doesn't do that at the pub."

Do what? she wondered at the same time as Jackson asked the question.

"Girls. Slavery. That kind of stuff," Hannibal answered, sending a shiver of fear through Rhea. While she hoped Selene was still alive, the thought of her having been trafficked...

"If someone asked for a recommendation for a restaurant—" Jackson began, but Hannibal quickly cut him off.

"I'd recommend the pub. Tell my boys to do the same. Family sticks together."

Jackson paused, but then challenged Hannibal. "Does family stick together enough to hide a murder? Or a kidnapping?"

The other man obviously didn't like the insinuation. "We're done here, Detective. You want to talk to me or my boys again, call my lawyer." Without missing a beat, the man walked away and back to the mechanic's bay. A second later, the sound of metal striking metal told them he was back at work.

Jackson peered at her. "Time to hit the pub."

The outside of the pub was not quite what she expected for a place of supposedly ill repute. The parking lot and grounds surrounding the building were clean and the landscaping welcomed with colorful flowers and neat bushes. The cedar shake siding, trim and doors had a fresh coat of paint.

When they entered there were very few patrons, but a couple of people were eating a late breakfast. The biggest feature in the space was a large horseshoe bar that separated the dining area from a section boasting cocktail-height tables, a dance floor and an upraised stage.

The place smelled faintly of yeasty beer, fried eggs and bacon, with a lingering hint of disinfectant, as if the floors and other areas had just been cleaned.

They had no sooner entered when a thirtysomething bearded man approached, a broad smile on his face. He stuck his hand out to Jackson and said, "Jax, dude, how are you doing?"

Jackson took the man's hand and pulled him in for a bro hug. "Marcus. What are you doing here?"

As the man stepped back from the embrace, he eyeballed Rhea and Jackson, as if to trying to figure out what they were doing together. "And you're…?"

She offered her hand to the man, and he shook it, politely and almost gently. "Rhea Reilly. Jackson and I are investigating my sister's disappearance."

Marcus lost a little of his earlier effusiveness and dipped his head respectfully. "Sorry to hear about that, but what brings you here?"

"We have some questions, Marcus. Is there somewhere—" Jackson peered all around the restaurant to see who might be listening "—more private."

Marcus nodded and swung his arm wide. "My office."

Marcus led the way, with Jackson and her following. As they walked, Jackson said, "Your office? You're working here?"

Marcus looked over his shoulder and shrugged. "After those fights you busted up last summer, the owner decided he needed to restore some law and order, so here I am."

Jackson explained for her. "Marcus used to be on the Regina police force, but decided to retire."

They had reached the door to a back office, and

Marcus unlocked it. They followed him down a hall past storage areas and a kitchen to an office at the farthest end of the hall. As he sat and invited them to join him, Marcus said, "Let's be honest, Jax. I had an alcohol problem, but thanks to you I've been sober for over a year and I have a new chance at life. I've been the manager since last September."

"I'm glad to hear that, but isn't it hard for you to work here?" Jackson asked and held his hands wide in emphasis.

A quick, tense shrug answered him. "Not easy at times, but this was a great opportunity, and it's been working as you may have noticed."

Jackson nodded. "Haven't been called out here for anything major."

"Good. Let's hope it stays that way. So how can I help you with your investigation?" Marcus leaned back in his chair, which creaked with the motion.

Jackson glanced at her, and she understood. "My sister may have been here the night she disappeared. We're trying to figure out if she met anyone that night."

Marcus shared an uneasy glance with Jackson before blurting out, "We get lots of women here, especially on the weekends. They come in for fun. Maybe meet someone."

"Selene, Rhea's sister, probably just stopped for dinner. She wasn't here for more than about forty minutes," Jackson said.

Marcus raised a brow as if to say it didn't take long for what most women in the pub wanted, but he was gentleman enough not to say it. "I don't know how we can help with more."

Rhea pointed out his door to another office where

she had noticed a number of monitors flashing images. "You have security cameras. Do you keep recordings from those cameras?"

Marcus leaned forward to track where she was pointing. He nodded and leaned back again, totally casual. "We do, but we only hold them for about two weeks. Unless there's some kind of incident. Then we label and store them."

"Would you possibly have any from November of last year? November 7, actually?" Jackson said.

Marcus immediately answered. "No, sorry."

"Are you sure?" Rhea asked, worried they were going to hit another dead end.

Marcus nodded. "I am. The PC for the recording system died on us right around then. Tech said it was toast and took it away. Set up a new system."

"Is it possible he still has that failed system?" Jackson asked.

"Possible," Marcus said and pulled open his desk drawer. He scrounged around, yanked out a wrinkled business card and handed it to Jackson. "Here's his info. I'll let him know you're coming."

"We truly appreciate that, Marcus. Thank you," Rhea said, grateful that the man hadn't been an obstructionist, which was what she'd been expecting after their earlier meeting with the gas station owner.

"My pleasure. Like I said before, we're trying to clean this place up, so anything to support our local police department," Marcus said as he rose and held his hand out to Jackson again. "I mean that, dude. You saved my life."

Jackson clasped the other man's hand in both of

his. "I'm glad to see you're doing well, Marcus. Just remember we're all here for you."

"You always were. If you don't mind, I've got some things to do before lunch," Marcus said and grimaced at the pile of papers on his desk.

"Totally get it and thanks again," Rhea said and hurried from the office to the restaurant, picturing Selene there. Wondering if someone had approached her. Someone who had decided to take her.

"Penny for your thoughts," Jackson said as they stepped outside and looked back at the pub. He smoothed a finger across the furrow in Rhea's forehead.

"Maybe something happened to her here. Someone who thought she was here for a hookup and decided to make that happen," Rhea said, worried that such an encounter may have turned into something violent.

"It's possible, Rhea. Although we've never had that kind of problem here," Jackson said.

Rhea crossed her arms and rubbed her hands up and down her arms. He hugged her close, offering comfort. Aware that, little by little, Rhea might be losing hope that Selene was still alive.

"Let's hit the road and see the tech."

The silence as they drove to the tech's offices weighed on him heavily, because Rhea was hurting. Luckily the office was just a block off Main Street and, as promised, Marcus had called ahead. The tech greeted them with no hesitation.

"Marcus says you want to look at their old system. I pulled it off the scrap pile for you." The tech walked to a large worktable in his back room. A computer tower sat there, a little dusty and worse for wear.

Jackson scrutinized it and then peered at the tech. "No chance of it working?"

The tech shook his head. "Tried, but there was a head crash. Head plinked around that disk like a marble in a pinball machine," he said and mimicked something bouncing around with his fingers. "That's why it was on the scrap pile. I keep the older units around in case I need power supplies, motherboards. That kind of thing."

"Mind if we take it?" Jackson said, earning a puzzled look from Rhea, and he explained, "My cousins in Miami are tech savants. Maybe they can get something off the unit."

"I'd be happy to pull the drive for you," the tech said and went into action, removing it from the system and packing it up.

"Good luck with it," the young man said and handed the box to Jackson.

"Thanks for all your help," Rhea offered, and Jackson echoed her sentiments.

"We appreciate the assistance."

Outside the tech's office, Jackson paused by his cruiser and whipped out his cell phone, wasting no time to call his cousins. Robert answered on the first ring. "Cuz, long time no hear," he said.

"Sorry, Robbie. I've just been a little busy. How are you and Sophie doing?"

"We're doing well. Let me put you on speaker," Robbie said and, a second later, the tone grew a little tinny as the speaker kicked in.

"I'm putting you on speaker also, Robbie. I have Rhea Reilly on the line with me. We're working on a case together."

"Hi, Robbie. Sophie," Rhea said.

"Nice to meet you," Sophie said. "What can we help you with?"

"You always cut to the chase, Sophie," Jackson teased and plowed on. "We have a hard drive with a head crash that may have information we need."

Robbie let out a low whistle. "Head crash is bad, man. That head hitting the disk probably took out some data."

"Some, but not all I gather," Jackson said, feeling optimistic that if anyone could get information from the disk it would be his cousins.

"Not all. Can you send it to us?" Sophie said.

"We can courier it to you for morning delivery," Jackson said, and his cousins clearly understood.

"We'll work on it immediately. Anything in particular?" Robbie asked.

"The hard drive was on a security system. We're looking for camera images from November 7. Anything from about 7:30 p.m. to 9:00 p.m.," he said.

"We're on it, Jax. If we can't get it for you, no one can," Sophie said.

"Thank you. It means a lot to me, since it may help us find out what happened to my sister," Rhea said.

"Family is important. Remember that, Jax," Robbie said, guilt heavy in his tone.

Miami was so not his style, but he understood. "I get it. When I have a vacation coming up I'll come visit my parents and swing by South Beach to see you."

"We'll hold you to that, Jax," Sophie said, and then the line went dead.

Rhea narrowed her eyes and glanced at him. "Somehow I can't picture you in South Beach."

Jackson sighed. "A little too city, hot and humid for me, but my parents have a place not far from there, and my uncle married into a Cuban family in Miami."

"And your cousins are there?" Rhea asked.

Jackson nodded. "Robbie and Sophie have their own tech company that develops apps and software, but my aunt's family has this high-powered private investigation and security company. The Liberty Agency. Robbie and Sophie often help them."

"I guess law enforcement runs in the family," Rhea said as Jackson opened the door to the cruiser.

Jackson slipped back into the driver's seat and, as he did so, he said, "And the military. Several of the members of the Gonzalez family that runs the Liberty Agency also served. Plus my Aunt Mercedes and Uncle Robert work for the NSA in D.C."

"Wow. Super-secret shadowy types," she teased.

He was about to start the car when a chirp announced he had a text message. With a quick look, he said, "Declan sent the photos of the bonfire." He held the phone so she could see the first photo. But as they swiped from one to the other, it was clear that the results of their experiment were not close to the crime scene photos of Matt's bonfire.

"There's a lot of dark residue and...bones," Rhea said with a frown.

Jackson nodded. "The experts pretty much told me to expect the residue from the body tissues."

With a rough breath, Rhea said, "I guess the cremation theory is out, isn't it?"

Jackson laid a hand on her shoulder and squeezed. "Tabled for now. Once we get this package off to my cousins, there's not much for us to do. Maybe review the materials again? Call Avalon PD for updates."

Rhea wasn't sure she could spend another night looking at the information and worrying about being disappointed or whether whoever was after her would try something else.

"I'd like to take the night off and return to Denver. Check in at my shop and maybe just get away from... everything," she said, and at his crestfallen face, she realized he'd interpreted it to include him. Speedily she added, "You're welcome to come with."

Peering at her, gray eyes squinted, awakening lines at the corners, he said, "It makes sense, because I want to make sure you're okay, but are you sure?"

She was and wasn't and hated that she couldn't figure out what she wanted with him. She punted and said, "You can use my guest room. Selene normally stays there."

He hesitated, but then nodded. "Let's get this package mailed and swing by my house to get our things."

"Sure," she said and sat there, anticipating what it would feel like to have him in her home. He was so big and masculine. Country. Her apartment was a lot like her. Artsy. Feminine. City.

In no time, they had run to the courier service and dropped off the hard drive, as well as made the trip to his house to pick up things for an overnight stay in Denver. Jackson also changed out of his police uniform into street clothes, and her heart did a little jump at the sight of him. The faded jeans hugged his powerful legs and trim waist. A pale blue button-down shirt brought out shards of blue in his gray eyes. But a loose denim jacket barely hid the bulge that told her he was wearing his holster and service weapon.

As they drove, she stayed silent, her thoughts bouncing around like the marble in the pinball game the tech had mentioned earlier.

She hadn't really expected to be staying in Jackson's home and the time spent there with him had provided her a whole new view of the detective she had nearly barreled over just a few days ago. He was a man who loved his family and obviously wanted one of his own, judging from the home he had built himself. He was honorable, even if it might cost him personally. And a leader, judging from the way Diego, Declan and even Marcus had assisted with the investigation. They clearly respected him, but he obviously cared about them, as well.

She was so lost in her thoughts that she hadn't realized they had entered the city limits until Jackson parked. They did the short walk to her building and she guided him toward the elevator at the back of the lobby. "I'm on the top floor."

Jackson took the time to appreciate Rhea's building. It was done in art deco style, with speckled black terrazzo floors and marbled walls. Sconces and other accents in shiny steel lightened all those dark colors as did the ornate wooden doors of the elevator.

As they stepped into the elevator, Rhea stuck a key into the panel to unlock the penthouse access and once they reached that floor, the elevator opened right into her home. A very feminine home filled with neutral-colored furniture with plush cushions and brightly colored accent pillows. The walls boasted an assortment of artwork, including some of Rhea's pieces. He recognized them immediately based on what he'd seen on her website. The paintings had that passion and life that jumped off the walls and called to him to take a closer look.

"Do you like?" she asked, hands clasped before her. A nervous seesaw from side to side while she waited for his opinion.

"I love it. You make the image come alive," he said and smiled. He turned and held his hands wide. "This is very nice. Full of life. Color."

"Thank you. It's taken some time to get it here, but I'm happy with it," she said and visibly relaxed, holding out a hand to him, which he took in his.

"I can see why. I know it's early, but how about a walk and dinner?" he said, splaying a hand across his stomach to hide the hunger grumble he felt building inside.

"I'd like that. One of my favorite places is just a few blocks away."

"I want to get to know what you like. How you live." She had intrigued him on multiple levels, from her determination and work on her sister's case, to her strength while in harm's way and the art on the walls that spoke of her passion for life. And, of course, the steel hidden beneath her delicate exterior that said she was the kind of woman he could have by his side. A woman who didn't wilt when faced with adversity.

"Great. I think you'll really like it." She tugged on his hand gently to steer him toward the door. He went willingly, eager for Rhea to have a distraction from her sister's case and the attacks against her, if only for the one night. Eager to get know more about her and how she lived.

Outside, they hurried away from the mall area and toward the Larimer Square historic district with its heritage buildings, eclectic shops and restaurants. With the warmer weather a number of the restaurants had created al fresco dining areas on the sidewalks. Edison lights had been strung overhead and across the street, creating a festive feel especially when combined with vibrant banners touting an upcoming music festival. Beneath trees boasting bright spring green leaves rested planters with vibrant blooms and small bushes that softened the urban feel of the buildings.

Rhea dragged him to the entrance to a steak place and, at his questioning look, she said, "I love a good piece of beef as much as you do."

He swung her arm playfully. "I'd tell you I'm vegan, but you already saw me chow down at Deck's."

"I did, and I hope you'll love this place also," she said, and with another tug, urged him into the restaurant.

The host at the podium, a youngish man in his late twenties, raised an eyebrow as Rhea came in with Jackson. The man swung around the podium to give her an effusive hug. "Rhea! So good to see you! And who's this?" he asked, shooting a warning glare in Jackson's direction.

With a playful shove, she pushed the host away. "Easy, Randy. This is Detective Whitaker. He's helping me with Selene's case."

Jackson shook the other's man hand and tried not to be too stung that Rhea hadn't said he was a friend. But then again, he wouldn't be too happy about being friend-zoned, either, since he wanted more from her.

"Your favorite table is free," Randy said, grabbed

some menus and guided them to a spot right by the windows where they could have dinner and people watch, as well.

After they were seated, Jackson leaned close and over the top of his menu whispered, "If you and Randy—"

Rhea chuckled and skimmed her hand across his forearm. "He's just a friend. A friend who's probably way more interested in you than me."

Jackson peered at the man, who smiled at him.

"Oh, okay. I was worried he might think I was competition or something."

Rhea smiled, and it was the smile of a seductress. Her crystal blue gaze darkened and her voice was husky, sexy, as she said, "No one can compete with you, Jax."

Wow, definitely not friend-zoned. "I can say the same about you, Rhea. My one wish is that we hadn't met the way we did, but I'm glad we've met."

"Me, too," she said and set her menu down.

The waiter approached at that moment and said. "Good to see you again, Rhea. The usual?"

"The usual, Sam," she answered and handed him the menu.

"What about you, sir?" the waiter said, his tone not anywhere near as friendly, warning that Rhea had another possible protector.

"The porterhouse. Medium rare," he said. As the waiter rushed away to place their orders, Jackson picked up his water glass and glanced at her over the rim. "You have a lot of defenders."

Rhea grinned and shook her head. "They're just not used to me bringing a man here," she said and then covered her mouth. He thought he heard her mutter,

"Stupid, stupid, stupid." It brought a smile to his face, since it made him special and since it confirmed that Rhea lacked guile.

He took hold of her hand. "I'm glad I'm special. I am special, right?"

With a chuckle, she twined her fingers with his. "And dense, if you don't know that yet."

Sam, the waiter, returned with a wine bottle and made quite a show of opening it. "Courtesy of Randy. One of our best cabernets."

They both offered their thanks, and Jackson took the first sip. "Excellent."

Sam filled their glasses and walked away to give them privacy. Jackson raised his glass and toasted. "To friendship."

She tapped her glass to his and surprised him again with her boldness. "To friendship and more, Jax."

With a dip of his head, he said, "To more."

Chapter 16

Jackson lounged on Rhea's sofa, his muscled arms resting along the top of the cushions. He'd taken off his denim jacket and carefully folded it to cradle the holster he also removed. The pile of the jacket and holster sat off to the side, a very masculine contrast to the brightly colored pillows tucked all around him.

Her belly was full with the fabulous filet mignon and wine she'd had for dinner, as well as the cheesecake slice she'd shared with Jackson. In truth, she was a little sleepy and, dare she say it, at peace for the first time in months.

Hard to believe, considering she still didn't know what had happened to Selene and someone was trying to either kill her or drive her off the investigation.

But with Jackson there...

So many different emotions raced through her in

addition to the peace. Comfort. Need, especially as he settled his gaze on her. His gray eyes were dark, almost black as he invited her to join him on the couch. Invited her to more.

She didn't hesitate, taking hold of his hand and snuggling into his side, her head pillowed against his chest. His heartbeat loud and beginning to race beneath her ear.

He skimmed his hand across her hair, smoothing it. Slipping beneath the hair at her shoulders to her neck, where he massaged her muscles and then shifted his hand downward again to hug her close.

She snuggled in tighter and higher, until her lips were barely inches from his. Laying her hand on his chest, she pressed upward to trace the edge of his jaw with her mouth. Beneath her hand, his muscles tensed.

She looked up at him. Found the question in his gaze. "I'm sure, Jax. I've never been more sure of anything in my life."

Her words released his control. Urgently he slipped his hands to her waist and urged her upward. Their first tentative kiss, one of invitation and acceptance, quickly flared into one of heat and passion. They kissed over and over, mouths meeting ruthlessly, hungrily.

As Jackson brought his hand around to cup her breast, she moaned and moved to straddle his thighs. His body was hard everywhere. Strong. So strong and insistent against hers.

She shifted on him, needing him. Needing to release her control and savor what this amazing man could provide.

Jackson groaned as Rhea moved on him. He clasped

her hips with his hands and urged her to still. "Rhea. Are you sure?"

"Yes, I am. Come with me." She eased from his lap and tugged him off the sofa.

He willingly followed, needing Rhea like he had no other woman. Wanting to explore the complex woman he'd only known for a few days. Humbled that he could feel so much for her in so short a time.

In her bedroom, she went straight to the bed and offered him a smile that was both welcoming and hesitant. He bent and tasted that smile. Accepted the invitation and hoped to ease her sudden reluctance, because if he couldn't...

He wouldn't pressure her.

He turned to sit on the bed, bringing her face-to-face with him.

Cupping her cheek, he gentled her and welcomed her into the V of his outspread legs. Gently he strummed his thumb across her cheek. Soothed his other hand up and down her side.

She laid her hands on his shoulders before leaning close and kissing him again. The kiss tentative at first until passion ignited need so intense, it was impossible to stop.

Kissing was interrupted only to remove clothes until flesh was against flesh, and Jackson slipped on protection. He covered her with his body, joining with her. Breaths caught with the union. Exploded as Jackson moved within her, pulling her ever higher. Pushing them closer and closer to the edge until, with a final thrust, they tumbled over the edge together.

Rhea cuddled tight to Jackson's side, her thigh tossed over his. Her head pillowed on his muscled chest. He draped his arm down her back, holding her near. He laid his other arm across hers, pinning it against his chest. His touch soothing as he grazed his hand along her upper arm.

"That was…nice," she said, unable to find the right word to describe what she was feeling. Satisfied. Peaceful. Expectant.

"Ouch. Just nice," he teased, laughter in his tone and in the shake of his body beneath hers.

She leaned an elbow on his chest and glanced up at him. "Okay, maybe more than nice. But don't let your ego get out of hand."

He inched a dark brow upward. "A lot more than nice?"

Chuckling, she settled back onto his chest and drifted her hand down his midsection and lower. "Maybe. Want to try for way more than nice?"

He rolled her beneath him. "Definitely."

They were heading back to Rhea's apartment after visiting her gallery the next morning when the call came from his cousin Sophie.

"I hope this is good news," Jackson said as he answered and paused by the entrance to the building.

"So nice to talk to you, too, *primo*," Sophie teased.

"Sorry, cuz. It is nice to hear from you. How are you?" he said and looked in Rhea's direction. With a dip of his head, he confirmed it was the call for which they'd been waiting.

"I'm fine, and so are you. Robbie and I managed to get some images off the hard drive of that woman whose photo you sent. It wasn't easy. We had to get the corrupted data off the drive, rebuild the FAT table and—"

"Sophie, English please," he said, teasing her about the geek speak.

Sophie chuckled and said, "I'm sending the photos via email, and I'll text them to you, as well." He heard the click-clack of keys to confirm the dispatch of the images.

"I owe you big time."

"You do, so how about you come visit and bring your lady friend, as well?" Sophie said, laying on the guilt.

"My mom told you to say that, didn't she?"

Sophie's husky laugh confirmed it. "Call us if you need anything else, *primo*."

"I will, Sophie. Thank Robbie for me," he said and hung up to peer at the images she had sent.

Jackson angled the phone so Rhea could see the grainy black-and-white photos. The first was of Selene inside the pub, sitting and eating. There were other patrons nearby, including two heavily bearded and long-haired men who seemed to be looking in Selene's direction. The second photo was similar to the first, but in this one there was no doubt that the men were staring at Rhea's sister. The last three images were from the exterior of the pub. Selene near her car and, after, another one showing her pulling away, but in the background, the two bearded men again. They were leaning against what looked like a Jeep. The final photo created a blast of memories through Jackson's brain.

The Jeep was backing out, providing a glimpse of its front bumper.

It was that bumper that had piqued his interest, since

it was way too similar to what he'd seen only moments before they'd been rammed and almost driven into the back of the logging truck.

"Is that—"

"The SUV that hit us? I think it might be," he said and used his thumb and forefinger to zoom the photo and enlarge the bumper section.

"A definite maybe," he said.

Rhea wiggled her forefinger at the phone. "Go back to the earlier images. I think I've seen that man before."

He did as she asked, and she nodded. "He was in the police station when I came to speak to the chief."

Jackson zoomed the image to focus on the faces of the two men. Their heavy beards and long hair hid many of their features, but there were some similarities in the shapes of their eyes, noses and lips. "They could be brothers," he said, tracing those features with his forefinger.

"They could be. And I had a witness who said she drove by and noticed another Jeep by Selene's car that night. We've been thinking that it was Matt's Jeep, but maybe it wasn't. Maybe it was this Jeep."

"There's only one way to find out. You have contact info for that witness, don't you?"

Rhea nodded and skimmed through the info on her phone. "I do. I guess we go see her."

"We do, only..." He wanted to tell her not to get her hopes up, but that would be unrealistic. The photos and connection to their attackers was beyond coincidence. It was a solid lead, and one they had to follow.

"Let's go," he said and held his hand out to her.

Her smile was grim as she slipped her hand into his. "I'm ready. Let's go."

Gail Frazier was a sixtysomething LPN who worked at an assisted living facility in Regina and volunteered with an organization that provided meals and companionship to seniors. She had been coming home from one of those volunteer assignments when she had seen Selene's car and the unidentified SUV.

"What time do you think you left Mrs. Wilson's home?" Jackson asked as they sat with the LPN in her workplace's cafeteria.

"Much later than normal. Mrs. Wilson was a little despondent that day since it was her husband's birthday. He passed several years ago," Gail explained.

Rhea nodded. "That was so nice that you stayed to cheer her up."

Gail sniffled, and her eyes filled with tears. "I lost my own husband two years ago and started volunteering to fill the empty hours. My assignments help me as much as I help them," she said and picked up her coffee mug that said "#1 Nurse." She took a sip and after said, "I think I was there until about nine. Maybe a little earlier. I got Mrs. Wilson settled in bed, cleaned up a bit and then drove home. That's when I saw the cars by the lake."

Jackson pulled out a photo of Selene's sedan. He laid it in front of Gail. "Is this the car you saw that night?"

Gail nodded, her head shifting up and down emphatically. "I think so. I didn't think anything about it that night since people stop to look at the lake at all hours."

"What made you reach out to me and not the police?" Rhea asked.

Gail shrugged and pointed to the photo. "At first I didn't think it was unusual. But then I ran across your

posts on Facebook asking for any additional information. It got me thinking about that night."

Jackson considered the older woman, judging her
sincerity. "So you suddenly remembered a second car
months later."

Another emphatic nod answered him. "I did. I wish
I had made the connection earlier, but I didn't. Like I
said, nothing seemed off until I saw Rhea's post and
started thinking about it."

Which would make her testimony in court totally
vulnerable to challenge. Any good defense lawyer
would chip away at it to attempt to prove she imagined the second car as a way to help Rhea. She was a
caregiver by nature and liked to volunteer to help others. Giving Rhea that info totally fit her nature, even
if the veracity of the information might be doubtful.

Jackson tried to push her some more. "You thought
the other car by the lake was a Jeep. One like this?" He
slipped a photo of Matt's Wrangler in front of the LPN.

She laid her hand on the photo and drew it near for
a closer inspection. With a shrug and a small frown,
she said, "Like this one, but not this new or nice. The
one I saw looked older. More beat-up."

Jackson shared a look with Rhea. If Gail was right,
Matt was moving further down on the suspect list with
each new bit of information they gathered. Opening
his folder, he drew out a photo that his cousins had
provided. "What about this SUV?"

Gail peered at the photo, squinting at the image. She
picked up the glasses hanging on a bejeweled chain
around her neck. Slipping on the cheaters, she said, "I
don't really need them, but use them just to be sure of
the directions on some of the patients' medications.

The print is just too small and this photo... Well, it's quite grainy."

With the cheaters in place, she perused the photo for a too-long minute before she set it down and gestured to it. "Like that one."

Rhea leaned toward the other woman and placed her hand on the photo. "Like that one? So you don't think this is the SUV you saw?"

Gail got snippy. "I didn't say that, did I, young lady?"

Rhea inhaled deeply, held her breath and then in a gentler tone said, "I'm sorry, Gail. I truly appreciate that you came forward so we can find out what happened to Selene."

Seemingly chastened by Rhea's statement, Gail picked up the photo once again and reexamined it. When she set it down, she said, "I think this was the car. I remember it having that weird bumper thing."

The same weird bumper thing that I saw just before we were rammed, Jackson thought.

"That's important, Gail. Thank you," Rhea said and shot Jackson a look, as if saying, *Tag, it's your turn*.

He ran with it. "Did you see anyone near the cars? Selene? Anyone else?"

She shook her head. "Just the cars. I didn't think to look at the lakeshore. Like I said, it didn't seem anything was out of the ordinary and truth be told, I was tired. I just wanted to get home and get some rest."

"We understand. You do hard work here and with the volunteering... You must be exhausted late at night." Rhea laid a hand on Gail's, offering her thanks with the touch.

"I am, but like I said before, it helps me, as well. If there's anything I can do, please let me know," Gail said and glanced at her watch. "I really should get back to my patients. It'll be lunchtime soon and I have to get their medications ready."

When she rose from her chair, Jackson and Rhea did the same. Jackson shook her hand and said, "We appreciate the time you took. If need be, would you be willing to testify to what you saw?"

Gail peered at Rhea and said, "I would and I'm so sorry for your loss. It must be difficult for you."

Rhea's lips were in a tight line, her voice choked with emotion as she said, "Thank you again, Gail. I appreciate you coming forward. It's been truly helpful."

With a quick nod, Gail slipped away to return to her patients, and Jackson and Rhea left the facility. At the cruiser, Jackson crossed his arms and leaned against the fender, facing Rhea. She stood before him, arms wrapped around herself defensively. "I know this is upsetting."

Rhea shook her head and her dangling silver earrings danced against her neck. "It is, but I can deal."

"Can you deal with the possibility Matt wasn't the one who killed Selene?" Jackson pressed, hating to hurt her, but needing her to acknowledge he was likely not their suspect any longer.

"She's not dead," Rhea said, which shouldn't have surprised him, but it did.

"Rhea, please," he urged and reached for her, but she brushed off his touch and stepped away from him.

Chin tilted up and ice in her crystal blue gaze, she said, "If we've eliminated Matt, then we move on to the other scenarios, and they include the possibility that Selene is alive, Detective. So what do we do next?"

Chapter 17

Ugh, detective-zoned. Far worse than friend-zoned, but he understood that Gail's information had upended what had been the most plausible explanation for what had happened to Selene. The others, including that Selene was alive...

He pushed off the bumper and opened the door for her. Meeting her gaze, he said, "We head back to the pub and speak to Marcus. Maybe he knows more about those two men."

Without waiting for her reply, he walked around and eased into the driver's seat. They were at the pub in no time. Quite a number of vehicles were in the parking lot, since it was almost lunch hour. Jackson parked, and Rhea and he entered. They located Marcus, who once again took them into his office to avoid prying eyes and gossip about Jackson's visit.

"How can I help you again?" Marcus asked with a tired sigh as he plopped into his chair.

"Rough morning?" Jackson asked, inching a brow upward in emphasis.

"Totally, dude. One of the chefs burned himself pretty bad, and we had a problem with one of the freezers, but I'm handling it," Marcus advised and skimmed his gaze from Rhea to him and back.

"You two look like your morning was as bad," Marcus said.

"You could say that," Rhea blurted out.

Marcus trained his gaze on Jackson, as if asking for his confirmation. Instead, Jackson took the photos from his folder and handed them to his former colleague. "What can you tell us about those two?"

Marcus shuffled through the photos and then gestured to Rhea with them. "This is your sister in the photos?"

Rhea nodded. "It is."

Marcus let out a low whistle. "You really are identical, aren't you?"

"Marcus, focus," Jackson said, and it brought back memories of working with the other man on the force. Although he'd been a good cop, he'd also been easily distracted.

"Easy, dude," Marcus warned and glanced at the photos again before handing them back to Jackson. Fingers laced, he laid his hands across his midsection and said, "They apparently come in every few months."

"Have you seen them lately?" Jackson asked.

Marcus tilted his head to the side and looked upward, searching his memory, and then shook his head. "Come to think of it, no. The staff calls them the 'Mountain Men.'"

Rhea jumped in with, "Why is that?"

With a shrug, Marcus said, "When they first came in, I got bad vibes. I asked the old-timers who gave me the skinny on them. That they seemed like recluses who only came down every few months. Kept to themselves. Creeped out some of the female customers."

"In what way?" Rhea asked, her gaze narrowed as she trained it on Marcus.

"I'm told they'd stare at them. Make comments. I wasn't around at the time, but they were asked to leave one night and got in the old manager's face. Pushed him around."

"Did you call the police? Is there a report possibly?" Jackson said, hoping that there would be so they might identify the men.

Marcus shook his head. "Sorry, but they didn't. It got handled, and no one was hurt."

"Do you mind if we ask your staff about them?" Jackson said.

Marcus frowned. "Dude, we're just about to start the lunch service. Can I send them to the station later?"

He glanced in Rhea's direction. She was bouncing her feet nervously, expectantly. She clearly would prefer to deal with it now as he would, but Marcus had been open and helpful, and he didn't want to push. Besides, they had things to do at the station anyway.

"We'll be there," he said, earning a quick hard glance from Rhea, but she remained silent.

"I appreciate that, Jax. I'll speak to my guys and ask them to go over after their shift. I'll make a list of who might have info also, just in case." Marcus stood as if to reinforce it was time for them to go.

"Just in case?" Rhea asked and stood, her face puzzled.

Marcus did a quick shrug. "Some of my guys... Let's just say they're not fans of the police. But I'll get them to you, I promise."

"Appreciate the help, Marcus. We truly do," Jackson said.

Once they were out in the restaurant, Jackson played it up as if to make it seem like their visit had been only a friendly one, since several eyes had turned in their direction. "Thanks for that donation to the PAL fund, Marcus. We truly appreciate it," he said, his voice loud enough to be overheard by those in the area.

Marcus smiled and chuckled. "You're welcome, Jax. Anything for a friend."

Rhea went up on tiptoes and brushed a kiss across his cheek, truly grateful for his assistance. "Thank you."

With a wink and a broad smile, Marcus said, "Anything for you, pretty lady."

Rhea returned the grin and suddenly felt the possessive press of Jackson's hand at the small of her back. Still angry, she glared at him and pushed away, eager to return to the police station. As she had told Jackson earlier, she thought she had seen one of the men at the station.

She hurried from the pub, the soft soles of her espadrilles creating a dull thud with each quick step. She shoved through the door to the cruiser and didn't wait for Jackson to do the gentlemanly thing. Grabbing the handle, she waited for the *kerthunk* to signal that he'd opened the lock, but when it didn't happen immediately, she turned to find him standing there.

"What?" she asked, wondering at his delay.

"I know you're angry," he began, but she shut him down with a sharp raise of a brow and the crossing of her arms. She lifted her face to stare at his, her chin tilted in defiance.

"My possibility is as plausible as any that remain."

Jackson jammed his hand on his hips, looked away from her penetrating gaze and sucked in deep breath. Blowing it out sharply, he said, "It is, Rhea. But it's the one that will bring you the most pain if it proves false. I don't want you to experience that kind of pain. Again."

His words mollified her anger, filled as they were with concern. "I'm a big girl, Jax. While it may be painful if I'm wrong, it brings me comfort to think she might be out there somewhere. To think we might be able to save her from suffering if she's alive."

He nodded, and while she sensed he had more to say, he bit his tongue. Literally, because she could swear she saw him wince before he unlocked the doors and walked around to his side of the cruiser.

She eased into her seat and buckled up, and Jackson took off for the police station. The trip was short, since Regina wasn't all that big. As they crossed Main Street, its beauty struck her once again and made her itch to finish the sketch she'd started the other day. When her gaze skimmed to Jackson, the sharp lines of his handsome face stole her breath and roused passion, both to finish his sketch and to be with him again.

At the station house, the desk sergeant who had been on duty the day Rhea had first come to see the chief was guarding the entrance again. Rhea smiled at her, and at the dip of Jackson's head, she buzzed them through.

But Jackson paused right past the barrier and turned to Rhea. "Do you see the officer here who had brought in one of our possible suspects?"

Rhea gazed around the various desks, looking for the middle-aged officer she thought she had seen with someone who looked like one of the Mountain Men, but she didn't spot him. But then two officers emerged with coffee from what must have been a break room. She pointed in their direction. "I think that's him. The one to the left."

Jackson nodded and called out to his colleague. "Officer Bellevue. Do you have a moment for us?"

The officer hurried over. "How can I help?" he said as he shook Rhea's hand and dipped his head in Jackson's direction.

Jackson opened his folder and handed a photo to Officer Bellevue. "Have you seen either of these men before?"

The man examined it and tapped on the face of one of the men. "Had this one in earlier this week."

Jackson shared a hopeful glance with Rhea. "Can you pull your report for us?"

A bright stain of color erupted across the officer's face. "I'm sorry, Jax, but I didn't file one. I brought him in for some minor shoplifting, but the owner said that if he paid for the items, she wouldn't press charges. He did, so I let him go with a warning."

Jackson dragged a hand through his hair in frustration. "You didn't get a name or address?"

"I did get a name, although it took some doing. Guy kept on muttering about how his brother would be so mad at him for getting in trouble. He did have a wallet, but no ID. " Officer Bellevue said and pulled a small notepad from his shirt pocket. Flipping through the pages, he stopped at one and said, "Wade Garrett."

"Thank you, officer. That's really helpful," Rhea said with a smile, trying to ease the officer's earlier upset about not filing a report.

"If you need me to run him down—"

Jackson held up a hand to stop the other man. "Thanks, but we'll do it. If there's anything else you can think of, please let us know."

"I will, Jax," he said and walked away to his desk.

"A name. I guess that's a start," Rhea said.

Since they'd almost made peace after that morning's upset, Jackson didn't want to tell her it wasn't much of a start, especially if the man had provided a fake name. "Let's go to my office, so we can try to track him down."

He laid a hand at her waist and was grateful she didn't shy away as she'd done before. With gentle pressure, he guided her to his office. Tossing the folder with the photos on his desk, he sat and explained to Rhea what he was doing on his computer. He couldn't let her see the screen once he logged on to the various police databases since she wasn't authorized, but he did turn the screen slightly as he added the photos his cousins had retrieved to their digital notebook and also updated the information from Gail Frazier.

"I'm going to run Wade Garrett through the state and federal databases to see if we get a hit," he said and moved the screen out of Rhea's line of sight.

"Do you think you will?" Rhea asked, worrying her

lower lip, her look expectant as she leaned toward him, almost as if urging him to get going.

Jackson shrugged. "Maybe."

He tapped away on the keys while Rhea sat there, almost bouncing up and down in her chair. The records he searched brought up several hits in various court cases, but as he skimmed through the available details it became clear a few of the cases dated to the early 1940s and involved an adult male.

"Got a few hits involving criminal cases, but the person would be way too old," he said, but quickly added, "Although it could be a parent."

After reviewing the last few entries, he leaned back in his chair and said, "Nothing here, and in Colorado vital records are considered confidential and not online. Plus, that assumes they're locals, and we don't know that. I'll search the DMV records, even though Bellevue said he didn't have a license. It might mean he just didn't have it with him."

But the DMV search didn't produce any hits and he advised Rhea of that. "Since that was a bust, I'm going to search through the national criminal databases that are available."

"Like which ones?" Rhea asked, craning her neck toward the screen, clearly wanting to be involved.

While Jackson entered his username and password into the first system, he said, "A whole alphabet soup of databases. NCIC. NICS."

A bright grin and chuckle relieved her earlier intensity. "Definitely alphabet soup. Which reminds me that we haven't had lunch yet." As if to reinforce her comment, her stomach grumbled noisily and she hastily laid a hand over her midsection to quiet the noise.

Jackson smiled and with a flip of his hand at the monitor, he said, "This may take a while. There are some chips and things in the break room, but also a nice sandwich shop just a few doors down on Main Street." He reached into this top desk drawer, found a take-out menu and handed it to her.

Rhea accepted the menu. The edges were ragged, and the paper was soft, as if it had been handled many times. "I guess you order from there a lot."

With a chagrined smile, Jackson said, "You have a lot of late nights in this job. Sandwiches make it easier to eat and work at the same time."

"But not healthier, mentally or physically. I'll take a walk and go get us something."

She placed the menu on his desktop, but as she moved away, he raised an index finger. "No salad. I'm allergic to green things."

She chuckled as he had intended and shook her head. "Got it. No salad."

Hurrying out to the street, she walked toward the center of town, where most of the stores and restaurants were located. She remembered seeing one place that sold pot pies with various fillings. They'd be a nice hearty lunch and force Jackson to take a break from the tedium of searching through the databases.

The shop had quite an assortment of fillings, from one mimicking a Cuban sandwich to the more traditional chicken and turkey pot pie variations. She chose the chicken for herself, but a chili-style filling for Jackson.

She had barely gone a block when she got that feeling

she was being followed. Turning quickly, she caught a glimpse of someone ducking into a small alley between two of the buildings.

The hackles rose down her neck and back, and she quickened her pace almost to a run. Turning every now and then to see if she was still being followed. She thought she caught another glimpse of someone as she hit the stairs for the police station, but safety was just a few steps away.

She stumbled on the last step, almost sending herself tumbling into the glass doors for the station, but she righted herself and managed not to drop their lunch while doing it.

Bursting through the doors, she immediately drew the attention of the desk sergeant who jumped to her feet, eyebrows knitted with worry. "Are you okay, Rhea?"

Rhea peered back over her shoulder. No one outside on the steps. Lifting her gaze to glance across the street, she thought she saw a big, bearded man again, one who looked too much like the one in the photos from the pub, but then he vanished.

Maybe it was all in her imagination. Her mother had told her on more than one occasion that she had a vivid imagination and, of course, it came part and parcel with being an artist.

"I'm okay. Just a little spooked."

The officer glanced past her and out the door, as well. "I'll buzz you through," she said after apparently determining that everything was in order.

"Thanks," she said and hurried to Jackson's door.

He was at work, but looked at her as she walked in.

He was immediately in action, coming to her side to take the package and guide her into a chair.

As he wrapped his arm around her, she realized for the first time that she was shaking.

"What happened, Rhea? You look like you've seen a ghost," he said, drawing her closer and brushing a kiss across her temple.

She wiggled her head, embarrassed. "Nothing, only... I thought someone was following me."

Jackson muttered a curse. "I'm sorry. I should have told you that I had one of our officers trailing you to make sure you were safe."

"Maybe that's why I felt I was being followed," she said with a shrug, wanting to alleviate the obvious guilt he was feeling.

"Maybe," he said, hugged her hard again and skimmed another kiss on her cheek.

A rough, overly loud cough, drew them apart.

She peered over her shoulder to find Jackson's boss staring at them intently. His face as hard and rough as the stone outcroppings on the mountains around Regina.

"Am I interrupting something?" the chief said and arched one bushy gray eyebrow.

"I just had a scare," Rhea said and slid to one side of her chair to create some distance from Jackson.

The chief crooked a finger in Jackson's direction and he rose, then stepped outside his office to speak to his boss. Bodies tilted toward each other, voices low, the two men spoke and, while she was unable to hear, their posture and the few chest pokes the chief gave Jackson said it all. He was clearly not happy with what he had just seen.

When the other man left, Jackson laid his hands on his hips and looked upward before entering his office and shutting the door for privacy.

"He's angry, isn't he?" she said as Jackson busied himself with removing the pot pies and cutlery from the bag. He ripped the bag open and spread it across the surface of the desk to act like a place mat.

"Jackson, talk to me," she said and placed her hand on his forearm to still his angry motion.

"Chief says I need to wrap this up. We're wasting too many man hours and resources. I'm letting it get too personal." His words were clipped and chilly.

She laced her fingers together and laid her hands in her lap. Peering at them, she said, "I'm sorry, Jax. I know how important becoming chief is to you—"

"But not more important than justice, Rhea. We're close. I can feel it," he said.

His body was stiff, and he had clearly shut himself off from her, so she decided not to press. They ate in silence, and while the food may have been scrumptious, she didn't taste a thing thanks to the emotions roiling inside.

Jackson gobbled his pie down in record time and swung back to his computer. Barely a second later, he returned to his two-fingered pecking at the keyboard. His brow furrowed as he paused, probably to review the information on the screen. That process was repeated over and over while Rhea picked at her pot pie, keeping herself occupied with counting the peas and carrots as she ate to keep from bothering Jackson.

A good hour went by like that until Jackson blew out a rough breath and pushed away from the computer. He leaned his elbows on the arms of his chair and steepled his fingers before his mouth, clearly unhappy.

"Nothing, right?" she said, reading his signals.

He nodded, his frustration apparent despite his earlier optimism that they were close to finding something. "Nothing. Nada. Zilch. Zero."

She was about to say something, she didn't know what, when he slapped his hands on his desk and said, "But that's not stopping me. Us. I'll be right back."

He rushed from his office and came back with a large roll of paper. She quickly cleared off the remnants of their lunch and threw them away so Jackson could unfurl the paper across his desk. A map of Regina and the adjacent mountain areas. He jabbed at the mountains and said, "Marcus said that it seemed as if the men had come down from the mountain. What if they did? What if they live in one of these nearby areas?"

"But these are all protected lands, right?"

"That doesn't stop poachers or squatters." He traced his index finger along the highway that ran along the base of the mountain peaks and near the lake where Selene had last been seen.

"They could have grabbed her here." He jabbed at the map by the lake. "And taken her somewhere on one of these mountains."

Rhea peered at the map. "That's a lot of territory to cover."

"For sure," Jackson said, but then grabbed his desk phone and tapped out a few numbers. "Dillon. Do you have a few minutes to help me?"

His smile confirmed Dillon would be over quickly, and within seconds, another officer was at Jackson's door. "You needed me, boss?"

Jackson nodded. "You're an expert hiker, aren't you?"

The other officer nodded and grinned. "I am. You need some advice on hiking trails?" he said and approached the desk. He barely looked old enough to be a cop, making her feel suddenly old, even though she was only twenty-eight.

Jackson gestured to the two mountains closest to Regina. "How hard would it be to hike up either of these peaks? Maybe even build yourself a little cabin. A private one."

Dillon let out a low whistle. "Depends on the time of year."

"Fall. November," Jackson said.

Dillon shot a quick glance in her direction and with a shrug said, "If there isn't snow on the ground, it's not so hard on this peak. There's actually a small road that goes up about halfway. You get some hikers who drive and then head to one of the lower peaks on foot. It takes more experienced climbers to actually reach the summit."

"So it gets enough traffic that it might be hard to hide?" Rhea asked. If she was trying to hide, she wouldn't want a lot of people traipsing nearby.

Dillon considered her comment and then nodded. "Enough traffic. Plus, there's a ski resort here," he said and gestured to the far side of the mountain, the area closest to where Selene disappeared.

Jackson stood, arms akimbo, perusing the map. He gestured to the other mountain. "What about this area?"

Dillon mimicked Jackson's pose and examined the map. With a nod of his head, he said, "That's a tougher hike for sure. Not many people do it."

"How would you get up there if you wanted to?" Rhea asked, leaning over to look at the map.

Dillon scratched his head. "Rumor has it there's an old logging trail, but it's been closed to the public for ages." He leaned his hands on the desk and shifted closer to the map, inspecting it more carefully. Running his finger along one stretch of highway, he said, "Somewhere around here."

"Satellite image might confirm it," Jackson said and hurried back to his computer. In no time, he had a map of the area up on the screen and turned it around so they could all see it. He zoomed in on the image and gestured to one section. "This looks like a trail, doesn't it? We could search in that area."

Dillon did another shrug of shoulders that still needed to fill out. "Maybe, but you're still talking a lot of area to search, boss. Acres and acres. It would take a lot of people to find anything in that wilderness."

Jackson laughed and leaned back in his chair. "I'm not talking people, Dillon."

Rhea narrowed her gaze and searched Jackson's features for some sign of what he was thinking, but failed. "What are you talking about, Jax?"

Chapter 18

"LIDAR."

"LIDAR? What's that?" Dillon asked.

Jackson clapped the young man on the back. "I thought you young guys were all about the tech," he teased and then explained, "It's like RADAR, but using laser light to make 3D images of an area."

"3D images of lots and lots of trees," Rhea said dejectedly.

"Actually not," Jackson said. "I've been reading about how you combine LIDAR images with software that can actually strip away vegetation to reveal any hidden structures."

Dillon mimicked opening the pages of a book. "Reading, like on paper."

"On paper and on the net. My cousins have been trying to keep me from becoming a Luddite," Jackson quipped.

"Can your cousins help us with the software part of it?" Rhea asked, losing a little bit of the glumness that had filled her tone a moment ago.

"I'm sure Robbie and Sophie can help us with the software. Maybe they even know someone in the area with drones equipped with LIDAR. Depending on what the images show, Dillon here can help us hike into the area. Maybe the forest service, as well. It is in their jurisdiction after all," Jackson advised.

Jackson's desk phone rang and he hit the button to engage the speaker. "What's up, Rodriguez?"

"I have a visitor for you. He says Marcus sent him over," Millie said.

"Perfect. Please put him in the conference room. We'll be over in a second," he said and disengaged the speaker.

"That's good news, right?" Rhea said, suddenly feeling more optimistic than she had barely minutes before.

Jackson nodded. "For sure." He turned to Dillon and shook his hand. "Thanks for the help. We'll let you know when we need you again."

Dillon did a little salute. "Anytime, boss."

He exited, and Jackson gestured for Rhea to follow him. Once in the hallway, he laid a hand at her back in a way that was becoming achingly familiar. It offered immediate comfort and a sense of protection.

He guided her toward the conference room where an older man sat, waiting for them. He looked familiar, and as she dug through her memory, she recalled that she'd seen him tending the bar at the pub.

He stood as they entered, and Jackson held his hand out for a shake. She guessed that his use of the conference room and friendliness were intended to put the man at ease and not make him feel as if he was being interrogated. "Bradley, right?" Jackson said.

The man dipped his head in greeting in her direction and said, "That's right. You have a good memory, Detective."

"Jackson, please. Thanks for coming by," Jackson said and sat kitty-corner to the man. Rhea sat beside Jackson, opposite the bartender.

"New manager says to come by, I come by. I don't want no trouble," the man said, hands clasped before him on the tabletop. His fingers were gnarly, arthritic. He also had assorted scars on his hands, nicks, cuts and even a larger silvery shape, like from a burn. Clearly the hands of a man who worked hard for his living. But also obviously a nervous man as he bounced those clasped hands on the surface of the table.

"I guess you know something about the two men we're interested in?" Jackson asked.

A slight lift of his shoulders was followed by, "Some, but not much. They come now and again. Usually when we're not as busy."

Which confirmed what Marcus had told them earlier, Rhea thought.

"Anything else?" Jackson pressed.

"They're rough. Not people persons. Mostly keep to themselves except…they've harassed some of the women," Bradley said.

"Marcus said they were booted from the place for that," Jackson said, trying to elicit more with the open question.

"They were. Not recently. After that they seemed to clean up their act, but they still creeped us out. The one brother seemed to be the leader and was just plain mean."

"Mean in what way?" Jackson said, obviously wondering as she was what had prompted that impression.

Bradley bounced his hands on the tabletop faster and, as if realizing what he was doing, suddenly pulled them down beneath the edge of the table. "He almost growls his orders. Never a smile. Never a tip, but I got the feeling they didn't have much money. Their clothes were raggedy and sometimes they smelled. Bad. If the girls didn't put out the pretzels and nuts in front of them fast enough, we'd hear it."

Jackson cupped his jaw and rubbed it thoughtfully. "Marcus said you all called them the 'Mountain Men.' Do you think they live up there?"

Bradley laughed and wobbled his head of salt-and-pepper hair back and forth. "It wouldn't surprise me if they hole up in a cave somewhere and, like bears, only come out of hibernation a couple of times a year."

Jackson continued with his questioning. "Anything else? Any names?"

The man shook his head, but then snapped his fingers. "I think the mean one called his brother 'Wade.' The older one was always warning his brother to stop one thing or another."

As if to confirm, Jackson said, "You think they're brothers?"

Bradley nodded vigorously. "I have an older brother, so I know how it goes. Totally brothers. And they look alike, I think. Hard to tell with all that hair."

Jackson peered in her direction for the briefest moment before returning his attention to the bartender. He rose and held his hand out to the other man. "Thank you so much for coming by, Bradley. You've been re-ally, really helpful. If by any chance you remember anything else or see these guys—"

"You'll be the first person I call, Jackson," the man said as he shook Jackson's hand and once again dipped his head in Rhea's direction. "Miss. I hope you find out what happened with your sister."

With that, the older man exited the room.

"What do we do now?" she asked, wondering, but Jackson clearly had no doubt about their next steps.

"We call Avalon PD and suspend what they're doing about Davis. Then I'll check with our Search and Res-cue guys to see if they have LIDAR and if not, time to talk to the cousins again."

"I hope those images we got for you were helpful," Robbie said.

"They were, cuz, but the thing is…they've taken us in a new direction in the investigation," Jackson ad-mitted and did a quick look at Rhea to gauge how she was handling that new direction.

"Wow, okay. I guess you need more help. Let me get Sophie on the line," Robbie said.

"Afternoon, Jackson," Sophie said as she came across the speaker.

"Our investigations are pointing to two suspects who may be squatting on federal lands. But it's a prob-lem to do a traditional search on foot. Too large an area and too much underbrush and vegetation," Jack-son explained.

Robbie let out a low whistle. "Tough luck, but there are ways to search using drones."

"And LIDAR," Sophie added.

Jackson smiled, and Rhea jumped in with, "Jackson thought we might be able to do it that way."

"You definitely can. First, you survey the area with drones equipped with LIDAR, and then you process that imagery to see what's beneath trees and other foliage," Sophie confirmed.

Jackson shared a look with Rhea. "We're hoping you can connect us to someone who can do the drone work."

The murmur of low voices drifted across the line. "We can do that, *primo*," Robbie said.

"And we have software to process that imagery for you," Sophie quickly added.

"Thank you so much! That would be fantastic," Rhea said, her tone excited and grateful.

"We need to call a couple of drone specialists to see who's free, but hopefully we can get back to you by later tonight," Robbie said.

"Appreciated, cuz. Your help has been invaluable. I don't know how we can repay you," Jackson said and prepared for what he was sure would come next.

"Bring your lady friend to Miami!" Sophie said enthusiastically.

Rhea glanced in his direction, and the heat in her look could have ignited a forest fire. It was easy to picture the two of them, holding hands and walking along Ocean Drive in South Beach.

Voice husky with desire, he said, "I'll definitely think about that. Thanks again, and we'll talk to you later."

He ended the call and peered at Rhea, hoping he hadn't misread her earlier signals. "I'm sorry my cousins involved you in the Miami thing."

Her gaze narrowed and grew a little more somber. "I guess you don't like that idea?"

He raised his hands to stop her from going somewhere negative. "I do like it. I'm just not sure where we're headed. I mean, we've kind of been forced together."

"Forced? Is that what happened last night?" she said, her tone getting harsher by the second.

"Hell, no, Rhea. Last night and this morning were amazing. But you're vulnerable right now, and I've got to think about—"

"Becoming police chief?" she said with an arch of her brow, the blue of her eyes becoming as chill as the ice on a winter lake.

"The investigation. And you. I never expected what's happening between us, but I don't regret it."

"I don't, either, Jax. But maybe we need to take a step back until this is all over," Rhea said.

He hated that she was right, but it made sense to bring things back into perspective until the investigation was done. And if his cousins could basically work a miracle and find something on the mountain that would lead them to their two new suspects, the investigation would quickly be coming to a close.

"I just want to update the digital notebook and reach out to my local contact at the Park Service and see how she wants us to handle this. I can have someone drive you home if you want," Jackson said.

Rhea shook her head. "I'll just hang out here and do some sketching."

She didn't give Jackson time to argue with her, since she grabbed her ever-present knapsack and pulled out her sketch pad and pencils. Balancing the pad on her knee, she went to work and he did, as well, adding all the information they'd gathered to his notes.

Rhea flipped to the sketch of Jackson that she had started just two days ago. It had the barebones lines of him lying on the sofa, but needed so much more to do justice to the man sitting across from her. Especially since she now had intimate knowledge of that body. The hard muscles sheathed in smooth skin. The scars of a warrior along his shoulder and back, making her wonder if that accounted for the pain she'd seen on occasion.

And his face. Lord, it was the face of a fallen angel, tempting a woman with his full lips, dimples and the slight cleft in his chin. Those features were balanced by the strong line of his jaw and sharp straight nose.

She worked on those elements, since she had an unfettered look at them as he worked, a slight furrow in his brow as he concentrated and pecked information into the computer. At one point he leaned back, rubbed his jaw with his hand, as if puzzled, but then he was back at work.

Smiling, she shifted her pencil lower, adding definition to the broad expanse of his chest and lean midsection. Capturing with her pencil and paper the details her hands had explored last night and this morning. Understanding, but regretting, that she wouldn't explore more of him tonight.

Caught up in her sketching, she was jolted back by the loud ring of Jackson's cell phone. He answered and said, "Hi, cuz. That's good news. Thanks."

With a swipe, he ended the call. "They've reached out to their contact and copied me on the email. Hopefully we'll be able to arrange to have the drone survey tomorrow."

"That's good news," she said, grateful and expectant, but also worried. As long as the investigation wasn't done, she'd be with Jackson and Selene was still alive. The next few days could change all that, but would it be for the better?

"Ready to go home?" he said, lacing his hands behind his head to stretch. A slight grimace skipped across his features, but he controlled it and brought his hands down to the arms of his chair to push to his feet.

"Back hurting?"

It was obvious he didn't want to appear vulnerable as he shrugged and said, "Just a kink. Too much sitting. They say sitting—"

"Is the new smoking," she finished for him with a chuckle. "We're both in professions where we do a lot of sitting."

"Too late for a hike, but maybe we can think of something else to do." His gaze met hers, the gray of it smoky, warning of the fire that might soon ignite.

"For sure," she said, despite her earlier reservations, and held her hand out to him in invitation.

As he slipped his work-rough hand in hers, she told herself not to worry about tonight or tomorrow. Whatever was meant to be was meant to be.

Even if it brought heartache.

The tension had been building ever since they'd left the police station and grabbed a quick bite for dinner in one of the restaurants along Main Street. Night had fallen as Jackson let them into his home, the ever-present police cruiser sitting in the driveway to warn off who-ever had burned down Jackson's shed.

Inside, they paused at the base of the stairs, the tension so thick it felt like a presence shimmering be-tween them.

With a wave of his hand, Jackson pushed away that sensation and said, "I have some things to do in my office. Why don't you go up and get settled?"

Coward! Rhea wanted to scream, hating that he'd put the onus on her to decide where she'd spend the night because, well, she was feeling as craven as he was. With a curt nod, she stomped up the stairs, an-noyed. Anxious. Needy. Despite knowing what was happening between them was so uncertain, she still wanted him. She wanted to not waste a minute with him because once the investigation was over...

She wouldn't think about that.

She wouldn't think about what she would do if Se-lene...

No, I won't think that. She's out there. Somewhere, she told herself and walked to the guest bedroom to get her nightshirt. A nice hot shower was bound to relax her and buy some time until Jackson came up and then...

She hurried into the shower, but took her time luxu-riating beneath the rain showerhead, working shampoo into a thick lather. Soaping up and running her hands across her skin. Letting the heat of the water sink into her bones. Thick steam gathered in the room, warning her she'd been in there for quite some time.

Reluctantly she shut off the water, grabbed a towel and dried off. Her skin seemed sensitized as the touch of the terry cloth across her body roused memories of the feel of the sheets beneath her, and Jackson above her, his big body driving into her.

The warmth on her skin from the water morphed into a different kind of heat deep within.

Rushing into Jackson's bedroom, she didn't even waste a moment to turn on the light. She slipped beneath the sheets and pulled them tight about her, the bed feeling empty without him. Her senses hyper, tuned to the slightest noise until she heard the first footfall on the steps.

She held her breath, waiting for him. Eager for his body next to hers.

The footfalls came closer and paused at the door. A breath seemed to burst from him, almost as if he'd been holding it in anticipation. A rush of steps came before his weight settled on the edge of the bed.

"Rhea," he said softly. Hesitantly.

She glanced at him. His face was in partial shadow, the only light that from the hallway. It made it hard to gauge what he was thinking. But then he cradled her jaw and tenderly ran his thumb across her cheek. Drifted it down to her lips, where he traced the edges of it, as powerful as any kiss. Stirring awake desire.

"Touch me, Jax," she said and covered his hand with hers. Urged it to her breast where her nipple pebbled beneath his rough palm.

"Rhea, this is crazy," he said, but he strummed his thumb across the hard tip and then reached beneath the sheets to find the hem of her nightshirt and draw it off her body.

With eager fingers she undid the buttons on his uniform shirt, baring his chest to her. Sitting up to drop kisses across the expanse until she tongued his masculine nipple and he groaned and held her head to him. With a little love bite, she brought her hands to his sides and urged him down to her, wanting his skin against hers. Wanting his hands on her.

"Please, Jax. Please," she pleaded.

Jackson moved away from her only long enough to remove the rest of his clothes and slip beneath the sheets with her.

She had her hands on him instantly, cupping him and stroking his hard length.

"I want you in me," she said and pressed him close.

"Bossy, aren't you?" he teased, drawing a chuckle from her as he fumbled in the nightstand for a condom. He had barely taken it out, and she was shifting, urging him to his back and taking it from him. She tore it open, took out the condom and, with delicious leisure, rolled it down over him, and now it was his turn to plead.

"Rhea. I need you," he said, and she didn't disappoint. She straddled him and sank onto him, slowly.

He laid his hands on her hips. Guided her to move on him, riding him. Thrusting into her forcefully, driving until the release washed over them, stealing their breaths.

Rhea wrapped her arms around him and laid her head against his chest. His heart beat rapidly beneath her ear, and his skin was damp. He smelled of man, leather and Jackson. She inhaled that aroma to commit it to memory. To remember it long past when this moment was done. He made her feel loved, but she told herself not to think too much about that.

There was still too much to do. Too many unknowns. And when the morning came, it might be the beginning of the end depending on what the drone footage revealed. Much like the end of the investigation would reveal if whatever she was feeling for Jackson was real.

Chapter 19

The drone sitting on the ground before them in the bright morning light was nothing like the small drones Rhea had seen at various events in Denver. The drone was easily a good three feet or more across, with large propellers to lift it high into the air. It sat on two up-raised legs and nestled at the center was something that looked like a camera, but she guessed was the LIDAR device, whatever that was. Projecting above the body of the drone, almost on antennae, were some pod-like pieces.

Jackson and the drone operator had gathered by the police cruiser, where Jackson had spread out the map of the mountain area above. He instructed the other man on what they wanted to survey. As she approached, she heard the drone operator issue a low whistle, look up toward the mountains and rub his head.

"Lots of dense vegetation, but hopefully the laser will be able to get through to get the data we need for Robbie and Sophie," the man said.

"What if there isn't enough data, Rick?" Jackson asked, taking the words right out of her mouth.

With a shrug, Rick said, "Robbie and Sophie are miracle workers. They can probably download topographical maps of the area and work them into any analysis to fill in gaps."

"Will it take long?" Rhea asked.

Rick peered up at the mountains again and said, "Your cousins sent me the specs for several flight plans. I've programmed them into my tablet, and once we send up the drone, it will fly those plans on its own to collect the data. My guess is a couple of hours."

"And then you send the data to my cousins?" Jackson said.

Rick nodded. "I'll transmit it to them, and they'll use their programs to get whatever images you want." Knowing what question would come next, Rick added, "With their supercomputers, it shouldn't take too long to process the data. You'd probably have it tomorrow if they jump right on it."

"Sounds good, and thanks again for doing this," Jackson said.

"Anything I can do. I can only imagine how hard it must be for you, Rhea. Hopefully we'll be able to help you find your sister," Rick said and walked to his tablet and remote controls. He picked up the controls, and a second later, the propellers whirred to life. With some swipes on the tablet, the drone lifted off and sped toward the mountains.

Jackson and she leaned against the cruiser and

watched the drone disappear up the mountain, but the hum of the propellers gave testament that it was still there, working its way along the first of the flight plans that Jackson's cousins had programmed. Rick walked back toward them, his gaze locked on his tablet. As he neared, he held it up for them to see the images that the drone was capturing.

"Lots and lots of trees," Rhea said, slightly worried that was all the imagery would capture.

Rick nodded, but seeing her concerns, he explained. "That's what our eyes and the camera see, but the LIDAR is getting a lot more. Trust me."

"We do," Jackson said and laid his arm over her shoulder to draw her near with a reassuring squeeze.

"We trust you, Rick," she added, almost in apology for having any doubts.

"Great. Let me get back to watching, just in case," he said and walked away to keep an eye on the drone's footage, the remote control nearby. She assumed that was just in case there was a problem with any of the flight plans.

The chill of morning faded as an hour passed, and then another, as the drone flew flight plan after flight plan. Jackson and she sat on a blanket spread beneath the shade of a large aspen, sipping coffee from the large thermos they'd brought with them. Taking over some coffee and breakfast pastries to Rick while he monitored the drone.

It was almost lunch hour when the drone came whirring back and landed just yards away from them. They approached as the blades stopped whirring, and Rick walked over to the machine. He worked quickly to remove the LIDAR device and store it in its protective luggage.

Jackson helped him with packing up the rest of the equipment, and once they were done, Jackson said, "What do you do next?"

Rick gestured to the luggage with the LIDAR device. "I'm going to connect that to my computer and get the data uploaded to the cloud. Once that's done, I'll let Robbie and Sophie know so they can generate the information for you."

Jackson nodded and shook the man's hand. "Thanks again. If there's ever anything we can do for you—"

"I'll let you know. Maybe help me score some BBQ from Declan's place. I hear it's the best in the area," Rick said.

Jackson smiled. "It is. Whenever you want to head over there, I'll let him know you're coming and it's on me. Whatever you want."

"Thanks, Jax. And good luck with everything. Rhea," the man said with a deferential nod.

Jackson and Rhea helped Rick load all the equipment containers in the back of his van. After another handshake from Jackson and hug from her, Rick drove off.

Rhea hoped that they'd gotten what they needed. With Matt virtually eliminated as a suspect, they had to focus on whether the two men at the pub had possibly had a part in Selene's disappearance, the attacks against her and the destruction at Jackson's home.

Jackson laid a hand on her shoulder and drew her near, comforting her. "This will work," he said with a playful nudge, trying to lighten the mood.

"It will," she said with more confidence than she

was feeling and with anticipation. His cousins' supercomputers couldn't work fast enough as far as she
was concerned, but she knew everyone involved would
work as quickly as possible.

But in the meantime, they had little to do and she
was too antsy to just sit around. She was even too antsy
to sketch, which rarely happened. Jackson must have
sensed her mood, since he said, "It's a beautiful day.
Feel like a walk around town?"

She'd love a walk, but didn't want to deal with having other people around. She wanted something more
private where it just the two of them. "Anywhere it can
be just the two of us?"

Jackson peered at her and nodded. "I know just the
place. How about we pick up a picnic lunch?"

She smiled. "That sounds nice. Thank you."

In just over fifteen minutes, they had a picnic lunch
from one of the restaurants in Regina and were back
on the road. Not far past the lake and nearby spillway,
Jackson turned off onto a side road that ran parallel to
the lake. Every now and then he'd look back, as if to
check if anyone was following, but apparently satisfied they were alone, he continued on their trek. To the
right of the paved road was what looked like a hiking
trail that ran for some distance.

Less than a quarter mile from the turnoff, they
pulled up in front of a large cabin that faced the lake. It
reminded her of Jackson's home, and when they pulled
into the driveway, she noticed the mailbox with the
owner's name: Whitaker.

"Is this your family's place?" she asked as Jackson
parked the cruiser.

"Mom and Dad's place. While they're in Florida, I

come up here every week or so to make sure everything is in order. It's got nice views of the lake. I figured we could have lunch up on the front porch and then do a short hike along the trail. If you want, that is."

"I'd like that," she said. She also liked that he asked and didn't assume, unlike her last boyfriend. An artist like her, it had started off well at first, but then he'd become more and more demanding. More controlling until she had finally put an end to the relationship. In the couple of years since then, she'd stayed out of the dating game, focusing on her artwork and building her business.

She wasn't sure she could call what was happening with her and Jackson dating, or call him her boyfriend. It was way more than that.

He grabbed the bag with their food from the back seat and swung around to open her door, ever the gentleman. The comforting touch of his hand came at her back, the pressure gentle as he guided her up the long set of steps up to the generous front porch for the cabin.

The porch wrapped around the cabin. In the front there were two large rockers and between them a small circular table where he set the bag with their lunch. As Rhea swept past him to one of the rockers, Jackson removed their sandwiches, chips and soda from the bag and laid it all out on the table.

They settled on the rockers to sit and eat, their words few as they satisfied their hunger, but maybe also possibly because they were both thinking about what had happened that morning and where it might lead.

For Rhea, there was no doubt the end was near. If the images found nothing, the investigation would go cold again. If there *was* something on the images…it would help them find her sister, and she refused to give up hope that Selene was alive.

Jackson took a last bite of his sandwich, scooped up a handful of chips and popped a few into his mouth. He chewed thoughtfully, swallowed and said, "I think it went well this morning."

"I think so, although I'm not really into tech. Not a Luddite, mind you, but I like doing things hands-on."

He raised an eyebrow and fixed his gaze on her. It was hot, so hot. "I like that you like that."

Rhea's cheeks burned with the heat ignited by his look. She shook her head and chuckled. "I'll have to remember that."

"And me? Will you remember me?" Jackson said, his mood growing more somber.

Remember him? How can I ever forget him? She reached over and laid her hand on his forearm. With a tender stroke, she said, "I could never forget you, Jax. What we have…it's complicated, isn't it?"

"It is, but you're very special to me, Rhea. Whatever happens…" He wagged his head in an almost defeated gesture, laced his fingers with hers and offered her a sad smile. "How about that hike?"

"Sounds nice," she said, eager to move away from a discussion that could only bring sadness.

Hand-in-hand they walked down the steps and across the one-lane road to a small path that led to the trail by the lake. Sunlight frolicked on the surface of the lake, glittering like silver and ice-blue confetti against the cerulean blue waters. Waters that lapped softly along the reeds at the lake's edges.

Ducks and geese swam here and there on the surfaces, dark shapes against the light dancing on the lake.
Far ahead of them, wading in the grasses on long stick-
like legs, a great blue heron stood still, patient. Waiting
to snare a meal. They carefully walked past so as not to
disturb the bird and pushed on, voices silent. Thoughts
loud, but calming slowly thanks to the beauty of the
nature around them. A little farther up the trail, the
sudden and loud flap of wings alerted them to a large
bird taking flight.

A bald eagle soared into view over the lake, majestic
and immense. With a few flaps of its wings the eagle
climbed ever higher, then glided on a burst of breeze,
reveling in its freedom.

Jackson watched the regal bird soar and dance on
the wind. Its flight graceful, but filled with strength.
In some ways, Rhea was like that bird. Elegant. Powerful. Free.

He had to remind himself of that. Free to choose her
own path. Free to leave when the time came, but much
like the bald eagles who left in late winter, sometimes
a pair would stay behind to nest and build a family.

They walked together for a good hour, enjoying the
many sights along the lake. The spring weather was
perfect for their walk, with a slight breeze to combat
the heat building from the bright sunlight. In the shade
of the trees on the trail, it was almost a little chilly and
when Rhea shivered, he wrapped an arm around her
shoulders and drew her close.

Hips bumping, they finally turned around and strolled
back toward his parents' home, peace filling him. Funny,

really, if you thought about it. He was in the middle of an active investigation. Someone was trying to hurt her, maybe even kill her, and yet what he felt was a peace that he hadn't experienced in years.

His heart was huge with that peace, with love for her, as they got back into the cruiser to head back to the police station for another look through their notes and to see if anyone needed his help on any other cases. The chief had warned him about how the investigation was taking too much of his time and the town's resources. With some downtime until his cousins came through with the information from the LIDAR footage, he had to give his attention to other cases his colleagues might be working on.

Back at the police station, he did just that, leaving Rhea comfortably tucked away in his office sketching while he checked in with the other officers on the force. He assisted one with recreating the scene of a hit-and-run. At another desk, an officer asked for advice about a burglary and that officer's version of the entry into the building.

Pleased with being of help to his colleagues, he was returning to his office when his police chief walked back into the station. If he remembered correctly, his boss had had a meeting with the mayor and some members of the town council about the police budget for the coming year.

"How'd it go, Bill?" he asked, hoping for positive news.

The police chief lifted his meaty shoulders in a careless way. "It's too soon to know, but at least it wasn't an immediate rejection."

Jackson heard the tone of worry in his chief's voice.

"Which might happen if they get a whiff of any issues. Like Selene's case, right?"

His boss glared at him. "Like that, Jax. I told you that when you first decided on this lunacy. Have you made any progress?"

Jackson clenched his jaw, biting back his anger. With a cleansing breath, he said, "We have. We've pretty much eliminated Matt Davis as a suspect. I've called Avalon PD to let them know that. We have photos of two possible suspects and a witness who saw their vehicle by the victim's sedan the night of her disappearance. Once we have the results of some drone imagery, we may know their whereabouts."

Taken aback, possibly shamed, the chief blustered, "Well, that all sounds good, Jax. Keep me posted."

The older man hurried away and Jackson returned to his office, where Rhea was still bent over her sketch pad, drawing.

"It's almost six. Are you ready to go? Maybe get dinner?" he said, but as he walked toward her his smartphone chirped. He grabbed it off his desk and realized it was his cousin Robbie calling.

"Hey, Robbie. Do you have good news for us?"

Rhea's head popped up at the sound of his cousin's name.

"Putting you on speaker," he said as he walked over to Rhea and sat in the chair beside her, the smartphone held between them.

"Okay. I've got Sophie here with me, and like I said, good news. We were able to process the LIDAR data and get some images for you. How about a video call and a bigger screen, so we can explain the information?"

"I'll arrange that. I'd also like to include one of my colleagues who is familiar with the area," he said.

"Great. I'll send a link to the meeting. Fifteen minutes?" Sophie asked.

"We'll be ready," Jackson said and hung up. He shared a look with Rhea and hoped she would be.

Chapter 20

Jackson had set up a large projection monitor in the conference room and sat next to her, a laptop before him ready to make the video call. Officer Dillon sat across from them at the table, poised with pen and paper to take notes if necessary.

Following the link Sophie had sent, Jackson began the video call. The almost musical beep-bloop-beep chime ended quickly as Robbie and Sophie answered and their smiling faces jumped onto the big screen in front of them.

Even if she hadn't been told that they were Jackson's cousins, she would have seen the family resemblance. They both had the same square jaw, straight nose and thumbprint cleft in their chins. Broad dimples bracketed their mouths, and like Jackson, they had light eyes, although it was hard to tell what color thanks to the quality of the video combined with the projection.

Jackson's hair was a light brown, but Robbie and Sophie both had coffee brown, slightly wavier locks. Robbie was handsome. Sophie beautiful, but not in a classic way. More like a warrior goddess, strong and sure of herself.

"Happy to see you, *primo*," she said.

"Happy to see the both of you, and thank you again. I've got Rhea and Officer Dillon with me," he said, although he was the only one visible on the video call thanks to the angle of the laptop's camera.

"Like I said before, we've got good news for you," Robbie said and, a second later, a photo replaced their smiling images.

"We took the LIDAR images, and this is the raw photo," Robbie said, describing the first image. "There's lots of forest on both mountains, except for the ski resort to the extreme right and an obvious trail near that area."

As Robbie spoke, the mouse highlighted the areas his cousin was describing. When he shifted to the path close to the resort, Dillon spoke up. "That's the trail that most hikers use."

After that, Robbie continued, pointing toward the middle of the photo. "Here there appears to be slightly less vegetation, but then it's quite dense to the left of it."

Dillon rose from his spot and walked toward the screen. Gesturing to the area where the forest was less dense, he said, "I think this is the old logging road I told you about. I'm not sure just how passable the road is nowadays, and I don't think many people use it."

"Thanks for that info, Officer Dillon," Sophie said. "There was clearly something there even before we processed the image with our software."

When she finished, another image immediately popped up on the screen, surprising them with the look of it. All vegetation had been cleared away, revealing the contours of the mountainside, as well as what appeared to be other features.

Robbie came back online and continued with his explanation. "We downloaded a topographical map so we could have reference points to assist us in determining what was natural and what was man-made. Beside the resort area that was visible before, the processed image reveals several buildings beneath the tree line close to the resort and the path of the nearby trail."

"Wow, way cool," Officer Dillon said.

Very, Rhea thought as Sophie took over, explaining the other features revealed by their work. "There is clearly a break of some kind on the second mountain. I think Officer Dillon mentioned it was an old logging trail. But fairly high up on the trail, there's a small structure. Maybe a lean-to of some kind."

"Would that be big enough to hide a vehicle?" Jackson asked.

"For sure," Sophie answered and pressed onward. "About two miles away there's another structure. A cabin. See this square at one side? Probably a chimney."

"You're sure that's a cabin?" Jackson asked.

"Without a doubt," Robbie said and then shifted to an image zoomed and enhanced to show the details of the structure. After that, he displayed several other photos, from slightly different angles, which helped to define the path of the logging trail, as well as a possible trail from the lean-to toward the cabin.

When he finished, he said, "We've sent you these

photos via email. If you need us to testify to them, we'd be happy to do that."

"We totally appreciate all you've done," Rhea said, suddenly feeling very optimistic about what the photos had revealed.

"We never say 'No' to family," Sophie said, which prompted a rough laugh from Jackson.

"Hint duly noted, as well as massive guilt, Sophie. I love you guys, and I hope to see you soon," Jackson said.

"Hope to see you soon *in Miami*, *primo*," Robbie said and ended the video call.

"They sure know how to lay on the guilt," Rhea teased, and Jackson laughed. He shot to his feet to turn on the lights in the conference room, leaned against the wall and crossed his arms. Peering at Dillon, he said, "You mentioned that logging road might be tough to traverse."

Dillon nodded. "Might be. We'd obviously need 4x4s and additional manpower. Those guys are probably armed."

Jackson nodded. "I spoke to the Parks Service, and they're leaving it up to us to take action. I'm thinking two other officers, SWAT possibly, if the chief approves of course."

"I agree. Weather tomorrow is supposed to be good," Dillon said.

Almost too eagerly, Rhea thought.

"I'll speak to the chief and ask him who will be our backup, but remember this, Dillon. These men are likely dangerous. Possibly murderers, or kidnappers if Selene is still alive," Jackson said in warning, like-

wise sensing the young officer's almost misplaced en-
thusiasm.

"Alive? It's been over six months, boss. Sorry, miss,"
Dillon said with a guilty look in her direction.

"It's okay, Officer Dillon. I understand." She peered
at Jackson as he continued to lean against the wall.

As her gaze met his, determination filled his gaze,
but also pain. They were possibly almost at the end of
their journey. It might end at a most dangerous place
tomorrow, after they made their ascent up the mountain
and to the structures the images had revealed.

"I'm going with you tomorrow, Jax. Make no mistake about that," she warned.

"We'll discuss this later. Right now, I have to get
the chief's approval for this operation."

He didn't wait for a reply from either her or Dillon.
He rushed out, his face dark with worry and hurt, gray
eyes as stormy as rainclouds. His lips a thin line in a
face as stony as granite. Closed off from her, and she
understood. He wasn't just preparing himself for the
danger to come.

He was preparing for her to leave.

He moved in her, his big body driving her toward
release. His gaze locked on her, wanting to see when
she went over and to hold that moment close before
he lost control.

Her blue eyes had darkened, were almost black with
desire. A soft moan escaped her with one thrust, and
he worried he might have hurt her until she dug her
fingernails into his skin and arched her back, deepening his penetration. He thrust again and she urged him
on, wrapping her legs around him.

Inside pressure built, his heart pounding harder and louder. Almost as if calling out what he was feeling. *Love you, love you, love you*, but the words never left his mouth, trapped by fear.

Beneath him, her body shuddered and tightened, and she called out his name, her release washing over her. Spilling onto him as he drove into her one last time. Her name escaped his lips and he fell over with her.

He held his weight off her, but then she reached up and cradled his shoulders. Invited him to rest on her, their bodies still united. But after a short minute, he rolled onto his side and took her with him, tucking her close.

They lay there in silence until Rhea stroked a hand across his chest. "It's going to be okay."

A rough laugh escaped him. "Funny. I thought that was supposed to be my line."

She didn't respond, she just moved closer, her hand resting over his heart.

He understood. As much as he had searched for the words since they'd left the police station earlier, he hadn't found them. Hadn't been able to figure out how to tell her that he loved her. How that had happened in just a few days. What he hoped for the future with her. If there even was a future.

Rhea rested beside him, her hand tucked over his heart, listening to the beat as it settled into a steady rhythm. She felt his tension growing. The muscles beneath her hand were tight, unyielding. The arm resting down her back, keeping her near, didn't exude that feeling of comfort or protection that his touch usually did.

It made her wonder if it would be okay, as she'd said earlier. If after tomorrow, no matter what happened, they could make this relationship work. If they could explore the love that had somehow blossomed between them at such an unlikely time. But it had taken hold and sunk its roots deep in her heart.

Has it done the same in him?

She refused to think that it hadn't, but tomorrow would tell. No matter what happened, they might have to go their separate ways.

But can we find our way back together?

Chapter 21

The turnoff to the logging road was blocked by a wall of underbrush, but the tire tracks in the soft dirt confirmed it had been recently used. Jackson and Dillon got out of the SUV and, after examining the tumble of vines and brush, pulled it away to allow them to pass.

They bumped their way up the uneven road, which was fairly navigable despite the large boulders and soft loose dirt at numerous spots along the path. At one point, the SUV behind them carrying the two members of the Regina SWAT team got bogged down in one of the softer ruts. Jackson got out, cut down some branches with his machete and tucked them under the tires, providing the traction to get them out of the rut.

Inside their SUV, Dillon manned a tablet with software that Robbie and Sophie had provided, which visualized exactly where they were based on the LIDAR images. As Dillon lifted the tablet, a 3D rendering of the area around them sprang to life. But as they got closer to the first structure identified by the drone imagery, they didn't need a tablet to tell them what was right before their eyes: the SUV from the photos at the pub.

Jackson got out of the car, stood on the running board and gestured to everyone to hold their positions with his upraised fist.

He hopped off the running board and carefully approached the lean-to, which housed the SUV, worried that anyone who had taken the time to hide the turnoff for the road might have created a booby trap to protect the vehicle.

He inched his way all around the area, searching for trip wires or hidden traps.

"All clear," he said and gave the hand motion to go.

Everyone exited the vehicles and came over to examine the SUV against the pub photo.

"Definitely the same car," said the one SWAT officer as he stood in front of the Jeep, his rifle slung across his chest.

Jackson squatted to examine the custom bumper. There were rough gouges and scratches in the thick steel, a testament to when they'd used the vehicle to ram them. There were even still some hints of white paint from the police cruiser's bumper.

"This is the vehicle that attacked us." He straightened and faced his team.

"These men are dangerous. They are likely armed. We need to use extreme caution on our approach and you—" he gestured to Rhea "—you hang back and stay close."

Jackson hated that she was even with them, but Rhea had insisted, and he knew it wouldn't have done any good to argue with her. They had come so far together, and it would end with them together. He walked over to her, cupped her jaw and said, "You understand, right? I don't want to see you hurt." For good measure, he checked the bulletproof vest and helmet she wore, making sure she'd be secure.

Rhea cradled his face. "I understand. I'll stay close, because I don't want to see any of you hurt."

He nodded and went to the head of his team. Gave the Move-out symbol.

There was a narrow trail from the SUV lean-to westward, and they hiked on it cautiously, watching for booby traps or alarms. Checking the tablet to see just how close they were to the cabin, which had been revealed by the LIDAR.

Jackson figured the structure was a good two miles from the logging trail. Not a long hike normally, but he and the other officers were in full protective gear. It was hot and sweaty beneath the body armor and helmets. Still they pressed on, navigating the trail until the cabin came into view, just where the LIDAR had said it would be.

He gave the Hold command and examined the clearing around the structure. Off to one side, there was an area with a woodpile and log with an ax buried in it.

One less weapon for them, Jackson thought.

Crude chairs fashioned from branches graced an equally crude and rustic porch, clearly an add-on to an otherwise solid log cabin. Curtains in an indiscriminate color hung on the windows, blocking his view into the building.

Wood smoke escaped the chimney, and the smell of it drifted over to them along with the scent of bacon. Someone was making a meal. Maybe a late breakfast.

A good thing. It meant they were home and maybe not paying too much attention to the exterior of the cabin.

He gestured to his team members to come close, and once they had gathered around him, he spoke to them in a low tone, directing each member to a different side of the structure. With a quick glance at Rhea, he said, "You stay down and close to me. Understand?"

Rhea nodded, comprehending Jackson's concerns. But there was no way she was going to miss this moment after all that they'd been through to get here.

She hung back, as close as she could so as not to hamper Jackson, and watched as the other team members fanned out. They had only gotten about halfway to their positions when a clanging sound rang out. A cow bell, warning anyone in the cabin that someone was outside.

The SWAT member who had tripped the alarm dropped to the ground, trying to avoid detection, but a second later came the sound of glass breaking and a shot rang out in his direction. Bark flew off a tree in his general direction.

A curtain shifted in the front of the cabin, and the glass shattered as a second rifle barrel poked out.

Jackson muttered a curse and shook his head. With a backward sweep of his arm, he tucked Rhea behind the protection of his back. Having been discovered, he had no choice but to shout, "Police. Drop your weapons and come out with your hands up."

A round of gunshots came in their direction, smashing into the trees and brush around them. One of their team returned fire, but Jackson radioed them and said, "Hold your fire. They could have a hostage in there."

He again called out to the men in the cabin. "We don't have to do this the hard way. Surrender, and I can speak to the DA to keep the sentence reasonable."

In response, a female face suddenly appeared in the window, but then was hauled back abruptly. "We'll kill her," someone shouted.

Selene. Alive. Selene's alive, Rhea thought and stood up slightly, her gut reaction to run to her sister.

Jackson hauled her back down and looked over his shoulder at her. Blood dripped from a cut on his cheekbone and a bit of bark stuck to his helmet. Eyes hard, he said, "Steady, Rhea."

Without missing a beat, he turned back toward the cabin and screamed, "You can make this easier for yourselves. Let the woman go, and I'll talk to the DA."

More gunfire erupted, but it was followed by shouting from inside the cabin. The thick log walls were enough to muffle whatever it was they were saying to each other, but Rhea hoped they were talking about surrendering. Her hopes were dashed as bullets tore into the underbrush and ground all around the SWAT officer who had tripped the cowbell.

A volley of gunfire erupted from the officer toward the side of the cabin. The dull thud of bullets striking wood reverberated through her.

Once again, Jackson reined in the response. "Hold your fire. Repeat, hold your fire."

"Copy that," echoed from all the officers.

The creak of the door drew their attention. It opened, almost in slow motion, providing a partial view of the interior of the cabin. But then suddenly, Selene stood in the doorway, hands held on top of her head.

She paused, a little wobbly. *Way too thin*, Rhea thought. The tattered shirt hung on her slim shoulders and was stained in various spots. Rhea had given her the shirt two Christmases ago. Her jeans were worn and torn, likewise dirty as if from soot or soil.

"Come forward slowly, hands up," Jackson shouted.

Selene took another hesitant step toward them onto the front porch. She squinted, as if the sunlight was too much for her, making Rhea wondered if it had been months since she'd been outside the walls of her prison.

"Walk forward slowly," Jackson said as another burst of shouting came from within the cabin.

A bearded face became visible in the window, and the man called out, "You have her. Now leave us alone."

More fighting followed that declaration, and with the door open, the words were a little more discernable. One voice, stronger and obviously in command. "Shut the door. Shut the damn door."

The second, weaker, almost stumbling. "B-b-b-ut—"

"Shut it," boomed the first person, and the door slammed closed.

Selene jumped, almost as if shot, and it was all Rhea could do not to run to her sister. But Jackson had his arm stuck out, a barrier keeping her back.

The shouting resumed inside the cabin, and Jackson took advantage of that to stand, exposing himself to gunfire. He held out his hand and motioned to Selene. "Here. Come here, Selene."

Her sister's eyes widened, but then she ran toward them and dropped to her knees, into Rhea's arms, when she got there.

Rhea kissed her sister's face and wrapped her arms around her, unable to believe she was really there. That she was alive.

"You've made this easier for yourselves, but you've got to surrender. Come out, hands up," Jackson commanded.

More yelling came from the cabin, followed by an assortment of crashes, as if someone was trashing the place. More shouts, and then silence. Finally, surprising all of them, the sound of a single gunshot.

Jackson sucked in a breath, trying to fathom what that single gunshot might mean. Especially as the door slowly opened again and a hesitant voice called out, "D-d-don't shoot. Please don't h-h-urt m-m-e."

There was almost a nervous quality to the voice, warning him that it might be the younger brother. A gentle hand on his forearm drew his attention back to where Rhea and Selene huddled, arms around each other. It was Selene's hand, and as he met her gaze, so much like Rhea's, he was taken aback for a moment. But only a millisecond in this life and death situation.

"It's Wade," Selene confirmed.

Jackson nodded. "Come out slowly, Wade. Hands on your head. We won't hurt you."

Finally, someone appeared in the doorway. One of the men in the photos. One of Selene's kidnappers.

"Slowly, Wade," he repeated as the man faltered on the front porch, clearly afraid as his gaze darted all around, seemingly uncomprehending.

Wade took a few more uncertain steps into the clearing in front of the cabin.

Over his shoulder, Jackson asked Selene, "What's his brother's name?"

"Earl," she said harshly, as if it pained her to say his name.

"On your knees, Wade. Where's Earl?" Jackson said, rising slightly so Wade could see him, but keeping behind the trunk of the tree for safety.

"Dead. Kilt himself," Wade said and whipped his head in the direction of the cabin.

Jackson radioed his team. "Visuals? Can anyone confirm?"

Dillon spoke up first. "I can see into the cabin. Looks like a body on the floor."

"Are you sure, Dillon?" Jackson pressed, wanting to avoid any additional bloodshed.

"I'm sure, boss."

Jackson commanded the two SWAT officers. "Levine. Anderson. Move in. Dillon, hang back and secure our suspect when possible."

"Copy that," all the officers confirmed.

Jackson waited, protecting the two women while his counterparts hurried toward the cabin, guns drawn. The SWAT officers paused at the door. Entry areas like that could be a fatal funnel, but as the one officer peered inside, he lowered his weapon slightly.

"Shot himself in the head. Going in to check on him. Cover my six, Anderson," Officer Levine said and entered the cabin. He emerged a second later and gave the All-clear motion.

Jackson stood and helped Rhea bring her sister to her feet. Together, they supported her to walk to a stump, where she sat and gazed up at them, tears streaming down her face.

"I thought I'd die here...like the others," she said,

and her gaze skittered back to the cabin for a second and then back to them.

"Others?" Jackson asked, hands on his hips as he focused on Selene's face, so much like Rhea's, but so much thinner from her captivity. The remnants of a bruise, going yellowish and purple, lingered along her right cheek. He clenched his jaw with anger at the thought of anyone striking her.

Selene nodded. "Wade let it slip that they'd taken other women, but I already knew. There were other feminine things in the cabin. Combs. Jewelry. Clothes. I think they killed them."

"Anderson. Dillon. Levine. Secure the area. I'm going to call in the Crime Scene Unit, since we may have other victims here," Jackson instructed and then stepped away to phone his chief and advise him on their status and the possibility they had multiple kidnappings and homicides.

"I have to say I'm surprised, Jax. That's just not the kind of thing that happens here," the chief said.

"I'm with you, Bill. I'm hoping Selene is wrong, and it was just Wade shoplifting things, like he did in Regina, but if not…" If not they had serial killers on their hands.

"I'll get them up there ASAP. How's the woman? Do you need transport to take her to the hospital?"

Jackson glanced back toward where Selene sat, Rhea kneeling beside her. "She's shaky, Chief. We may need transport, but give me a little more time to talk with her and see what she wants."

Jackson returned to the two women and was once again struck by how identical they were. Same intelligent crystal-blue eyes and full lips. The dark, almost black hair, although Selene's was far longer and dull. As he neared, they both looked toward him, the motion of their bodies in unison.

"CSU will be coming up to search the scene and preserve evidence. I'd like to take you to the hospital—"

"No, I want to go home," Selene said, shaking her head furiously.

Jackson looked toward Rhea, who did a little dip of her head. "I think that would be best."

Blowing out a rough breath, Jackson said, "We need to take some photos of you and get a statement. Are you up for doing that?"

Selene nodded. "I am. Anything you need me to do."

"I'm grateful for that, Selene. I can call for a transport chopper—"

"I can walk. I just want to get out of here," she said, wrapped her arms around herself and began to rock, like a child trying to comfort itself during a nightmare.

Rhea hugged her sister and kissed her temple, trying to calm her. "It's okay, Selene. It's over. You'll be home soon."

"With you. I want to go with you," Selene cried and grabbed hold of Rhea's arm.

"With me, sis. Don't worry. You can stay as long as you need to," Rhea said.

"Let me just give my men some other instructions and then we'll head back to Regina," Jackson said.

He returned, leaving Dillon to guard Wade in the hopes he would provide more information to the CSU. They read him his Miranda rights, using Dillon's body cam to preserve it and anything else he said as evidence. He worried that if they didn't record it, it might not hold up in court, but his top priority, beside getting

Selene home, was discovering if Wade and his brother had kidnapped and killed other women.

Together, Rhea and he supported Selene for the hike back to their vehicle. As they walked, she seemed to grow stronger, her back straightening and her head lifting from its earlier cowed droop. Halfway through the walk, she began her story.

"Matt and I had another fight, and he hit me again. I ran, afraid of him. Scared of myself and what I was becoming. I was driving to you, Rhea, but it was late and I got hungry. I stopped for gas and when I asked the clerk about a place to eat, he recommended the pub." She stopped to draw a shaky breath and then continued, "I ordered a burger and was eating when Earl and Wade came by. They started making comments. Eyeing me. When I left, they followed me out and catcalled me again, but I ignored them, got in my car and drove away.

"When I got to the lake, it called to me, so I parked and walked toward the shore. Stood there thinking about my life and decided it was time to leave Matt. Time to follow my dreams like you had, Rhea." She glanced at her sister and offered her a smile.

Like Rhea, Selene is even more beautiful when she smiles, Jackson thought.

"Is that when you texted me?" Rhea asked.

Selene nodded. "It is. I was going to come to you that night, but as I turned, someone grabbed me and covered my mouth. Someone else took hold of my feet to haul me back toward the road. I was kicking and trying to scream, but I couldn't breathe and passed out."

"Earl and Wade took you to the cabin?" Jackson said.

"They expected me to service them and if I didn't..."

Selene's voice cracked then, and tears came to her eyes and spilled downward, but she swiped them away furiously. "They'd rape me once or twice a week. Wade really didn't want to, but Earl would bait him and say that he wasn't a real man if he didn't."

Walking beside Selene, Rhea was likewise crying, obviously thinking about everything her sister had suffered in the months she'd been held captive. The two sisters held each other, offering support. Offering comfort to each other as they finished the hike and reached the police SUVs.

Jackson helped the women into the back and got behind the wheel. It was time to return Selene to civilization. Back to her real life.

Away from Regina, he thought, but reined in his emotions. Selene was alive and free, but there might be other women who had not been so lucky.

Now it was his job to speak for them and to give their families relief. Everything else would have to wait.

Chapter 22

Rhea had sensed his withdrawal with every mile that took them away from the cabin and to Regina. Upon their arrival, he was the consummate professional, arranging for one of the female officers to take photos of Selene and afterward getting her statement on video while he took notes. While she understood he had a job to do, it only reinforced her earlier fears that once this case was over, they'd be over.

But her pain was dimmed by the joy that Selene was alive. *Alive*, she thought and hugged her sister hard. Gazing at her, Rhea examined Selene, taking note of how she'd changed in the many months she'd been gone. There was something in her gaze that was older somehow, and there were tiny scars, the remnants of scratches and cuts, in addition to the very-visible remnants of a bruise along her cheek.

As Rhea continued her perusal, she noted additional

bruising along her collarbone and bruises that looked like fingerprints on her upper arms.

Selene's gentle touch came to Rhea's jaw, urging her gaze away from the bruises. Selene was smiling, a sad smile that didn't quite reach her eyes. "I knew you wouldn't give up. I knew you'd come for me."

Rhea's gaze grew hazy with unshed tears and emotion choked her throat. She fought past it and said, "I knew you were alive. I felt it, in here." She tapped her chest.

Selene nodded. "Me, too, and I feel your pain now," she said softly and peered toward Jackson as he stood outside the interrogation room, speaking with his chief. "He's special to you, isn't he?"

Rhea closed her eyes to fight the tears and wagged her head. "He is. Very special."

"It will be all right, Rhea. Believe that," Selene said, but fell silent as Jackson returned to the room.

He laid the file in his hand on the table. It contained Selene's statement, his notes and the photos they'd taken of her various injuries. With a heavy sigh, he said, "I think we're done here, but I hope that if we need more information, you'll make yourself available."

"I will," Selene said and skipped her gaze between Jackson and her. "Do you two need a moment?"

"Yes," Rhea said at the same time that Jackson said, "No."

Rhea's heart plummeted with that, but she refused to show it. "I guess we should go now."

Jackson nodded, but didn't look at her. Instead, he focused on Selene and said, "I think you should go to the hospital."

Rhea was looking away, but she caught sight of Selene peering between them as she said, "If you think so, but what about you two—"

"Rhea wants to make sure you're safe and sound also," he replied and grabbed hold of his file. "If you don't mind, I have to head back to the cabin. The CSU team has found other victims there."

He hurried from the room, but before he did so, he gazed at her like a hungry man at a king's feast, igniting hope that he really did care. That he really wanted more for them despite his behavior.

And then he was gone to do his job, and she had her own responsibilities to fulfill. She needed to get her sister to the hospital and make sure she was fine. Once they were home, she needed to help Selene rebuild her life and get on with her own.

The police station still looked picture perfect, the craftsman building nestled harmoniously with the other shops along Main Street. The flowers on either side of the wide steps leading to the door had grown larger in the month since she'd last been there. As a warm breeze swept past, the petals waved at her in welcome as they had a month ago.

She only hoped she would be as welcome inside, because so much had happened in the last few weeks.

Jackson and his team had found the bodies of three other women buried a short distance from the cabin. The jewelry and other items had helped to confirm their identities. One of the women had been missing for nearly four years, and based on the date of her disappearance, as well as the others, it seemed as if the brothers had taken a new woman every year. The other victims had been taken from farther away, which was why neither the Regina nor Avalon police departments had noticed a pattern. It had kept them from being criticized in the press. If anything, Jackson and his team, as well as her, had been praised for the police work that had brought closure to the other cases and families.

Wade had confirmed that it was Earl who had been at the inn, wanting to grab Rhea so they'd have both sisters under their control. When he'd realized Rhea was no pushover, he'd decided to scare her away or kill her if need be.

Entering the building, the familiar sight of the desk sergeant was a relief. Millie would know who she was, and she suspected the other woman would know who she was there to see. She wasn't wrong, as the young police officer smiled and buzzed her through the barrier. Rising, Millie said, "It's good to see you again, Rhea. Or, at least, I hope it's a good thing."

She nodded. "It is, Millie. Wish me luck."

Millie smiled and gestured toward the back of the station. "I think you know where his office is."

"I do," she said and, without waiting, headed to see Jackson.

As she neared the door, she passed Dillon who said, "Better be careful, Rhea. He's as cross as a bear with a thorn in its paw."

Jackson's door was closed. She knocked and heard his grumbled "I'm busy" through the door.

She'd come too far to be ignored that easily. She pushed through the door and shut it behind her.

A look of surprise filled Jackson's face before he schooled his features and stood.

He took her breath away, much like he had the first

time she'd seen him. His police blues seemed a little looser around his body, and his face was thinner, as well. His shortly cropped brown hair had grown out a little and the gray of his eyes was muddled, like the sky during a rainstorm. He clenched and unclenched his jaw as he stood there, clearly uneasy.

She charged on, "It's good to see you again, Jax."

"Nice to see you again, Rhea," he said, although nothing about his tone and stance said he was happy to see her.

"I know we left things on a weird note," she began, and he laughed harshly, rocked back and forth on his heels.

"That's an understatement. How is Selene? How is she doing?" he asked and relaxed a little. He invited her to sit, but she was too nervous. And too anxious about what she intended to say to him.

"She's doing well. She divorced Matt and has been seeing a therapist and going to a support group. She's also been singing at some of the local clubs."

"Sounds good." He paused, jammed his hands in his pockets and said, "How about you? You okay?"

This was the moment she'd been waiting for and she didn't hesitate to grab it with both hands. "I'm miserable. I miss you. I hated how it ended with us because... I don't want it to end, Jax. I'm in love with you."

He reared back as if he'd been struck, but then he rushed toward her and embraced her in a bear hug. "You can't imagine how many times I dreamed you'd come back and say that."

She laughed, dropped a kiss on his jaw and said, "You dreamed of me?"

"Every night, Rhea. But when we started you were

so vulnerable, and I felt so guilty that I might have taken advantage. That's why I forced myself to make you leave that day. You needed space. So did I."

She playfully elbowed him and then urged him to sit with her in the chairs in front of his desk. "I was so hurt that day, but once I was back in Denver, helping Selene, I realized I needed to find out if what we had was real."

He arched a brow and took hold of her hand, lacing his fingers with hers. "And did you?"

She nodded without hesitation and squeezed his hand. "I did. I want to be with you, Jax. That is if you want to be with me."

He leaned close and laid his forehead against hers. Kissed her cheek. "I want to be with you, but your life is in Denver."

"It *was* in Denver," she said. She broke away from him only long enough to remove a key from her purse. She dangled it in front of him and, at his questioning look, she said, "I rented a storefront on Main Street for a new gallery."

"Are you sure?" Jackson asked, unable to believe that what he'd dreamed of for the last month was actually coming true. That Rhea was back. For good this time.

Rhea smiled and said, "I'm sure. I love you, Jax."

As he perused her features, her love beamed from her crystal-blue gaze, dispelling any remaining doubts he might have had.

"I love you, Rhea. I can't wait for our life together to begin."

"Why wait?" she said and pulled him up from the chair and toward the door.

Jackson laughed, but stopped at the door to kiss her. Hard. Demanding. But he tempered the kiss, worried they might not make it out of the station. As they broke apart, he cradled her face and said, "Have I ever said how much I love that you don't give up?"

"I think you called me stubborn, but that's okay, because I won't ever give up on us, Jax."

He smiled and kissed her again. "I think I can live with that. Forever, Rhea."

"Forever, Jax," she said and pulled him out the door and into the rest of their lives.

* * * * *

Cindi Myers is the author of more than fifty novels.
When she's not plotting new romance plots, she
enjoys skiing, gardening, cooking, crafting and
daydreaming. A lover of small-town life, she lives with
her husband and two spoiled dogs in the Colorado
mountains.

Books by Cindi Myers

Harlequin Intrigue

Eagle Mountain: Search for Suspects

Disappearance at Dakota Ridge

The Ranger Brigade: Rocky Mountain Manhunt

Investigation in Black Canyon
Mountain of Evidence
Mountain Investigation
Presumed Deadly

Eagle Mountain Murder Mystery: Winter Storm Wedding

Ice Cold Killer
Snowbound Suspicion
Cold Conspiracy
Snowblind Justice

Visit the Author Profile page
at Harlequin.com for more titles.

ICE COLD KILLER

Cindi Myers

Chapter 1

Snow hid a lot of things, Colorado State Patrol Trooper Ryder Stewart mused as he watched the wrecker back up to the white, box-shaped clump near the top of Dixon Pass. Christy O'Brien, a sturdy blonde with chin-length hair beneath a bright red knit beanie, stopped the wrecker a few inches from the snow clump, climbed out and brushed at the flakes with a gloved hand, revealing the bumper of a brown delivery truck. She knelt and hooked chains underneath the truck, then gave Ryder a thumbs-up. "Ready to go."

Ryder glanced behind him at the barrier he'd set up over the highway, and the Road Closed sign just beyond it. Ahead of Ryder, a cascade of snow flowed over the pavement, part of the avalanche that had trapped the truck. "You're clear," he said.

Slowly, Christy eased the wrecker forward. With

a sound like two pieces of foam rubbing together, the delivery truck emerged from its icy cocoon. When the truck was fully on the pavement, the wrecker stopped. The door to the delivery truck slid open, clumps of snow hitting the pavement with a muffled *floof*. "Took you long enough!" Alton Reed grinned as he said the words and brushed snow from the shoulders of his brown jacket.

"How many times is this, Alton?" Ryder asked, looking the driver up and down.

"First one this year—fourth overall." Alton surveyed the truck. "Got buried pretty deep this time. I'm thinking it's going to be a bad year for avalanches."

"The weather guessers say it's going to be a bad snow year." Ryder studied the pewter sky, heavy clouds like dirty cotton sitting low on the horizon. "This is the second time this week we've had to close the highway. Might not open again for a few days if the weather keeps up."

"You people ought to be used to it," Alton said. "It happens often enough. Though I can't say I'd care for being cut off from the rest of the world that way."

"Only four days last winter," Ryder said.

"And what—three weeks the year before that?"

"Three years ago, but yeah." Ryder shrugged. "The price we pay for living in paradise." That was how most people who lived there thought of Eagle Mountain, anyway—a small town in a gorgeous setting that outsiders flocked to every summer and fall. The fact that there was only one way in and out of the town, and that way was sometimes blocked by avalanches in the winter, only added to the appeal for some.

"Guess I'll have to find a place in town to stay until

the weather clears," Alton said, eyeing the cascade of snow that spilled across the highway in front of them.

"You ever think of asking for a different route?" Ryder asked. "One that isn't so avalanche prone?"

"Nah." Alton climbed back into his van. "After the first scare, it's kind of an adrenaline rush, once you realize you're going to be okay. And this route includes hazard pay—a nice bonus."

Ryder waved goodbye as Alton turned his truck and steered around the barriers, headed toward town. He and the other commuting workers, delivery drivers and tourists trapped by the storm would find refuge at the local motel and B&Bs. Ryder shifted his attention to Christy, who was fiddling with the chains on her wrecker. "Thanks, Christy," he said. "Maybe I won't have to call you out anymore today."

"Don't you want me to pull out the other vehicle?" she asked.

The words gave him a jolt. "Other vehicle?" He turned to stare at the snowbank, and was stunned to see a glint of red, like the shine of a taillight. The vehicle it belonged to must have been right up against the rock face. Alton hadn't mentioned it, so he must not have known it was there, either. "Yeah, you'd better pull it out, too," he said. "Do you need any help?"

"No, I've got it."

He shoved his hands in the pockets of his fleece-lined, leather patrolman's jacket and blew out a cloud of breath as he waited for Christy to secure the vehicle. When she'd brushed away some of the snow, he could make out a small sedan with Colorado plates.

Wedged farther back under the packed snow, the car took longer to extricate, but it was lighter than the delivery van, and Christy's wrecker had tire chains and a powerful engine. She dragged the vehicle, the top dented in from the weight of the snow, onto the pavement.

Snow fell away from the car, revealing a slumped form inside. Ryder raced to the vehicle and tried the door. It opened when he pulled hard, and he leaned in to take a look, then groped for the radio on his shoulder. "I need an ambulance up at the top of Dixon Pass," he said. "And call the medical examiner."

Even before he reached out to feel for the woman's pulse, he knew she wouldn't be needing that ambulance. The young, brown-haired woman was as cold as the snow that surrounded them, her hands and feet bound with silver duct tape, her throat slit all the way across.

He leaned back out of the car and tilted his head up into the cold, welcoming the feel of icy flakes on his cheeks. Yeah, the snow hid a lot of things, not all of them good.

Darcy Marsh ran her fingers through the silky fur of the squirming Labrador puppy, and grinned as a soft pink tongue swiped at her cheek. For all the frustrations that were part of being a veterinarian, visits like this were one of the perks. "I'd say Admiral is a fine, healthy pup," she told the beaming couple in front of her. High school teacher Maya Renfro and Sheriff's Deputy Gage Walker returned the smile. "We'll keep an eye on that little umbilical hernia, but I don't expect it will cause any problems."

"Can Casey hold him now?" Maya asked, smiling at her young niece, Casey, who was deaf. The little girl's busily signing fingers conveyed her eagerness to cuddle her puppy.

"Yes, I think he's ready to come down." Darcy handed over the pup, and Casey cradled him carefully.

"You'll need to bring him back in a month for his second set of puppy vaccinations," Darcy said as she washed her hands at the exam room sink. "If you have any concerns before then, don't hesitate to give us a call."

"Thanks, Doc," Gage said. The family followed Darcy to the front of the office. "Are you all by yourself today?"

"It's Dr. Farrow's day off," Darcy said. "And I let Stacy go early, since you're my last client for today."

"Not quite the last," Maya said. She nodded toward the open waiting room door. An auburn-haired man in the blue shirt and tan slacks of a Colorado State Patrolman stood at their approach.

"Ryder, what are you doing here?" Gage asked, stepping forward to shake hands with the trooper.

"I just needed to talk to the vet for a minute," the officer, Ryder, said. He looked past Gage. "Hello, Maya, Casey. That's a good-looking pup you have there."

"His name is Admiral," Maya said as Casey walked forward with the now squirming dog.

Ryder knelt and patted the puppy. "I'll bet you two have a lot of fun together," he said, speaking slowly so that Casey could read his lips.

Darcy moved to the office computer and printed out an invoice for Maya, who paid while Gage and Ryder made small talk about dogs, the weather and the upcoming wedding of Gage's brother, Sheriff Travis Walker. "We're thinking of throwing some kind of bachelor party thing in a couple of weeks," Gage said. "I'll let you know when I have all the details. We may have to stay in town, if the weather keeps up like this."

"That should be an exciting party—not," Maya said as she returned her wallet to her purse. "All the local law enforcement gathered at Moe's pub, with the entire town keeping tabs on your behavior."

"This is my brother we're talking about," Gage said. "Travis isn't exactly known for cutting loose."

Laughing, they said goodbye to Ryder and left.

"What can I do for you?" Darcy leaned back against her front counter and studied the trooper. He was young, fit and good-looking, with closely cropped dark auburn hair and intense blue eyes. She had only been in Eagle Mountain four months, but how had she missed running into him? She certainly wouldn't have forgotten a guy this good-looking.

"Are you Dr. Darcy Marsh?" he asked.

"Yes."

"Is Kelly Farrow your business partner?"

"Yes." The room suddenly felt at least ten degrees colder. Darcy gripped the edges of the front counter. "Is something wrong?" she asked. "Has Kelly been in an accident?" Her partner had a bit of a reckless streak. She always drove too fast, and with this weather...

"I'm sorry to have to tell you that Ms. Farrow— Dr. Farrow—is dead," Ryder said.

Darcy stared at him, the words refusing to sink in. Kelly...dead?

"Why don't you sit down?" Ryder took her by the arm and gently led her to a chair in the waiting room, then walked over and flipped the sign on the door to Closed. He filled a paper cup with water from the cooler by the door and brought it to her. At any other time, she might have objected to him taking charge that way, but she didn't see the point at the moment.

She sipped water and tried to pull herself together. "Kelly's really dead?" she asked.

"I'm afraid so." He pulled a second chair over and sat facing her. "I need to ask you some questions about her."

"What happened?" Darcy asked. "Was she in an accident? I always warned her about driving so fast. She—"

"It wasn't an accident," he said.

She made herself look at him then, into eyes that were both sympathetic and determined. Not unkind eyes, but his expression held a hint of steel. Trooper Stewart wasn't a man to be messed with. She swallowed hard, and somehow found her voice. "If it wasn't an accident, how did she die?" Did Kelly have some kind of undiagnosed heart condition or something?

"She was murdered."

Darcy gasped, and her vision went a little fuzzy around the edges. This must be a nightmare—one of those super-vivid dreams that felt like real life, but wasn't. This couldn't possibly be real.

Then she was aware of cold water soaking into her slacks, and Ryder gently taking the paper cup from her hand. "I need to ask you some questions that may help me find her murderer," he said.

"How?" she asked. "I mean, how was she…killed?" The word was hard to say.

"We don't have all the details yet," he said. "She was found in her car, buried in an avalanche on top of

Dixon Pass. Do you know why she might have been up there?"

Why wasn't her brain working better? Nothing he said made sense to her. She brushed at the damp spot on her pants and tried to put her thoughts into some coherent order. "She told me she was going shopping and to lunch in Junction," she said. Leaving Eagle Mountain meant driving over Dixon Pass. There was no other way in or out.

"When was the last time you spoke to her?" Ryder asked.

"Yesterday afternoon, when we both left work. Today was her day off."

"Was that unusual, for her to take off during the week?"

"No. We each take one day off during the week so we can both work Saturdays. My day off is Wednesday. Hers is Tuesday."

"How long have you known her?"

Darcy frowned, trying to concentrate. "Five years? We met in college, then were roommates in vet school. We really hit it off. When she was looking for a partner to start a vet business here in Eagle Mountain, I jumped at the chance."

"Are you still roommates?" he asked.

"No. She lives in a duplex in town and I have a place just outside town—on the Lusk Ranch, out on County Road Three."

"Do you know of anyone who would want to hurt her?" he asked. "Does she have a history of a stalker, or someone from her past she's had a rocky relationship with?"

"No! Kelly got along with everyone." Darcy swallowed past the lump in her throat and pinched her hand, hard, trying to snap out of the fog his news had put her in. She couldn't break down now. Not yet. "If you had ever met her, you'd understand. She was this outgoing, sunny, super-friendly person. I was the more serious, quiet one. She used to say we were good business partners because we each brought different strengths to the practice." She buried her face in her hands. "What am I going to do without her?"

"Can you think of anyone at all she might have argued with recently—an unhappy client, perhaps?"

Darcy shook her head. "No. We've only been open a few months—less than four. So far all our interactions with clients have been good ones. I know, realistically, that won't last. You can't please everyone. But it's been a good experience so far. Well, except for Dr. Nichols." She made a face.

"Ed Nichols, the other vet in town?"

"Yes." She sighed. "He wasn't happy about our coming here. He said there wasn't enough business in a town this small for one vet, much less three. He accused us of undercutting his prices, and then I heard from some patients that he's been bad-mouthing us around town. But he never threatened us or anything like that. I mean, I can't believe he would want to kill one of us." She wrapped her arms around herself, suddenly cold.

"Where were you this morning, from nine to one?" Ryder asked.

"Is that when she died? I was here, seeing patients. We open at eight o'clock."

"Did you go out for lunch?"

"No. We had an emergency call—a dog that had

tangled with a porcupine. I had to sedate the poor guy to get the quills out. I ended up eating a granola bar at my desk about one o'clock."

"So you usually spend all day at the office here?"

She shook her head. "Not always. One of us is usually here, but we also treat large animals—horses and cows, mostly, but we see the occasional llama or donkey. Sometimes it's easier to go out to the animal than to have them brought here. That was something else Dr. Nichols didn't like—that we would do house calls like that. He said it set a bad precedent."

"Was Kelly dating anyone?" Ryder asked.

"She dated a lot of people, but no one seriously. She was pretty and outgoing and popular."

"Did she ever mention a man she didn't get along with? A relationship that didn't end well—either here or where you were before?"

"We were in Fort Collins. And no. Kelly got along with everyone." She made dating look easy, and had sometimes teased Darcy—though gently—about her reluctance to get involved.

"What about you? Are you seeing anyone?"

"No." What did that have to do with Kelly? But before she could ask, Ryder stood. He towered over her—maybe six feet four inches tall, with broad shoulders and muscular thighs. She shrank back from his presence, an involuntary action she hated, but couldn't seem to control.

"Can I call someone for you?" he asked. "A friend or relative?"

"No." She grabbed a tissue and pressed it to her eyes. "I need to call Kelly's parents. They'll be devastated."

"Give me their contact information and I'll do that," he said. "It's part of my job. You can call and talk to them later."

"All right." She went to the office, grateful for something to do, and pulled up Kelly's information on the computer. "I'll go over to her house and get her cats," she said. "Is it okay if I do that? I have a key." Kelly had a key to Darcy's place, too. The two looked after each other's pets and were always in and out of each other's homes.

"Yes. I already stopped by her place with an evidence team from the sheriff's department. That's how we found your contact information."

She handed him a piece of paper on which she'd written the names and numbers for Kelly's parents. He took it and gave her a business card. "I wrote my cell number on there," he said. "Call me if you think of anything that might help us. Even something small could be the key to finding out what happened to her."

She stared at the card, her vision blurring, then tucked it in the front pocket of her slacks. "Thank you."

"Are you sure you're going to be okay?" he asked.

No. How could she be okay again, with her best friend dead? And not just dead—murdered. She shook her head but said, "I'll be all right. I'm used to looking after myself."

The intensity in his gaze unnerved her. He seemed genuinely concerned, but she wasn't always good at reading people. "I'll be fine," she said. "And I'll call you if I think of anything."

He left and she went through the motions of closing up. The two cats and a dog in hospital cages were doing well. The dog—the porcupine victim—would be able to go home in the morning, and one of the cats, as well. The other cat, who had had surgery to remove a tumor, was also looking better and should be home by the weekend. She shut down the computer and set the alarm, then locked up behind her.

Outside it was growing dark, snow swirling over the asphalt of the parking lot, the pine trees across the street dusted with snow. The scene might have been one from a Christmas card, but Darcy felt none of the peace she would have before Ryder's visit. Who would want to hurt Kelly? Eagle Mountain had seemed such an idyllic town—a place where a single woman could walk down the street after dark and never feel threatened, where most people didn't bother to lock their doors, where children walked to school without fear. After only four months she knew more people here than she had in six years in Fort Collins. Kelly had made friends with almost everyone.

Was her killer one of those friends? Or a random stranger she had been unfortunate enough to cross paths with? That sort of thing was supposed to happen in cities, not way out here in the middle of nowhere. Maybe Eagle Mountain was just another ugly place in a pretty package, and the peace she had thought she had found was just a lie.

Chapter 2

A half mile from the veterinary clinic, Ryder almost turned around and went back. Leaving Darcy Marsh alone hadn't felt right, despite all her insisting that he go. But what was he going to do for her in her grief? He'd be better off using his time to interview Ed Nichols. Maybe he would call Darcy later and check that she was okay. She was so quiet. So self-contained. He was like that himself, but there was something else going on with her. She hadn't been afraid of him, but he had sensed her discomfort with him. Something more than her grief was bothering her. Was it because he was law enforcement? Because he was a man? Something else?

He didn't like unanswered questions. It was one of the things that made him a good investigator. He liked figuring people out—why they acted the way they did. If he hadn't been a law enforcement officer, he might have gone into psychology, except that sitting in an office all day would have driven him batty. He needed to be active and *doing*.

Ed Nichols lived in a small, ranch-style home with dark green cedar siding and brick-red trim. Giant blue spruce trees at the corners dwarfed the dwelling, and must have cast it in perpetual shadow. In the winter twilight, lights glowed from every window as if determined to dispel the gloom. Ryder parked his Chevy Tahoe at the curb and strode up the walk. Somewhere inside the house, a dog barked. Before he could ring the bell, the door opened and a man in his midfifties, thick blond hair fading to white, answered the door. "Is something wrong?" he asked.

"Dr. Nichols?" Ryder asked.

"Yes?" The man frowned.

"I need to speak with you a moment."

Toenails clicking on the hardwood floors announced the arrival of not one dog, but two—a small white poodle and a large, curly-haired mutt. The mutt stared at Ryder, then let out a loud *woof*.

"Hush, Murphy," Dr. Nichols said. He caught the dog by the collar and held him back, the poodle cowering behind, and pushed open the storm door. "You'd better come in."

A woman emerged from the back of the house— a trim brunette in black yoga pants and a purple sweater. She paled when she saw Ryder. "Is something wrong? Our son?"

"I'm not here about your son," Ryder said quickly. He turned to Nichols. "I wanted to ask you some questions about Kelly Farrow."

"Kelly?" Surprise, then suspicion, clouded Nichols's

expression. He lowered himself into the recliner and began stroking the big dog's head while the little one settled in his lap. "What about her?"

"You might as well sit down," Mrs. Nichols said. She perched on the edge of an adjacent love seat while Ryder took a seat on the sofa. "When was the last time you saw Kelly Farrow?" he asked.

Nichols frowned. "I don't know. Maybe—last week? I think I passed her on the street. Why? What is this about? Is she saying I've done something?"

"What would she say you've done?"

"Nothing! I don't have anything to do with those two."

"Those two?"

"Kelly and that other girl, Darcy."

"I understand you weren't too happy about them opening a new practice in Eagle Mountain."

"Who told you that?"

"Is it true?"

Nichols focused on the big dog, running his palm from the top of its head to the tip of its tail, over and over. "A town this small only needs one vet. But they're free to do as they please."

"Has your own business suffered since they opened their practice?" Ryder asked.

"What does that have to do with anything?" Mrs. Nichols spoke, leaning toward Ryder. "Are you accusing my husband of something?"

"You can't come into my home and start asking all these questions without telling us why," Nichols said.

"Kelly Farrow is dead. I'm trying to find out who killed her."

Nichols stared, his mouth slightly open. "Dead?"

"Ed certainly didn't kill her," Mrs. Nichols protested. "Just because he might have criticized the woman doesn't mean he's a murderer."

"Sharon, you're not helping," Nichols said.

"Where were you between nine and one today?" Ryder asked.

"I was at my office." He nodded to his wife. "Sharon can confirm that. She's my office manager."

"He saw patients all morning and attended the Rotary Club meeting at lunch," Sharon said.

"Listen, Kelly wasn't my favorite person in the world, but I wouldn't do something like that," Nichols said. "I couldn't."

Ryder wanted to believe the man, who seemed genuinely shaken, but it was too early in the case to make judgments of guilt or innocence. His job now was to gather as many facts as possible. He stood. "I may need to see your appointment book and talk to some of your clients to verify your whereabouts," he said.

"This is appalling." Sharon also rose, her cheeks flushed, hands clenched into fists. "How dare you accuse my husband this way."

"I'm not accusing him of anything," Ryder said. "It's standard procedure to check everyone's alibis." He nodded to Nichols. "Someone from my office will be in touch."

Ryder left the Nicholses' and headed back toward Main. He passed a familiar red-and-white wrecker, and Christy O'Brien tooted her horn and waved. Weather like this always meant plenty of work for Christy and her dad, pulling people out of ditches and jump-starting cars whose batteries had died in the cold.

Ryder pulled into the grocery store lot and parked.

He could see a few people moving around inside the lit store—employees who had to be there, he guessed. People who didn't have to be out in this weather stayed home. The automatic doors at the store entrance opened and a trio of teenage boys emerged, bare-headed and laughing, their letter jackets identifying them as students at the local high school. Apparently, youth was immune to the weather. They sauntered across the lot to a dark gray SUV and piled in.

Ryder contacted his office in Grand Junction to update them on his progress with the case. Since state patrol personnel couldn't reach him because of the closed road, he had called on the sheriff's department to process the crime scene. After the medical examiner had arrived at the scene and the ambulance had transported the body to the funeral home that would serve as a temporary morgue, he had had Kelly's car towed to the sheriff's department impound lot. But none of the forensic evidence—blood and hair samples, fingerprints and DNA—could be processed until the roads opened again. Eagle Mountain didn't have the facilities to handle such evidence.

"The highway department is saying the road won't open until day after tomorrow at the earliest," the duty officer told Ryder. "It could be longer, depending on the weather."

"Meanwhile, the trail gets colder," Ryder said. "And if the killer is on the other side of the pass, he has plenty of time to get away while I sit here waiting for the weather to clear."

"Do what you can. We'll run a background check on this Ed Nichols and let you know what we find. We're also doing a search for similar crimes."

"I'm going to talk to the sheriff, see if he has any suspects I haven't uncovered."

He ended the call and sat, staring out across the snowy lot and contemplating his next move. He could call it a night and go home, but he doubted he would get any rest. In a murder investigation it was important to move quickly, while the evidence was still fresh. But the weather had him stymied. Still, there must be more he could do.

A late-model Toyota 4Runner cruised slowly through the parking lot, a young man behind the wheel. He passed Ryder's Tahoe, his face a blur behind snow-flecked glass, then turned back out of the lot. Was he a tourist, lost and using the lot to turn around? Or a bored local, out cruising the town? Ryder hadn't recognized the vehicle, and after two years in Eagle Mountain, he knew most people. But new folks moved in all the time, many of them second homeowners who weren't around enough to get to know. And even this time of year there were tourists, drawn to backcountry skiing and ice climbing.

Any one of them might be a murderer. Was Kelly Farrow the killer's only victim, or merely the first? The thought would keep Ryder awake until he had answers.

Darcy parked in front of Kelly's half of the duplex off Fifth Street. Kelly had liked the place because it was within walking distance of the clinic, with easy access to the hiking trails along the river. Darcy let herself in with her key and when she flicked on the light, an orange tabby stared at her from the hall table, tail flicking. *Meow!*

"Hello, Pumpkin." Darcy scratched behind the cat's ears, and Pumpkin pressed his head into her palm.

Mroww! This more insistent cry came from a sleek, cream-colored feline, seal-point ears attesting to a Siamese heritage.

"Hello, Spice." Darcy knelt, one hand extended. Spice deigned to let her pet her.

Darcy stood and looked around at the evidence that someone else—Ryder, she guessed—had been here. Mail was spread out in a messy array on the hall table, and powdery residue—fingerprint powder?—covered the door frame and other surfaces. Darcy moved farther into the house, noting the afghan crumpled at the bottom of the sofa, a paperback romance novel splayed, spine up, on the table beside it. A rectangle outlined by dust on the desk in the corner of the room indicated where Kelly's laptop had sat. Ryder had probably taken it. From television crime dramas she had watched, she guessed he would look at her emails and other correspondence, searching for threats or any indication that someone had wanted to harm Kelly.

But Kelly would have said something to Darcy if anyone had threatened her. Unlike Darcy, Kelly never held back her feelings. Darcy blinked back stinging tears and hurried to the kitchen, to the cat carriers stacked in the corner. Both cats watched from the doorway, tails twitching, suspicious.

She set the open carriers in the middle of the kitchen floor, then filled two dishes with the gourmet salmon Pumpkin and Spice favored, and slid the dishes into the carrier. Pumpkin took the bait immediately, scarcely looking up from devouring the food when Darcy fastened the door of the carrier. Spice was more wary, tail twitching furiously as she prowled around the open carrier. But hunger won over caution and soon she, too, darted inside, and Darcy fastened the door.

She was loading the second crate into the back of her Subaru when the door to the other half of the duplex opened. A man's figure filled the doorway. "Darcy, is that you?"

"Hello, Ken." She tried to relax some of the stiffness from her face as she turned to greet Kelly's neighbor. Ken Rutledge was a trim, athletic man who taught math and coached boys' track and Junior Varsity basketball at Eagle Mountain High School.

He came toward her and she forced herself not to pull away when he took her arm. "What's going on?" he asked. "When I got home from practice two cop cars were pulling away from Kelly's half of the house." He looked past her to the back of her Forester. "And you're taking Kelly's cats? Has something happened to her?"

"Kelly's dead. Someone killed her." Her voice broke, and she let him pull her into his arms.

"Kelly's dead?" he asked, smoothing his hand down her back as she sobbed. "How? Who?"

She hated that she had to fight so hard to pull herself together. She tried to shove out of his arms, but he held her tight. She reminded herself that this was just Ken—Kelly's neighbor, and a man Darcy herself had dated a few times. He thought he was being helpful, holding her this way. She forced herself to relax and wait for her tears to subside. When his hold on her loosened, she eased back. "I don't know any details," she said. "A state patrolman told me they found her up on Dixon Pass—murdered."

"That's horrible." Ken's eyes were bright with the

shock of the news—and fascination. "Who would want to hurt Kelly?"

"The cops didn't stop to talk to you?" she asked.

"When I saw the sheriff's department vehicles I didn't pull in," he said. "I drove past and waited until they were gone before I came back."

"Why would you do that?" She stared at him.

He shrugged. "I have a couple of traffic tickets I haven't paid. I didn't want any hassle if they looked me up and saw them."

She took a step back. "Ken, they're going to want to talk to you," she said. "You may know something. You might have seen someone hanging around here, watching Kelly."

"I haven't seen anything like that." He shoved his hands in his pockets. "And I'll talk to them. I just didn't feel like dealing with them tonight. I mean, I didn't know Kelly was dead."

She closed the hatch of the car. "I have to go," she said.

He put a hand on her shoulder. "You shouldn't be alone at a time like this," he said. "You're welcome to stay with me."

"No. Thank you." She took out her keys and clutched them, automatically lacing them through her fingers to use as a weapon, the way the self-defense instructor in Fort Collins had shown her.

His expression clouded. "If it was someone else, you'd accept help, wouldn't you?" he said. "Because it's me, you're refusing. Just because we have a romantic history, doesn't mean we can't be friends."

She closed her eyes, then opened them to find him glaring at her. Were they ever going to stop having this conversation? They had only gone out together three times. To her, that didn't constitute a *romantic history*, though he insisted on seeing things differently. "Ken, I don't want to talk about this now," she said. "I'm tired and I'm upset and I just want to go home."

"I'm here for you, Darcy," he said.

"I know." She got into the driver's seat, forcing herself not to hurry, and drove away. When she glanced in the rearview mirror, Ken was still standing in the drive, frowning after her, hands clenched into fists at his sides.

Dating him had been a bad idea—Darcy had known it from the first date—but Kelly had pressured her to give him a chance. "He's a nice man," she had said. "And the two of you have a lot in common."

They did have a lot in common—a shared love of books and animals and hiking. But Ken pushed too hard. He wanted too much. After only two dates, he had asked her to move in with him. He had talked about them taking a vacation together next summer, and had wanted her to come home to Wisconsin to meet his parents for Christmas. She had broken off with him then, telling him she wasn't ready to get serious with anyone. He had pretended not to understand, telling her coming home to meet his family was just friendly, not serious. But she couldn't see things that way.

He had been upset at first—angry even. He called her some horrible names and told her she would regret losing a guy like him. But after he had returned from visiting his folks last week, he had been more cordial. They had exchanged greetings when she stopped by to see Kelly, and the three of them spent a couple of hours one afternoon shoveling the driveway together.

Darcy had been willing to be friends with him, as long as he didn't want more.

She turned onto the gravel county road that led to the horse ranch that belonged to one of their first clients. Robbie Lusk had built the tiny house on wheels parked by the creek as an experiment, he said, and was happy to rent it out to Darcy. His hope was to add more tiny homes and form a little community, and he had a second home under construction.

Darcy slowed to pull into her drive, her cozy home visible beneath the golden glow of the security light one hundred yards ahead. But she was startled to see a dark SUV moving down the drive toward her. Heart in her throat, she braked hard, eliciting complaints from the cats in their carriers behind her. The SUV barreled out past her, a rooster tail of wet snow in its wake. It turned sharply, scarcely inches from her front bumper, and she tried to see the driver, but could make out nothing in the darkness and swirling snow.

She stared at the taillights of the SUV in her rear-view mirror as it raced back toward town. Then, hands shaking, she pulled out her phone and found the card Ryder had given her. She punched in his number and waited for it to ring. "Ryder Stewart," he answered.

"This is Darcy Marsh. Can you come out to my house? A strange car was here and just left. I didn't recognize it and I... I'm afraid." Her knuckles ached from gripping the phone so hard, and her throat hurt from admitting her fear.

"Stay in your car. I'll be right there," Ryder said, his voice strong and commanding, and very reassuring.

Chapter 3

Ryder met no other cars on the trip to Darcy's house. Following the directions she had given him, he turned into a gravel drive and spotted her Subaru Forester parked in front of a redwood-sided dwelling about the size of a train caboose. She got out of the car when he parked his Tahoe beside her, a slight figure in black boots and a knee-length, black puffy coat, her dark hair uncovered. "I haven't looked around to see if anything was messed with," she said. "I thought I should wait for you."

"Good idea." He took his flashlight from his belt and played it over the ground around the house. It didn't look disturbed, but it was snowing hard enough the flakes might have covered any tracks. "Let me know if you spot anything out of place," he said.

She nodded and, keys in hand, moved to the front

door. "I know most people around here don't lock their doors," she said. "But I'm enough of a city girl, I guess, that it's a habit I can't break." She turned the key in the lock and pushed open the door, reaching in to flick on the lights, inside and out.

Ryder followed her inside, in time to see two cats descending the circular stairs from the loft, the smaller, black one bounding down, the larger silver tabby moving at a more leisurely pace. "Hello, guys." Darcy shrugged off her shoulder bag and bent to greet the cats. "The black one is Marianne. Her older sister is Elinor." She glanced up at him through surprisingly long lashes. "The Dashwood sisters. From *Sense and Sensibility*."

He nodded. "I take it you're a fan of Jane Austen?"

"Yes. Have you read the book?"

"No." He couldn't help feeling he had failed some kind of test as she moved away from him, though she couldn't go far. He could see the entire dwelling, except for the loft and the part of the bathroom not visible through the open door at the end, from this spot by the door—a small sitting area, galley kitchen and table for two. The space was organized, compact and a little claustrophobic. It was a dwelling designed for one person—and two cats.

Make that four cats. "I stopped by Kelly's place and picked up her two cats," she said. "Will you help me bring them in?"

He followed her back to her car and accepted one of the cat carriers. The cat inside, a large gold tabby, eyed him balefully and began to yowl. "Oh, Pumpkin, don't be such a crybaby," Darcy chided as she led the way back up the walk. Inside they set the carriers side by side on the sofa that butted up against the table on one side of the little house. "I'll open the carrier doors and they'll come out when they're ready," she said. "They've stayed here before."

"I'll go outside and take a look around," he said, leaving her to deal with the cats.

A closer inspection showed tire tracks in the soft snow to one side of the gravel drive, and fast-filling-in shoe prints leading around one end of the house to a large back window. He shone the light around the frame, over fresh tool marks, as if someone had tried to jimmy it open. Holding the light in one hand, he took several photos with his phone, then went back inside.

"I put on water for tea," Darcy said, indicating the teakettle on the three-burner stove. "I always feel better with a cup of tea." She rubbed her hands up and down her shoulders. She was still wearing her black puffy coat.

Ryder took out his notebook. "What can you remember about the vehicle you saw?" he asked.

"It was a dark color—dark gray or black, and an SUV, or maybe a small truck with a camper cover? A Toyota, I think." She shook her head. "I'm not a person who pays much attention to cars. It was probably someone who was lost, turning around. I shouldn't have called you."

Ryder thought of the 4Runner that had cruised past him in the grocery store parking lot. "There are fresh footprints leading around the side of the house, and marks on your back window, where someone might have tried to get in."

All color left her face, and she pressed her lips together until they, too, were bleached white. "Show me," she said.

She followed him back out into the snow. He took her arm to steer her around the fading shoe prints, and shone the light on the gouges in the wooden window frame. "I'm sure those weren't here before," she said. "The place was brand-new when I moved in four months ago."

"I'll turn in a report to the sheriff's office," he said. "Have you seen the vehicle you described before?"

"No. But like I said, I don't pay attention to cars. Maybe I should."

"Have you seen any strangers out here? Noticed anyone following you? Has Kelly mentioned anything about anyone following her?"

"No." She turned and walked back into the house. When he stepped in after her, the teakettle was screaming. She moved quickly to shut off the burner and filled two mugs with steaming water. Fear seemed to rise off her like the vapor off the water, though she was trying hard to control it.

"I know this is unsettling," he said. "But the fact that the person didn't stay when you arrived here by yourself tells me he was more likely a burglar who didn't want to be caught, than someone who wanted to attack you."

"I was supposed to be safe here," she said.

"Safe from what?"

She carried both mugs to the table and sat. He took the seat across from her. "Safe from what?" he asked again. "I'm not asking merely to be nosy. If you have someone you're hiding from—someone who might want to hurt you—it's possible this person confused you and Kelly. It wouldn't be the first time something like that happened."

"No, it's not like that." She tucked her shoulder-length brown hair behind her ear, then brought the mug to her lips, holding it in both hands. When she set it down again, her eyes met his, a new determination in their brown depths. "I was raped in college—in Fort Collins. I moved in with Kelly after that and she really helped me move past that. My mother and I aren't close and my father has been out of the picture for years."

He thought of what she had said before—that she was used to looking after herself. "Women who have been through something like that often have a height-ened awareness of danger," he said. "It's good to pay attention to that. Have you seen anyone suspicious, here or at Kelly's or at your office? Have you felt threatened or uneasy?"

"No." She shook her head. "That's why I thought Eagle Mountain was different. I always felt safe here. Until now."

He sipped the tea—something with cinnamon and apples. Not bad. It would be even better with a shot of whiskey, but since he was technically still on duty, he wouldn't bring it up. He wondered if she even had hard liquor in the house. "I stopped by and talked to Ed Nichols and his wife after I left the clinic," he said.

Fine lines between her eyes deepened. "You don't really think he killed Kelly, do you?"

"I haven't made up my mind about anything at this point. He said he was at the clinic all morning, and then at the Rotary Club luncheon."

"How did she die?" Darcy asked. "You told me you found her up on Dixon Pass, but how?"

"Do you really want to know?"

"I have a very good imagination. If you don't tell me, I'll fill in too many horrid details of my own." She took another sip of tea. "Besides, the papers will be full of the story soon."

"She was in her car, over to the side, up against the rock face at the top of the pass. Her hands and feet were bound with duct tape and her throat had been cut."

Darcy let out a ragged breath. "Had she been raped?"

"I don't know. But her clothes weren't torn or disarrayed. We'll know more tomorrow."

"So someone just killed her and left her up there? Why there?"

"I don't know. Maybe he—or she—hoped what did happen would happen—an avalanche buried the car. We might not have found it for weeks if a delivery truck wasn't buried in the same place. When we pulled out the delivery driver, we found Kelly's car, too."

"Did you talk to her parents?"

"Yes. They wanted to fly down right away. I told them they should wait until the road opens."

"When will that be?"

"We don't know. A storm system has settled in. They're predicting up to four feet of new snow. Until it stops, no one is getting in or out of Eagle Mountain."

"The sheriff and Lacy Milligan are supposed to get married in a few weeks," she said.

"The road should be open by then," he said. He hoped so. He wasn't going to get far with this case without the information he could get outside town.

"When I moved here and people told me about the road being closed sometimes in winter, I thought it sounded exciting," she said. "Kind of romantic, even—

everyone relying on each other in true pioneer spirit. Then I think about our weekly order of supplies not getting through, and people who don't live here being stuck in motels or doubling up with family—then it doesn't sound like much fun." She looked up at him. "What about you? Do you live here?"

"I do. I'm in a converted carriage house over on Elm."

"No pets? Or are you a client of Dr. Nichols's?"

Her teasing tone lifted his spirits. "No pets," he said. "I like dogs, but my hours would mean leaving it alone too long."

"Cats do better on their own." She turned to watch Pumpkin facing off with Marianne. The two cats sniffed each other from nose to tail then, satisfied, moved toward the stairs and up into the loft.

"I should let you go," she said. "Thank you for stopping by."

"Is there someone you could stay with tonight?" he asked. "Or you could get a motel room, somewhere not so isolated."

"No, I'll be fine." She looked around. "I don't want to leave the cats. I have a gun and I know how to use it. Kelly and I took a class together. It helped me feel stronger."

He was tempted to say he would stay here tonight, but he suspected she wouldn't welcome the offer. He'd have to sleep sitting up on her little sofa, or freeze in his Tahoe. "Keep your phone with you and call 911 if you feel at all uneasy," he said.

"I will. I guess I should have called them in the first place."

"I wasn't saying I minded coming out here. I didn't. I don't. If you feel better calling me, don't hesitate."

She nodded. "I guess I called you because I knew you. I'm not always comfortable with strangers."

"I'm glad you trusted me enough to call me. And I meant it—don't think twice about calling me again."

"All right. And I'll be fine." Her smile was forced, but he admired the effort.

He glanced in the rearview mirror as he drove away, at the little house in the snowy clearing, golden light illuminating the windows, like a doll's house in a fairy-tale illustration. Darcy Marsh wasn't an enchanted princess but she had a rare self-possession that drew him.

He parked his Tahoe on the side of the road to enter his report about the vehicle she'd seen and the possible attempted break-in at her home. He was uploading the photos he'd taken when his phone rang with a call from the sheriff's department.

Sheriff Travis Walker's voice carried the strain of a long day. "Ryder, you probably want to get over here," he said. "We've found another body."

Chapter 4

Christy O'Brien lay across the front seat of her wrecker, the front of her white parka stained crimson with blood, her hands and feet wrapped with silver duct tape. The wrecker itself was nose-down in a ditch at the far end of a gravel road on the outskirts of town, snow sifting down over it like icing drizzled on a macabre cake.

Ryder turned away, pushing aside the sickness and guilt that clawed at the back of his throat. Such emotions wouldn't do anyone any good now. "I just saw her," he said. "Less than an hour ago."

"Where?" Sheriff Travis Walker, snow collecting on the brim of his Stetson and the shoulders of his black parka, scanned the empty roadside. Travis was one of the reasons Ryder had ended up in Eagle Mountain. He had visited his friend at the Walker ranch one summer and fallen in love with the place. When an opening in this division had opened up, he had put in for it.

"I was in the grocery store parking lot," Ryder said. "She passed me. I figured she was on a call, headed to pull someone out of a ditch."

"This probably happened not too long after that." Travis played the beam of his flashlight over the wrecker. "Maybe the killer called her, pretended his car wouldn't start—maybe a dead battery. When she gets out of the wrecker to take a look, he overpowers her, tapes her up, slits her throat."

"Then shoves her into the wrecker and drives it into the ditch?"

"He may not have even had to drive it," Travis said. "Just put it into gear and give it a good push in the right direction. Then he gets in his own car and drives away."

"Who called it in?" Ryder asked.

"Nobody," Travis said. "I was coming back from a call—an attempted break-in not far from here. I turned down this road, thinking the burglar might have ducked down here. When I saw the wrecker in the ditch, I knew something wasn't right."

"An attempted break-in?" Ryder asked. "Where? When?"

"Up on Pine." Travis indicated a street to the north that crossed this one. "Maybe twenty minutes ago? A guy came home from work and surprised someone trying to jimmy his lock. He thought it was a teenager. He thought he saw an Eagle Mountain High School letter jacket."

"I saw three boys in letter jackets at the grocery store just after Christy's wrecker passed me," Ryder said. "And someone tried to break into Darcy Marsh's place this evening—I was leaving there when you called me."

Travis frowned. "I don't like to think teenagers would do something like this, but we'll check it out." He turned back toward the wrecker. "I'll talk to the people in the houses at the other end of the road, and those in this area. Maybe someone heard or saw something."

"There would be a lot of blood," Ryder said.

"More than is in the cab of the wrecker, I'm thinking. It was the same with Kelly, did you notice? She wasn't killed in that car—and it was her car."

"I did notice," Ryder said. "There was hardly any blood in the car or even on her."

"I think she was killed somewhere else and driven up there," Travis said.

"So the killer had an accomplice?" Ryder asked. "Someone who could have followed him up to the pass in another car, then taken him away?"

"Maybe," Travis said. "Or he could have walked back into town. It's only about three miles. We'll try to find out if anyone saw anything." He walked to the back of his cruiser and took out a shovel. "I don't think Christy was killed very far from here. There wasn't time. I want to see if I can find any evidence of that." He followed the fast-filling tracks of the wrecker back to the road and began to scrape lightly at the snow.

Ryder fetched his own shovel from his vehicle and tried the shoulder on the other side of the road. The work was slow and tedious as he scraped, then shone his light on the space he had uncovered. After ten minutes or so, the work paid off. "Over here," he called to Travis.

The blood glowed bright as paint against the frozen ground—great splashes of it that scarcely looked real.

Travis crouched to look. "We'll get a sample, but I'm betting it's Christy's blood," he said.

"Whoever did this would have blood on his clothes, maybe in his vehicle," Ryder said.

Travis nodded. "He could have gone straight home, or to wherever he's staying, and discarded the clothes— maybe burned them in a woodstove or fireplace, if he has one. There's no one out tonight to see him, though we'll ask around." He stood. "You said you were at Darcy's place?"

"Right. When she got home tonight, there was a strange vehicle leaving. I found signs that someone tried to break in."

"What time was this?" Travis asked.

Ryder checked his notes. "Seven forty."

"The person or persons who tried to break in to Fred Starling's place might have come from Darcy's, but I don't see how they would have had time to drive from Darcy's, kill Christy, then break in to Fred's," Travis said. "We'll see what the ME gives us for time of death." He glanced down the road. "He should be here soon."

"I didn't like leaving Darcy alone out there," Ryder said. "It's kind of remote."

"I've already called in one of our reserve officers," Travis said. "I'll have him drive by Darcy's place and check on her. Why did she call you?"

"I gave her my card when we spoke earlier and told her to call if she needed anything." Ryder shifted his weight, thinking maybe it was time to change the subject. Not that he thought Travis was a stickler over jurisdiction, but he didn't think Darcy would welcome any further attention from the sheriff. "What are you doing, pulling the night shift?" he asked. "Doesn't the sheriff get any perks?"

"The new officer who's supposed to be working tonight has the flu," Travis said. He shrugged. "I figured I'd make a quick patrol, then spend the rest of the night at my desk. I have a lot of loose ends to tie up before the wedding and honeymoon."

"I hope the weather cooperates with your plans," Ryder said. "The highway department says the pass could be closed for the next two or three days—longer if this snow keeps up."

"Most of the wedding party is already here, and the ones who aren't will be coming in soon," Travis said. "My sister, Emily, pulled in this afternoon, about half an hour ahead of the closure."

He turned to gaze down the street, distracted by the headlights approaching—the medical examiner, Butch Collins, followed by the ambulance. Butch, a portly man made even larger by the ankle-length duster and long knitted scarf he wore, climbed out of his truck, old-fashioned medical bag in hand. "Two dead women in one day is a little much, don't you think, Sheriff?" He nodded to Ryder. "Is there a connection between the two?"

Ryder checked for any lurking reporters, but saw none. He nodded to the ambulance driver, who had pulled to the side of the road, steam pouring in clouds from the tailpipe of the idling vehicle. "Both women had their hands and feet bound with duct tape, and their throats slit," he said. "It looks like they weren't killed in the vehicle, but their bodies were put into the vehicles after death."

Collins nodded. "All right. I'll take a look."

Ryder and Travis moved to Travis's cruiser. "Darcy said Kelly was going shopping today," Ryder said. "She couldn't think of anyone who would want to hurt Kelly. No one had been threatening her or making her feel uneasy. You're a little more tied in with the town than I am. Do you know of anyone who might have had a disagreement with her—boyfriend, client or a competitor?"

"I didn't know her well. My parents had Kelly or Darcy out to the ranch a few times to take care of horses. I remember my mom said she liked them. I knew them well enough to wave to. I don't think she was dating anyone, though I'll ask Lacy. She keeps up with that kind of gossip more than I do." Travis's fiancée was a local woman, near Kelly's age. "I never heard anything about unhappy clients. As for competitors, there's really only Ed Nichols."

"What do you know about him?" Ryder asked. "Darcy said he wasn't too happy about them opening up a competing practice."

"Ed's all right," Travis said. "He might have grumbled a little when the two women first arrived, but it's understandable he would feel threatened—two attractive, personable young women. I imagine it cut into his business."

"I talked to him and his wife this afternoon," Ryder said. "He seemed genuinely shaken by the news that Kelly was dead."

"It's hard to picture Ed doing something like this," Travis said. "But we'll check his alibi for the time of Christy's death."

"What about a connection between Kelly and

Christy?" Ryder asked. "Were they specific targets, or random?"

"Maybe Kelly was the target and the killer went after Christy because she was the one who pulled the car with Kelly's body in it out from its hiding place?" Travis shook his head. "It's too early to make any kind of hypothesis, really."

"I've got a bad feeling about this."

"I don't like to use the words serial killer," Travis said. "But that could be what we're looking at."

"After I found Kelly's body, I was worried her murderer had gotten away before the road closed," Ryder said. "If he did, we might never find him."

"Looks like he didn't get out," Travis said. "Which could be a much bigger problem."

"I hear you," Ryder said. As long as the road stayed blocked, the killer couldn't leave—but none of his potential victims could get very far away, either.

Darcy considered closing the clinic the next day, out of respect for Kelly. But what would she do, then, other than sit around and be sad? Work would at least provide a distraction. And the clinic had been her and Kelly's shared passion. Keeping it open seemed a better way to honor her than closing the doors.

The morning proved busy. Most of the people who had come in had heard about Kelly and were eager to share their memories of her. Darcy passed out tissues and shed a few tears of her own, but the release of admitting her grief felt good. Knowing she wasn't alone in her pain made it a tiny bit more bearable.

The office manager, Stacy, left for lunch, but Darcy stayed behind, claiming she had too much work to do. If she was being honest with herself, however, she could admit she didn't want to go out in public to face all the questions and speculation surrounding Kelly's murder, especially since one of her last patients of the day had told her the newest edition of the *Eagle Mountain Examiner* had just hit the stands, with a story about the two murders filling the front page. The editor must have stayed up late to get the breaking news in before the paper went to the printer.

Murder. The word sent a shiver through her. It still seemed so unreal. Who would want to harm Kelly? Or Christy? Darcy hardly knew the other woman, but she had seemed nice enough. Not that nice people didn't get killed, but not in places like Eagle Mountain. Maybe she was wrong to think that, but she couldn't shake her belief that this small, beautiful town was somehow immune to that kind of violence.

She was forcing herself to eat a cup of yogurt from the office refrigerator when the phone rang. She should have let it go straight to the answering service, but what if it was Ryder, with news about Kelly? Or Kelly's parents, wanting to talk?

She picked up the receiver. "Hello?"

A thin, quavering voice came over the line. "Is this the vet?" The woman—Darcy thought it was a woman—asked.

"Yes. This is Dr. Marsh. Who is this?"

"Oh, my name is Marge. Marge Latham. You don't know me. I'm in town visiting my cousin and I got trapped here by the weather. Me and my dog, Rufus. Rufus is why I'm calling."

"What's the problem with Rufus?" Darcy called up

the scheduling program on the office computer as she spoke.

"He's hurt his leg," the woman said. "I don't know what's wrong with it, but he can't put any weight on it and he's in a lot of pain. It's so upsetting." Her voice broke. "He's all I have, you see, and if something happens to him, I don't know what I'd do."

"If you can bring Rufus in at three today I can see him," Darcy said. The patient before that was routine vaccinations, so that shouldn't take too long. The patient after might have to wait a little, but most people understood about emergencies.

"I was hoping you could come here," Marge said. "He's such a big dog—he weighs over a hundred pounds. I can't possibly lift him to get him into the car."

"What kind of dog is Rufus?" Darcy asked.

"He's a mastiff. Such a sweet boy, but moving him is a problem for me. I was told you do house calls."

"Only for large animals," Darcy said. "Horses and cows." And llamas and goats and one time, a pig. But they had to draw the line somewhere. Most dogs were used to riding in the car and would climb in willingly—even mastiffs.

"Well, Rufus is as big as a small horse," Marge said.

"Is there anyone who can help you get him to the office?" Darcy asked. "Maybe your sister or a nephew—"

"No, dear, that isn't possible. Won't you please come? The other vet already said no and I don't know what I'll do. He's all I have." She choked back a sob and Darcy's stomach clenched. She couldn't let an animal suffer—or risk this old woman hurting herself trying to handle the dog by herself.

"I could stop by after work tonight," she said. "But we don't close until six today, so it would be after that."

"That would be wonderful. Thank you so much."

The address the woman rattled off didn't sound familiar to Darcy, but that wasn't unusual. Four months was hardly enough time to learn the maze of gravel roads and private streets that crisscrossed the county. "Let me have your number, in case I'm running late," Darcy said.

"Oh, that would be my sister's number. Let me see. What is that?" The sounds of shuffling, then Marge slowly read off a ten-digit number. "Thank you again, dear. And Rufus thanks you, too."

Darcy hung up the phone and wrote the woman's information at the bottom of the schedule, and stuffed the notes she had taken into her purse.

Five and a half hours later, Darcy drove slowly down Silverthorne Road, leaning forward and straining her eyes in the fading light, searching for the address Marge had given her. But the numbers weren't adding up. She spotted 2212 and 2264 and 2263, but no 2237. Had Marge gotten it wrong?

Darcy slowed at each driveway to peer up the dark path, but usually she couldn't even make out a house, as the drive invariably turned into a thick tunnel of trees. Growing exasperated, she pulled to the side of the road and took out her phone and punched in the number Marge had given her. A harsh tone made her pull the phone from her ear, and a mechanical voice informed her that the number she had dialed was no longer in service or had been changed.

Darcy double-checked the number, but she had it right. And she was sure she hadn't written it down wrong. So was Marge completely confused, or was something else going on? "I should have asked her sister's name," Darcy muttered. "Then maybe I could have looked up her address."

Or maybe there wasn't a sister. A cold that had nothing to do with the winter weather began to creep over her. No. She pushed the thought away. There was no reason to turn this into something sinister. It was simply a matter of a confused old woman, a stranger in town, getting mixed up about the address. Darcy would go into town and stop by the sheriff's department. The officers there knew the county front to back. They might have an idea where to find a visitor with an injured mastiff and her sister.

With shaking hands, Darcy put the car in gear and eased on to the road once more, tires crunching on the packed snow, even as more of the white stuff sifted down. As soon as she found a place to turn around, she would. But houses were far apart out here, and the narrow driveways difficult to see in the darkness. She missed the first drive, but was able to pull into the next, and carefully backed out again and prepared to return to town.

She had just shifted the Subaru into Drive when lights blinded her. A car or truck, its headlights on bright, was speeding toward her. She put up one hand to shield her eyes, and used the other hand to flash her high beams. Whoever was in that vehicle was driving much too fast, and didn't he realize he was blinding her?

She eased over closer to the side of the road, annoyance building, but irritation gave way to fear as she realized the other car wasn't slowing, and it wasn't moving over. She slammed her hand into the horn, the strident blare almost blocking the sound of the racing engine, but still, the oncoming vehicle didn't slow or veer away.

Panic climbed her throat and she scarcely had time to brace herself before the other car hit her, driving her car into the ditch and engulfing her in darkness.

Chapter 5

Travis had offered one of the sheriff's department conference rooms as a temporary situation room for the investigation into the murders of Kelly Farrow and Christy O'Brien. Until the roads opened and Colorado State Patrol investigators could take over, Ryder would work with Travis and his officers.

On Wednesday evening, he met with Travis and deputies Dwight Prentice and Gage Walker, to review what they knew so far. Travis yielded the whiteboard to Ryder and took a seat at the conference table with his officers.

"Our interviews with neighbors and our calls for information from anyone who might have seen anything in the vicinity of both crime scenes have turned up nothing useful," Ryder began. He had spent part of the day talking to people in houses and businesses near where the crimes had taken place. "That's not terribly surprising, considering both murders took place in isolated areas, during bad weather."

"That could mean the murderer is familiar with this area," Dwight said. "He knows the places he's least likely to be seen."

Ryder wrote this point on the whiteboard.

"It's a rural area, so isolated places aren't hard to find," Gage said.

"Point taken," Ryder said, and made a note. He moved on to the next item on his list. "We didn't find any fingerprints on either of the vehicles involved."

"Right. But everyone wears gloves in winter," Dwight said.

"And even dumb criminals have seen enough movies or television to know to wear gloves," Gage said.

"What about the tire impressions?" Ryder asked. "There was a lot of fresh snow at both scenes."

"We don't have a tire impression expert in the department," Travis said. "But we know how to take castings and photographs and we've compared them to databases online."

Dwight flipped pages in a file and pulled out a single sheet. "Best match is a standard winter tire that runs on half the vehicles in the county," he said. "We've even got them on one of the sheriff's department cruisers."

"And the snow was so fresh and dry that the impressions we got weren't good enough to reveal any unusual characteristics," Travis said.

Ryder glanced down at the legal pad in his hand for the next item on his list. "We have blood samples, but no way to send them for matching until the roads open up," he said.

"Could be tomorrow, could be next week," Gage said. "One weather station says the weather is going to clear and the other says another storm system is on the way."

Impatient as the news made him, Ryder knew there was no point getting stressed about something he couldn't control. "What about the duct tape?" He looked at the three at the table.

"Maybe a fancy state lab would come up with something more," Gage said. "But as far as we could tell, it's the standard stuff pretty much everybody has a roll of."

Ryder nodded. He hadn't expected anything there, but he liked to check everything off his list. "Have we found any links between Kelly and Christy?" he asked.

"Christy had a cat," Gage said. "Kelly saw it one time, for a checkup."

"When was that?" Ryder asked.

"Three months ago," Gage said.

"Anything else?" Ryder asked. "Did they socialize together? Belong to the same groups or organizations?"

The other three men shook their heads. "I questioned Christy's mom and dad about who she dated," Gage said. "I thought I might be able to match her list to a list of who Kelly went out with. I mean, it's a small town. There are only so many match-ups. But I struck out there."

"How so?" Ryder asked.

"Christy is engaged to a welder over in Delta," Gage said. "They've been seeing each other for three years. I talked to him on the phone. He's pretty torn up about this—and he couldn't have gotten here last night, anyway, since the road was still blocked."

"What about Kelly's dating history?" Ryder asked. "Anything raise any questions there?"

Gage shook his head. "That was harder to pull together, but Darcy gave me some names. One of them moved away two months ago. The other two have alibis that check out."

Ryder had to stop himself from asking how Darcy was doing. She obviously hadn't had any more trouble from whoever had tried to break into her place. He might find an excuse to stop by there later, just to make sure.

"Ed Nichols was home with his wife, watching TV last night when Christy was killed," Travis said.

"I'm guessing he wasn't too happy to see you," Ryder said, recalling his own less-than-warm reception in the Nicholses' home.

"Ed was okay, but his wife is furious," Travis said. "But I think they were telling the truth. There was six inches of snow in the driveway when I pulled in last night, and no sign that Ed's truck or her car had moved in the last few hours."

Ryder consulted his notes again, but he had reached the end of his list. "What else do we have?" he asked.

"I questioned some of the high school kids this afternoon," Gage said. "And I talked to the teachers. No one knew anything about any guys in letter jackets who might have been out last night, trying to break into homes. I got the impression some of the students might not have been telling me everything they knew, but it's hard to see a connection between attempted break-ins and these murders."

"If students were in that area last night, they might have seen the killer, or his vehicle," Travis said. "I want to find and talk to them."

"Anything else?" Ryder asked.

"The ME says both women had their throats cut with a smooth-bladed, sharp knife," Travis said. "No defensive wounds, although Christy had some bruising, indicating she might have thrashed around quite a bit after the killer taped her hands and feet."

"So the murderer was able to surprise the women and bind them before they fought much," Dwight said.

"Might have been two men," Gage said. "No woman is going to lie still while you tape her up like that."

"One really strong man might be able to subdue a frightened woman," Travis said.

"Or maybe they were drugged," Dwight said. "A quick jab with a hypodermic needle, or chloroform on a rag or something."

Ryder frowned. "I don't think there are any facilities here to test that," he said. "And even if we collect DNA from the bodies, we don't have any way of testing or matching it here."

"Right," Travis said. "We'll have to hold the bodies at the funeral home until the roads open."

Meanwhile, whoever did this was running free to kill again. "I spoke with the friends and family of both women," Ryder said. "None of them were aware of anyone who had made threats or otherwise bothered Kelly or Christy."

"There was no sexual assault," Travis said. "Whoever did this was quick. He killed them and got out of there. No lingering."

"We can't say they weren't targeted killings, but right now it feels random," Ryder said.

"Thrill killings," Gage said. "He did it because he could get away with it."

"If that's the case, he's likely to kill again," Travis said.

The others nodded, expressions sober. Ryder's stomach churned. He felt he ought to be out doing something to stop the murderer, but what?

Travis's phone buzzed and he answered it. "Sheriff Walker." He stilled, listening. "When? Where? Tell the officer we'll be right there."

He ended the call and looked to the others. "A 911 call just came in from Darcy Marsh. Someone attacked her tonight—ran her car off the road."

"Darcy! Darcy! Wake up, honey." Darcy struggled out of a confused daze, wincing at the light blinding her. She moaned, and the light shifted away. "Darcy, look at me."

She forced herself to look into the calm face of a middle-age man who spoke with authority. "What happened?" Darcy managed, forcing the words out, the effort of speaking exhausting her.

"You were in a wreck. I'm Emmett Baxter with Eagle Mountain EMS. Can you tell me what hurts?"

"Everything," Darcy said, and closed her eyes again. She had a vague recollection of dialing 911 earlier, but her memories since then were a jumbled mess.

"Don't go to sleep now," Emmett said. "Open your eyes. Can you move your feet for me?"

Darcy tried to ignore him, then the sharp odor of ammonia stung her nose and her eyes popped open. "That's better." Emmett smiled. "Now, tell me your name."

"Darcy Marsh."

He asked a few more questions she recognized as an attempt to assess her mental awareness — her address, birthdate, telephone number and the date.

"Now try to move your feet for me," he said.

Darcy moved her feet, then her hands. The fog that had filled her head had cleared. She took stock of her surroundings. She was in her car, white powder coating most of the interior, the deflated airbag spilling out of the steering wheel like a grotesque tongue. "My face hurts," she said.

"You're going to have a couple of black eyes and some bruises," Emmett said. He shone a light into each eye. "Does anything else hurt? Any back or neck pain, or difficulty breathing?"

She shook her head. "No."

He released the catch of Darcy's seat belt. "I'm going to fit you with a cervical collar just in case." He stripped the plastic wrapping from the padded collar and fit it to her neck, the Velcro loud in her ears. "How do you feel about getting out of the car and walking over to the ambulance?" he asked. "I'll help."

"Okay." Carefully, she swung her legs over to the side of the car, Emmett's arm securely around her. They both froze as the bright beams of oncoming headlights blinded them.

"I'm not sure why the state patrol is here," Emmett said.

Ryder, a powerful figure in his sharp khaki and blue, emerged from the cruiser and strode toward the car. His gaze swept over the damaged vehicle and came to rest on Darcy's face. The tenderness in that gaze made her insides feel wobbly, and tears threatened. "Darcy, are you okay?" he asked.

She clamped her lips together to hold back a sob and managed, almost grateful for the pain the movement caused. At least it distracted her from this terrible need to throw her arms around him and weep.

"We're just going to get her over to the ambulance where we can get a better look at her," Emmett said.

"Let me help." Not waiting for a response, Ryder leaned down and all but lifted her out of the car. He propped her up beside him and walked her to the back of the ambulance, then stepped aside while Emmett and a female EMT looked her over.

"You're going to be pretty sore tomorrow," Emmett pronounced when they were done. "But there's no swelling or indication that anything is broken and I can't find any sign of internal damage. How do you feel? Any nausea or pain?"

"I'm a little achy and still shaken up," Darcy said. "But I don't think I'm seriously injured."

"With the highway still closed, we can't transport you to the hospital, but I'd recommend a visit to the clinic in town. They can do X-rays and maybe keep you overnight for observation."

"No, I really don't think that's necessary," she said. "I think I just had the wind knocked out of me. If I start to feel worse, I promise I'll see a doctor."

Emmett nodded. "Don't hesitate to call us if that changes or you have any questions." He glanced over his shoulder at Ryder, who stood, arms folded across his chest, gaze fixed on Darcy. "Your turn."

For the first time Darcy realized there were other

people at the scene—Travis and another man in a sheriff's department uniform, and several people in jeans and parkas who might have been neighbors. Ryder sat beside her on the back bumper of the ambulance while Travis came to stand beside them. "What happened?" he asked.

She took a deep breath, buying time to organize her thoughts. "I got a call at lunchtime today," she said. "When I was alone in the office. A woman who said her name was Marge asked me if I could make a house call to look at her mastiff who had hurt his leg. She said she was staying with her sister and had been trapped by the weather. She gave me an address on this street, but I couldn't find the number. I tried to call her, but the phone number she had given me wasn't a working number. I turned around and started to head back toward town when this vehicle blinded me with its headlights and ran into me." She put a hand to her head, wincing. "I must have blacked out for a minute, then I guess I came to and called for help, then passed out again. I didn't come to completely until the ambulance was here."

"A man backing out of his driveway saw the accident and called 911, too," Travis said. "He didn't get a good look at the vehicle that hit you, though he thinks it was a truck. He said it drove off after it put your car in the ditch."

Darcy looked toward her car, which was canted to one side in a snowbank. "He hit me almost head-on," she said. "My car's probably ruined."

"Had you ever heard from this Marge person before?" Ryder asked.

"No. She said her name was Marge Latham. I didn't think to ask for her sister's name."

"What was the address she gave you?" Travis asked.

"Two two three seven Silverthorne Road," Darcy said. "She said her dog's name was Rufus. She sounded really old, and said he was a mastiff, and too big for her to lift."

"You say you were alone in the office when the call came in?" Ryder asked.

"Yes. I had just sent Stacy to lunch. I stayed in to catch up on some work."

"So anyone watching the office would have known you were alone," Ryder said.

She stared at him. "Why do you think someone was watching the office? Why would they do that?"

His grim expression sent a shiver of fear through her. "I think someone made that call to get you out here, so they could run you off the road," he said. "The neighbor backing out of his driveway probably scared him off."

She hugged her arms across her stomach, fighting nausea. "Do you think it's the same person who killed Kelly and Christy?"

Ryder and Travis exchanged a look. "Is there anyone you can stay with for a while?" Ryder asked.

"No," she said. If Kelly was still alive, Darcy might have stayed with her, but that wasn't possible now. And the thought of leaving her little home was wrenching. "I don't want to leave the cats. I'll be fine."

A young uniformed officer approached. "The wrecker is here," he said. "Where do you want the car towed?"

All three men looked at Darcy. "Oh. Is there a mechanic in town?"

"There's O'Brien's," the officer said. "That's where the wrecker's from."

"Then I guess tow it there," she said.

"I'll drive you home," Ryder said.

There was no point in refusing—she didn't have any other way to get home, and she could see he wasn't going to take no for an answer. He helped her to his Tahoe and she climbed in. They rode in silence; she was still numb from everything that had happened. At the house he took the keys from her and opened the door, then checked through the house—which took all of a minute—the cats observing him from their perches on the stairs to the loft.

Darcy unbuttoned her coat and Ryder returned to her side to help her out of it. He draped it on the hook by the door, then hung his leather patrolman's jacket beside it. "Sit, and I'll make you some tea," he said.

She started to protest that he didn't have to wait on her. He didn't have to stay and look after her. She wanted to be alone. Instead, she surrendered to her wobbly knees and shakier emotions and slid onto the bench seat at the little table and watched while Ryder familiarized himself with her galley kitchen. Within minutes he had a kettle heating on the stove and was opening a can of soup.

"You don't have to stay," she said.

"No." He took two bowls from a cabinet and set them on the counter. "You've had a fright. I figured you could use some company." His eyes met hers. "And I'd rather stay here than go home to my empty place and worry about you out here alone."

"I'll be fine," she said. "I can see anyone coming, the locks are good and I have my gun and my phone."

"Use the phone first."

"Of course." She shivered. She had only ever fired the gun at the range. Could she really use it on a person? Maybe. If her life depended on it. "But I think I'm safe here." If she kept repeating the words, she might make them true.

"You should install an alarm system," he said.

"That's a great idea. But the nearest alarm company is in Junction—on the other side of Dixon Pass." Not accessible until the road reopened.

He stirred the soup, the rhythmic sound calming. Elinor the cat settled onto the bench next to Darcy, purring. She stroked the cat and tried to soak in all this soothing comfort. "Why is this happening?" she asked.

"Have you thought of anything at all that's happened the past few weeks that's been out of the ordinary?" he asked. "A client who was difficult, a man who leered at you in the grocery store—anything at all?"

"No."

"And no one who might have a grudge against you, or resentment—other than the other vet."

She hesitated. There was Ken, but he didn't really hate her. He had only had his feelings hurt because she had refused to continue dating him. But she had never felt threatened by him. Ryder turned toward her. "Who are you thinking of?"

She sighed. "There was a guy I went out with a few times—Ken Rutledge. He lives next door to Kelly, in the other half of the duplex. I thought he was getting too serious too quickly, so I broke things off. He wasn't happy about it, but I can't believe he would *kill* anyone. I mean, he's just not the violent type." She would have said the same about the man who raped her, too, though.

"I'll have a talk with him," Ryder said. He poured soup into the two bowls and brought them to the table. "I won't tell him you said anything. If he was Kelly's neighbor, I need to talk to him, anyway."

"Thank you." She leaned over the bowl of soup and the smell hit her, making her mouth water. Suddenly, she was ravenous. She tried not to look like a pig, but she inhaled the soup and drained the cup of tea, then sat back. "I feel much better now," she said.

Ryder smiled. His eyes crinkled at the corners when he did so. A shadow of beard darkened his chin and cheeks, giving him a rakish look. "You're not as pale," he said. "Though I bet you're going to be pretty sore tomorrow."

"But I'll heal," she said. "I'm not so sure about my car. And how am I going to get to work?" Her predicament had just sunk in. "It's not as if Eagle Mountain has a car rental agency."

"I'm pretty sure Bud O'Brien keeps a couple of loaner vehicles for customers," Ryder said.

"I hate to bother him," Darcy said. "The man just lost his daughter." Her stomach clenched, thinking of the woman who had been murdered.

"The people who work for him will be there," Ryder said. "Too many people would be left stranded in this weather if they closed their doors. Call them in the morning and someone will work something out for you. If not, give me a call and I'll put out some feelers."

"Thanks."

Ryder insisted on staying to help clean up and do the dishes. They worked side by side in her tiny kitchen.

He seemed too large for the compact space, and yet comfortable in it, as well. Finally, when the last dish was returned to its place in her cabinets, he slipped on his jacket.

"You're sure you'll be comfortable here by yourself?" he asked.

He was standing very close to her so that she was very aware of his size and strength. She wasn't exactly uncomfortable, but her heart beat a little too fast, and she had trouble controlling her breathing.

"Darcy?"

He was looking at her, waiting on an answer. She cleared her throat. "I'll keep my phone with me and I'll call 911 if I see or hear anything suspicious."

"Call me, too," he said. "I'm going to have the phone company try to track the number the call came from, but if you hear from Marge again, you'll let me know."

It wasn't a request—more of an order. "I will," she said. "Part of me still hopes it was a mistake—a confused woman who wasn't familiar with the area gave me the wrong address and phone number."

"It would be nice if that were the case," he said. "But I think it's better to act as if it was a genuine threat and be prepared for it to happen again."

His words sent a shudder through her, but she braced herself against it and met his gaze. "I'll be careful," she said.

He rested his hand lightly on her shoulder. "I'm not trying to frighten you," he said.

She wanted to lean into him, to rest her cheek against his hand like a cat. Instead, she made herself stand still and smile, though the expression felt weak.

"I know. I'm already frightened, but I won't let the fear defeat me."

"That's the attitude." He bent and kissed her cheek, the brush of his lips sending a jolt of awareness through her. She reached up to pull him to her, but he had already turned away. She leaned in the open doorway.

He strode to his car, his boots crunching in the snow. He lifted his hand in a wave as he climbed into the Tahoe, then he was gone. And still she stood, with the door wide open. But she didn't feel the cold, still warmed by that brief kiss.

Chapter 6

Ryder's first impression of Ken Rutledge was an over-grown boy. On a day when the temperatures hovered in the twenties, Rutledge wore baggy cargo shorts and a striped sweater, and the sullen expression of a teen who had been forced to interact with dull relatives. "You're that cop who's investigating Kelly's murder," he said by way of greeting when he opened the door to Ryder.

"Ryder Stewart." Ryder didn't offer his hand—he had the impression Rutledge wouldn't have taken it. "I need to ask you some questions."

"You'd better come in." Rutledge moved out of the doorway and into a cluttered living room. A guitar and two pairs of skis leaned against one wall, while a large-screen TV and a video gaming console occu-pied most of another. Rutledge clearly liked his toys.

Rutledge leaned against the door frame of the entrance to the kitchen, arms folded across his chest. "What do you want to know?" he asked.

"How well did you know Kelly Farrow?" Ryder asked.

"Pretty well. I mean, we lived right next to each other. We were friends."

"Did you ever date her?"

Rutledge grinned. "She flirted with me. I think she would have gone out with me if I'd asked, but she wasn't my type."

Ryder wondered if this meant he'd asked her out, but Kelly had turned him down. "What is your type?"

"I like a woman who's a little quieter. Petite. Kelly had too much of a mouth on her."

Quiet and petite—like Darcy. Ryder took out his notebook and pen—more to have something to do with his hands than to make notes. He wasn't likely to forget anything this guy said. "You dated Darcy Marsh," he said.

Rutledge shifted, uncrossing his arms and tucking his thumbs in the front pockets of the cargo shorts. "We went out a few times."

"She says you weren't too happy when she broke it off."

"Yeah, well, she would say that, wouldn't she?"

"What do you mean?"

"Women always try to make themselves look like the victim."

"So what did happen between you two?" Ryder asked.

"I was really busy—I teach school and coach basketball. Darcy was a little too needy. I didn't give her the attention she wanted." He shrugged. "I let her down easy but I guess I hurt her feelings, anyway."

Ryder pretended to consult his notebook. "Where were you last night about six thirty?" he asked.

"Why? Did they find another body?"

"Answer the question, please."

"Yeah, sure. Let's see—there was a game at the high school. The varsity team—I coach JV—but I was there to watch."

Ryder made a note of this. It ought to be easy enough to check. "What about Tuesday night?" he asked.

"I was home, playing an online game with a couple of friends."

"I'll need their names and contact information."

"Sure. I can give that to you." He moved to a laptop that was open on a table by the sofa and manipulated a mouse. While he made notes on a sheet of paper torn from a spiral notebook, Ryder looked around the room. There were no photographs, and the only artwork on the wall was a framed poster from a music festival in a nearby town.

"Here you go." Rutledge handed Ryder the piece of paper. "And since I know you're going to ask anyway, the day Kelly was killed, I was teaching school. That'll be easy for you to check."

Ryder folded the paper and tucked it into the back of his notebook. "Do you have any idea who might have wanted to kill Kelly Farrow?" he asked. "Did she ever mention anyone who had threatened her, or did you ever see anyone suspicious near the house?"

Ken shook his head. "It could have been anybody, really," he said.

Most people said things like "everybody liked Kelly" or "she never made an enemy." "Why do you say that?" Ryder asked.

"Like I said, she had a mouth on her. And she dated lots of men—though none for very long. Maybe she said the wrong thing to one of them."

"And you think that would justify killing her?"

Ken took a step back. "No, man. I'm just saying, if the wrong guy had a hair trigger—it might be enough to make him snap. There are a lot of sick people in this world."

Ryder put away the notebook and took out one of his cards. "Call me if you think of anything," he said. Though Rutledge's alibis sounded solid enough, he couldn't shake the feeling the man was hiding something. Ryder would be keeping an eye on him.

At seven thirty Thursday morning a mechanic from O'Brien's Garage delivered a battered pickup truck in several shades of green and gray to Darcy's door. "She looks like crap, but she runs good," the young man said as he handed over the keys. He rode off with the friend who had followed him to her place, and Darcy hoisted herself up into the vehicle, wishing for a step stool, it was so high off the ground. She felt tiny in the front seat—even the steering wheel felt too big for her hands. But as promised, the truck ran smoothly and carried her safely into town.

She had discarded the cervical collar that morning. While much of her was sore, none of the aches and pains felt serious. Her patients might all have fur or feathers, but she considered herself competent to assess her own injuries.

She stopped by Eagle Mountain Grocery, hoping the store would be mostly empty this time of morning. All she needed was a deli sandwich, since she planned to eat lunch at her desk again. She had layered on makeup in an attempt to hide the worst of the bruising, but she was sure she faced a day full of explaining what had happened to her.

As hoped, the store was mostly empty when she arrived. She hurried to the deli and ordered a turkey sandwich on cranberry bread, and debated adding a cookie while the clerk filled her order. A few more minutes and she'd be safely out of here.

"Darcy Marsh, you've got a lot of nerve!"

The strident voice rang through the store like a crack of thunder. Darcy turned to see Sharon Nichols steering her grocery cart toward her. For a tense moment Darcy thought Sharon intended to run her over. She had a flash of herself, pinned to the glass-fronted deli case by the cart.

But Sharon stopped a few inches short of hitting Darcy. "Haven't you done enough to hurt us?" she demanded, lines etched deeper in her face than Darcy remembered.

"I don't know what you're talking about." Darcy spoke softly, hoping Sharon would lower her voice, as well. As it was, the two workers in the deli had both turned to stare.

"You complained about my husband to that cop and now he won't leave us alone." Sharon leaned closer, but didn't lower her voice. "He had the nerve to suggest Ed murdered those girls. Ed—who wouldn't hurt a fly! Why do you hate us so much?"

Darcy took a step back, desperately wanting to get away from Sharon and the angry words, which battered her like a club. "I don't hate you," she said. "And I never suggested Ed killed anyone. I don't believe that."

"You should go back to wherever you're from and leave us alone. Ed has lived here all his life. He had a good business, taking care of the animals in this county, then you and your friend had to move in and try to take over."

"We didn't try to take over. There's room enough in Eagle Mountain for all of us."

"That's a lie and you know it!" Sharon inched closer until the end of her cart pressed against Darcy's hips. "You came in with your fancy new office and pretty faces, undercutting us, trying to put us out of business."

"That's not true." If anything, the fees she and Kelly charged were higher than Ed's, but there was no use pointing that out to Sharon. Darcy glanced around. Two women peered from the end of one aisle, and one of the checkout people and a stocker had gathered to watch, as well. "I think you should go," she said softly.

"You won't run us out of town," Sharon said, tears streaming down her face. "You won't. We'll force you to leave first."

She turned and, seeing her chance, Darcy fled. She fumbled the keys into the ignition of the truck and drove out of the lot, scarcely seeing her surroundings, her mind too full of the image of Sharon Nichols's furious face.

Her final words, about making Darcy leave town, left a sick feeling in the pit of Darcy's stomach. She had never seen anyone so angry. Was Ed that angry, too? Were the Nicholses angry enough to kill?

Ryder stepped into the clinic and was greeted by furious barking from a small white terrier, who strained on the end of its leash. "I'm sorry about that." A middle-age woman with red curly hair scooped up the barking dog. "He thinks he has to protect me from everyone."

"Hello, Officer." The receptionist, a blue-eyed blonde with long, silver-painted fingernails, greeted him from behind the front counter. "What can I do for you?"

"I'd like a word with Darcy, if she's free."

"Wait just a few minutes."

He took a seat. The terrier glared at him from the redhead's lap. The office smelled of disinfectant. A brochure rack on the wall offered information on various ailments from arthritis to kennel cough, and a locked cabinet displayed a variety of cat and dog food and treats.

The door to the back office opened and a gray-haired couple emerged, the man toting a cat carrier. Darcy followed them out. "Bring her back on Tuesday and we'll remove the bandage," Darcy said. "And don't let her near any more mousetraps." She looked over Ryder's shoulder and sent him a questioning look.

He stood and as the couple moved to the front desk to pay, he slipped through the door and followed her into a small exam room where she sprayed the exam table with disinfectant and began to wipe it down. "Stacy said you wanted to talk to me," she said.

He shut the door to the room behind him. "Just to tell you that I talked to Ken Rutledge and his alibis for last night, and the times of the murders check out." Several people remembered seeing Ken at the basketball game, his online buddies had vouched for the times he had been involved in their game and he had had a full load of classes the day Kelly was murdered, including lunchroom and bus duty.

"I'm glad to hear it." She all but sagged with relief. "I hated to think I'd misjudged him so badly—that he was capable of something like that."

"He had a different story about your relationship, though," Ryder said.

"Oh?" She went back to wiping down the table and counters.

"He says he broke it off because you were too clingy."

She let out a bark of laughter. "That's not what happened, but if it makes him feel better to say so, it doesn't make any difference to me."

"He also said Kelly flirted with him, but she wasn't his type."

"Oh, please. Kelly was gorgeous. She was nice to everyone, which I guess some men take as flirting, but she wasn't interested in Ken." She tucked the bottle of disinfectant back in a cabinet over the sink and dropped a handful of used paper towels in the trash can by the door. "To tell you the truth, I think she introduced him to me as a way to get him off her back."

"So he may be a jerk, but I don't think he's the person who's harassing you." He leaned against the end of the counter. "Have you heard any more from Marge?"

"No. And I doubt I will."

"I checked with Ed Nichols. He says he never got a call from a woman about a large dog that needed a house call."

A shadow passed over her face as if she was in pain. "What is it?" Ryder asked. "What's wrong?"

She glanced over his shoulder as if making sure the door was still closed. "I ran into Sharon Nichols at the grocery store this morning," she said. "She cornered me and demanded to know why I was trying to ruin her husband's life. She was so furious, she was almost...unhinged."

Ryder tensed. "Did she threaten you?"

"Not exactly."

"What did she say—exactly?"

"She said I wouldn't run them out of town—that they would make me leave first."

"She didn't elaborate?"

"No. And I really think she was just talking. She was so upset."

"I'll have a word with her."

"No." She grabbed his arm. "Please. You'll only make things worse."

His first inclination was to deny this. If the Nicholses had any intention of harming Darcy, he wanted to make it clear he would see they were punished, swiftly and harshly.

But the pleading look in Darcy's eyes forced him to calm down. "I won't say anything to them," he said. "But I will keep an eye on them."

She took her hand from his arm. He wanted to pull it back—to pull her close and comfort her. Last night he had kissed her cheek on impulse, but he had wanted to kiss her lips. Would she have pushed him away if he tried?

"I need to get back to work," she said, glancing toward the door again.

"Just one more question," he said. "Though you may not like it."

"Oh?"

"What happened with the man who raped you?"

She hadn't expected that, he could tell. "If he's not in

prison, I think it would be worth tracking him down," he said. "Just to make sure he isn't in Rayford County."

She nodded. "He was caught. I testified at the trial. I think he's still in prison."

"What was his name?"

"Jay Leverett. You don't think he's come after me again—not here?" Her skin had turned a shade paler.

"I'm just going to check."

She nodded. "This whole thing scares me. But I can't let that stop me from living my life."

"I don't like you out there at that little house by yourself." He'd meant to keep his fears to himself, but suddenly couldn't.

"It's my home. And my cats' home." She frowned. "Ken asked me to move in with him. I told him no way."

If Ryder asked her to move in with him, would she lump him in the same category as Ken? "You could move into Kelly's place," he said. "It's right in town, with more people around."

"No. I can't make you understand, but it's important to me to be strong enough to stay put. One thing I learned after I was raped was that fear was my worst enemy. Let me put it this way—if you were the one being threatened, would you move out of your home?"

"Probably not." He wanted to argue that he was a trained professional—but that wasn't what she wanted to hear. "I'll be keeping an eye on you," he said. "And keep your phone charged and with you at all times, with my number on speed dial. Call 911 first, then call me."

"I will. And thank you." She reached past him for the doorknob. "Now I have to get back to my patients."

The terrier growled at him as he passed. He ignored

the dog and went back outside. Snow swirled around him in big white flakes. The sun that had shone earlier had disappeared and there was already an inch of snow on his Tahoe. The city's one snowplow trundled past him as he waited to turn onto Main Street. From the looks of things, the highway wouldn't be opening back up today. Was the killer getting antsy, looking for his next victim? If he was the person who went after Darcy last night, he had failed. How long would he wait before trying again?

Chapter 7

Friday afternoon Darcy watched the young woman lead the horse the length of the barn and back and nodded. "I think she's more comfortable with the leg wrapped, don't you?" she said.

"Yes, I do." Emily Walker, younger sister to Travis and Gage Walker, brushed back a sweep of long, dark hair and smiled at Darcy. "Thanks so much for coming out here to look at her." She rubbed the horse's nose. "I've only ridden her once since I got here and she was fine then. I couldn't believe it this morning when I came out and found she'd gone lame."

"Keep the wrapping on, let her rest and give her the anti-inflammatories I prescribed," Darcy said. "If she's not better in a couple of days, call me and we can do some more extensive testing, but I think she'll be okay."

"I hope so." Emily gave the horse another pat, then

both women exited the stall. "Thanks again for driving out here. I wasn't really looking forward to pulling a horse trailer on these snowy roads."

"I take it you're here for the wedding?" Darcy asked.

"It's my winter break, so I'd probably be here, anyway, but of course I'm staying over for the wedding." Emily grinned. "It's going to be so beautiful. I adore Lacy and though my big brother likes to play it all serious and unemotional, I can tell he's over the moon in love. I'm so happy for them both."

"You're from Denver?" Darcy asked.

"Fort Collins. I'm in grad school at Colorado State University."

"That's where I went to school," Darcy said.

"I love it there," Emily said. She stretched her arms over her head. "But I can't tell you how great it is not to have to think about classes and data analysis and lab reports and all of that for a few weeks. I'm determined to make the most of my time at home, snow or no snow." She put a hand on Darcy's arm. "What are you doing tomorrow?"

"I have office hours until noon." With Kelly gone, she was working six days a week—six long days, since she was handling all the office visits as well as house calls. She had rearranged her schedule this afternoon in order to make this call, but she had a full slate of patients for the rest of the afternoon. She hadn't had time to think much about how she was going to manage to keep up with such a schedule.

"Come here for the afternoon," Emily said. "I'm hosting a snowshoe scavenger hunt for the wedding party and any other young people I can get up here.

We might all be trapped by the snow, but that doesn't mean we can't enjoy it."

Kelly would have jumped at that kind of invitation—she adored parties and meeting new people. Darcy, on the other hand, had been looking forward to an afternoon curled up on the sofa with the cats around her and a good book. "Oh, thanks so much," she said. "But I don't think I'll be able to make it. Since my partner died I'm pretty much buried under work." Not a lie.

Emily looked as disappointed as a child who had been told she couldn't have a puppy. "I was so sorry to hear about Kelly." She squeezed Darcy's arm. "If you change your mind, come anyway. The more the merrier."

They emerged from the barn and Darcy was startled to see Ryder striding toward them. Dressed in his uniform with the black leather coat, he somehow didn't look all that out of place in the corral. "Hello, Emily, Darcy." He nodded to them. "Is everything all right?"

"It is now," Emily said. "Darcy has taken very good care of my favorite mare." She touched Darcy's arm. "Darcy, do you know Ryder Stewart? He's one of Travis's groomsmen."

"We know each other," Ryder said. A little current of heat ran through Darcy as his eyes met hers.

"If you're looking for Travis, he went somewhere with Dad," Emily said. "But they should be back pretty soon for supper. Our cook, Rainey, doesn't like it if people are late for meals, and Dad doesn't like to cross her."

"I'll catch him later," Ryder said. "It's not that important."

"Well, I'm glad you stopped by, anyway," Emily said. "You've saved me a phone call. I'm having a get-together for the wedding party and friends tomorrow afternoon—a snowshoe scavenger hunt." She turned to Darcy. "I'm trying to talk Darcy into coming, too."

"You should come," Ryder said. "It'll be good to be around other people."

She heard the unspoken message beneath his words: no one is going to bother you with half a dozen law enforcement officers around. And maybe socializing would be a good way to distract herself from worries about everything from the business to her own safety. "All right. I guess I could come."

"Wonderful," Emily said. She looked past Ryder, toward the ranch house. "My mom is waving to me—she probably needs my help with something for the wedding. With most of the wedding party staying here, you wouldn't believe how much there is to do." She waved goodbye to both of them and hurried away.

Ryder fell into step beside Darcy as they headed for the parking area near the stables where she had left the borrowed truck. Ryder laughed when he saw the green and yellow monster. "I saw this outside your office," he said, "But I had no idea it was yours."

"It's the official loaner vehicle for O'Brien's Garage," she said. "A little horrifying, but it runs well. I was glad to get anything at all, since my car will need some pretty major repairs."

"I think anyone will have a hard time running you off the road in that," Ryder said.

"Good point." The idea cheered her. She took out the keys and prepared to hoist herself into the cab, then paused. "Is everything all right?" she asked. "You aren't here to see Travis about a development in the case?"

He shook his head. "He asked me to help find extra chairs for the wedding guests and I wanted to get a look at the space where the ceremony will be. I have a couple of places that have agreed to loan some chairs, and I wanted to see what would work best."

"That's nice of you," she said.

"I'm the backup plan, really," he said. "They have a wedding planner out of Junction who's supposed to supply all that stuff, but this is in case the roads don't open in time."

"But the wedding is still over three weeks away," Darcy said. "Surely, the road will be open by then."

"Probably," he said. "But it's probably not a bad idea to plan, just in case."

"I need to go through our medical supplies and make sure we have enough of everything," she said. "I can see it will be a good idea to keep extra stock on hand in the winter." She climbed into the truck.

Ryder shut the door behind her. "Have a good evening," he said. "See you tomorrow."

"Yeah. See you tomorrow." While part of her still longed for that quiet afternoon at home, curled up with a book, she could see the sense in spending her free time around other people. That one of those people would be Ryder made the prospect all the more pleasing.

Ryder had just turned onto Main Street when his phone rang with a call from Travis. "I was just up at your place, looking at the wedding venue," Ryder said.

"I ended up getting detoured to the office," Travis said. "When you get a chance, swing by here. I've got something to show you."

"I'll be right over."

Adelaide Kinkaid, the seventy-something woman whose title Ryder didn't know, but who kept the sheriff's department running smoothly, greeted Ryder as he stepped into the station lobby. "Trooper Stewart," she said. "We're seeing so much of you lately we should make you an honorary deputy."

"Do I get to draw double pay?" Ryder asked.

Adelaide narrowed her blue eyes behind her violet-rimmed glasses. "I said *honorary*. To what do we owe the pleasure of your company today?"

"I need to speak with the sheriff."

"Of course you do. You and half the county. Don't you people know he has a wedding to prepare for?"

"I thought the bride did most of the work of weddings," Ryder said.

Adelaide sniffed. "We live in a new age, haven't you heard? Men have to pull their weight, too."

"I'm more concerned about this case than the wedding right now." Travis stood in the hallway leading to the offices. "Come on back, Ryder."

Instead of stopping at his office, Travis led the way down the hall to a conference room. He unlocked the door and ushered Ryder inside. Items, some of which Ryder recognized as being from the crime scenes, were arrayed on two long folding tables. He followed Travis around the tables. "When we originally towed Kelly's car, our intention was to secure it and leave it to the state's forensic team to process," Travis said. "After

Christy's murder, with the road still closed, we felt we no longer had that luxury, so I put my team on it."

He picked up a clear plastic envelope. "They found this in Kelly's car, in the pocket on the driver's side door."

Ryder took the envelope and studied the small rectangle of white inside. A business card, with black letters: Ice Cold. "What does that mean?" he asked. "Is it supposed to be the name of a business?"

"We don't know. We didn't turn up anything in our online searches. It's not a business that we can find."

Ryder turned the packet with the card over. The back was blank, but on closer inspection, he could see that the edges of the card were slightly uneven, as if from perforations. "It looks like those blanks you can buy at office supply stores," he said. "To print your own cards at home."

"That's what we think, too," Travis said. "We think it was printed on a laser printer. The card stock is pretty common, available at a lot of places, including the office supply store here in town, though the owner doesn't show having sold any in the past month. But it could have been purchased before then."

Ryder laid the envelope back on the table. "We don't know how old it is, either," he said. "Kelly could have dropped it months ago."

"Except we found another card just like this in Christy's wrecker." Travis moved a few feet down the table and picked up a second envelope.

The card inside was identical to the one in the first envelope. A brief tremor raced up Ryder's spine. "We found it wedged between the cushions of the driver's seat," Travis said.

"Whoever left it there had to know we'd find it," Ryder said.

"I don't think he's going to stop with two murders," Travis said. "He's going to want to keep playing the game."

Ryder thought of Darcy, her car run off the road, and felt a chill. "Darcy could have been the third."

"Maybe," Travis said. "But Christy's murder, at least, feels more like a crime of opportunity. She was one of the few people out that night. The killer saw her and decided to make her his next victim."

"How do we stop him?" Ryder asked.

"I'm putting every man I can on the streets, and I'm asking the newspaper to run a story, warning everyone to be careful about stopping for strangers, suggesting they travel in pairs, things like that. I don't want to alarm people, but I don't want another victim."

"That may not be enough," Ryder said. "Some people think they're invincible—that a place like Eagle Mountain has to be safe."

"I'm trying to make it safe," Travis said. "We'll do everything we can, but we're at a disadvantage. The killer knows us and that we're looking for him." He picked up the business card again. "We'll keep trying to track down the meaning of Ice Cold."

"I'll get folks at state patrol working on it, too. We can transmit the images electronically. At least we've still got that. Did you find anything else in the vehicles that we can use?"

"Nothing. No fingerprints, no hair. Of course, with the weather, he was probably bundled up—cap, gloves, maybe even a face mask."

"Which makes it even more certain the business

card was left deliberately." Anger tightened Ryder's throat. "He's treating this like some kind of game—taunting us."

"It's a game I don't intend to lose," Travis said.

Ryder nodded. But the cold knot in his stomach didn't loosen. If whoever did this killed again, someone would lose. Someone—probably a woman—would lose her life. And the awful reality was that he and Travis and the other officers might not be able to stop it from happening.

A late cancellation allowed Darcy to keep her pledge to take an inventory of veterinary supplies at her office Friday afternoon. To her relief, she was well stocked on most items, though her stockpile of some bandages and Elizabethan collars were running low. Fortunately, Kelly kept overflow supplies in her garage and Darcy was sure she could find what she needed there.

After closing up that evening, she drove to Kelly's duplex. She parked the truck in the driveway, then let herself in with her key and switched on the living room light. Already, the house looked vacant and neglected. Kelly's furniture and belongings were still there, of course, but dust had settled on the furniture, and the air smelled stale. She swallowed back a knot of tears and forced herself to walk straight through to the connecting door to the garage. She would get what she needed and get out, avoiding the temptation to linger and mourn her missing friend.

Darcy flipped the switch for the garage light, but only one bulb lit, providing barely enough illumination to make out the boxes stacked along the far wall.

Without Kelly's car parked inside, the space looked a lot bigger. Darcy wondered what would happen to the duplex now. The rent was presumably paid up through the end of the month. Once the road opened, she assumed Kelly's parents would clean the place out.

The boxes of supplies on the back wall contained everything from paper towels and toilet paper for the veterinary office restrooms to surgical drapes and puppy pads. The friends had found a supplier who offered big discounts for buying in bulk, and had stocked up on anything nonperishable.

The bandages and plastic cones she needed were in two separate boxes on the bottom of the pile, the contents of each box noted on the outside in Kelly's neat handwriting. Darcy set her purse on the floor and started moving the top layer of boxes out of the way. At least all this activity would warm her up a little. The temperature had hovered just above freezing all day, plunging quickly as the sun set. The concrete floor of the garage might as well have been a slab of ice, radiating cold up through Darcy's feet and throughout her body.

She shifted a heavy carton labeled surgical supplies and set it on the floor with a rattling thud. The noise echoed around her and she hurried to pull out the box of bandages. She'd carry the whole thing out to the truck, then come back for the collars. She only needed a few of them, in small and medium sizes.

She picked up the bandage carton—who knew all that elastic and cloth could be so heavy?—and headed back toward the door to the kitchen. She had her foot on the bottom step when the door to the kitchen opened and the shadowy figure of a man loomed large. "What do you think you're doing?" he demanded. A flashlight blinded her, then someone knocked the box from her hand and she was falling backward, a scream caught in her throat.

Chapter 8

Darcy tried to fight back, but the man's arms squeezed her so tightly she could scarcely breathe. She kicked out and clawed at his face, screaming and cursing. Then, as suddenly as he had grabbed her, the man let go. "Darcy! Darcy, are you okay? I had no idea it was you."

Eyes clouded with angry tears, she stared at Ken, who stood at the bottom of the steps leading into the house, a flashlight in one hand, the other held up, palm open. Darcy swiped at her eyes and straightened her clothes. "What are *you* doing here?" she asked. "And why did you attack me?"

"I didn't know it was you." He looked truly flustered. "I saw the truck in the driveway and didn't recognize it. Then I heard a noise in the garage—I thought someone was trying to rob the place."

She gathered up the scattered contents of the carton

of bandages, trying to gather up a little of her dignity, as well. "Let me help you with that," Ken said, bounding down the stairs to join her. "Why are you driving that old truck?"

"My car is in the shop," she said. "Someone ran me off the road the other night."

"Oh, Darcy." He put a hand on her shoulder and looked into her eyes. "You need to be careful. Do you think it was the serial killer?"

"Serial killer?" The word struck fear into her. Could he be a serial killer if he'd only killed two people? Or had Ryder and the sheriff discovered others?

"That's what the paper is saying," Ken said. "They even printed a statement from the sheriff, telling everyone to be careful around people they don't know, and suggesting people not go out alone."

She clutched the box to her chest, pushing down the flutters of panic in her stomach. "I'm being careful," she said. So careful she was beginning to feel paranoid, scrutinizing the driver in every car she passed, looking on every new male client with suspicion.

"You shouldn't be out at your place alone," Ken said. "The offer is still open to stay with me."

"I'm fine by myself," she said. "And I couldn't leave the cats."

She pushed past him and he let her pass, but followed her into the living room. "I talked to that cop," he said. "That state trooper."

She set the box down and pulled on her gloves. "Oh?"

"He thinks I had something to do with Kelly and Christy's deaths—that I killed them, even."

She looked up, startled. "Did Ryder say that? Did he accuse you of killing them?" He had told her that

Ken's alibis for the times of the murders checked out, but maybe he had only been shielding her. Or maybe he even thought she might share information with Ken.

"He didn't have to. He grilled me—asking where was I and what was I doing when the women were killed. And he wanted to know all about my relationship with Kelly."

"He just asked you the same questions he asked everyone who knew Kelly," she said. "He wasn't accusing you of anything. And you haven't done anything wrong, so why be upset?"

"Cops can frame people for crimes, you know," he said. "Especially people they don't like, or who they want to get out of the way."

"Don't be ridiculous." She regretted the words as anger flashed in his eyes. "I mean, why would he do that?" she hastened to add. "Ryder doesn't even know you."

"He wanted to know about my relationship with you, too," Ken said. "I think he's jealous that we're friends. That we used to date."

Darcy didn't think three dates amounted to a relationship, but she wasn't going to argue the point now. "I think he's just doing his job," she said.

"I think that cop is interested in you," Ken said. "You should be careful. What if he's the serial killer?"

"Ryder?" She almost laughed, but the look on Ken's face stole away any idea that he was joking.

"It's not so far-fetched," he said. "Crooked cops do all kinds of things. And he was the one who found Kelly's body."

"Ryder was with me when Christy was killed," she said.

Ken's eyes narrowed to slits. "What was he doing

with you?" He took a step closer and she forced herself not to move away, though her heart pounded so hard it hurt.

"Someone tried to break into my house," she said. "He came to investigate."

Ken's big hand wrapped around her upper arm. "I told you it's not safe for you out there," he said, squeezing hard.

She cried out and wrenched away. She searched for her car keys and realized she had left her purse in the garage. She could do without the collars if she had to, but she couldn't go anywhere without her keys. "You can go home now," she said. "I'll let myself out."

Not waiting for an answer, she pushed past him and all but ran to the garage where she retrieved her purse, threaded half a dozen plastic, cone-shaped collars over one arm and returned to the living room. Ken had picked up the box of bandages. "I'll carry these for you," he said.

At the truck, he slid the box onto the passenger seat. She dropped the collars onto the floorboard and slammed the door, then hurried around to the driver's side. "You look ridiculous in this big old wreck," he said, coming around to the driver's side as she hoisted herself up into the seat.

"I've got more important things to worry about." She turned the key and the engine roared to life.

"Be careful," he said. "And be careful of that cop. I don't trust him."

"I do," she said, and slammed the door, maybe a little harder than necessary. She drove away, but when she looked in the rearview mirror, Ken was still standing there, watching her. She didn't think he was a killer, but she was glad she had decided not to date him anymore. She had never been completely comfortable with him. And while she trusted Ryder to have her best interests at heart, she couldn't say the same about Ken.

On Saturday afternoon the parking area around the ranch house at the Walker Ranch was so packed with vehicles that a person could have been forgiven for thinking the wedding day had been moved up, Darcy thought as she maneuvered the truck into a parking spot. A steady stream of young people made their way to the bonfire in front of the house where Darcy found Emily Walker greeting everyone.

Ryder caught her eye from the other side of the bonfire and joined her. "Are all these people in the wedding party?" Darcy asked. She recognized Tammy Patterson, who worked for the *Eagle Mountain Examiner*, and Fiona Winslow, who waited tables at Kate's Kitchen. Dwight and Gage from the sheriff's department were there, and Dwight's new wife, Brenda Stinson. A few other people looked familiar, though she couldn't name them.

"Some of them. Others are people from town, and some visitors." He indicated a dark-haired man in a sheepskin jacket and cowboy hat. "That's Cody Rankin, a US Marshal who's one of the groomsmen. To his left is Nate Hall. He's a fish and wildlife officer—another groomsman."

"We ought to be safe here with all these law enforcement officers," she said.

"When you're in the profession, you end up hanging out with others in the profession a lot," Ryder said. "But there are plenty of civilians here, too." He nodded toward a pair of men in puffy parkas, knit caps pulled down low over their ears. "Those two are students Emily knows from Colorado State University. They came to Eagle Mountain on their winter break to ice climb and got trapped by the snow."

As she was scanning the crowd, Ken arrived. He saw her standing with Ryder and frowned, but didn't approach. Darcy was glad. After their uncomfortable encounter last night, she intended to avoid him as much as possible.

Emily climbed up on a section of tree trunk near the fire and clapped her hands. She wore a white puffy coat, and a bright pink hat, skinny jeans tucked into tall, fur-topped boots. Her long, dark hair whipped in the wind and her face was flushed from excitement or the fire, or both. "All right, everybody. I think everyone's here," she said. "I think you all know each other, but I wanted to introduce Jamie Douglas. She's been in town for a while, but she's the newest deputy with the Rayford County Sheriff's Department."

A rosy-cheeked brunette, who wore her hair in twin braids, waved to them.

"And last, but not least, we have Alex Woodruff and Tim Dawson." Emily indicated the two men Ryder had pointed out. "They live in Fort Collins and go to school at CSU."

Everyone waved or said hello to Alex and Tim, who returned the greetings. "All right," Emily said. "Let's get this party started." She pulled a handful of cards from her coat pocket. "I want everyone to form teams of two to three people each. Here are the lists of items you need to find. The first team to find all the items on the list wins a prize. Gage, please show everyone the prize."

Gage stepped forward and held up a liquor bottle. "What if you don't like Irish cream?" someone in the crowd asked over the oohs and ahhs of other guests.

"Then you give it to me, because it's my favorite," Emily said. She held up her phone. "It's two o'clock now. Everybody meet back here at four and we'll see who has the most items. We have plenty of food and drinks to enjoy around the bonfire, too. Now, come get your lists."

Ryder took Darcy's arm. "Let's team up together," he said.

"All right."

He went forward and got one of the cards, then rejoined her and they leaned in close to read it together. "A bird's nest, animal tracks, red berries, spruce cones, old horseshoe, mistletoe," Ryder read. "How are we supposed to collect animal tracks?"

"We can take a picture," Darcy said. "Where are we going to find a rock shaped like a heart with all this snow?"

"Maybe down by the creek." He handed her the list. "Did you bring snowshoes?"

They retrieved their snowshoes and put them on, then set out in the wake of other partygoers, everyone laughing and chattering. For once it wasn't snowing. Instead, the pristine drifts around them sparkled in the sun, the dark evergreens of the forest standing out against an intensely turquoise sky. "Emily must live a charmed life to get weather like this for her party," Darcy said as she tramped across the snow alongside Ryder.

"I'm hoping this break in the weather lasts," Ryder said. "The highway department is blasting the avalanche chutes today, and they've got heavy equipment in to clear the roads. With luck they can get everything open again by Monday morning."

"Will that help you with your case?" she asked. "Having the roads open?"

He glanced at her. "It will. But I don't want to talk about that today." He pointed a ski pole toward an opening in the woods. "Let's head to the creek, see if we can find that rock. And maybe the bird's nest, too."

"Are birds more likely to nest along creeks?" she asked.

"I have no idea. You're the animal expert here."

She laughed. "I can tell you about dogs and cats, some livestock, and a little about ferrets and guinea pigs. I don't know much about wild birds except they're pretty."

"Did you always want to be a veterinarian?" he asked.

"I wanted to be a ballerina, but short, awkward girls don't have much a chance at that," she said. "Then I wanted to be a chef, an astronaut or the person who ran the roller coaster at Elitch Gardens. That was just in third grade. I didn't settle on vet school until I was a sophomore in college, after I got a part-time job working at an animal hospital. I thought I would hate it, but I loved it."

"It's good to find work you love."

"What about you?" she asked. "Do you love your job?"

He glanced down at her, his expression serious. "I

do. I like doing different things every day and solving problems and helping people."

"Is it something you've always wanted to do?" she asked.

"I went to college to study engineering, but attended a job fair my freshman year where the Colorado State Patrol had a booth. I'd never even thought about a law enforcement career before, but after I talked to them, I couldn't let go of the idea. I talked to some officers, did a couple of ride-alongs—and the rest is history." He stopped and bent to peer into the underbrush. "There's red berries on that list, right?"

"Yes."

He leaned forward and reached into the brush, and came out with a half dozen bright red berries clustered on a stem. "That's one down," he said. He handed the berries to her. "Stash those in my pack."

She had to stand on tiptoe—not an easy feat in snowshoes—in order to unzip the pack and put the berries inside. He crouched a little to make it easier. "Ready to keep going?" he asked.

She nodded and fell into step behind him this time as the woods closed in and the path narrowed. "How did you meet the sheriff?" she asked.

"We met in the state police academy," he said. "We just really hit it off. We kept in touch, even after he signed on with the sheriff's department in Eagle Mountain and I went to work for CSP. I visited him here on a vacation trip and fell in love with the place. When a job opening came up, I jumped on it." He looked over his shoulder at her. "How did you end up in Eagle Mountain?"

"Kelly visited here and came back and told me it

was the perfect place to open a practice," she said. "There were a lot of people moving in, a lot of area ranches, and only one solo vet, so she thought we'd have plenty of business. I was ready to get out of the city so I thought, why not give it a try?"

"Will you stay, now that she's gone?"

She stopped. "Why wouldn't I stay?" Leaving hadn't crossed her mind.

He turned back toward her. "I hope you will stay," he said. "I just didn't know if it was something you'd want to do—or be able to afford to do."

She nodded. "Yeah, the money thing might be a problem. But I'm going to try to find a way to make it work. This is home now."

"An awfully tiny home," he said.

She laughed. "It's cozy and it's cheap," she said. "Maybe it wouldn't be practical for a family, but it's perfect for me right now."

The clamor of shouts ahead of them distracted her. Something crashed through the underbrush toward them, and Tim Dawson emerged onto the trail just ahead of them. "It's mine!" he shouted, waving what at first appeared to be a ball of sticks over his head. As he neared them, Darcy realized it was a bird's nest. Laughing and whooping, he ran past her, followed by his friend, Alex Woodruff.

She and Ryder started forward again, only to have to move off the trail again to allow Ken and Fiona to pass. "That jerk stole our bird's nest," Fiona said as she passed them.

"It was a jerk move, but there are probably other nests," Ryder said.

Fiona stopped, panting. "That's what I told Ken, but

he's too furious to listen to reason." She bent forward, catching her breath. "Fortunately, those two are too fast, so I don't think he'll catch them."

"Do you want to hunt with us, instead?" Darcy asked. Not that she wasn't enjoying spending this time alone with Ryder, but she knew enough about Ken in a bad temper that she didn't want Fiona's afternoon ruined.

"Good idea to switch teams," Fiona said. She straightened. "It's sweet of you to offer, but I saw Tammy and Jamie up the creek a ways. I think I'll join them." She waved and headed back the way she had come.

Ryder and Darcy set out again and in another few minutes they reached the creek. The area near the trail was deserted, but tracks in the snow veered to the left along the bank. Ryder turned right. A few minutes later he stopped, putting an arm out to stop Darcy. "Animal tracks," he said, pointing to a row of tiny paw prints in the snow.

While he pulled out his camera and took several photographs, Darcy crouched to examine the tracks more closely. "I think they might be a weasel or something."

"I thought you didn't know about wild animals," he said.

"No. But they look a lot like a ferret. And ferrets are related to weasels."

Ryder pocketed his phone. "We have berries and animal tracks. What else is on the list?"

"The bird's nest and the rock shaped like a heart. A horseshoe—I don't think we're going to find that here."

"We can save the horseshoe for last. I know where the Walkers put all their old ones."

"Then we also need a spruce cone and mistletoe."

He scanned the trees around them, then took a few steps forward and plucked an oval brown cone from a tree. "One spruce cone," he said and handed it over.

She closed her hand around the cone and turned toward his backpack, but froze as her gaze landed on a familiar clump of leaves in the tree over their heads. "Isn't that mistletoe?" she asked.

Ryder looked up, and a grin spread across his face. "It is."

"How are we going to get it down?" It had to be ten feet up the tree.

He looked down again, into her eyes, and her heart fluttered as if she'd swallowed butterflies as she realized they were standing very close—so close she could see the rise and fall of his chest as he breathed, and make out the individual lashes framing his blue eyes. He put a hand on her shoulder and she leaned in, arching toward him, and then he was kissing her—a slow, savoring caress of his lips, which were warm and firm, and awakening nerve endings she hadn't even known she had.

She moaned softly and darted her tongue out to taste him, and the gentle pressure of the kiss increased until she was dizzy with sensation, intoxicated by a single kiss. She opened her eyes and found he was watching her, and his mouth curved into a smile against his. She pulled back a little, laughing. "That's some really powerful mistletoe," she said.

"I'm thinking we have to get some to keep now." He

looked up at the green clump of leaves, which grew at the end of a spindly branch of fir.

"You can't climb up there," Darcy said. "The tree would never support your weight. And there aren't any branches down low to hold on to."

"Maybe I can throw something and knock some down."

"Throw what?"

"I don't know. A big rock?"

She looked toward the creek. Though snow obscured the banks and ice glinted along the edges, the water in the center of the channel was still flowing, and lined with rocks. "I'm not going to stick my hand in that freezing water," she said.

He stripped off his gloves and handed them to her. "I will."

"A picture is probably good enough," she said as he kicked out of his snowshoes.

"I told you, I like to solve problems." He took a step forward and immediately sank to his knees in the soft snow.

She put a hand over her mouth, trying to suppress a giggle. "Ryder, I really don't think—"

A scream cut off her words—an anguished keening that shredded the afternoon's peace and tore away the warmth Darcy had wrapped herself in after Ryder's kiss. "Who is that?" she asked.

Ryder fought his way out of the drift and shoved his boots back into the snowshoes. "It came from downstream," he said and headed out, leaving Darcy to keep up as best she could.

Chapter 9

The screams had died down by the time Ryder reached the crowd of people on the stream bank. Gage turned at Ryder's approach, his expression grim. Next to him, his sister Emily stood with her face in her hands, drawing in ragged breaths, clearly trying not to cry. Tammy and Jamie both knelt in the snow, Tammy sobbing loudly.

"What's going on?" Ryder asked Gage. But then he saw the woman half-submerged in the shallow creek, hands and feet bound with silver duct tape, blood from the gash at her throat staining the water pink.

Behind him, Darcy made a choking noise. He turned to look at her, but Emily had already put her arm around her and was leading her away. "Travis is on his way," Gage said. "And Dwight. And probably Cody and Nate, too."

Ryder made himself look at the body in the water

again. Fiona's knit cap had come off and her shoulder-length brown hair was spread out around her head, moving in the current of the stream as if blown by a gentle wind. "This must have just happened," he said, keeping his voice low. "Darcy and I saw her maybe half an hour ago. She and Ken Rutledge were chasing those two college guys—Tim and Alex—down the trail. She said Tim had stolen a bird's nest they had found. Ken was going after them. She decided to turn around and try to find Tammy and Jamie." He nodded to the two women kneeling in the snow. Emily and Darcy were beside them now, urging them up and away from the creek.

Tammy's sobs had quieted, and Jamie helped her to stand, then joined Gage and Ryder on the bank. "We didn't touch anything," she said. "I looked and I didn't see anyone else around here, or any obvious tracks."

Thrashing sounds in the brush heralded the arrival of Travis. "I sent Dwight to round up the rest of the guests and get them to the house," Travis said. He scowled at the scene beside the creek. "We need to get everybody out of here," he said.

"I'll take the others up to the ranch house," Emily said. Pale, but composed, she took Darcy's hand. "Darcy will help me."

The lawmen stood beside a large cottonwood, the bare branches forming a skeletal canopy over their heads while Emily and Darcy persuaded Tammy to come with them. When the others were out of sight up the trail back to the house, they began to work.

Gage and Jamie cordoned off the scene while Ryder took photographs. All the blood had washed away by now, leaving Fiona looking more like a mannequin than a human, her skin impossibly pale. Or maybe it only helped to think of her that way. She looked cold, sprawled in the icy water, though he knew she couldn't feel the chill anymore. She would never feel anything again, and the fact that she had been killed minutes after he saw her, when he was located less than a quarter mile away, gnawed at him.

Travis returned from a walk down the creek bank and the lawmen gathered under the tree once more. "The snow is churned up on this side of the creek for a good five hundred yards," he said. "There are some indistinct snowshoe tracks—probably from the guests on the scavenger hunt. No tracks on the opposite bank that I could find. My guess is the murderer walked in the water when he had to, and on trampled ground the rest of the time."

"So we're looking for a person or persons with blood on his clothes and wet feet," Gage said.

"He might not have any blood on him," Jamie said. "If he had her in the creek, facing away from him, he could reach in front of her, cut her throat and all the spray would go out in front and into the water."

"You say she was with Ken when you and Darcy met her on the trail?" Travis asked Ryder.

"He passed us first," Ryder said. "Well, Tim and Alex ran past us, and a few seconds later Ken ran past. Fiona was a few seconds behind him. She stopped to talk to us for a few more seconds, then turned and went back the way she came. She said she was going to catch up with Tammy and Jamie and hunt with them."

"She never found us," Jamie said. "We didn't hear or see anything of her until we came across her body."

Ryder was silent, recreating the scene in his head.

"When Darcy and I got to the creek, where the trail stops at the creek bank, all the other tracks had turned left," he said. "We turned right and didn't see any other tracks."

"Could she have turned off the trail before she reached the creek?" Travis asked.

"I don't think so," Ryder said. "The brush is pretty thick on either side of the trail in there. She was wearing snowshoes, like us, so it would have been tough to maneuver through the underbrush."

"Emily and I were searching along the creek and we saw Jamie and Tammy ahead of us," Gage said. "We stopped to talk to them, and then started all searching together. We didn't see Fiona until we stumbled over her body."

"Did you see anyone else?" Travis asked.

Gage shook his head. "No."

"I told Dwight not to let anyone leave until we've questioned them," Travis said. "I want to know where everyone was and what they were doing when she was killed."

"The murderer isn't necessarily one of your guests," Ryder said. "It wouldn't have been that hard to find out this party was going on up here this afternoon. The killer might have taken it as a personal challenge to kill under a bunch of cops' noses, so to speak."

"Or maybe it's a copycat," Jamie said. "Someone with a grudge decides to get rid of Fiona and make it look like a serial killing."

"We'll look into Fiona's background," Travis said. "But I never heard anything about her having trouble with anyone."

"Why doesn't anyone around here get killed in a

nice warm building?" Medical Examiner Butch Collins
trudged into view, his booming voice the only clue to
his identity, the rest of him concealed by a calf-length
leather duster, a yards-long red wool scarf wrapped
several times around his throat, the ends trailing down
his back, a black Stetson shoved low over his ears,
oversize dark glasses shading his eyes. He stopped in
front of them and whipped off the glasses. "And while
I'm ordering up the perfect murder, it needs to happen on a weekday, when coming to see you people is
a good excuse for getting out of the office, instead of
away from a nice warm fire in my own home."

"When we catch the killer, we'll be sure to pass
along your request," Gage said.

Butch surveyed the body in the creek. "I hope you
catch him soon," he said. "I'm tired of looking at lovely
young women whose lives have been cut short." He
shrugged out of his backpack and set it in the snow.
"I'll be done here as soon as I can, so we can all get
warm."

"Ryder, I want you and Gage to go up to the house
and start questioning people," Travis said. He didn't
say *before one of them tries to leave* but Ryder knew
that was what he meant.

The two men didn't say anything on their trek to
the ranch house. Ryder's mind was too full of this new
development. How had the killer been so close, and he
hadn't had any inkling? Was one of the people waiting for him at the ranch house responsible for this and
the other murders?

Emily must have been watching for them. She
met them at the front door. "Everyone is in the living
room," she said. "I had Rainey make hot chocolate for

everyone—with whiskey or schnapps if they wanted— and plenty of snacks."

Conversation rose from behind them. "They don't sound too upset," Gage said.

"They were, at first," Emily said. "Then I had everyone show their scavenger hunt finds and got them to talking. It's not that everyone isn't horrified, but I didn't see any point in dwelling on the tragedy—and I didn't think you'd want them talking about it amongst themselves. Not before you'd had a chance to question them."

"Good thinking." Gage patted her shoulder. "Is everyone here?"

"Everyone," she confirmed.

A woman appeared in the doorway behind Emily. Nearly six feet tall, her blond hair pulled back in a tight ponytail, blue eyes lasering in on them from a weathered face. "These are for you," she said, pushing two mugs of hot chocolate toward them. "Get those coats and boots off and warm up by the fire before you go to work."

"Ryder, this is our cook, Rainey Whittington," Gage said. "In case you haven't noticed, she's bossy."

"Hmmph." She turned and left the room.

Ryder sipped the chocolate—it was rich and creamy. His stomach growled—he'd have to snag some of the hors d'ouevres he'd spotted on trays around the room to go with the chocolate.

He and Gage left their boots and coats in the foyer and moved into the next room—a large space with windows on two sides, a massive stone fireplace, soaring ceilings and oversize cushioned sofas and chairs. Almost every seat was filled with men and women, who looked up when Gage and Ryder entered.

Some of the women looked as if they had been crying. Most of the men showed tension around their eyes. "What's going on out there?" Ken Rutledge demanded.

"The medical examiner is at the scene," Gage said. He sipped his chocolate, watching the others over the rim of his cup. The two college guys, Alex and Tim, fidgeted. Tammy looked as if she was going to cry again. Ken prodded the fire with the poker.

Darcy cradled a mug with both hands and met Ryder's gaze. She looked calm, or maybe a better word was resigned.

"We're going to need to question each of you," Gage said. "To find out where you were and what you were doing shortly before Fiona's body was found."

"You don't think one of us killed her, do you?" Alex asked.

"You might have seen or heard something that could lead us to the killer," Gage said.

Rainey appeared in the doorway with a fresh tray of hors d'ouevres, a thin, freckled young man behind her with a second tray. She began passing the food. The young man walked up to Ryder with his tray. "I'm Rainey's son, Doug," he said.

Ryder took a couple of the sausage balls from the tray. "Thanks."

Gage shook his head and Doug moved on. "Ken, why don't you come in the library with me and Ryder," he said.

Ken jumped up and followed them down a short hallway to a small room just past the area where everyone had gathered. "You think because I was teamed up with Fiona that I had something to do with her death," he said. "But I don't know what happened to her. She didn't even tell me she wanted to split up—she just left."

"Why don't you sit down?" Gage motioned to an armchair. He and Ryder arranged the desk chair and another armchair to face him. Ken looked flushed and agitated, his face pale. His jeans, Ryder noted, were wet from the knees down.

"When I saw you on the trail, you were chasing Alex and Tim," Ryder said. "What was that about?"

"They stole the bird's nest Fiona and I found by the creek," Ken said. "I wasn't going to let them get away with that, so I chased them."

"Did you catch them?" Gage asked.

Ken looked sullen. "No. They must have veered off the trail into the woods."

"How far did you chase them?" Gage asked.

"I don't know. Not that far, I guess. It's too hard to run in snowshoes."

"What did you do after you stopped chasing them?" Ryder asked.

"I went looking for Fiona. I figured she'd be waiting for me, back on the trail, but she'd disappeared."

"Did that upset you?" Gage asked. "When you couldn't find her?"

"I was a little annoyed, sure. But I didn't kill her."

"You were annoyed because she ditched you," Ryder said.

"I thought maybe she got lost or something. Most women aren't good with directions."

Gage and Ryder both stared at him. "What?" Ken asked. "It's true."

"Okay, so you were by yourself, for how long?" Gage asked.

"I don't know. Twenty minutes? I was trying to find the others."

The desk chair squeaked as Gage shifted his weight. "Did you find them?" he asked.

"No," Ken said. "I finally gave up and came back here. That's when I heard what happened to Fiona. I feel sick about it."

"How did your pants get so wet?" Ryder asked.

Ken flushed. "I fell in the creek getting the bird's nest out of the tree. That's when those jerks came along and got it, while I was in the water. Fiona was screaming at them to stop and they just laughed."

"How did you and Fiona come to team up?" Ryder asked.

"I asked her to come with me. She wasn't here with anybody, so I figured, why not?"

"Had the two of you ever dated?" Ryder asked.

"Nah. We'd flirted some, when I had dinner at Kate's Kitchen. I was thinking about asking her out. I figured this would be a good way to get to know each other better."

"While you were looking for Fiona, did you see anyone else?" Gage asked. "Talk to anyone?"

He shook his head. "No. Not until I got back to the house. Travis was here, and his fiancée. Maybe some other people." He shrugged. "I just wanted to get inside and get warm. Then they told me about Fiona and I couldn't believe it. I mean, I thought this guy killed women in their cars. What's he doing out in the woods?"

Good question, Ryder thought. They sent Ken on his way. "What do you think?" Gage asked when he and Ryder were alone again.

"I don't know," Ryder said. "Maybe he's telling the truth. Or maybe he caught up with Fiona and slit her throat."

"But first he bound her wrists and ankles with duct tape and no one else saw or heard a thing?" Gage grimaced. "I'm thinking it had to be a job for two people."

"Let's talk to Tim and Alex," Ryder said.

Tim Dawson and Alex Woodruff had the easy-going, slightly cocky attitudes of young men for whom everything in life came easy. They dressed casually, in jeans and fleece pullovers and hiking boots, but the clothes were from expensive designers. They had straight teeth and stylish haircuts, and Alex wore a heavy copper and gold bracelet that wouldn't have looked out of place in an art gallery. He and Tim shook hands with Ryder and Gage, and met their gazes with steady looks of their own. "You've certainly got your hands full, investigating something like this," Alex said. "I don't imagine a sheriff's department in a place like Eagle Mountain is used to dealing with serial murderers."

"You might be surprised," Gage said, which had the two younger men exchanging questioning looks.

"How did you two end up in Eagle Mountain?" Gage asked when they were all seated in the library.

"We heard the ice climbing here was good," Tim said.

"Tim heard the ice climbing was good and wanted to come," Alex said. "I sort of invited myself along."

"Why is that?" Gage asked.

Alex shrugged. "I didn't have anything better to do. Getting away for a few days sounded like a good idea."

"We didn't plan on getting stuck here," Tim said.

"But we're making the best of it," Alex said.

"What are you studying at the university?" Ryder asked.

"Business," Tim said.

"Psychology." Alex's smile flashed on and off so quickly Ryder might have imagined it. "So this whole case interests me—as an observer."

"How did you come to be invited here today?" Gage asked.

"We know Emily from school," Alex said.

"Alex knows her," Tim said. "He introduced me when we ran into her in town a few days ago and she invited us to come." He shrugged. "It was fun until that girl was killed."

"Did you know the woman who died?" Gage asked.

They both shook their heads.

"Take us through the afternoon," Gage said. "What you did and when."

The two exchanged glances. Alex spoke first. "We got the list and decided to head to the creek. I guess a lot of people did that, but we ran to get ahead of them."

"Why the creek?" Ryder asked.

"It seemed to me that a lot of the items on the list could be found there," Alex said. "And I was right. We found the heart-shaped rock and the red berries right away. And then we got the bird's nest."

Tim made a noise that was almost like a snicker. "Where did you find the bird's nest?" Ryder asked.

"That big blond guy—Ken—was standing on the creek bank in the snow, trying to get to this nest up high. He had hold of a branch and was trying to bend the tree down toward him."

"Except he slipped and fell into the water," Alex said. "When he let go of the branch, the tree sprang back upright, and the nest flew out of it and landed practically at Tim's feet."

"So I picked it up and ran," Tim said. "The guy was screaming bloody murder, and so was the woman, too, but hey, I figure 'finders keepers.'"

"Losers weepers," Alex added.

"What happened next?" Ryder asked.

"You know," Tim said. "You saw. We took off, with the blond coming after us. He couldn't run that fast in snowshoes, and he gave up pretty quick."

"What did you do next?" Gage asked.

"We kept on finding the stuff on the list," Tim said. "We had everything but the horseshoe when the cops herded everyone back to the house."

"We figure we must have more items than anyone else," Alex said. "We're bound to win the prize."

"Did you see Fiona or Ken again after you ran off with the bird's nest?" Ryder asked.

"No," Alex said. "We didn't see anyone until that cop told us to go back to the house." He stretched his arms over his head. "Are you going to keep us here much longer?"

"Do you have somewhere else you need to be?" Gage asked.

"Not really." Alex grinned. "But it's Saturday night. We thought we'd go out, have a few beers, maybe meet some women."

"Where are you staying?" Gage asked.

"My aunt has a little cabin on the edge of town," Tim said. "It's a summer place, really, but it's okay. At least we're not paying rent."

Gage took down the address and both men's cell

phone numbers. "That's all the questions I have." He looked at Ryder.

"That's all I have for now," Ryder said.

Tim and Alex stood. "You know where to find us if you need more," Alex said.

They ambled out of the room, shutting the door softly behind them. Gage let out a sigh. "Both of them working together could have done it," he said.

"They could have," Ryder said. "Or they could just be a couple of cocky college guys who didn't do anything but swipe a bird's nest that really didn't belong to anyone, anyway. They're not wet from being in the creek and they don't have blood on them."

"They might have a change of clothes in their vehicle or their pack," Gage said. "And Jamie was right about the blood—if they were careful, they wouldn't get much, if any, on them."

"We'll check their backgrounds, maybe talk to the aunt and their neighbors at that cabin," Ryder said.

A knock on the library door interrupted him. "Come in," Gage called.

Travis stepped inside and closed the door behind him. "How's it going?" he asked.

"Not much to go on yet," Gage said. "We've talked to Ken and Tim and Alex. That's all the non-law enforcement men. Except for Doug, the cook's son. I guess we'd better talk to him."

"I sent Jamie back early and she and Dwight interviewed the women," Travis said. "None of them saw or heard anything."

"Anything turn up at your end?" Ryder asked.

"We'll go over the body more closely tomorrow, but we found this." He took an evidence envelope from the inside pocket of his jacket and passed it over. Ryder stared at the single square of water-soaked pasteboard. A business card, the words Ice Cold barely legible on the front.

"It's the same killer," Ryder said. "Not a copycat. The same man or men who killed Kelly and Christy."

"It's the same one," Travis said. "He's challenging us right under our noses now."

Chapter 10

Darcy arrived home to a chorus of complaining cats and the beginnings of more snow. She dealt with the cats by serving up fresh seafood delight all around, and dispensed with the snow by turning her back on it, drawing the shades and standing under the strong stream of a hot shower until the icy chill that had settled over her hours ago had receded and the tension in her shoulders and neck began to relax.

She and Ryder had exchanged a brief goodbye as she filed out of the ranch house with the rest of the non-law-enforcement guests. Earlier she had given her version of their encounter on the trail with Ken and Fiona to the female deputy, Jamie. "I'll call you when I can," Ryder said, and squeezed her hand.

She checked the locks on her doors and windows again, turned on the outside lights and settled on the sofa with a fresh cup of tea and a peanut butter sandwich—her idea of comfort food. She had just picked up a favorite Regency romance novel and turned to the first chapter when strains of Vivaldi sounded from her cell phone.

Spirits lifting, she snatched up the phone, but her mood dropped again when she saw that the call wasn't from Ryder as she had hoped, but from Kelly's mother. "Darcy, I hope I haven't caught you at a bad time." Cassidy Farrow spoke with a tremor as if she was very old, though she was probably only in her early fifties.

"Not at all." Darcy tucked her feet up beside her and pulled a knitted blanket up to her knees. "What can I do for you?"

"I don't know, really. I just… I just wondered if you've heard anything about…about Kelly's case. If they're any closer to finding out who did this awful thing." Her voice caught, and Darcy pictured her struggling to regain her composure.

"I know the officers are working very hard to find out who killed Kelly," Darcy said. Should she mention the other women who had died? No. That would only be more upsetting, surely.

"I hate to keep calling the Colorado State Patrol," Mrs. Farrow said, "They're always very nice, of course. And they tell me they'll contact me when they know something, but then I don't hear anything, and we can't even get there to see our girl, or to take her…her body for the funeral. It's just so awful."

"It is," Darcy said. "It's the most awful thing I can imagine." She grieved terribly for her friend—how much worse the pain must be for Kelly's mother.

"It doesn't even seem real to me." Mrs. Farrow's

voice was stronger now. "I don't think it will be until I see her. I keep dreaming that there's been some mistake, and that she's still alive."

"I catch myself thinking that, too," Darcy said. "I wish she were still here. I miss her all the time."

"The officer I spoke to said they were sure the woman they found was Kelly."

"Yes," Darcy said, speaking softly, as gently as she could. "It really was Kelly."

The sobs on the other end of the line brought tears to her own eyes. As if sensing her distress, Elinor crawled into her lap, and the other cats arranged themselves around her, a furry first-aid team, offering comfort and protection.

"I'm sorry," Mrs. Farrow said. "I didn't mean to call and cry like this. I just wanted to talk to someone who knew her, who understood how wonderful she was."

"Call anytime," Darcy said. "It helps to talk about her. It helps me, too."

"Thank you. I'll say goodbye now, but we'll be in touch."

"Goodbye."

She ended the call and laid the phone back on the table beside her. She turned back to her book but had read only the first page when headlights swept across the windows, and the crunch of tires on her gravel drive made her clamp her hand around the phone again. She glanced toward the loft where the gun lay in the drawer of the table beside her bed. Then she shook her head and punched 911 on her phone. She wouldn't hit the send button yet, but she'd be ready.

The car stopped and the door creaked open. Darcy wanted to look out the window, but she didn't want to let whoever was out there know her location in the house. Footsteps—heavy ones—crossed to the house and mounted the steps to her little front porch, then heavy pounding shook the building. "Darcy, it's me, Ken. Please let me in. I need to talk to someone."

Her shoulders sagged, and annoyance edged out some of her fear. "Ken, I really don't want to have company right now," she said.

"Just let me in for a few minutes," he said. "Today has been so awful—for us both. I just need to talk."

She wanted to tell him no—that she just wasn't up to seeing him right now. But he sounded so pitiful. Fiona had been his partner in the scavenger hunt—to have her killed must have been a shock to him. Sighing, she unlocked the door and let him in. "You can only stay a few minutes," she said. "I really am exhausted."

He had changed clothes since leaving the ranch and wore baggy gray sweatpants and a University of Wisconsin sweatshirt. His hair was wet as if he had just gotten out of the shower. "Thanks," he said. "I was going crazy, sitting at the house with no one to talk to."

"Do you want me to make you some tea?" Darcy asked.

"No. That's okay." He began to pace—four steps in one direction, four in another. "I can't believe this is happening," he said.

"I can't believe it, either." Darcy settled on the sofa and hugged a pillow to her chest. Three women dead—it was hard to accept.

"That cop as good as accused me of murdering that woman."

Of course. Ken wasn't upset because Fiona had died. He was agitated because he had been questioned. "He's just doing his job," she said. "The cops questioned everyone."

Ken stopped and faced her. "Why are you defending him? Is there something going on between you two?"

"No!" But her cheeks warmed at the memory of the kiss they had shared under the mistletoe. Maybe *something* was happening with her and Ryder—but she wasn't clear what that something might be. Or what it might turn into.

Ken began to pace again, running his fingers through his hair over and over, so that it stood straight up on his head, like a rooster's comb. "You shouldn't be here by yourself," he said. "You should come and stay at my place. No one will bother you with me around."

"No one is going to bother me here."

"You can't know that."

She wasn't going to waste her breath arguing with him. She picked up her now-cold tea and sipped, waiting for him to calm down so she could ask him to leave.

More headlights filled her window. "Who's that?" Ken demanded.

"I don't know." She stood and went to the door. A few moments later a light knock sounded. "Darcy? It's me, Ryder."

Relief filled her and she pulled open the door. She wanted to throw her arms around him, but thought better of it, feeling Ken's stare burning into her back. "What are you doing here?" Ken asked, his tone belligerent.

"I wanted to make sure Darcy was all right after the upsetting events of this afternoon," Ryder said. He moved into the room and shut the door, but kept close to Darcy. "Why are you here?"

"Darcy and I are friends. I wanted to make sure she was all right, too."

"Thank you for checking on me, Ken," Darcy said, hoping to defuse the situation by being gracious. "I'll be fine. You can go now."

"Is he staying?" Ken asked.

"That really isn't your concern," she said. She patted his arm. "Go home. Try to get some rest."

He hesitated as if he intended to argue, then appeared to think better of it and moved past Ryder and out the door. As he pulled out of the drive, Ryder gathered Darcy close. "Your heart is pounding," he said into her hair. "Did he frighten you?"

"No. Just annoyed me." She looked up at him. "I think he has a habit of rubbing people the wrong way."

"What did he want?"

"He was upset. He seemed to think you believe he killed those women."

"We haven't identified anyone as our main suspect."

"Ken is annoying, but I can't believe he's a killer," she said. "And you said his alibis checked out."

"Alibis can be faked," he said. "And right now it's my job to be suspicious of pretty much everyone."

She started to protest again that Ken couldn't be the murderer—but how much of that was a true belief in his innocence, and how much was her desperate desire not to be wrong again about a man she had trusted? She probably would have defended the man who raped her, too—until he turned on her. Was she making the same mistake with Ken?

She put her hand on his shoulder, the leather of his jacket cold beneath her palm. "You're freezing," she said. "And you must be exhausted."

"I'm all right," he said.

"At least let me fix you some tea or soup."

"I wish I could stay, but I need to get over to the sheriff's department. I just wanted to make sure you were okay."

"You're going back to work?" she asked. "Does this mean you have a suspect?"

He shook his head. "I couldn't tell you if I did, but no. No suspects yet. We need to look at the evidence we gathered today and see if we find something we've missed before."

"You don't really think one of the party guests is the killer?" she asked. Everyone had seemed so nice—people she either already thought of as friends, or whom she looked forward to getting to know better.

"We just don't know." He kissed her cheek. "All you can do is be extra careful."

He started to pull away, but she wrapped her arms around his neck and tugged his lips down to hers. She hadn't intended to kiss him so fiercely, had only wanted to prolong the contact between them, but as soon as their lips met the last bit of reserve in her burned away in the resulting heat. She lost herself in the pleasure of that kiss, in the taste of him, in the power of his body pressed to hers, and in her own body's response.

He seemed to feel the same, his arms tightening around her, fitting her more securely against him, his lips pressed more firmly to hers, his tongue caressing. She felt warmed through, safer and happier than she had felt in a long time. They broke apart at last, both breathing hard, eyes glazed. He stroked his finger down her cheek. "I wish I didn't have to go," he said.

"I wish you didn't have to go, either."

He stepped back, and she reluctantly let him. "Lock the door behind me," he said.

"I will."

"If Ken comes back here, don't let him in," he said.

"All right," she said.

She didn't want to let anyone in—into her home, or her life, or her heart. That had been her policy for years. But Ryder had breached those barriers and the knowledge both frightened and thrilled her. He wasn't a killer. Ryder would never hurt her. She knew that, but that didn't mean he didn't have the power to hurt her. Maybe not physically, but if you gave your heart to someone, you risked having it broken. She had been so wrong about a man before—would she ever really be able to trust her judgment again?

Ryder was the last to arrive in the situation room at the sheriff's department. He filled a mug from the coffeepot at the back of the room, then settled at the table next to Gage. Like Ryder, most of the others still wore the clothes they had had on that afternoon. Only the sheriff and Dwight were in uniform—Ryder assumed because they were on duty.

"Let's get started," Travis said from the front of the room. "I've asked Cody and Nate to sit in, since they were at the ranch this afternoon."

US Marshal Cody Rankin and Department of Wildlife officer Nate Hall nodded to the others.

Travis moved to the whiteboard. "Let's start by summarizing the information we learned this afternoon," he said. "Jamie, you helped interview the women. Anything there?"

"Ryder and Darcy appear to be the only people who

saw Fiona after she and Ken set out on the scavenger hunt," Jamie said. "No one thought it was odd for her to be with him. Several said they were laughing together when they split up from the rest of the group to start the hunt. No one saw any strangers or anything they thought was odd or out of place."

Travis nodded. "About what we got from the men, too."

"I don't think any of the women had the physical strength to overcome Fiona," Jamie said. "Even two women working together would have had a hard time, and she would have fought and screamed. Someone would have heard."

"There were no signs of struggle in the stream or on the bank," Dwight said.

"There were a lot of footprints in the soft snow," Ryder said. "Too many to tell who they belonged to."

Travis picked up a sheet of paper from a stack on the end of the conference table. "The medical examiner says Fiona was struck on the back of the head," he said. "It wasn't enough to kill her, but it probably would have knocked her out, at least long enough to restrain her."

"So whoever killed her comes up behind her, hits her in the head with a big rock before she can say anything," Gage said. "She falls, he wraps her up in duct tape, slits her throat and leaves."

"That's different from the way he handled Kelly and Christy," Ryder said.

"Probably because he was in a hurry," Gage said. "He was out in the open, with lots of people around. He needed to get her down quickly."

"So we're pretty sure it's a man," Travis said. "I

think it's safe to rule out the law enforcement personnel who were at the party."

"That leaves Ken, Alex and Tim," Ryder said.

Travis wrote the names on the whiteboard. "Ken was the last person seen with Fiona," he said. "He's big and strong enough to take her down without too much trouble, and he was alone with her. Alex and Tim could have worked together. They're new to the area, and we don't know much about them."

"Ken has strong alibis for the other two murders," Ryder said. "And we're assuming all three women were murdered by the same person because of the business card."

"Do we have any idea what the significance of Ice Cold might be?" Jamie asked.

"I've been working on that." Dwight, who had been rocked back in his chair, straightened. "Online searches haven't turned up anything—no businesses by that name. Maybe the killer is bragging about how 'cool' he is."

"Or how fearless and unfeeling?" Jamie suggested. "Nothing can touch him because he's ice cold."

"We know this guy likes to show off," Ryder said. "Leaving the cards at the scene of each killing is a way of bragging. And killing Fiona when he was pretty much surrounded by cops is pretty arrogant."

"Tim and Alex struck me as arrogant," Gage said.

"Let's check their alibis for the other two killings," Travis said. He glanced at his note. "And there's one other man on the scene we need to check."

"Doug Whittington," Gage said.

"Right," Travis said.

"The cook's son," Ryder said, remembering.

"It would have been fairly easy for him to slip away from the house and follow Fiona and Ken into the woods," Travis said.

"What do you know about him?" Ryder asked. "Has he worked for your family long?"

"Rainey has been with us for at least ten years," Gage said. "Doug only showed up a couple of months ago."

"My parents agreed he could stay to help Rainey with the extra workload of so many wedding guests," Travis said. "She promised to keep him in line."

"What do you mean, *keep him in line*?" Ryder asked.

"He has a record," Travis said. "In fact, he just finished a fifteen-month sentence in Buena Vista for assault and battery."

"He beat up his girlfriend," Gage said. "Broke her jaw and her arm."

Jamie made a face. "So a history of violence against women. That definitely moves him up my list."

"Let's check him out," Ryder said. "But be careful. Make it seem routine. Not like we suspect him."

"We'll keep a close eye on all our possible suspects," Travis said. "Whoever did this may think he can kill right under our noses, but he'll find out he's wrong." He laid aside the marker he'd been using to make notes on the whiteboard. "Dwight, I want you and Ryder to interview Doug tomorrow. Since his mother is so closely associated with our family, Gage and I should keep our distance for now."

"I want to talk to Alex and Tim tomorrow, too," Ryder said. "Double-check their alibis for the other murders."

"If the roads open up tomorrow, we'll have someone rush the forensic evidence we've collected to the lab," Travis said.

"I wouldn't hold your breath on that," Gage said. "The snow is really coming down out there."

"We'll do what we can," Travis said. "For now the rest of you go home and think about what we know so far. Maybe you'll come up with an angle we haven't examined yet."

Ryder said good-night to the others and climbed into his Tahoe. But instead of driving to the guest house he rented on the edge of town, he turned toward the address for the cabin Alex and Tim said belonged to their aunt. He wouldn't stop there tonight; he just wanted to check it out and see what those two might be up to. And if they weren't home, he might take a little closer look at the place.

He had just turned onto the snow-covered forest service road that led to the cabin when he spotted a dark gray SUV pulled over on the side of the road. The vehicle was empty, as far as he could tell, but there were no houses or driveways nearby. Had someone broken down and left the car here? An Eagle Mountain Warriors bumper sticker peeked out from the slush that spattered the vehicle's bumper. Where had he seen this vehicle before?

He parked his Tahoe in front of the SUV and debated calling in the plate, which was almost obscured by slush. He climbed out of his vehicle and walked back toward the SUV to get a better look. He had just pulled out his flashlight when shouting to his right made him freeze. A cry for help, followed by cursing and what might have been jeers. He played the light over the side of the road and spotted an opening in the brush. It appeared to be a trail. As the shouting continued, he sprinted down the narrow path into the woods.

Chapter 11

The trail ended in a clearing at the base of ice-covered cliffs. Ryder shut off his light and stopped, watching and listening. Moonlight illuminated two young men in Eagle Mountain High School letter jackets standing at the base of a frozen waterfall, while a third young man dangled precariously from the ice. "Help!" the man stranded on the ice called.

"Chicken!" one of his companions jeered.

"You don't get credit unless you make it all the way up," the third man said.

"This ice is rotten," the first man said. "This was a stupid idea."

"You took the dare," the second man said. "That's the rules. To get credit, you have to complete it."

Ryder switched on the light, the powerful beam freezing the three teens. They stared at Ryder, expressions ranging from defiance to fear. Ryder moved toward them. "I heard the shouting," he said. "What's going on?"

"Just doing some climbing." The first young man—blond, with acne scars on his cheeks—spoke. He slouched, hands in pockets, not meeting Ryder's eyes.

Ryder played the beam of light over the young man on the ice. He balanced on a narrow ledge on one foot, hands dug into the ice in front of his chest. "You okay up there?" he called.

"I'm fine." The man spoke through clenched teeth.

"Odd time of night to be climbing," Ryder said. "And shouldn't you have ropes and a helmet?"

"He said he's fine." The second young man spoke. "Why don't you leave us alone?"

"He doesn't look fine." Ryder pulled out his phone. "I'm going to call for help."

"No!" The man on the ice sounded frantic. "I'll be okay. I just need to find the next footho—" But the word ended in a scream as the ledge holding him broke and he slid down the ice.

Ryder sprinted forward, though the young man's companions remained frozen in place. He was able to break the kid's fall, staggering back under the sudden weight, then dropping hard to his knees on the snowy ground, the young man collapsed against him. They stayed that way for a long moment, catching their breath.

The sound of an engine roaring to life made Ryder jerk his head around. The climber's companions were gone. "Looks like your friends ditched you," he said.

The young man grunted and tried to stand, but his left leg buckled when he tried to put weight on it.

Ryder knelt beside him. "You're hurt," he said. "Lie still. I'll call for help."

"I don't need help." The young man tried to stand and succeeded this time, though he favored his left leg. "It's just a sprain." He glared at Ryder. "I would have been fine if you hadn't interfered."

"I'd better take you home," Ryder said.

Sullen, the young man limped ahead of him down the trail. Ryder waited until he was buckled into the passenger seat of the Tahoe before he spoke. "What's your name?" he asked.

"Greg Eicklebaum," he said. "You can drop me off at the school. I'll walk home from there."

"You can't walk home with a bad ankle." Ryder started the Tahoe. "What's your address?"

Greg reluctantly rattled off an address in one of Eagle Mountain's more exclusive neighborhoods. "My parents are going to freak when a cop shows up at the door," he said.

"What did your friends back there mean about the climb not counting if you didn't finish?" Ryder asked.

"It was nothing. Just stupid talk."

"I gathered you made the climb on a dare."

Greg said nothing.

"What other dares have the three of you tried?" Ryder asked.

Greg stared out the window. "I don't know what you're talking about."

"Did you decide to break into some houses on a dare? Maybe the tiny house out at Lusk Ranch where the veterinarian lives? Or the Starling place on Pine Drive? Fred Starling said he thought the guy he surprised was wearing a letter jacket like the one you've got on."

Greg slumped down farther in his seat. "I don't have to talk to you," he said. "I'm a minor and you can't question me without my parents around."

"You're right. Let's wait and talk to your parents. I'm sure they'll be interested in hearing about this dare business."

Greg sat up straighter. "We're not doing anything wrong," he said. "It's just, you know, a way to pass the time. So we dare each other to do stuff, like climbing without ropes. Stupid, maybe, but it's not against the law."

"Attempting to break in to someone's home is against the law."

"I don't know anything about that."

"What other kinds of dares have you done?" Ryder asked.

"Gus ate a live cricket." Greg grinned. "It was disgusting."

"So there's you and Gus. Who's the third kid?"

Greg's expression grew closed off again. "I don't have to say."

"That's okay. I'll run the plate on his vehicle and find out."

Greg glared at him, then slumped down in his seat.

"The night of those break-ins, a woman was murdered," Ryder said.

"Are you trying to pin that one on us, too?" Greg asked.

"The murder wasn't far from the Starling house. The weather was bad and there weren't many people out. The person or persons who attempted the break-in might have seen the murderer, or his car."

"Can't help you."

"Think about it," Ryder said. "The sheriff might be willing to overlook an attempted burglary charge in exchange for evidence that helps us track down a killer."

"Right."

When Ryder pulled into the driveway at the Eicklebaum house, no lights showed in the windows. Greg unsnapped his seat belt and was opening the door before Ryder came to a complete stop. "Looks like nobody's home," he said. "Thanks for the ride." Then he was out of the Tahoe and sprinting up the drive.

Ryder waited until the young man was in the house, the door shut behind him. He could have waited for the parents to return, or he could come back later to talk to them, but he doubted they would be able to shed any light on the situation. He'd run the plates on the SUV, and let Travis and his men know about the three young men and their series of dares. He couldn't prove they were the ones behind the break-in at Darcy's house, but it felt right. And if he could find the right pressure to put on them, they might have some evidence that could help break this case.

"Good morning, Trooper Stewart."

Ryder was startled to be greeted by Adelaide Kinkaid when he entered the sheriff's office Sunday morning. "What are you doing working on a Sunday?" he asked.

"No rest for the wicked," she said.

"She doesn't think we can manage without her," Gage said as he joined Ryder in the lobby.

"You can't," she said. "And as long as there's a killer terrorizing my town, I don't see any sense sitting at home twiddling my thumbs. It's not as if at my age I'm going to take up knitting or something."

"I have a job for you," Ryder said. He handed her a piece of paper on which he'd written the license plate information from the SUV Greg's friends had driven. "Find out who this vehicle is registered to."

Adelaide studied him over the top of her lavender bifocals. "Does this have something to do with the killer?"

"Probably not. But I still need to know."

"All right. But next time call it in to the highway patrol."

"Yes, ma'am." Ryder grinned, then followed Gage into his office where Dwight was already slouched in the visitor's chair.

Dwight straightened and stifled a yawn. "I guess you're here to go with me to interview Doug Whittington," he said.

"That's the plan." Ryder leaned against the doorjamb. "No rush. I'd like to get the information on that license plate from Adelaide first."

"What's up with the plate?" Gage asked.

Ryder told them about his encounter the night before with Greg Eicklebaum. "The plate belongs to the SUV they were in. His friends drove off without him, so I didn't get their names, though I take it one of them has the first name of Gus."

"Gus Elcott." Adelaide spoke from the doorway. "The SUV is registered to his father, Dallas, but Gus is the one who drives it."

"What do you know about Gus?" Ryder asked her. Adelaide was known for having her finger on the pulse of the town.

"He's the star forward on the high school basketball team. An only child of well-off parents, which means he's spoiled, but aren't they all these days?" Her eyes behind the bifocals narrowed. "Why? What's he done?"

"Nothing that I know of," Ryder said. "I caught him and some friends ice climbing in the dark without safety equipment. One of them fell and sprained his ankle and I took him home."

"Oh. Well, I suppose if that's the worst trouble they get into, we should be thankful." She left them.

Gage moved over to the door and shut it. "Now, tell us what's really going on," he said.

"I'm not sure," Ryder said. "Greg said something about a series of dares they were doing, and apparently there's some kind of point system. I take it whoever racks up the most points wins. Wins what, I don't know, and Greg wouldn't elaborate. But I think Greg and Gus and one other kid, whose name I don't know yet, were behind the attempted break-ins at Darcy's house and at Fred Starling's the night Christy O'Brien was killed."

"Fred said he thought the burglar wore a high school letter jacket," Gage said.

"Yeah," Ryder said. "And Darcy said the car that pulled out of her driveway that night was a dark SUV. And I saw three high school boys at the grocery store not long before the break-ins."

"It doesn't sound like we have enough evidence to charge them with anything," Dwight said.

"No," Ryder agreed. "But there's a chance those boys saw something that night that could help us track down the murderer—a vehicle, or maybe the murderer himself. We just have to find a way to make them talk."

"Maybe we gather more evidence about the burglaries and use that to put pressure on them," Gage said. "Offer to make a deal."

"It's worth a try," Ryder said. "Right now we don't have much else."

Dwight stood. "Maybe after today we'll have more," he said. "You ready to go interview Doug?"

"Be warned that Rainey isn't going to welcome you with open arms," Gage said. "She's very protective of her son."

"Any particular reason why?" Ryder asked.

"Apparently, his dad was out of the picture early on, and she raised him by herself. It really broke her heart when he went to jail. She's determined to keep him from going back." He pulled a folder from a stack on the corner of his desk. "Take a look at this before you go out there. Dwight's already seen it."

Ryder read through the file. Doug Whittington had been convicted two years previously of beating up his girlfriend during a drunken argument. He broke her jaw and her arm and cracked several ribs. She had ended up in the hospital, and he had ended up in jail. After he had served fifteen months of a two-year sentence, he was eligible for parole. He looked up at Gage. "Did he come to the ranch right after he was paroled?"

Gage nodded. "Rainey begged my parents to let him stay with her on the ranch until he could get on his feet again. He had completed both anger management and alcohol rehab while behind bars, and wasn't going to mess up in a household with two lawmen as part of the family."

"If he is the killer, he's taking a big risk, murdering women while two lawmen are in and out of the house practically every day," Dwight said.

"This particular killer seems to enjoy taking risks and taunting lawmen," Ryder said. "So he would fit that pattern."

Gage took the folder Ryder handed him. "I hope he has nothing to do with this. It's going to be messy for my folks if he does, but we have to check it out. Still, Rainey isn't going to be happy."

Twenty minutes later Ryder parked in front of the ranch house and he and Dwight made their way up a recently shoveled walkway. Emily answered their knock, dressed in ripped jeans and a button-down shirt, her hair piled in a loose knot on her head and her feet bare. "Mom and Dad are away, but Travis told me you were coming," she said, ushering them inside. "He asked me not to say anything to Doug. He and Rainey are both in the kitchen."

She showed them into the kitchen, a modern, light-filled space with expanses of cherry cabinets and black granite countertops. The cook, Rainey, was rolling dough on the kitchen island while Doug chopped carrots by the sink. Rainey looked up as they entered, her gaze sweeping over them. "Hello, officers," she said, her tone wary.

"You remember Sergeant Stewart and Deputy Prentice from my party yesterday, don't you?" Emily asked.

"We need to ask Doug a few questions," Ryder said.

At the sink, Doug stopped chopping and raised his head, but he didn't turn around.

"Doug can't tell you anything," Rainey said.

"You don't know what we need to ask him," Ryder said.

"It doesn't matter." Rainey went back to rolling dough. "He doesn't socialize with folks in town. He stays here at the ranch with me and keeps his nose clean. He's had culinary training, you know. He plans to open his own restaurant one day, or maybe do catering. He's been a big help to me, preparing for this wedding."

"If he hasn't done anything wrong, then he doesn't have anything to worry about," Dwight said.

Rainey sniffed. "Go ahead and ask, then. He doesn't have anything to hide, do you, Doug?"

Doug wiped his hands on a dish towel and turned to face them. He had a square, freckled face under closely cropped hair, his nose off-kilter as if it had been broken and not set properly. "What do you want to know?" he asked.

"I'll leave you all to it," Emily said and slipped out the door.

Ryder turned to Rainey. "If you could excuse us a moment," he said. "This won't take long."

"It's my kitchen and I'm not leaving." She assaulted the dough on the counter with vigorous strokes from her rolling pin. "And he's my son. Anything you want to ask him, you can ask in front of me."

Ryder and Dwight exchanged looks. They could always insist on taking Doug down to the sheriff's department to interview, but that would no doubt cause trouble for the sheriff and his family. And it might be interesting to see how Rainey reacted to their questions. There was still the possibility that the killer had

had an accomplice. "All right," he said and took out his notebook. "During the party yesterday, what were you doing?"

"I worked with Mom, in the kitchen here," he said. "We made snacks for the party."

"Did you take a break from the work anytime?" Ryder asked. "Maybe step outside for a cigarette?"

Doug looked at his mother, who had given up all pretense of rolling out dough and stood with her arms crossed, watching them. "Mom doesn't like me to smoke," he said.

"But did you smoke?" Ryder pressed. "Maybe stepped outside to grab a quick cigarette?"

Doug nodded slowly.

"When?" Ryder asked.

"I dunno. A couple of times. But I didn't go far." He nodded toward the back door. "Just behind the wood-pile out there."

Ryder walked to the door and looked out the glass at the top. A wall of neatly stacked wood extended from the corner of the house, forming a little alcove between the back door and the side of the house. "Did you see anyone while you were out there?" he asked. "One of the party guests, or maybe someone who wasn't sup-posed to be there? Did you speak to anyone?"

"No. I try to stay back, so no one sees me."

"How long were you out there?" Dwight asked.

"A few minutes. Maybe ten. As long as it takes to smoke a cigarette."

"What about last Tuesday?" Ryder asked. "What were you doing that day?"

He looked again to his mother, his gaze questioning. "I dunno," he said. "I guess I was here."

"That's the day they found those women," Rainey said. "And yes, he was here. With me. What are you implying?"

Ryder ignored the question. "You were here all day?"

"Are you calling me a liar?" Rainey moved around the counter toward him. She was almost as tall as Ryder, and though she had left the rolling pin on the counter, he was aware that it was still within reach, as were half a dozen knives in a block on the edge of the counter.

"If you can't remain quiet, Mrs. Whittington," Ryder said, "I'll have to ask you to leave."

She said nothing, but didn't advance any farther toward him.

Trusting Dwight to keep an eye on her, Ryder turned his attention to Doug. "Did you know Kelly Farrow or Christy O'Brien or Fiona Winslow?" he asked.

"No," Doug said.

"You'd never seen any of them around town, or spoken to them?" Ryder asked.

"I saw Fiona at the restaurant where she worked," he said. "She waited on my table once."

"Did you speak to her?" Ryder asked.

"I maybe said hello." He shifted his weight and shoved his hands in the pockets of his jeans. "There's no law against that."

"She was a very pretty woman," Ryder said.

"They were all pretty," Doug said.

An innocent statement, maybe, but it gave Ryder a chill. "I thought you said you didn't know Kelly or Christy."

"I saw their pictures in the paper."

"Did you ask Fiona to go out with you?" Ryder asked.

"What makes you think that?" Doug asked.

"Just a guess. Maybe you asked her out and she turned you down. When you saw her at the party, it reminded you of that and made you angry. Maybe you followed her into the woods and confronted her."

"No!" Doug and Rainey spoke at the same time.

"How dare you make up lies like that about my son," Rainey said. "Just because he made a mistake once, people like you want him to keep paying for the rest of his life. Instead of going out and finding the real killer, you can just pin these murders on him and your job is done."

"I haven't accused your son of anything," Ryder said.

"Does the sheriff know you're here?" she asked. "I can't imagine he'd put up with you bullying someone who is practically a member of his own family."

"Can Mr. or Mrs. Walker, or someone else, confirm that you didn't leave the ranch on Tuesday?" Ryder asked Doug.

"I don't know," he said. "I guess you'd have to ask them."

"Please don't ask them." Rainey's tone had turned from strident to pleading. "You'll only embarrass all of us. Doug was here because he was with me. I make it a point to keep him busy. He doesn't need to go to town for anything."

"He obviously went to town at some point and met Fiona at the restaurant," Dwight said.

"He was with me that day," Rainey said. "I keep him with me."

Dwight returned his notebook to his pocket. "That's all for now," he said. "I may have more questions later."

They left the kitchen. The living room was empty, so they let themselves out of the house. Ryder stopped on the way back to the Tahoe and looked around. Four cars were parked in front of the house, with another couple of trucks over by the horse barn. "A lot of vehicles," he said.

"The Walkers and Emily live here, along with Rainey and Doug, a ranch foreman and a couple of cowboys," Dwight said. "Cody Rankin is staying here until the wedding, and there are probably people in and out all day—delivery people, the veterinarian and farrier, other service people."

"So it would be easy for Doug to have slipped away while his mother was busy," Ryder said.

"Maybe," Dwight said. "But what's his motive?"

"He thought the women who were killed were pretty. If they turned down his advances, he might have taken it personally."

"He served time for assaulting a woman," Dwight said. "Not a stranger, but a woman he knew. And the crime was more violent and spontaneous. These crimes feel more planned out to me."

Ryder nodded. "His mother is worried about something," he said and resumed the walk to his vehicle. "Something to do with Doug."

"I got that feeling, too," Dwight said. "He might not be guilty of murdering Fiona and the others, but she thinks he's guilty of something."

"Or maybe she's lying about Doug having been with her every day, all day," Ryder said. "Her guilt over the lie is what I'm picking up on."

"She said she keeps him on the ranch with her, and pretty much doesn't let him out of her sight," Ryder said. "But it might be possible he could slip out without her knowing."

"Anything is possible," Dwight said. "We could get a warrant to search his room. Maybe we'd get lucky and find a stack of Ice Cold calling cards."

"I don't think we have enough evidence to get a warrant," Ryder said. "Right now he has an alibi we can't disprove for all the killings. We don't have a motive, and the crime he was convicted of isn't similar enough to these murders to justify a search—at least not from a judge's point of view."

"I wonder if he has access to a computer and printer?" Dwight asked.

"I'll bet there's one somewhere in that house." Ryder glanced over at the big ranch house. "But without a warrant, we can't legally find out what's on it."

"We don't have much of anything, really," Dwight said. "That's the problem with this case—lots of guys who might be a killer, but no proof that any of them are."

"Yeah." Ryder's hands tightened on the steering wheel. "It feels like we're in a race, hurrying to catch this guy before he strikes again." A race that, right now at least, they were losing.

Chapter 12

By Monday Darcy was feeling much calmer. Fiona's murder had been very upsetting, but Darcy had managed to bring her feelings under control and focus on her work. "You've got a new patient in room two," Darcy's receptionist, Stacy, said when Darcy emerged from the kennels that afternoon where she'd been checking on a corgi who had had a bad tooth removed that morning. Churchill the corgi, more familiarly known as Pudge, was sleeping peacefully in a kennel, cuddled up on his favorite blanket, supplied by his indulgent owner.

"Oh?" Darcy accepted the brand-new patient chart, labeled Alvin. The information sheet inside listed a three-month-old Labrador puppy, Spike.

"The pup is adorable," Stacy said. "I should prepare you for the owner, though."

Darcy checked the sheet again. The puppy's owner was listed as Jerry Alvin. "What about him?" Had he given Stacy trouble already?

"He seems very nice," Stacy said. "But he's recovering from some kind of accident—his face is all bandaged and one arm is in a sling. I thought I should prepare you since it's a little shocking when you first see him."

"Oh, okay. Thanks." She closed the folder, then opened the door to exam room two.

Jerry Alvin's appearance was indeed a little shocking. Most of his head—with the exception of his eyes, ears and chin, was wrapped in bandages, and his left arm was enclosed in a black sling. He wore a black knit hat pulled down to his ears, tufts of blond hair sticking out from beneath it. "Hello, Dr. Marsh," he said, rising to greet her, and offering his hand.

"Hello, Mr. Alvin." She turned to greet the dog. "And hello, Spike."

Spike, a dark brown ball of fur, seemed thrilled to see her, jumping up and wagging his whole body. Darcy rubbed behind his ears and addressed his owner once more. "What's brought you in to see me today?"

"I was in a car accident." Alvin indicated the bandages. "Got pretty banged up. Spike was thrown from the car. He acts okay, but I just wanted to make sure he isn't hurt."

"When did this accident happen?" Darcy asked.

"Yesterday. I hit an icy spot on the highway and ran off the road, hit a tree. My head went through the windshield. I guess I'm lucky to be alive."

Darcy knelt and began examining Spike. The pup

calmed and let her run her hands over him. "You say he's acting fine," she said. "No limping or crying out?"

"No. He landed in a snowbank, so I guess that cushioned his fall."

Spike certainly looked healthy and unharmed. Darcy picked him up and put him on the exam table. "He has a little umbilical hernia," she said. "That's not uncommon with some puppies. Chances are he'll outgrow it, but we should keep an eye on him."

"I'll do that. Thanks."

The hernia made her think of another puppy she had seen recently, with an almost identical umbilical hernia. Gage Walker's lab puppy was a twin to this dog—same age and size. He even had the same cloverleaf-shaped white spot on his chest. A chill swept over Darcy as she continued to examine the dog. If this wasn't the same puppy Gage had brought to her, then it was an identical twin. She glanced at Alvin. "Is something wrong?" he asked, leaning toward her.

"Nothing." She picked up the puppy and cradled it to her chest. "I'm going to check something in the back right quick. It won't take a minute." Before he could stop her, she exited the room and hurried to the back. She found her microchip reader in the drawer of the lab table and switched it on. With shaking hands, she ran it over the pup's shoulder. A number appeared on the screen. Darcy made note of the number, then carried the puppy to an empty kennel and slid it inside. The pup whined at her. "You'll only be in here a minute," she said and shut the door and slid the catch in place.

Then she hurried to the front office. "What's going on?" Stacy asked. "Did something happen back there?"

"What do you mean?" Darcy pulled Gage Walker's folder from the filing cabinet and spread it open on the desk.

"Mr. Alvin just ran out of here—without his dog."

Darcy looked up. "What?"

"He couldn't get out of here fast enough," Stacy said.

Darcy went to the window and peered out at the parking lot. Only her and Stacy's cars were visible. "Did you see what he was driving?" she asked.

"No." Stacy folded her arms. "Are you going to tell me what's going on or not?"

"Just a second." Darcy returned to the folder and compared the code the microchip scanner had displayed with the code registered to the microchip she had implanted in Gage's puppy, Admiral. They matched.

Stacy peered over her shoulder. "What are you doing with Gage's folder?"

"The puppy back there—the one Jerry Alvin called Spike—is Gage Walker's new dog."

"You mean that guy stole it?" Stacy's eyes widened. "So all those bandages must have been a disguise. But why bring it here?"

"I don't know." Darcy picked up the phone and punched in Gage's cell number. He answered on the third ring.

"Darcy," he said. "What can I do for you?"

"Gage, I have your puppy, Admiral, here at the office," she said.

"What? What happened? Where's Maya?"

"A man who said his name was Jerry Alvin brought him in to see me," Darcy said. "He was calling the dog Spike. As soon as I went into the back to check the dog's microchip, he ran out the front door."

"I'll be right over," Gage said.

Darcy went to the back and retrieved the puppy from the kennel. She wasn't comfortable letting it out of her sight until its real owner arrived. Ten minutes later Gage walked into the office, along with Maya and Casey. The little girl squealed and ran to envelop the puppy in a hug.

"We got in from school just a few minutes ago," Maya said. "We were frantic when we couldn't find Admiral. Gage called while we were looking for him."

"He's perfectly fine," Darcy reassured them. "Whoever took him didn't hurt him."

Gage took a small notebook from the pocket of his uniform shirt. "Tell me about this Alvin," he said. "What did he look like?"

"That's the thing," Darcy said. "I can't really tell you." She explained about the bandages and sling.

"It looked like a Halloween costume," Stacy said. "He said he'd been in a car wreck."

"He told me he ran off the road and hit a tree," Darcy said. "Even when he said that, I was thinking it didn't sound right. He said his face went through the windshield, but wouldn't the airbag have protected him from that? And even if he wasn't wearing a seat belt, it seemed he would have been hurt worse. And do they really bandage people up like that—like mummies?"

"How tall was he?" Gage asked. "What kind of build?"

Darcy and Stacy exchanged glances. "Just—average," Darcy said.

"Maybe five-ten," Stacy said. "Not too big, not too little."

"Hair color?" Gage asked. "Eye color?"

"He had a knit cap pulled over his hair, but there were some blond strands sticking out," Darcy said. "And I was so distracted by the bandages, I didn't notice his eyes."

"How was he dressed?" Gage asked.

"Jeans, a dark blue or black parka and the hat," Darcy said. "I didn't notice his shoes."

"The bandages and sling really drew all your attention, you know," Stacy said. "I guess that was the idea."

"Did you get a look at his car?" Gage asked.

Both women shook their heads.

Gage pocketed the notebook. "I'll ask the neighbors if they saw anyone around the house this afternoon."

"I'm so glad you thought to check the microchip," Maya said. She held the puppy now, stroking the soft brown fur. "I don't know what we'd have done if we lost him."

The front door opened and Ryder entered. "Darcy, are you all right?" he asked.

"I'm fine," she said. "Why wouldn't I be?"

"I stopped by the sheriff's department and Adelaide told me a guy showed up at your office who had stolen Gage's dog."

"He did, but he ran away when I took the dog into the back room to check the microchip," she said.

"I don't understand," Stacy said. "Why bring the dog here in the first place? It wasn't sick or hurt, and he had to have realized that in a town this small, the odds were good we had already seen the puppy." She tapped her chin. "You know, the more I think about it, the more I think this guy was trying to seem older than he was. Like—I don't know—a kid playing dress-up."

"You think this was a kid?" Darcy stared at her.

Stacy scrunched up her nose. "Not a little kid, but maybe a teenager?"

"I have an idea," Ryder said. "Maya, do you have a high school yearbook at your house?"

"Sure," Maya said. "I have a copy of last year's."

"Could you bring it to us? Now?"

"Oh. Okay." She took Casey's hand. "Come on, honey. Let's take Admiral home and get a book Trooper Stewart wants to look at."

"Why do you want to look at the school yearbook?" Darcy asked.

"Just a hunch I have about who might have done this. You take care of your next patient and I'll call you when Maya gets back with the book."

Darcy vaccinated a dachshund, and Maya and Gage returned together with the Eagle Mountain High School yearbook. "You think those daredevil high school students were behind this?" Gage asked as he handed over the yearbook.

"I think it's a possibility." Ryder opened the book. "What year is Greg Eicklebaum?" he asked.

"He's a junior," Maya said.

Ryder flipped to the pages for the junior class and found Greg's picture and showed it to Stacy and Darcy. They both peered at it, then shook their heads. "I was paying attention to the dog, not its owner," Darcy said.

"That's not the guy," Stacy said. "The hair was a lot lighter, and I'm pretty sure at least some of it was real."

"Try Gus Elcott," Gage said.

Ryder found Gus's picture, but it got a no also. "Try Pi Calendri," Maya said.

"Who names their kid Pie?" Ryder asked as he turned pages.

"It's short for Giuseppe," Maya said. "Apparently, a lot of Italians settled in this area at the turn of the last century to work in the mines. The Calendris have been here for generations. The story I heard is that Giuseppe is Italian for Joe. Someone started calling him Joe Pi, then it got shortened to Pi." She shrugged. "He hangs out with Dallas and Greg."

Ryder studied the photograph of a mature-looking blond. He turned the page toward Stacy. "What about him?"

"Bingo." She nodded. "That's him."

Darcy leaned over to take a look. "I think it could be him," she said. "Something about the chin..."

Ryder closed the book. "Why would Pi Calendri steal our dog?" Maya asked. "He's not even in any of my classes."

"Why don't we go talk to him and find out," Gage said.

Chapter 13

The Calendri home was in the same neighborhood as the Eicklebaums', though the house was larger, with more spectacular views. An attractive blonde answered the door, and her carefully groomed brows rose at the sight of two law enforcement officers on her doorstep. "Is something wrong?" she asked.

"Mrs. Calendri?" Ryder asked.

She nodded. "We'd like to speak to Pi," Ryder said. "Um, that is, Giuseppe."

"What is this about?"

"We have a few questions for him," Gage said. "We'd like you and your husband, if he's home, to be present while we talk to him, of course."

"My husband isn't here," she said. "Should I call our lawyer?"

"It's just a few questions," Ryder said. "May we come in?"

She stepped back and allowed them to pass, then shut the door behind them. "Excuse me," she said and hurried up the stairs to their left. A few moments later not-so-muffled tones of argument sounded overhead, though the words were too garbled for Ryder to make them out. A few seconds later mother and son descended the stairs.

"Hello, officers." A handsome young man, neatly dressed in jeans and a button-down shirt, stepped forward and offered his hand. "My mother said you wanted to speak to me. Is this about that fender bender in the school parking lot yesterday afternoon? I'm afraid I wasn't there. I had practice."

"Pi is rehearsing for the school's production of *Guys and Dolls*," Mrs. Calendri said. "He has the male lead."

"So you're in drama," Gage said. He and Ryder exchanged looks. A drama student would know how to change his appearance and assume a different identity.

"Yes, sir. You're Ms. Renfro's husband, aren't you?" Pi asked.

"Yes."

"Come into the living room and have a seat and tell us what this is all about." Mrs. Calendri led them into a room that looked straight out of a top-end designer's showroom—all leather and hammered copper and carved cedar. A fire crackled in a massive gas fireplace. A large white dog rose from a bed in front of the fire and padded over to greet them, tail slowly fanning back and forth.

"Beautiful dog," Ryder said, scratching the animal's ears.

"That's Ghost," Pi said. He sat on the end of the sofa.

Ryder and Gage took chairs facing him. The dog sat beside the young man, who idly patted its back.

"You like dogs, I see," Ryder said.

"Sure," Pi said. "Who doesn't?"

"What is this about?" Mrs. Calendri asked.

"I have a dog," Gage said. "A chocolate Lab puppy, Admiral."

"Labs are great dogs," Pi said. "Do you plan to train him to hunt?"

"I hope to." Gage scratched his chin. "Funny thing, though. Someone took Admiral out of my yard this afternoon."

"That's terrible." Pi looked suitably shocked, though Ryder thought he wasn't ready for his professional acting debut just yet. "Do you know who did it?"

"We have a very good idea," Ryder said. "And we think you do, too."

"Are you accusing Pi of taking your dog?" Mrs. Calendri poised on the edge of her seat as if prepared to leap up and do battle on behalf of her child.

"Funny thing about cops," Gage said. "We're very security conscious. And when you have a family, you can't be too careful. Lots of us install security cameras in our homes." Ryder noticed that Gage hadn't said that he personally had a security camera, though he wanted Pi to think so.

"Not to mention, the receptionist at the vet clinic where you tried to pass off Admiral as your own made you for a teenager right away," Ryder said.

Pi tried to hold his expression of surprise, but Ryder's words broke his resolve. He slumped, head in his hands. "It was just supposed to be a joke," he said. "I would never have hurt your dog, I promise. I would have returned him to your house before you even knew he was gone."

"Giuseppe! What are you saying?" Mrs. Calendri glared at her son. "You stole this officer's dog? Why?"

"You did it on a dare, didn't you?" Ryder asked.

Pi nodded. "At first, the dare was just to snatch the dog. But there's nothing really difficult or dangerous about taking a dog out of someone's yard." He sent Gage an apologetic look. "We didn't know about the security camera. So then we decided it would be worth more points if I tried to pass the dog off as my own. So we thought I should take it to the vet. If I could have fooled her, I'd be way ahead of the other guys on points."

"How many points would breaking into someone's house be worth?" Ryder asked.

Pi flushed. "I don't know anything about that."

"Pi, what are you talking about?" Mrs. Calendri asked. "What other guys?"

"Greg Eicklebaum and Gus Elcott," Ryder said. "They've been egging each other on in a series of dares, to see who can get away with various stunts without getting caught." He turned back to Pi. "Who's ahead?"

"Right now Gus is," Pi said. "After he put the bear statue from the city park on the high school gym roof the week after Christmas. He was sure nobody could beat that. That's why I had to do something really outrageous to top him." He buried his head in his hands. "Am I in big trouble for taking your dog? I promise I wouldn't have hurt him."

"You could be," Gage said. "That depends on whether or not you're willing to help us in another matter."

"Of course he'll help you," Mrs. Calendri said.

Pi sighed. "What do you want?"

"The night Christy O'Brien was killed—Tuesday, the fifth," Gage said. "You and Greg and Gus were out that night, in the snowstorm."

"I saw you in the parking lot of the grocery store," Ryder said. "You stood out because almost no one else was out in that weather."

"So? There's no law against being out at night," Pi said.

"Who else did you see that night? You may have seen the murderer, or his car."

"We didn't see anybody," Pi said. "That's the point, you know? Not to see anyone and not to let them see you."

"Except the veterinarian, Darcy Marsh, came home and surprised you trying to break in to her house, and a little while later Fred Starling did the same," Ryder said.

"I don't know what you're talking about," Pi said.

"We don't care about that right now," Gage said. "We want to know if you saw anyone else out that night. Any other car on the road, especially near Fred Starling's place."

"We weren't near Fred Starling's place," Pi said. "I can't help you."

"How do you know where Fred Starling lives?" Ryder asked. "We didn't mention an address."

Pi scowled. "This town is like, three blocks wide. I grew up here. I know where everyone lives. Mr. Starling was my Cub Scout leader when I was in second grade."

"He said he doesn't know anything that can help

you." Mrs. Calendri stood. "If you want to talk to him anymore, you'll have to wait and do it when his father and our lawyer are present."

Ryder and Gage rose also and followed Mrs. Calendri to the door. In the hallway Gage turned back to Pi. "If you think of anything that might be helpful, call anytime," he said. "Oh, and if anything else happens to my dog, I'll come looking for you, and I won't just ask questions."

"I would never hurt a dog," Pi said. "I promise you."

Gage nodded, and both officers left.

When they were in Ryder's Tahoe again, he leaned back against the driver's seat and let out a long breath. "Those boys were responsible for both those attempted break-ins," he said.

"We'll never prove it," Gage said. "But at least we know it wasn't the murderer targeting Darcy."

"The boys didn't pretend to be an old woman with a dog, and I don't think one of them ran her off the road," Ryder said. "All three of them were playing on the varsity basketball team that night. I saw the roster when I checked Ken Rutledge's alibi."

"Right," Gage said. "I'm still holding out hope they saw something that night that can help us. We'll try questioning all three of them, but we'll have to be careful—probably bring them in to the station with their parents and their attorneys. I'll talk to Travis and see what he thinks."

"Good idea." Ryder started the Tahoe. "Want me to drop you at the station or your house?"

"My vehicle is at my house. And I need to check in with Maya and Casey. Casey isn't going to want to let Admiral out of her sight for the next month."

"I'm glad your dog is okay," Ryder said.

"Me, too. I believe Pi when he said he wouldn't hurt him, but we need to stop these stunts before somebody does get hurt." He was silent a moment, then chuckled.

"What's so funny?" Ryder asked.

"I can't believe a high school kid got that bear statue up on the roof of the gym. The statue is made of bronze. It must weigh a ton. I took the call and the look on the principal's face was priceless. It was all I could do to keep a straight face."

"Maybe we can declare Gus the winner of the contest and put an end to the dares," Ryder said.

"Yeah," Gage agreed. "We've got better things to do than deal with high school delinquents." They had a murderer to stop, and Ryder hated that it didn't feel like they were any closer to him than they had ever been. It was only a matter of time before he struck again, and every woman in town was vulnerable—even, or especially, Darcy.

Darcy wasn't surprised to see Ryder waiting for her as she ushered her last patient of the day back into the lobby. She busied herself removing her lab coat and smoothing her hair while the woman paid her bill. As soon as the door shut behind the woman, Stacy demanded, "Well? Did you find out who took Gage's pup?"

"It was a high school kid," Ryder said.

"I knew it!" Stacy pumped her fist.

"What did he want with Gage's dog?" Darcy asked.

"He did it on a dare." Ryder came around the counter to join them in the little office space. "We think he and his friends were behind the attempted break-in at your house, and at another house, the night Christy O'Brien was killed."

Darcy sagged against the counter. "That's a relief," she said. "I mean, to know it was just a bunch of kids." And not the killer—though she couldn't bring herself to say the words out loud.

"Yes and no," Ryder said. "The kids aren't dangerous, but this does show how vulnerable you are to someone who could mean harm. Especially while we've got a killer running loose, you should be wary of new clients."

"I'm not going to turn away paying customers—or hurt animals," Darcy said.

He opened his mouth to protest and she rushed to cut him off. She wasn't going to debate her business practices. "I've already made a policy of not going on any more house calls for new patients," she said. "And I won't see anyone if I'm here alone."

"I'll start asking every new patient for a copy of their driver's license," Stacy said. "They do it at my doctor's office—I don't see why I can't do it here."

"That's not a bad idea," Darcy said. "We'll be careful, I promise."

Ryder studied her, clearly displeased, but not saying anything. Stacy slung her purse over her shoulder. "I think I'll head home now." She looked from Ryder to Darcy. "You two don't need me here."

When she was gone Darcy steeled herself to argue with Ryder. "I can't shut down my business or put my life on hold because of the killer," she said. "Of course I'll be careful, but teenagers playing pranks don't have anything to do with that. They're a nuisance, but they're not dangerous."

"They aren't the ones who ran you off the road when you went on that bogus call," Ryder said. "We still don't know who was responsible for that. They might try again."

Her stomach hurt, the old fear squeezing at her. But she couldn't let fear run her life. If Ryder had his way, he'd want her to shut down the practice and move into a spare cell at the sheriff's department. As pleasant as it was to know he was concerned for her, she couldn't live like that. "I'll be careful," she said, softening her voice. "It's all any of us can do."

He nodded. "That doesn't mean I won't worry."

"And I think your worrying is sweet." She reached for her coat and he took it and held it while she slipped her arms into the sleeves. It was a little gesture, but it touched her. She turned and put her hands on his chest. "It means a lot to me," she said. "Knowing you care. But it unsettles me a little, too. I'm not used to that."

He covered her hands with his own. "I hope you could get used to it."

"Maybe I can. But I need time. And I need space, too. Okay?"

He looked into her eyes. Searching for what? she wondered. He stepped back. "Okay," he said. "I'll walk you to your car, then I have to get back to work. I won't rest easy until we've found this guy."

"I think all of us can say that," she said. And she wouldn't deny that it was comforting to have him walk her to her car—to have him watching over her.

Ryder reminded himself that Darcy was a smart, careful woman who would be on her guard against anyone who might harm her. She was perfectly capable of looking out for herself, and he really ought to be concentrating on the case. He'd always made it a point to seek out easy, uncomplicated relationships—that worked out best for everyone involved. But there was nothing easy or uncomplicated about Darcy. Yet, the thought of distancing himself from her set up a physical ache in his chest.

He tried to push the thought aside as he headed back to the sheriff's department—his home away from home these days, since his regular office on the other side of Dixon Pass was off-limits due to the still-closed roads. Gage saluted him with a slice of pizza. "There's more in the break room, if you hurry," he said.

Ryder helped himself to the pizza. "I thought you'd be home with your dog," he said when he rejoined Gage in his office.

"I'm on duty this evening," Gage said. "And the dog is fine—being showered with treats by Maya and Casey, who have vowed not to let him out of their sight."

Ryder sank into the chair across from Gage's desk. "I don't even know why I'm here," he said. "Except I keep hoping for a break in the case."

"You can help sort through the calls we've had from the public." Gage picked up the top sheet from a stack of printouts on his desk. "'My neighbor has a lot of guns and looks at me funny whenever I go out to my car. Maybe he's your killer.'" He tossed that sheet aside and selected another. "'I overheard a man at the café the other morning tell his wife that Fiona Winslow probably got in trouble because she was such a big flirt. I didn't get a good look at him, but if you find him, maybe he knows something.'"

"Are they all like that?" Ryder asked.

"So far. But we have to look at them all. Someone might come up with something. Oh, and I almost forgot." He pulled another sheet of paper from a different stack. "This came into the office for you this morning."

Ryder set aside the half-eaten slice of pizza and took the paper—a printout from the Colorado Department of Corrections. "Who is Jay Leverett and why do you want to know if he's been released from prison or not?" Gage asked.

"It's a man Darcy dated in Fort Collins," Ryder said. "The relationship didn't end well."

"And you thought he might have tracked her down here?"

"It's always possible." He glanced up. "You saw what he served time for?"

Gage nodded. "Sexual assault. And he was released two months ago."

"And the DOC has no idea where he is now." Ryder tossed the paper back onto the desk. "Do you know of anyone in town who fits his description?"

"Not offhand," Gage said. "But we have a lot of strangers stranded here by the storms. He could be one of them."

"And he could be our killer," Ryder said. "Or not. But it's one more lead to follow."

Adelaide appeared in the doorway. "If you men are finished stuffing your faces, there's someone here who wants to speak with an officer," she said. "Actually, two someones. Tourists."

"I'll take this," Gage said.

Ryder and Dwight followed Gage and Adelaide to the lobby, where Tim and Alex stood, studying the photographs displayed on the walls. "Hey, long time no see," Alex said.

"Adelaide said you wanted to talk to an officer?" Gage asked.

"Yeah," Tim said. "We want to report a crime."

"What sort of crime?" Gage asked.

"Someone tried to kill us," Alex said. "You've got a lunatic running around in your little town."

Chapter 14

"You say someone tried to kill you?" Ryder studied the two men before him. Tim looked visibly shaken, but Alex was red-faced with anger. "What happened?"

"Come take a look at this." Alex motioned them toward the door.

Ryder, Dwight and Gage followed Alex and Tim out into the small front parking lot. Alex led the way to a gray Toyota 4Runner. "Some maniac tried to run us off the road," Tim said. "Look what he did to my ride." He walked around the car and indicated the bashed-in driver's side front quarter-panel.

"Was it a traffic accident, or was it deliberate?" Gage asked.

"Oh, it was deliberate," Alex said. "He aimed right at us."

"Come inside and tell us what happened," Gage said. He led the way to an empty conference room. He sat on one side of the table, with Alex and Tim on the other. Dwight sat next to him, while Ryder stood by the door. This wasn't his case—the two men had come to the sheriff's department to report a crime. But his interest in the men as suspects in his case made it reasonable for him to be present for the interview, though he planned to keep quiet and let Gage take the lead.

Gage leaned over and switched on a digital recorder that sat in the middle of the table. "I'm going to make a record of this," he said. "We'll transcribe your statements later and have you sign them. All right?"

Both men nodded. "Okay," Gage said. "Tell us what happened—where were you, when and all the details you can remember."

"We were out near Tim's aunt's cabin," Alex said. "On County Road Five. We were headed into town for dinner when this guy in a dark pickup truck turned out of a side road and headed toward us. He was driving really fast."

"Yeah, like maybe eighty miles an hour," Tim said. "Crazy, because the road has a lot of snow on it—packed down and drivable, but not that fast."

"Tim laid on the horn and moved over as far as he could, but the guy just kept coming," Alex said.

"It was like he was playing chicken or something," Tim said. "He headed straight for us and at the last minute sideswiped us."

"If he was going that fast and hit you, why didn't he lose control and go crashing into the trees?" Dwight asked.

Tim glanced at Alex. "He was lucky, and a good driver," Alex said.

"It would have been better if you had remained at

the scene and called us," Gage said. "We'll send some-one out to take a look. We may be able to determine his speed by skid marks."

"Good luck with that," Alex said. "It's all snow out there."

"You can see where we went into the ditch," Tim said. "And there's, like, glass and stuff from my busted headlight."

"All right," Gage said. "We'll check. In the mean-time, can you tell us where you were Tuesday?"

Tim laughed. "I can't even remember what I had for breakfast yesterday."

"That was the day after that first big snowstorm, right?" Alex said. "The day those two women were killed."

"Yes," Gage said. "What were you doing that day?"

"We were hanging out at Tim's aunt's place, moan-ing about being stuck here for who knows how long," Alex said.

"Did you go out to a restaurant or bar or maybe to the store to buy groceries?" Gage asked. "Did you see or talk to anyone else?"

"Nah. We stayed in and got drunk," Tim said.

"No offense, but the idea of being stuck here with nothing to do when we could be back in the city, hang-ing out with friends, really bummed us out," Alex said.

"I thought you came here to ice climb," Gage said.

"Sure. But you can't even do that when it's snowing so hard you can't see in front of your face," Alex said.

"Yeah," Tim agreed. "We've pretty much climbed all the good local routes, so doing them again would be kind of lame."

"How have you been occupying your time while you're stranded here?" Dwight asked.

"Watching a lot of TV, playing video games," Tim said.

"That's why it was so nice of Emily Walker to invite us to her party," Alex said. "It was a lot of fun until that poor woman was killed."

"Did you get a good look at the driver of the truck that hit you?" Gage asked. "Did you get a license plate number?"

"I'm pretty sure the vehicle didn't have a front license plate," Alex said. "And the windows were tinted. I had the impression of a big person—probably a man, with broad shoulders. He was wearing some kind of hat, like a ball cap."

Gage looked at Tim, who shrugged. "Like he said, the windows were tinted. And I was too terrified to notice much of anything. I really thought we were going to be killed."

"Were either of you hurt by the impact?" Gage asked.

"My neck is pretty sore." Alex rubbed the back of his neck. "I think I might have whiplash."

"I'm just generally banged up," Tim said. "No permanent damage, I don't think."

"Your airbag didn't deploy," Dwight said.

Again, the two friends exchanged a look. "No," Tim said. "I wondered about that. Maybe it's defective."

"We were both wearing seat belts," Alex said. "I'm sure that saved us from more serious harm."

"We'll get someone out to the site and check it out," Gage said. "We don't have a lot to go on, but we'll do what we can, though I think you realize we're a small department, and we have more pressing concerns at the moment."

"I wanted to ask you about that," Alex said. He smiled, a tight grimace that made Ryder think he didn't use the expression often. "I think I told you I'm studying psychology at the university. I have a special interest in serial killers. I'm actually thinking of pursuing a career as a profiler, helping law enforcement."

"I really can't talk about the case," Gage said.

"Oh, I get that," Alex said. "I wouldn't ask you to reveal anything confidential. But I read in the paper that the killer has been leaving cards with the bodies of his victims—cards that say Ice Cold. I wonder what you think the significance of that might be. Is he trying to send a particular message? And to whom? Does he kill women because he sees them as emotionally cold? Does he think this about all women or do his victims symbolize a particular woman?"

"I don't have any answers for you," Gage said. He stood. "If you could stop by the station again tomorrow, we'll have your statements ready for you to sign, and we may have some photographs from the scene for you to look at and verify. Thanks for stopping by."

He and Dwight escorted the two out to the truck and watched them leave. When they returned to the lobby, Ryder asked, "What do you make of that?"

"They're lying about something," Gage said.

Dwight nodded. "I got that, too," he said.

"The truck was damaged," Ryder said.

"It was," Gage said. "I'm just not sure the damage happened the way they said."

"What about those questions he asked?" Ryder asked. "About the killer?"

"Lots of people are fascinated by serial killers," Dwight said. "I imagine most psychology students find the topic interesting."

"How did the information about those cards get in the paper?" Ryder asked.

"Tammy Patterson was at the party at the ranch Saturday," Gage said. "She's a reporter for the paper. She probably heard about the cards there."

"I wish she hadn't publicized it," Ryder said.

"Nothing we can do about it now." Gage shoved his hands in his pockets. "Alex raised some interesting points," he said. "Ones we should look at."

"They don't have an alibi for the day Kelly and Christy were killed," Ryder said.

"No," Gage said. "But the weather was bad that day. Most people were probably staying at home, watching TV, playing video games and drinking. It doesn't prove they were guilty of anything."

"We aren't getting anywhere with this case," Ryder said.

"When we find out what those two are lying about, maybe we'll have something to work with," Gage said.

"I am not going to let you eat lunch cooped up here in the office again." Stacy, purse in hand, handed Darcy her coat after she had sent her last patient of the morning on her way Tuesday.

"I don't mind staying in." Darcy slipped out of her lab coat and hung it on a peg by the door. "It's a good time to catch up on paperwork." Since Kelly's death, she had fallen into the habit of bringing food from home or from the grocery store deli, and eating at her desk.

"Lunch is supposed to be a break from work," Stacy

said. "So you come back in the afternoon refreshed. Besides, if you go to lunch with me, neither one of us is alone. It just seems safer to me for women to travel in groups around here, at least until that Ice Cold Killer is caught."

"Ice Cold Killer?" The name gave her a jolt. "Where did you get that?"

"That's what the paper is calling him. Apparently, he leaves a business card with those words on it with each of the bodies of the women he's killed." She shuddered. "Creepy. I wouldn't stay anywhere by myself for ten seconds, much less a whole lunch hour."

"I'm sure I'm perfectly safe here," Darcy said, though even as she uttered the words, a shiver of fear ran through her. "I keep the door locked."

"You keep thinking that way if it helps you sleep at night," Stacy said. "As for me, I'm scared half to death, and I'd appreciate the company."

Though Stacy's tone was joking, Darcy sensed some truth behind her words. She hadn't read the latest issue of the paper, but news of a serial killer snowed in with the rest of the town had everyone on edge. And she had noticed an uptick of men accompanying the women who brought their pets in to see her. Maybe she and Stacy keeping each other company wasn't such a bad idea. She collected her purse from the bottom drawer of the filing cabinet. "All right. I'll go to lunch with you."

They headed for Kate's Kitchen, always a favorite. But the black ribbons adorning the door reminded them that Fiona Winslow had worked here, which momentarily quieted their conversation. Stacy waited until they had placed their orders before she spoke. She stripped the paper off a straw and plopped it into her glass of diet soda. "It's just so weird that a serial killer would end up here, in little Eagle Mountain. What's the attraction?"

"I guess killers take vacations and go to visit relatives, like anyone else," Darcy said. "He got caught by the snow like a lot of other people."

"And while he's here he decides he should kill a few people?" She grimaced. "It's beyond creepy."

"I know the sheriff's department and every other law enforcement officer in the area is working really hard to track him down," Darcy said. "They're bound to catch him soon. There aren't that many people in this town, and he can't leave."

"Yeah. You have to hope the killer really is a stranger who got stuck here—and not someone we've all known for years. That would freak me out. I mean, how could someone hide that side of himself?"

"It happens all the time," Darcy said. The man who had raped her had seemed like another good-looking, charming fellow student—until he had refused to let her leave his apartment one night, and had turned what had started as a pleasant date into a nightmare.

"I guess it does," Stacy said. "I mean, the news reports always have some neighbor talking about 'He was such a nice, quiet man. He kept to himself and didn't hurt anybody.'"

The waitress—an older woman whose name tag identified her as Ella—delivered the soup and sandwiches they had both ordered. Darcy picked up her spoon.

"Speaking of law enforcement officers," Stacy said. "What's the story with you and Ryder?"

Darcy blinked. "Story?"

"He's not hanging around the office so much because of the case," Stacy said. "Or at least, that's not the only reason." She picked up half a sandwich. "And didn't the two of you team up at Emily Walker's party last Saturday? How was that?"

"It was fun." Darcy sipped her own drink. "Until it wasn't."

"Yeah, not the most romantic of circumstances," Stacy said. She leaned across the table, her voice lowered. "Still, you have to admit he is one gorgeous man. And I can tell he's really into you."

How can you tell? Darcy wanted to ask, but she didn't. Because it didn't really matter what someone else thought was going on. The only gauge that counted was what she and Ryder felt. She could assess her own feelings, but the emotions of the other party in a relationship were impossible to plumb. Probably even people who had been together for years had a tough time of it.

So what about her feelings for him? Ryder was gorgeous. And his kisses certainly hadn't been casual pecks on the lips. But they had been thrown together under such odd circumstances. How much of her attraction to him was fueled by fear? If anyone could protect her from this Ice Cold Killer, surely it was a lawman who wore a gun pretty much all the time. And what if she was mistaking his sense of duty to protect her for something more? "I like him," she said. "But it's not as if we've even had a real date." The party had been a good start, but they had been interrupted before they had spent all that much time together.

"You can fix that," Stacy said.

"Fix what?"

"Not having had a date. Ask him out."

"Oh. Well, he's really busy right now."

"He can't work all the time," Stacy said. "He has to eat, right? Take him to dinner. Or better yet, offer to cook at your place."

Yes, she and Ryder had shared tea and conversation and even soup at her place, but it wasn't a real date. A real date, where she dressed up and cleaned the house and put some effort into a meal, felt like too much just yet. Too intimate and confining.

Maybe a little too reminiscent of her date-turned-nightmare with the man who had raped her.

"Okay, you're not digging that idea," Stacy said. "I can see it on your face. So what about an activity? Maybe something outdoors? Go ice-skating at City Park."

"I don't know how to skate." A broken bone didn't sound very romantic.

"Then something else. You're smart. You can think of something."

"What if he says no?"

"He won't." Stacy pointed her soup spoon at Darcy. "Don't be a coward. And hey, think of it this way— when you're out with a cop, Mr. Ice Cold isn't going to come anywhere near you."

Chapter 15

As the highway closure stretched to its second week, what had been a fun, short-term adventure began to wear on everyone's nerves. Tempers were shorter, complaints were louder and signs on the doors of stores and restaurants warned of limited menus and items no longer available. All the fresh milk and bread in town were gone, though a couple of women were making a killing selling their home-baked loaves, and the local coffee shop had converted more than a few people to almond milk and soy milk lattes. One of the town's two gas stations was out of gas. The city had made the decision to not plow the streets, and people made the best of the situation by breaking out cross-country skis for their commutes.

Darcy figured she had enough fuel to take her through another week. Weather prognosticators were predicting a break in the storms any day now—but they had been saying that for a while.

Four days had passed since Fiona's murder, and though tensions in town were still high, Darcy had stopped flinching every time the door to the clinic opened, and she had stopped looking over her shoulder every few seconds as she drove home in the evening.

"Ryder is here." Stacy made the announcement Wednesday afternoon in a singsong voice reminiscent of a schoolgirl on the playground teasing another girl about her crush.

Darcy finished vaccinating Sage Ryan's tortoise-shell cat and frowned at Stacy. They'd have to have a discussion about interrupting Darcy while she was with a client.

"Do you mean that hunky highway patrolman?" Sage asked as she gathered the cat—Cosmo—into her arms once more. "He's easy enough on the eyes that I might not even mind getting a ticket from him."

"Cosmo should be good for another three years on his rabies vaccine," Darcy said. "He's a nice, healthy cat, though it wouldn't hurt for him to lose a few pounds. I'll ask Stacy to give you our handout on helping cats lose weight."

"Oh, he's just a little pudgy, aren't you, honey?" Sage nuzzled the cat, who looked as if he was only tolerating the attention in hopes it would pay off with a treat. "He's so cute, I can't help but spoil him."

"Try spoiling him with toys and pats instead of treats," Darcy said. "He'll be much better for it in the long run."

"I'll try." She caught Darcy's eye, her cheeks reddening slightly. "And I'm sorry if I said anything out of line about your boyfriend. I promise I didn't mean anything by it."

Darcy opened her mouth to protest that Ryder was not her boyfriend, but the eager look in Sage's eyes changed her mind. No sense providing more fuel for the town gossips.

She followed Sage out to the front. "Now's your chance," Stacy whispered as Darcy passed.

In the waiting room, Ryder rose from the chair he had taken by the door. Dressed in his sharp blue and buff uniform, tall leather boots accenting his strong legs and the leather jacket with the black shearling collar adding to the breadth of his shoulders, he definitely was *easy on the eyes*, as Sage had said. "I didn't mean to interrupt," he said.

"I can give you a few minutes," she said and led the way past Stacy, who didn't even pretend not to stare, into the exam room she'd just exited. "What can I do for you?" she asked, picking up the bottle of spray disinfectant.

"I just wanted to see you, make sure you haven't had any more suspicious customers or disturbances at your home," he said.

"No." She sprayed down the metal exam table. "I promise I'll let you know if anything happens."

"I know." He leaned against the wall, relaxed. "I guess I just wanted to see you. I've been so busy we haven't seen much of each other the past couple of days."

The knowledge that he missed her made her feel a little melted inside. "It's really good to see you, too." She set aside the spray bottle. Her palms were sweating, but it was now or never. "I've been meaning to call you," she said.

"Oh?"

"I wondered if you wanted to go skiing this weekend. I mean, if you're free. I know you're putting in a lot of overtime on the case, but I thought—"

He touched her arm. "I'd love to," he said. "Unless something urgent comes up, I can take a day off. When?"

"Sunday? The office is never open then, and the forecast is for clearing weather."

"Sounds great. I'll pick you up. Is ten o'clock good?"

"Sure." She couldn't seem to stop grinning. "I hope nothing happens to keep you from it. Things have been pretty quiet lately, right?"

"Yeah. But it feels like we're waiting for the other shoe to drop. We know the killer hasn't gone anywhere, because he can't."

"Maybe he's decided to stop killing people."

"That's not usually the way it works with serial killers. I think he's waiting for something."

"Waiting for what?"

"I don't know." He patted her shoulder, then kissed her cheek. "Don't let down your guard," he said. "And I'll see you Sunday morning."

She opened the door of the exam room just wide enough to watch him saunter down the short hallway to the door to the lobby. Now she would be the one waiting, anticipating time alone with Ryder and where that might lead

The snow that had been falling when Ryder awoke Sunday morning had all but stopped by the time he reached Darcy's house, and patches of blue were starting to show through the gray clouds. But Darcy, dressed in a bright yellow and blue parka and snow pants, would have brightened even the dreariest day. Ryder's heart gave a lurch as she walked out to meet him, her smile lighting her face. Oh yeah, he was definitely falling for this woman, though it was harder to read what she felt for him.

At least she looked happy enough to see him today, though maybe it was just the break in the snow that had her smiling. "I'm so relieved to see a change in the weather," she said.

"This was a great idea," he said, opening up the back of the Tahoe and taking the skis she handed to him. "Nothing like getting out in the fresh air to clear away the cobwebs."

"I've been looking forward to a little time off from work," she said, handing him her ski poles.

"I guess it hasn't been easy, handling the practice by yourself," he said. On top of grieving the loss of her friend, she was having to do the work of two people.

"In some ways it's been a blessing." She stepped back and tucked a stray lock of hair beneath her blue stocking cap. "I haven't had too much time to brood. But I haven't had much time off, either. One day soon I need to sit down and draw up a new schedule. I can't keep the office open ten hours a day, six days a week by myself."

"You could bring in another partner," he said.

She wrinkled her nose. "That would be hard to do. The partnership with Kelly worked because we had been such good friends for years. I don't know if I could bring in a stranger. If it were the other way around—if Kelly was the one having to look to replace me—it wouldn't be so hard. She loved meeting new people and she got along with everyone. It takes me a lot longer to warm up to people."

Her eyes met his and he wondered if she was warning him off—or letting him know how privileged he was to be invited closer to her.

She looked away and moved past him to deposit her backpack next to the skis. "I imagine you could use a break, too," she said. "With the roads closed, you're the only state patrol officer in town."

"Yes, though most of my patrol area is closed due to the snow," he said. "Which isn't so bad. It's left me more time to concentrate on the case."

Worry shadowed her face. "You're probably tired of people asking you if you have any suspects."

"I only wish I had a better answer to give than no." He shut the back of the Tahoe. "Maybe a day in the woods will give me a new perspective on the case."

They climbed into the truck and he turned back onto the road. "Where should we go skiing?" she asked. "I know the trails up on Dixon Pass are popular."

Ryder shook his head. "The avalanche danger is too high up there right now. I thought we'd head down valley, to Silver Pick Recreation Area. There are some nice trails through the woods there, sheltered from the wind."

"Kelly and I hiked there this fall," she said. "Right after we moved here. The color in the trees was gorgeous." She settled back in her seat and gazed out the side window. "One of the things I love about living here is there are so many places to go hiking or skiing or just to sit and enjoy nature. The city has plenty of parks, but it's not the same." She glanced at him. "And before Kelly died, I always felt safe out here, even when I was alone. I guess I couldn't imagine any harm could come to me in such a peaceful place."

He tightened his grip on the steering wheel. "I hate

that this killer has taken that peace away from you—
and from a lot of other people."

"I guess we're naive to think small towns are immune from bad things and bad people," she said. "Or
maybe, because crime is so rare in a place like this, it
has a bigger impact."

"You would think that a killer hiding in a small
population like this would be easier to find," he said.
"But that isn't proving to be the case."

She leaned over and squeezed his arm, a gentle, reassuring gesture. "Today let's try not to think about
any of that," she said. "Let's just enjoy the day and
each other's company."

He covered her hand with his own. "It's a deal."

There were several cars and trucks parked at the recreation area, including a couple of trailers for hauling
snow machines. "Snowmobilers have to use the trails
on the other side of the road," Ryder said. "We'll probably hear them, but the trails on this side are only for
skiers and snowshoers."

They unloaded their skis and packs and set out up
an easy groomed trail. After a few strides they fell into
a rhythm. The snow had stopped altogether now, only
the occasional cascade of white powder sifting down
from the trees that lined the trail. The air was sharp
with cold, but the sun made it feel less biting and more
invigorating.

They had traversed about a half mile up the trail
when a loud boom shook the air. Darcy started. "What
was that?"

Ryder looked in the direction the explosion had
come from. "Sounds like avalanche mitigation up on
the pass," he said. "That's good news. The weather

forecast must call for clear weather and they're working to get the roads open."

"Oh." Darcy put a hand to her chest. "I guess I knew they used explosives—I just didn't expect for them to sound so loud."

"Sound carries a long way here. And those howitzers they use can be pretty loud."

"Howitzers?" she asked. "As in military weapons?"

"Yeah. They're actually on loan from the army. A lot of the avalanche control crews are ex-military. Their experience with explosives comes in handy. They'll try to bring down as much snow as possible, then get heavy equipment in to haul it off."

"So the highway could be open soon?"

"Maybe as early as tomorrow."

She grinned. "Everyone will be glad to hear it. You wouldn't think a whole town could feel claustrophobic, but it can. And it'll be good to restock all the stores."

"Hopefully the roads will stay clear for all the wedding guests who'll be arriving at the Walker ranch over the next few weeks," Ryder said. "Since some of the party live far away, the family has asked them to stay for an extended visit. They're making kind of a reunion of it, I guess."

"That sounds nice," she said. "It should be a beautiful wedding."

"Would you like to come to the ceremony and reception?" he asked. "I'm allowed to bring a date."

"Oh. Well…"

He cringed inwardly as her voice trailed off. Had he asked too much too soon?

"Yes. I'd love to come with you," she said.

"Good." He faced forward and set out again, though it felt as if his skis scarcely touched the snow.

They paused several times to rest and to take pictures. She snapped a shot of him posed near a snowman someone had built alongside the trail, then they took a selfie in front of a snow-draped blue spruce.

Their destination was a warming hut at the highest point of the trail. They reached it just after noon and raced to kick off their skis and rush inside. The rough-hewn log hut contained a wooden table, several benches and an old black iron woodstove that someone had stoked earlier in the day, so that the warmth wrapped around them like a blanket when they entered.

They peeled off their jackets and Ryder added wood to the stove from the pile just outside the door, while Darcy unpacked a thermos of hot cocoa, two turkey and cheese sandwiches, clementines and peanut butter cookies.

"What a feast," Ryder said as he straddled the bench across from her. He sipped the cocoa, then bit into the sandwich. "Nothing like outdoor exercise to make such a simple meal taste fantastic."

She nodded her agreement, her mouth full of sandwich, laughter in her eyes. A few moments later, when they had both devoured about half the food, she said, "Kelly and I didn't hike this far in the fall. I didn't even know this was up here."

"At the solstice a bunch of people ski or hike up here and have a bonfire," he said. "You should come."

"Maybe I will."

Maybe she would come with him. It felt a little dangerous to think that far ahead, but satisfying, too. Maybe the two of them would have what it took to make it as a couple. This early in their acquaintance, when they were just feeling their way, getting to know each other, anything felt possible.

"Did you make these?" he asked, after taking a bite of a soft, chewy cookie.

She nodded. "I like to bake."

"They're delicious."

They sat side by side on a bench in front of the hut's one window, a view of the river valley spread out before them. "Road closure or not," he said, "I can't think of anywhere I'd rather be right now than here." He turned to her. "With you."

"Yes," she said. "I feel the same."

There wasn't anything more that needed saying after that. They sat in companionable silence until the cocoa and cookies were gone. "Ready to ski back down?" he asked.

"Yes. I want to stop near the river and take some more pictures of the snow in the trees."

They traveled faster going downhill, racing each other to the flat section of the trail along the river where they stopped and she took more pictures. By the time they started out again, the light was already beginning to fade, the air turning colder and the wind picking up.

When Ryder first heard the snowmobile, he mistook the noise for the wind in the trees. But Darcy, skiing ahead of him, stopped abruptly. "Is that a snowmobile?" she asked. "It sounds like it's heading this way."

"The snow and the trees can distort sound," he said. "All snowmobile traffic is on the other side of the road."

They skied on, but the roar of the machine increased as they emerged into an open area just past the river.

"It's probably someone headed to the parking lot," Darcy called over her shoulder.

Ryder started to agree, then saw a flash of light over Darcy's shoulder. The snowmobile emerged from the trees ahead, a single headlight focused on them, a great rooster tail of snow arcing up behind the vehicle.

"What is he doing?" Darcy shouted as the machine bore down on them. She sidestepped off the main trail, but there was nowhere they could go that the snowmobile wouldn't be able to reach. The driver, face obscured by a helmet, leaned over the machine and gunned the engine. He was headed straight for them and showed no sign of veering away or slowing down.

Chapter 16

Darcy stared at the snowmobile charging toward them. The roar of the engine shuddered through her, and the stench of burning diesel stung her nose. *Move!* a voice inside her shouted, but her limbs refused to obey, even as the machine closed the gap between them with alarming speed.

And then she was falling as Ryder slammed into her. They rolled together, a tangle of skis and packs and poles. The snowmobile roared past, a wave of snow washing over them in its wake.

"We've got to get out of these skis!" Ryder shouted. He reached back and slammed his hand onto the release of her skis, then untangled his own legs and pulled her to her feet. The snow off the trail was deep and soft, and she immediately sank to her knees, but Ryder held on to her, keeping her upright. "We have to get into the trees!" he shouted.

She followed his gaze behind them and her stomach turned over as the snowmobile driver made a wide turn and headed back toward them.

"Come on." Ryder tugged on her arm. In his other hand, he held a gun. Was he really going to shoot the driver? If he did, would that even stop their attacker in time?

The snowmobile bucked forward, and she lurched ahead, as well, Ryder still gripping her arm tightly. They fought their way through heavy snow, every step like walking in a dream, her legs heavy, trapped in the snow. They were in an open field, the line of trees fifty yards or more away, the roar of the snowmobile ever louder as it raced toward them again.

"He's crazy!" she shouted. "How can he hit us without wrecking?"

Ryder shook his head but didn't answer, all his energy divided between breaking a path for them through the drifts and keeping an eye on the snowmobile.

We aren't going to make it, Darcy thought, when she dared to look back and saw the snowmobile only a few dozen yards from them.

The report of Ryder's gun was deafening, and she screamed in spite of herself. The snowmobile veered, then righted. Ryder fired again, and the bullet hit the windscreen, shattering it.

The snowmobile wobbled, then righted itself once more, then the driver turned and headed back the way he had come, away from them.

"I have to go after him," Ryder said. He tucked the pistol into the pocket of his parka. "Can you make it back to the parking lot okay on your own? I'll meet you there."

She nodded, too numb to speak.

He half jogged through the snow, back to the trail and his skis, then took off, kicking hard, making long strides, and was soon out of sight.

She moved much more slowly, her legs leaden. By the time she reached the trail she had begun to shake so hard it took her half a dozen tries to put on both skis. Then she started slowly back toward the parking lot, her movements more shuffle than glide, tears streaming down her face, her mind replaying over and over the sight of that snowmobile bearing down on them.

Ryder met her near the end of the trail. He took her pack from her and skied beside her all the way to the Tahoe, saying nothing. Then he helped her out of her skis and into the truck. "He was gone by the time I got here," he said. "I followed his tracks across the road, but he disappeared into the woods."

"Do you think you hit him when you fired?" she asked, struggling to keep her voice steady.

"No. I hit the machine, but not him."

Neither of them spoke on the drive back to her house. Ryder turned the heat up and Darcy huddled in her seat, unable to get warm. At the house he took her keys and unlocked the door, then she followed him inside.

He closed the door behind them, then pulled her close. They stood with their arms wrapped around each other for a long moment.

"I thought we were going to die," she said, unable to keep her voice from shaking.

He cupped her face in his hands and stared into

her eyes. "We didn't die," he said. "We're going to be okay."

She slid her hands around to the back of his head and pulled his mouth down to hers. She kissed him as if this might be the last chance she ever had of a kiss. Need surged through her—the need to be with him, to feel whole again with him.

She had wasted so much time being cautious, waiting to be sure. Sure of what? What was more sure than how much she wanted him right this minute? What could be more sure than the regret she would have if she didn't seize hold of this moment to live fully?

Ryder returned the kiss with the same ferocity, sliding his hands down to caress her ribs, then bringing them up to cup her breasts. She leaned into him and moved her own hands underneath his sweater, tugging at the knit shirt he wore underneath the wool.

His stomach muscles contracted at her touch, and heat flooded through her. She spread her fingers across his stomach, then slid up to his chest, the soft brush of his chest hair awaking every nerve ending.

He nipped at her jaw, then pulled her fleece top over her head and tossed it aside, followed by her silk long underwear top. Then he began kissing the top of her breasts where they swelled over her bra, and her vision lost focus and she sagged in his arms.

He paused and looked up at her. "How far do you want this to go?" he asked. "Because if you want me to leave, I should probably stop now."

She hugged him more tightly. "Don't leave." Smiling, she reached back and unhooked her bra, then sent it sailing across the room. Out of the corner of her eye, she watched as one of the cats—Pumpkin, she thought—pounced on the lacy toy, which only made her grin more broadly.

The look in Ryder's eyes was worth every bit of the cold chill that made her nipples pucker. He started to reach for her, but she intercepted his hands. "Come on," she said, and led the way to the stairs to the loft.

The stairs were steep and narrow, but they negotiated them in record speed. In the loft Ryder had to duck to avoid hitting his head on the ceiling, but once sprawled on the queen-size bed, his height didn't matter so much. They wasted no time divesting each other of their clothes, then, naked, they slid under the covers.

"This is nice and cozy," he said, pulling her close. "I like the flannel sheets."

"Not as sexy as silk, maybe, but a lot warmer," she agreed.

"Trust me, with you in them, flannel is incredibly sexy." He kissed her, long and deep, while his hands explored her body, learning the shape and feel of her while she did the same with him.

Their leisurely movements gradually became more intense and insistent. Ryder leaned back to study her face. "I probably should have asked this before," he said. "But do you have any protection?"

Smiling, she rolled away from him and opened the drawer in the bedside table. She handed him the box of condoms.

"This has never been opened," he said. "Did you buy them just for me?"

"That's right," she said. "I've been planning to seduce you for weeks now." Then she grew more serious. "Actually, Kelly gave them to me in a whole box of things when I moved into this place. She said coming here was my chance to get out of my shell and improve my social life. I told her she was being overly optimistic, but maybe I was wrong."

"She was a good friend," Ryder said. "I wish I'd known her better."

"Ha! If you had known her, you never would have looked twice at me," she said. "Men took one look at her blond hair and knockout figure and they couldn't see anything else."

"I prefer brunettes." He took a condom from the box. "And your figure definitely knocks me out."

She sat up and watched him put on the condom, almost dizzy with desire, and then he started to push her back down on the mattress. She stiffened in spite of herself, then tried to force herself to relax. This was Ryder. He wasn't going to hurt her. Everything was going to be fine.

Ryder stilled, then took his hands from her and sat back. "What's wrong?" he asked.

"Nothing's wrong."

"Something's wrong. I felt it. Tell me what I did so I won't do it again."

She looked away, ashamed, and then angry at the shame. "I just... I don't like someone looming over me. A man. I... I can't relax."

Understanding transformed his face. "I should have realized," he said. "I'm sorry."

"No, it's okay." She sat up, arms hugged across her stomach, fighting back tears. Things had been going so well, and she had to ruin it.

"Hey." He touched her shoulder lightly. "It's okay." He lay down and patted the sheet beside him. "We don't have to rush. We'll take our time and do what feels good for both of us."

Hesitantly, not trusting herself, she lay down beside him again. He stroked her arm, gently, then moved her hand to rest on his chest. "Feel that?" he asked.

She waited, then felt the faint beat of his heart beneath her palm. She looked into his eyes. "Your heartbeat," she said.

He lifted her palm and kissed it, the brush of his tongue sending a jolt of sensation through her. "That's the sound of me, wanting you," he said.

She closed her eyes and he kissed her eyelids, then she was kissing his forehead, his cheek, his ear. They began to move together, desire rebuilding, but somehow deeper, more intense, this time. Facing him, she draped her thigh over his and, eyes open, watching him, she guided him into her. She didn't feel afraid or overwhelmed or anything but aware of her own body and of his—of the tension in his muscles and the heat of her own skin and the wonderful sensation of being filled and fulfilled.

She kept her eyes open as they moved together, and when her climax overtook her, he kissed her, swallowing her cries, and then she saw his face transform with his own moment of release. They held each other, rocking together and murmuring words that weren't really words yet that conveyed a message they both understood.

When at last he eased away from her to dispose of the condom, she let him go reluctantly. When he returned, he pulled her close again, her head cradled on his shoulder, his arm securely around him. The steady beat of his heart lulled her to sleep, the message it sent more powerful than any words.

Chapter 17

Ryder breathed in the perfume of Darcy's hair, and reveled in her softness against him. The comfortable bed in this cozy loft seemed a world apart from the snowy landscape outside where a murderer might lurk. But he could only hide from that world so long, before duty and his conscience drove him to sit up and reach for his clothes.

"You're not leaving, are you?" Darcy shoved up onto one elbow, one bare shoulder exposed, tousled hair falling across her forehead. She looked so alluring, he wondered if he really had the strength to resist the temptation to dive back under the covers with her.

"I'm not leaving," he said, standing and tugging on his jeans. "But I have to call in a report about that snowmobiler." Later he'd have to file a report for his commander, explaining why he had discharged his weapon. "I should have called it in earlier."

"We were both a little distracted," she said, and the heated look that accompanied these words had him aroused and ready all over again.

"I'll, uh, be right back," he said, grabbing a shirt and heading for the stairs.

Three of the four cats met him at the bottom of the steps, studying him with golden eyes, tails twitching. "It's okay," Ryder said, stepping past them. "I'm not the enemy."

He punched in Travis's number and while he waited for the sheriff to answer, he studied the view out the window. The sun was setting, slanting light through the trees and bathing the snow in a rosy glow. It was the kind of scene depicted in paintings and photographs, or on posters with sayings about peace and serenity—not the kind of setting where one expected to encounter danger.

"Ryder? What's up?" Travis's voice betrayed no emotion, only brisk efficiency.

"Darcy and I were skiing over at Silver Pick rec area and a snowmobiler tried to run us down," Ryder said. "I fired off a couple of shots and he fled. I followed, but I lost him on the snowmobile trails on the other side of the road."

"When was this?" Travis asked.

Ryder looked around and spotted the clock on the microwave, which read four thirty. "Around three o'clock," he said.

"And you're just now calling it in?"

"Yes."

Travis paused as if waiting for further explanation, but Ryder didn't intend to offer any. "All right," the sheriff said. "Can you give me a description of the guy, or his snowmobile?"

"It was a Polaris, and one of my shots hit the windscreen and shattered it. The driver was wearing black insulated coveralls and a full helmet, black. That's all I've got."

"Let me make sure I'm clear on this," Travis said. "You and Darcy were on the ski trails, on the east side of the highway, closest to the river, right?"

"Right. We were headed back to the parking lot and were in that open flat, maybe a quarter mile from the parking area. He came straight toward us. We bailed off the trail and tried to make it through the woods, but the snow there is thigh-deep and soft. He missed us his first pass, then turned and came back toward us. That's when I fired on him."

"How many shots?" Travis asked.

"Three. One hit the windscreen and two went wide."

"Hard to hit a moving target like that with a pistol," Travis said. "This doesn't sound like our serial killer. For one thing, running over someone with a snowmobile is a pretty inefficient way to kill someone."

"If he had hit us, chances are he'd have been injured himself," Ryder said. "He probably would have wrecked his machine and could have been thrown off it, too."

"So maybe he wasn't trying to hit you," Travis said. "Maybe he was playing a pretty aggressive game of chicken."

"Maybe," Ryder said. "But he sure looked serious to me."

"Ed Nichols has a Polaris snowmobile," Travis said.

"Gage saw it when he interviewed him about his alibi for Kelly's murder."

Nichols. Ryder hadn't focused much attention on the veterinarian after all his alibis had checked out. Clearly, that had been a mistake. "We need to find out what he was doing this afternoon," Ryder said. "And check the windscreen of his snowmobile. Maybe he was the one who ran Darcy off the road that night, too."

"He has an alibi for that evening," Travis said. "He was cooking for a church spaghetti supper."

"It doesn't seem likely we'd be dealing with two different attackers," Ryder said. What could Darcy have done to make herself such a target?

"Question Darcy again," Travis said. "See if she can come up with anyone who might want to get back at her for something. Maybe she failed to save someone's sick dog, or someone disagreed with her bill—it doesn't take much to set some people off."

"I'll do that," Ryder said. "Let me know if you spot any snowmobiles with the windscreens shot out."

He ended the call and turned to find Darcy, wrapped in a pink fleece robe, standing at the bottom of the steps, watching him. "Do you have to go?" she asked.

"No." He pocketed the phone. "I can stay if you want."

"I'd like that." She moved to him and put her arms around him. He kissed the top of her head, wondering how she'd react if he suggested they go back to bed.

"I'd like to take a shower," she said, pulling away from him. "Unfortunately, my shower isn't big enough for two people."

"You go ahead," he said. "I'll clean up when you're done."

She nodded and headed for the bathroom. Once the water was running, Ryder called into his office. His supervisor was out, but he made his report to the duty officer and promised to follow up with the appropriate paperwork. When Darcy emerged from the shower, pink-cheeked, damp hair curling around her throat, he was studying a photo of her standing with an older couple. "Are these your parents?" he asked.

"My mom and her boyfriend." Darcy came to stand beside him. "That was taken the day I graduated from veterinary school."

"Where does she live?" Ryder asked.

"Denver. Though she isn't home that much. She travels a lot. Right now she's in China, I think. Or India?" She frowned. "It's hard to keep up. We're not close."

"I'm sorry," he said and meant it. Though he didn't see them often, he had always felt embraced by his own family.

"It's okay," she said.

"Where is your father?" he asked.

"I have no idea. He and my mother divorced when I was six months old. I never knew him."

His instinct was to tell her how sad this was, but clearly, she didn't want any sympathy. "What about your family?" she asked.

"My mom and dad are in Cheyenne," he said. "I have a brother in Seattle and a sister in Denver. We're all pretty close."

"That's nice." She patted his arm. "The shower is all yours."

When he emerged from the shower—which, in keeping with everything else in the house, was tiny—

she handed him a glass of wine. "I don't have anything stronger in the house," she said. "I figured we could both use it."

She sat on the sofa, legs curled up beneath her robe, and he moved aside a couple of throw pillows and sat beside her, his arm around her shoulders. She snuggled close. "What a day, huh?" she said.

He stroked her shoulder. "Are you okay?"

"Better." She sipped the wine, then set the glass on the low table in front of them. "I can't promise I won't have nightmares about that snowmobile headed straight for us. I mean, it was scary when that guy ran me off the road, but this was worse. I felt so vulnerable, out there in the open. And he seemed closer, without a vehicle around him. The attack seemed so much more personal." She shuddered, and he set aside his glass to wrap his other arm around her.

They were both silent for a long moment. Ryder wondered if she was crying, but when she looked up at him, her eyes were dry. "Why is someone trying to kill me?" she asked.

"Kill you—or frighten you badly," Ryder said. He leaned forward and handed her her wineglass and picked up his own. "I know I've asked you this before, but can you think of anyone who might want to hurt you? A client or someone who wanted to rent this place and you beat them to it? Anything like that?"

She shook her head. "I've thought and thought and there isn't anyone."

"We checked on Jay Leverett," he said, not missing how she stiffened at the mention of the name.

"Oh?" she asked.

"He was released from prison two months ago. We're still trying to find out where he went after that."

"I'm sure I would recognize him if he was here in Eagle Mountain," she said. She set her now-empty wineglass aside and half turned to face Ryder. "Why would he come after me now—after all this time? It's been six years since he raped me, and I wasn't the first woman he had hurt—or the only one. Mine wasn't even the crime he was sentenced for—he was caught when he broke into a girls' dorm and attacked one of the women there. Why would he come after me?"

"What he did to you before didn't make sense, either," Ryder said. "And this may have nothing to do with him. We just need to be sure."

"Did whoever is after me kill Kelly and Christy and Fiona, too?" she asked.

"We don't know," Ryder said. "Your attacker could be someone different. As far as we know, Kelly and the others were never pursued prior to their deaths."

"How did I get to be so lucky?" She tried to smile but failed, and her voice shook.

He took both her hands in his—they were ice cold. "We can find you a safe place to stay until we've tracked this guy down," he said. "Travis's family probably has room at their ranch—or you could stay with me. My place isn't much, but you'd be safe there."

She nodded. "Maybe it's time for something like that," she said. "I mean, I don't want to be stupid about this—I just hate being chased out of my own home."

"I understand." He admired her independence, but was relieved she was smart enough to accept help. "My place isn't set up for cats, but if you tell me what you need…"

"I think I'll leave them here," she said. "I can come by and check on them every day."

"Do you want me to call Travis and have him ask his parents if you can stay with them, or are you comfortable moving in with me?"

"I'll stay with you." She leaned toward him once more, her hands on his shoulders. "I think I can trust you."

He knew how much those words meant, coming from her. He pulled her close. "We don't have to be in any hurry," he said. "What would you think if I spent the night here tonight?"

A slow smile spread across her lips. "I think that's a very good idea," she whispered and kissed him, a soft, deep kiss that hinted at much more to come.

Half of Darcy's clients canceled their appointments the next day. The highway had opened at last, and everyone was anxious to drive over the pass to do shopping and run errands. A steady stream of delivery trucks flowed into town. The prospect of new supplies, along with the abundant sunshine, had everyone in a jubilant mood.

"If I call the patients who still have appointments today and convince them to come in early, do you think we could close up ahead of schedule?" Stacy asked after yet another client called to move their appointment to another day. "I'd really like to get over to Junction and do some shopping."

"That sounds like a good idea," Darcy said.

"You could come with me, if you like."

"Thanks, but I've got plenty to keep me busy here." She and Ryder had agreed that she would head back to her place after work, pack up whatever she thought she needed for the next few days, make sure the cats were settled, then drive over to his house.

It's only temporary, she reminded herself. *It's not as if we're really moving in together.* After all, they had known each other only a few days, even though it felt as if he already knew her better than anyone ever had. He had learned to read her moods and anticipate her thoughts, attuned to her in a way that was both touching and awe-inspiring.

When they reopened the office after lunch, Darcy was surprised to find Ken waiting outside the clinic. "What can we do for you?" Stacy asked as she waited for Darcy to unlock the door. "Are you overdue for your rabies shot?"

"Very funny." He followed them into the clinic. "I just stopped by to see how you're doing," he said to Darcy.

"I'm fine." Had word somehow gotten out about her encounter with the homicidal snowmobiler the day before?

"Why wouldn't she be fine?" Stacy asked.

Ken glared at her. "Don't you have work to do?"

"It's much more fun to annoy you."

Ken turned his back on her. "The sheriff's department and that highway patrolman haven't done anything to stop this Ice Cold Killer. Everyone is wondering who he's going to kill next."

"The local law enforcement officers are working very hard to try to stop the killer," Darcy said.

"But they aren't getting anywhere, are they? They don't have any suspects, do they?" He stared at her as if expecting an answer.

"I wouldn't know," she said.

"I thought you might, since you and that highway patrolman are so cozy."

He looked as if he expected her to confirm or deny this. She did neither. She certainly wasn't going to tell Ken she was moving in with Ryder. She had decided not to share their plans with anyone. Not because she was ashamed, but because she and Ryder had agreed the fewer people who knew where she was, the safer she would be.

She took her white coat from its peg and put it on. "Thanks for stopping by," she said. "I have to get ready to see my afternoon patients."

"I know the female teachers at my school are terrified," he continued. "The male teachers have agreed to walk them to their cars, kind of like bodyguards."

"That's very thoughtful of you," Darcy said.

"You should do something like that here," he said.

"I'm being careful."

"Now that the highway is open, maybe the killer will take the opportunity to get out of here," Stacy said. "Maybe he's already gone."

"I guess that would be good," Ken said.

"I'd rather see him caught and stopped," Darcy said. "I hate to think of him moving on to somewhere else to kill more women."

"Now that the road is open, maybe they'll get some experts in who can track him down," Ken said.

Darcy resisted the impulse to defend Ryder. She sensed Ken was only trying to bait her, and she wasn't going to waste energy sparring with him.

He shifted his weight to his other hip, apparently prepared to stay until she ordered him away. "I guess now that the road is open, Kelly's parents will be coming to clear her things out of the duplex," he said.

"I guess so." She frowned, thinking of all the clinic supplies in the garage. "I'll need to clear out the garage," she said. "And find some place to store all that stuff here."

"Why don't you just move in, instead?" Ken asked. "My landlord would be happy to find a renter so easily. You'd be closer to work and town and you could still use the garage for storage."

"I like the place where I am now," she said.

"Sure. But it's not safe for you out there. You're way too vulnerable without other people around. If you lived in town, I'd be right next door, and there are other neighbors nearby."

She couldn't tell him that having him right on the other side of her living room wall wasn't something she looked forward to. "I'll be fine. And now I really do need to get ready for my patients." Not waiting for an answer, she turned and walked into the back room, closing the door from the waiting room firmly behind her.

A few moments later Stacy joined her in the section of the big back room they used as their in-house laboratory, where Darcy was unpacking a new supply of blood collection tubes. "Poor Ken," Stacy said. "He's still crazy about you. He can't get over losing you."

"He never had me to lose," Darcy said. "We only went out three times." And she had only agreed to the third date so that she could tell him to his face that she didn't have romantic feelings for him and didn't believe she ever would. She had tried to let him down gently, but she had also been clear that she didn't want to date him again.

"Still, I feel sorry for him," Stacy said. "He's one of these guys who tries too hard."

"Then you date him."

"I'm married, remember?" She leaned back against the lab table. "I didn't say I thought you ought to go out with him. Ryder is a much better guy for you." She grinned. "How did your date go yesterday?"

"It went...well."

"Uh-oh. I distinctly heard a 'but' in there. What happened?"

Darcy pushed aside the half-empty box of tubes. "You can't tell anyone, okay?"

"Cross my heart." She made an X across her chest with her forefinger.

"We had a great time," Darcy said. "It was a beautiful day and we skied up to the warming hut at the top of the hill and had lunch."

Stacy looked disappointed. "That's not a 'but.'"

"I'm getting to the bad part." She took a deep breath. Better to just come out with it. "On the way back down, a guy on a snowmobile tried to run us over."

"I thought snowmobiles weren't allowed on the ski trails," Stacy said.

"They're not. But he deliberately tried to kill us. When he missed the first time, he turned around and headed for us again."

"Sheesh, woman! What is with you and guys trying to run you down?" She touched Darcy's arm. "Sorry. I wasn't trying to be insensitive. Are you okay?"

Darcy nodded. "I was terrified at the time. But

Ryder pulled his gun and shot at the guy and he raced off. Ryder tried to follow, but he got away."

"Do you have any idea who it was?"

"No. He was wearing a full helmet with a visor. There was no way to know."

The bells on the front door announced the arrival of their first afternoon patient. A dog's insistent bark confirmed this. "That will be Judy Ericson and Tippy," Stacy said. She squeezed Darcy's arm. "I'm so glad you're okay. And I hope they find out who it was."

"One of Ryder's bullets hit the windshield of the snowmobile," Darcy said. "He's hoping that will help him find the guy."

"Ryder should talk to Bud O'Brien—he rents snowmobiles out of his garage," Stacy said. "If this maniac was a tourist who's stuck here, he might not have his own snowmobile. He'd have to rent one."

"That's a great idea. I'll pass it on."

Stacy headed to the door, but stopped before she opened it and turned to face Darcy again. "I think I agree with Ken on this one—you shouldn't be out at your place by yourself. You're welcome to stay with me and Bill."

"I'll be fine," Darcy said. "I promise."

Stacy nodded. "At least you have one thing going for you," she said.

"What's that?"

"You've got Ryder on your side. That's worth a lot."

Chapter 18

"Now that the highway is open, the Colorado Bureau of Investigation is sending in its own team to investigate the murders," Ryder told Travis when they met at the sheriff's department Monday morning.

"So I hear," Travis said. "Good luck to them. So far we don't have a lot to go on."

"When I spoke with my boss this morning, he told me to deliver the physical evidence to the state lab in Junction as soon as possible," Ryder said. "I had to tell him we didn't have any physical evidence—no blood, no hair or fibers, no prints."

"I checked with Ed Nichols about his whereabouts yesterday afternoon," Travis said. "He says he was home with his wife, watching television."

"That's a hard alibi to disprove if his wife backs him up," Ryder said. "What about the snowmobile?"

"It wasn't there," Travis said. "He said it's at O'Brien's Garage, waiting on a part."

"A new windscreen?"

"I don't know. O'Brien's was closed when I went by there, and the phone goes to an answering machine. Bud didn't answer his home phone, either."

"I'll go by his house," Ryder said. "He'll want as much as anyone to get to the bottom of this. But first, I want to interview Tim and Alex again. I want to see what they were up to yesterday afternoon."

"There was only one man on that snowmobile," Travis said.

"Maybe it was one of them—maybe it wasn't," Ryder said.

"The problem I have is with motive," Travis said. "Why go after Darcy?"

Gage joined them. "I heard about what happened yesterday," Gage said. "Is Darcy okay?"

"She's holding up," Ryder said. He turned to Travis once more. "She tried again to think of someone who might have a grudge against her and came up with nothing." He hesitated. He wanted to honor the trust Darcy had placed in him by revealing her past, but he couldn't keep information pertaining to the case from Travis. "She does have an ex-boyfriend who went to jail after kidnapping and raping her," he said. "It happened six years ago, and he was released from prison two months ago, after serving time for another crime. I received a report about him yesterday—no current address. But Darcy is sure she hasn't seen him here in town."

"He could have avoided her," Travis said. "He wouldn't want her to know he was behind the attacks."

"Right. His name is Jay Leverett," Ryder said. "I gave his description to the other officers, and it's on your desk."

"We'll be on the lookout for him," Travis said. He turned to Gage. "I need you to contact Bud O'Brien," he said. "Find out why Ed Nichols's snowmobile is at his garage, how long it's been there and if it has a damaged windscreen."

"Will do," Gage said.

Travis turned back to Ryder. "I'll go with you to interview Tim and Alex."

"We should try to get Darcy into a safe house," Travis said when he and Ryder were in Travis's cruiser. "I can make some calls…"

"She'll never go for that," Ryder said. "And she has a business to run here in town."

"I can try to run extra patrols out her way, but I don't really have the personnel," Travis said.

"It's okay. I talked her into moving in with me."

Travis glanced at him, one eyebrow quirked, but all he said was, "All right, then."

No vehicles were parked in the driveway at the cabin where Alex and Tim were staying, and no one answered Travis's knock. "Maybe they left town already," Ryder said. He scanned the snow-covered yard. A black plastic trash can on rollers sat against the house, next to a half cord of firewood. No snowmobile.

Travis walked along the narrow front porch and peered into a window. "If they did, they left behind most of their stuff," he said.

Ryder cupped his hands against the windowpane and studied the clothing, shoes, beer cans, half-empty bags of chips and video game controllers scattered across the sofa and coffee table. "Yeah, it doesn't look like they went back to Denver yet," he agreed.

The two men returned to Travis's cruiser. "What now?" Ryder asked.

"I need to run up to my folks' ranch," Travis said. "I've got a couple of guests that are supposed to arrive now that the road is open. One of them is the caterer and I want to make sure she has everything she needs."

"Rainey and Doug Whittington aren't doing the food for the wedding?"

"They wanted to, but this woman is a friend of Lacy's. It was important to her to have her do the wedding and I wasn't going to argue. And Rainey is always complaining about how much work all the wedding guests are for her, so she should appreciate the help."

Rainey struck Ryder as the type who wouldn't want to share her kitchen with anyone, but he kept that opinion to himself. "Speaking of the Whittingtons, does Doug have a snowmobile?" he asked.

"He doesn't own one," Travis said. "But he certainly has access to several. I'll check on that while I'm up there."

Ryder glanced back toward the house. "I'll swing by here later and try to catch these two — try to find out what their plans are." He started to mention the lack of a snowmobile but was interrupted by the insistent beeping from his shoulder-mounted radio. "Report to Dixon Pass for one-vehicle accident. Vehicle is blocking the road."

"Guess that means the pass is closed again," Travis said. "It's going to be a long winter."

Ryder nodded. "It's already too long for me."

* * *

Darcy waved goodbye to Stacy and headed for the Green Monster. As long as she still had the truck, she might as well move the boxes from Kelly's garage to the office. She told herself she was being practical, tackling the job now, and tried to ignore the voice in the back of her head that said she was only delaying taking her things to Ryder's house.

Not that she wasn't looking forward to spending more time with him—she definitely was. And she knew she would be much safer with what amounted to her own personal bodyguard. But moving in with a man, even temporarily, was a big step. One she wasn't sure she was ready to take. She certainly wouldn't be doing this now when they had known each other so little time, if circumstances—or rather, a deranged man who was possibly a killer—hadn't forced her hand.

She pulled into the driveway of the duplex, relieved to see no sign of Ken or his truck. The house looked even more neglected when she stepped inside, the air stale, the furniture lightly covered with dust. She made her way to the garage and opened the automatic door from the inside, then set about transferring boxes to the back of the truck. Fortunately, none of the cartons was particularly heavy, though by the time she had filled the truck bed, she felt as if she had had a workout. She slammed the tailgate shut and surveyed the full bed. She had managed to get everything in.

Something cold kissed her cheek and she looked up into a flurry of gently falling white flakes. More snow felt like an insult at this point, but she reminded herself this was what winter in the mountains was all about. She needed to get used to it.

She went back inside, stopped just inside the doorw time she was ever in this house many memories. She and Kelly had evenings here, drinking wine and eating watching television or planning the next step veterinary practice. She could almost see her in seated in the corner of the sofa, a bowl of popcorn her lap, her hair pulled up in a messy ponytail, head thrown back, laughing. The memory made her smile, even as unshed tears pinched at her throat.

From the living room she walked down a short hall-way to the master bedroom, the bed unmade as it al-most always was, clothes thrown over a chair, shoes discarded just inside the doorway. She bent and picked up a red high heel. Kelly loved shoes, and was always encouraging Darcy to go for prettier, sexier footwear. She understood Darcy had no desire to call attention to herself with provocative clothing, but she tried to do whatever she could to help her friend get over the fear behind those inhibitions.

The two had met only a few months after Darcy's rape. Kelly had come in late to a class and taken the vacant seat next to Darcy. In the next five minutes she had borrowed a pen, some notepaper, shared half a car-rot cake muffin and invited Darcy to have lunch with her. Swept along in what she later thought of as Hur-ricane Kelly, Darcy had found herself befriended by this vibrant, fearless woman. Though their personali-ties were so different, they bonded quickly. When Kelly learned about Darcy's traumatic experience, she had become her biggest cheerleader and defender.

When she had first visited Darcy's apartment and

...earned that
...ough it made
...y to move in
...he confidence
...found a thera-
...ictims, and had
...intment.

...g and protective,
...ome dependent on
...ed Darcy to try new
...her boundaries. She

...to shut the garage door,
...ay. This might be the last
...a place that held so
...d spent countless
...pizza, binge-
...s for the
...iend,

453

could be ov... ...o friends had had their
share of disagreemen... ...e end Kelly had saved
her. It grieved Darcy beyond words that she hadn't been
able to save her friend.

She shook her head, set the shoe on the dresser and
left the room. Time to get on with it. As she passed
through the kitchen on her way to the garage, she decided to check Kelly's pantry for more cat food. No
sense letting it go to waste. She found an unopened bag
of dry food, and half a dozen cans, as well as a brand-
new catnip mouse. The cats would appreciate a new
toy, and it would help assuage her guilt at abandoning
them while she stayed with Ryder.

She was searching for a bag to put the food in, hum-
ming to herself, when pain jolted her. The cat food cans
tumbled from her arms and rolled across the kitchen
floor as blackness overtook her.

Chapter 19

The eighteen-wheeler had slid sideways across the highway near the top of Dixon Pass, until the back wheels of the trailer slipped off the edge, while the rest of the truck sprawled across both lanes. The driver had somehow managed to stop, and gravity and one large boulder had prevented the rig from sliding farther. The road was at its narrowest here, with almost no shoulders and no guardrails. The driver, who had bailed out of the cab, now stood in the shelter of a rock overhang, staring through a curtain of falling snow, hands shoved in the pockets of his leather coat, while they waited for a wrecker to come and winch the rig all the way back onto the road.

"The wrecker should be here in about ten minutes," Ryder told the driver, ending the call from his dispatcher. "What are you hauling?"

"Insulation." He wiped his hand across his face.

"Yesterday I had a load of bottled water. All those heavy bottles probably would have shifted and taken me on over the side." His hand shook as he returned it to his pocket.

"You got off lucky," Ryder said.

"Yeah. I guess so."

Ryder moved away and, shoulders hunched against the falling snow, hit the button to call Darcy. He needed to let her know he was going to be late. She should let herself into the house with the key he had given her and make herself at home. Even though they had both agreed this stay would only be temporary, he wanted her to feel she could treat his place as her own. He let the call ring, then frowned as it went to voice mail. Maybe she was with a late patient and couldn't be interrupted. He left a message and stowed the phone again as a man in a puffy red coat and a fur hat strode toward him through the falling flakes.

"How much longer is the road going to be closed?" the man asked in the tone of someone who is much too busy to be stalled by petty annoyances.

"Another hour at least," Ryder said. "Maybe more. It depends on how long it takes to move the truck."

"You people need to do a better job of keeping the highway open," the man said. "Isn't that what we're paying you for?"

"I'm charged with keeping the public safe," Ryder said.

"They should keep these big rigs off the road when the weather is like this," the man said. "They're always causing trouble."

Ryder could have pointed out that passenger cars had more accidents than trucks, but decided not to waste his breath. "A wrecker is on the way to deal with this truck," he said. "If you don't want to wait, you can turn around."

"I can't turn around," he said. "I have business in Eagle Mountain."

"Then you'll need to go back to your vehicle and wait."

The man wanted to argue, Ryder could tell, but a stern look from Ryder suppressed the urge. He turned and stalked back toward his SUV. Ryder didn't even give in to the urge to laugh when he slipped on the icy pavement and almost fell.

Ryder's phone rang and he took the call from Travis. "I checked at the ranch and none of our snow machines are damaged," Travis said. "And Rainey swears Doug was helping her in the kitchen all yesterday afternoon. I haven't heard yet from Gage about Ed's snowmobile."

"Thanks for checking," Ryder said. "Did your caterer make it?"

"She called Lacy a little while ago and told her she's stuck in traffic. Apparently, a wreck has the highway closed again."

"Yeah. We're going to get it cleared away in an hour or two." He looked up at the gently falling snow. "I'm hoping the highway department can keep it open. Looks like we've got more snow."

"I'll try to get by Alex and Tim's place tomorrow to talk to them," Travis said.

"I'll do it on my way home this afternoon," Ryder said. "It's on my way." He really wanted to talk to those two before they slipped out of town.

Two hours later the wrecker had winched the eighteen-wheeler to safety. The driver, and all the cars that had piled up behind him, were safely on their way, and a Colorado Department of Transportation plow trailed along behind them, pushing aside the six inches of snow that had accumulated on the roadway. As long as the plows kept running and no avalanche chutes filled and dumped their loads on the highway, things would flow smoothly.

Ryder turned traffic patrol over to a fellow officer and headed back into Eagle Mountain. He tried Darcy's phone again—still no answer. Maybe she'd forgotten to charge it, or was simply too busy to answer it, he told himself. He resisted the urge to drive straight to his house, hoping to find her there, and stuck with his plan of interviewing Tim and Alex.

But first, he had to stop for gas. He was fueling the Tahoe when a red Jeep pulled in alongside him. "Hello, Ryder," Stacy said.

"Hi, Stacy," he said. "You're getting off work a little late, aren't you?"

"Oh, I've been off hours," she said, getting out of her car and walking around to the pump. "We closed up early and I went into Junction to do some shopping. I made it back just before the road closed again, but then I had more errands to run here in town." She indicated the back of the Jeep, which was piled high with bags and boxes. "It's been a while."

If she had closed the clinic early, then Darcy probably hadn't been with a patient when he called earlier. So why wasn't she answering her phone? "Do you know where Darcy headed after you closed?" he asked.

"She said she had things to do," Stacy said.

"Did she say what?"

"Easy there, officer. Is something wrong?"

He reined in his anxiety. "I've tried to call her a couple of times and she isn't answering."

Stacy frowned. "That isn't like her. She said something earlier about needing to get all the clinic supplies out of Kelly's duplex. I guess now that the highway is open again, Kelly's parents want to come and clean it out. Maybe she decided to take care of that."

Maybe so. Though that still didn't explain why she hadn't answered his calls.

He headed for Tim's aunt's cabin next, determined to get that interview out of the way. The gray Toyota with the dent in the front quarter-panel sat parked in the driveway of the cabin, a frosting of snow obscuring the windows. Ryder parked his Tahoe behind the Toyota and made his way up the unshoveled walk to the vehicle. A deep indentation ran the length of the driver's side front quarter-panel, the metal gouged as if by a sharp object.

Ryder straightened and made his way to the front door. Alex answered his knock, dressed in black long underwear pants and top. "Hey," he said. "What you need?"

"Can I come in?" Ryder asked. "I need to ask a few questions."

Alex shrugged. "I guess so." He held the door open.

Tim was sprawled across the sofa, wearing green-and black-check flannel pants and a Colorado State University sweatshirt, a video game controller in his hands. He sat up and frowned at Ryder. "What do you want?"

"The highway is open," Ryder said, stepping around a pile of climbing gear—ropes and packs and shoes.

"I figured the two of you would be headed back to Denver."

"We took advantage of the great weather to go climbing." Alex sat on the end of the sofa and picked up a beer from the coffee table. "We don't have to be back in class until the end of the month, anyway."

"What do you care?" Tim asked, his attention on the television screen, which was displaying a video game that seemed to revolve around road racing.

"What did the two of you do Sunday?" Ryder asked.

"What did we do Sunday?" Tim asked Alex.

"We went climbing." Alex sipped the beer.

"Where did you go?" Ryder asked.

"Those cliffs over behind the park," Alex said. "And before you ask if anyone saw us, yeah, they did. Two women. We went out with them that night."

"I'll need their names and contact information," Ryder said.

"Why?" Tim asked. "Did another woman get iced?" He laughed, as if amused by his joke.

"Have you visited Silver Pick Recreation Area while you've been in town?" Ryder asked.

"We checked it out," Alex said. "We didn't see any good climbing."

"Good snowmobile trails," Ryder said.

"We talked about renting a couple of machines," Tim said. "Too expensive. Climbing's free."

"Since when are you concerned about us having a good time?" Alex asked.

"We're looking for a snowmobiler who threatened a couple of people out at Silver Pick Sunday afternoon. He tried to run them down with his snowmobile."

"It wasn't us," Alex said.

"Maybe it was the same idiot who smashed my truck," Tim said.

"Yeah," Alex said. "What are you doing about trying to find that guy?"

"I don't think there's a guy to find," Ryder said.

"What?" Tim sat up straight. "Are you calling us liars?"

"I took another look at that dent on your truck," Ryder said. "It's too low to the ground to have been made by another car. And too sharp."

"It is not," Tim said.

"The more I think about it, the more it looks like it was made by those big chunks of granite that edge the parking lot near the ice climbing area out on County Road Fourteen," Ryder said. "It's easy enough to do—don't pay attention to what you're doing and you can run into one of them, scrape the heck out of your car."

"You can't prove it," Tim said.

"I'll bet if I went out there, I'd find paint from your truck on one of the rocks," Ryder said.

Tim and Alex exchanged looks. "Why would we bother making up a story and getting the police involved if it wasn't true?" Alex asked.

"If someone else caused the damage to your car, maybe you thought you could get your insurance to pay for it under your uninsured motorist coverage," Ryder said. "It works like that in other states—for instance, in Texas, where you said you were from. But it doesn't work that way in Colorado. In Colorado you have to have collision coverage in order for the insurance to pay."

"No way!" Tim looked at Alex. "You told me we

could get the insurance company to pay. Now what am I going to do?"

Alex ignored his friend. He looked at Ryder. "If you think you can prove something, have at it. Otherwise, why don't you leave us alone?"

"I'll leave for now," Ryder said. "But you'll be hearing from me again." Tomorrow he would go to the parking lot and try to find the rock they had hit. Filing a false report to a peace officer was at best a misdemeanor, but the charge would be a hassle for the two young men, and having to deal with it might teach them a lesson.

From the cabin to the place Ryder rented was only a short drive. His heart sank when he saw that the driveway was empty. He hurried into the house, hoping to see some sign that Darcy had been there, but everything was just as he had left it. No suitcases or bags or any of Darcy's belongings. He pulled out his phone and dialed her number again. Still no answer. What was going on?

Darcy woke to familiar surroundings, sure she was in her own bed, but with the terrible knowledge that something was very wrong. When she tried to sit up, she discovered that her hands were tied to the headboard, and her ankles were bound together. She began to shake with terror, almost overwhelmed with the memory of another time when she had been tied to a bed, unable to escape her tormentor.

"Don't struggle now. You don't want to hurt yourself." Ken leaned over her, his smile looking to her eyes like a horrible grimace.

"What are you doing?" she asked. The memory of

being in Kelly's kitchen flooded back. She had been looking at cat food and the next thing she knew, she woke up here. "Did you hit me on the head?"

"It was for your own good," Ken said. "If you had listened to me when I offered to let you move in with me, it wouldn't have been necessary."

"Let me go!" She struggled against the ropes that held her. The bed shook and creaked with her efforts, but she remained trapped.

"No, I can't do that," Ken said. "If I do that, you'll only call the sheriff, or that state trooper, Ryder. Then I'd have to leave and you'd be here all alone and unprotected."

"I don't need protection," she said.

"But you do. There's a serial killer in town who's murdering young women just like you. You don't want to be his next victim, do you?"

She stared at him, searching for signs that he had lost his mind. He looked perfectly ordinary and sane. Except every word he uttered chilled her to the core.

He sat on the side of the bed, the mattress dipping toward her. "What are you doing?" she asked, trying to inch away from him.

He put his hand on her leg. "I'm going to protect you."

"Did you kill Kelly and those other women?" she asked. If he was the murderer, was confronting him this way a mistake? But she had to know.

His hand on her leg tightened. "Is that what you think of me?" he asked. "That I'm a killer? A man who hates women?" He slid his hand up her leg. "I love women. I love you. I've loved you since the first time I saw you with Kelly. I kept waiting for you to see it, but you couldn't. Or you wouldn't." His fingers closed around her thigh, digging deep.

"Stop!" She tried to squirm out of his grasp. "You're hurting me."

"I decided I had to do something to wake you up," he said, continuing to massage her thigh painfully. "To make you see how much I love you."

"If you loved me, you wouldn't frighten me this way," she said. "You wouldn't hurt me."

"I won't hurt you." He leaned over her, his voice coaxing. "In fact, I'm going to show you how gentle I can be." He moved his hand to the waistband of her slacks.

She closed her eyes and swallowed down a scream. There was no one to hear her, and if she screamed, she might give in to the panic that clawed at her. Hysterics wouldn't help her. She had to hang on. She had survived before, and she would survive again.

How long before Ryder came looking for her? He would be expecting her at his house, but what if he had to work late? She had no idea what time it was, though the window at the end of the loft showed only blackness. If could be seven o'clock or it could be midnight—she couldn't tell.

But no matter the hour, she had to find a way out of this situation. So far Ken hadn't threatened her with a gun. As far as she knew, he didn't own one. He was counting on his size and strength to overpower her, and so far it was working for him, but she had to find some advantage and figure out a way to use it against him.

"You need to untie me," she said, surprised at how calm she sounded. "I can't relax and…and I can't focus on you if I'm tied up."

"You don't like being tied up?" He looked genuinely puzzled. "I thought it would be fun." He grinned. "A little kinky."

She swallowed nausea. "I just… I want to put my arms around you," she said.

He sat back, searching her face. "You won't try to fight me?"

"Of course not," she lied.

"I'll untie your hands," he said and leaned forward to do so. "But I'll leave your feet the way they are. I don't want you running away."

She forced herself to remain still while he fumbled with the knots at her wrists. "Maybe you need a knife," she said.

"Good idea." He stood, then winked at her. "Don't go away. I'll be right back."

"I'll be waiting." Saying the words made her feel sick to her stomach. But she would be waiting when he returned with the knife—then she would do everything to get her hands on that blade. He thought she was passive, but he would learn she was a fighter.

Chapter 20

The parking lot of the veterinary clinic was empty, the only tracks in the smooth coating of snow the fresh ones made by Ryder's Tahoe. He tried the door, anyway, and peered through the glass. A single light behind the front desk illuminated the empty counter. The only sound was the crunch of his own boots on the snow.

He tried Darcy's phone again, and this time the call went straight to voice mail. He hung up without leaving a message, stomach churning. Where was she?

He headed for her house, but since Kelly's duplex was on the way, decided to swing by there first. Stacy had mentioned that Darcy had planned to pick up some supplies from there. Maybe she had gotten distracted, or the task took more time than he would have thought. But even as he thought these things, instinct told him something was wrong.

The driveway to the duplex was vacant, and no lights shone from either half. The snow was falling harder now, filling in Ryder's tracks on the walkway to the door within minutes of his passing. He knocked on Kelly's door, then tried the knob. It was locked. With a growing sense of urgency, he moved to Ken's door and pounded on it. "Ken, it's Ryder! I need to talk to you."

He turned and headed back across the porch and up the walk toward his Tahoe. But a dark bulk along the side of the duplex caught his eye. He unclipped the flashlight from his utility belt and shone it over a tarped snowmobile. Heart pounding, he stepped through the deepening snow to the snowmobile and unhooked the bungie cord that held the tarp in place.

His flashlight illuminated first the Polaris emblem. Then he arced the beam upward to the spiderweb of cracks in the windscreen that spread out from the neat, round bullet hole.

Ken cut the plastic ties that had bound Darcy's wrists and laid the knife on the floor beside the bed. She stretched her arms out in front of her, wincing at the pain, and struggled to sit up. Ken pushed her back onto the bed with one hand, reaching for the fly of his jeans with the other.

"Wait," she cried, squirming into a sitting position. She forced a smile to her trembling lips. "Let's talk a little bit first. You know—get in the mood."

He frowned but moved his hand away from his fly. "What do you want to talk about?"

"Were you the one on the snowmobile on the ski trail at Silver Pick Sunday afternoon?"

"What about it?"

"I just wondered." She swallowed, trying to force some saliva from her dry mouth. "I figure you were trying to show me how dangerous it was," she said. "How much I need to depend on you to protect me."

His expression lightened. "That's it." He sat beside her and took her hand in his. "I didn't want to frighten you, but I had to make you see the danger you were in. I did it to protect you."

"And were you the one who ran me off Silverthorne Road?" she asked. "You pretended to be that woman with the hurt mastiff?"

He laughed. "That was pretty clever, wasn't it?" He leaned closer. "If only you weren't so stubborn. You would have saved us all so much trouble if you had accepted my help from the first."

She pushed him gently away, trying hard to hide her revulsion and fear. "Did you try to break in to this place, the night Kelly was killed?"

He frowned. "No. I wouldn't do something like that."

Hitting her over the head and kidnapping her, not to mention threatening her with both a truck and a snowmobile, apparently weren't as bad as jimmying a lock? But she believed him when he said he hadn't tried to break in that night. But was he the killer?

Ken forced his lips onto hers and slid his hands under her sweater. Her stomach churned and she wondered if it was possible to vomit from fear. Would that be enough to scare him off?

"I'm ready now." He stood and, so quickly she hardly registered what was happening, shoved his jeans down. She reacted instinctively, drawing up her legs, ankles still bound together, and shoving hard against his chest. He stumbled back and she dove for the floor, grabbing for the knife.

He straddled her, hands around her throat, choking her, as she felt blindly for the knife, which had slid under the bed. Her fingers closed around the handle, as he shoved his knee into her back, forcing her flat onto the floor. And all the while his hands continued to squeeze until her vision fogged and she felt herself slipping away.

A mighty crash shook the whole house, and the pressure on her throat lessened. "What the—"

"Darcy!" Ryder's shout was followed by pounding footsteps as he vaulted up the stairs.

His weight still grinding her into the floor, Ken swiveled to face the entrance to the loft. Darcy tightened her grip on the knife.

"Darcy!" Ryder shouted again.

"I'm here," she said, her voice weak, but she thought he heard.

"Get off her!" he roared.

"You can't have her." Ken stood, bringing her with him, and clasping her in front of him like a shield. She held the knife by her side, half-hidden in the folds of her trousers, and prayed he was too focused on Ryder to notice.

Less than six feet away, Ryder stood at the top of the stairs, both hands steadying his pistol in his hands. His eyes met Darcy's, and there was no mistaking the fear that flashed through them. He lowered the gun. "Don't do anything stupid," he said.

"You're the one who's stupid." Ken moved sideways, away from the bed. "Thinking you could have her. She belongs with me."

"I don't want to be with you!" She squirmed, but he held her so tightly her ribs ached.

"Get out of the way," Ken told Ryder. "Let us pass. And if you try anything, I'll kill her."

Why did he think *he* got to determine who she wanted to be with and what happened to her? Rage at the idea overwhelmed her. In one swift movement, she brought the knife up and plunged it into his thigh. It sank to the hilt, blood gushing. Ken screamed and released her.

Ryder grabbed her hand and thrust her away from the other man. She slid to the floor as Ryder shoved Ken against the wall, the gun held to his head. "Don't move," Ryder growled. "Don't even breathe hard."

"I'm bleeding!" Ken cried. "Do something."

"Sit down," Ryder ordered, and Ken slid to the floor.

Ryder pulled cuffs from his belt and cuffed Ken's hands behind him, then grabbed a pillow from the bed and held it over the bleeding. He looked over at Darcy. "Are you okay?"

She nodded. She felt sick and shaky, but she was alive. She had fought back. She would be okay—eventually.

He slipped a multi-tool from his belt and slid it across the floor to her. "Can you cut the ties on your ankles?"

Though her hands were still unsteady, she managed to sever the ties and stand. "I should call 911," she said.

"Do that." He saw her hesitation and softened his voice. "I'll be okay," he said.

She went downstairs and found her phone and made the call, then collapsed on the sofa and began to sob. She didn't know why she was crying, exactly, except that it had all been so horrible, and she was so relieved it was over.

She didn't know how long it was before Ryder came to her. He wrapped her in a blanket, then drew her into his arms and held her tightly. She clung to him, sobbing. "I was s-so scared," she said through her tears.

"You were great," he said, gently kissing the side of her face. "It's over now. You're safe."

Some time after that the ambulance came, along with Travis and Gage Walker. A paramedic checked out Darcy and gave her a sedative, while two others carried a howling and complaining Ken down the narrow stairs and out to the ambulance. "What will happen to him?" Darcy asked, the medication having soothed the hard, metallic edge of fear.

"He's under arrest," Travis said. "For kidnapping and menacing and probably a half a dozen other charges we haven't sorted out yet. He'll be placed under a guard at the clinic here and when the road opens again we'll transport him to jail to await his trial."

"The road's closed again?" Ryder asked.

Travis nodded. "I'm afraid so."

"I found a snowmobile at Ken's duplex, with the windscreen shot out," Ryder said.

"He admitted he tried to run us down at Silver Pick," Darcy said. "And he was the one who pretended to be an old woman with a mastiff, who ran me off Silverthorne Road that night." She studied the faces of all three lawmen, trying to figure out what they were thinking. "I don't think he killed Kelly or the others," she said. "Maybe I'm wrong, but…"

"I don't think he killed them, either," Ryder said.

"He was teaching a class full of students when Kelly was killed."

"He was supposedly at a basketball game when that truck ran Darcy off the road," Gage said.

"That one was easy enough to fake," Ryder said. "He went to the basketball game, made sure he saw and talked to a lot of people, then slipped out. People would remember he was there, but they wouldn't necessarily remember the exact time they saw him. The classroom is tougher to fake. Everyone we talked to said he was there the whole time."

"So the killer is still out there?" Darcy asked.

"Maybe," Travis said. "Or maybe he took advantage of the break in the weather and left town."

"I'm still hoping Pi and his friends saw something that will help us," Ryder said.

"So far they're still not talking," Travis said. "But I've contacted all their parents and they all agreed this business of daring each other to do risky things has to stop. They've agreed that the boys should spend their spare time for the next few weeks doing community service."

"What kind of service?" Darcy asked.

"They can start by shoveling snow. We have a lot of it to move at the school and at the homes of elderly residents. That should keep them out of trouble."

"So what do you do about the killer?" Darcy asked.

Ryder's arm around her tightened. "We wait."

Darcy was surprised to learn it was only a little after seven o'clock when Ryder had arrived at her house. By nine, the two of them had moved her belongings—including all four cats—into the house he rented on the other side of town. She had located the cats hidden in various places around the house—behind books on a shelf, under a sofa cushion, in a cubby in the kitchen. She dosed them all with an herbal sedative and Ryder helped her stow them in their carriers and gather their food, treats, toys and litter boxes. He didn't ask why she had changed her mind about leaving the cats at the house, merely helped her move them. She hoped it was because he understood she needed them with her. They were part of her home—and the tiny house would never feel like home again.

When they had unloaded the cats and her belongings at Ryder's place, he made macaroni and cheese and served it to her with hot tea spiked with rum. "This tastes better than anything I've ever eaten," she said, trying hard not to inhale the bowl full of orange noodles that had to be the ultimate comfort food.

"I'm not a gourmet cook, but you won't starve while you're here," he said.

She wouldn't have to be afraid while she was here, either, she thought.

After supper he persuaded her to leave the dishes until the next day, and he built a fire in the fireplace. Then they settled on the sofa and he wrapped a knitted throw around them both. "Do you want to talk about what happened?" he asked, his voice quiet.

"The sheriff said I'll need to give a statement to him tomorrow."

"You can wait until then if you like," he said. "We can try to find a victim's advocate for you to talk to, too. You don't have to tell me anything."

"I want to tell you." It was true. She laced her fingers through his. "Talking can help. I learned that before—

after Jay kidnapped and raped me." It had taken her a long time—years, really—before she had been able to name the crimes done against her so boldly. But naming them was a form of taking control, she had learned.

Ryder settled her more firmly against him. "All right," he said. "I'm listening."

So she told him everything—from the moment in the kitchen through everything that had happened until his arrival at her house. Reciting the facts, along with admitting her terror in the moment, made her feel stronger. "As bad as it was, it could have been so much worse," she said. "That's one reason I don't think Ken is the one who killed Kelly and the others. He's a terrible man, but I don't think he's a murderer."

"No, I don't think so," Ryder agreed. "But I'm glad he's behind bars now—or will be, as soon as his doctors okay his release. And I'm not sure I can put into words how relieved I am that you're safe."

She turned into his arms and kissed him, a kiss that banished the chill from the last cold places within her. "Ken was right about one thing," she said.

"What is that?"

"I was wrong to insist on continuing to stay out at that isolated house by myself. Not that I would have ever accepted his offer to stay with him, but I could have gone to Stacy's."

"I'm glad you're here right now," he said.

"I'm going to stay as long as you'll have me," she said.

"How about forever?"

She stared at him, her heart having climbed somewhere into her throat. "I love you," he said. "And I want to keep on loving you. But I don't want to pressure you or control you or ever have you think I'm like Ken or Jay or anyone else who would try to hurt you."

She put her fingers over his lips. "Shhh. I know the difference between you and those others." She moved her hand and kissed the place where her fingers had been. "I love you, too," she said. "And I want to be with you." She kissed him again.

"To forever," he said and kissed her, softly and surely.

"Forever," she echoed. Saying the word was like uttering a magical incantation that opened the last lock on her heart. She felt lighter and freer—and more safe and secure—than she ever had.

* * * * *

SPECIAL EXCERPT FROM

⊕ HARLEQUIN

INTRIGUE

*Thanks to a car accident, Melanie Blankenship has
returned to Kelby Creek with no memory of why she'd go
back to the place that turned against her. And when she's
reunited with Sheriff Sterling Costner, who vows to help
her uncover the truth, she's happy to have him by her side
for protection. And is more than surprised at the sparks
still flying between them after all these years…*

*Keep reading for a sneak peek at
Accidental Amnesia,
part of The Saving Kelby Creek Series,
from Tyler Anne Snell.*

Five years of memories didn't compare an ounce to the man
they'd been made about. Not when he seemingly materialized
out of midair, wrapped in a uniform that fit nicely, topped
with a cowboy hat his daddy had given him and carrying
some emotions behind clear blue eyes.

Eyes that, once they found Mel during her attempt to flee
the hospital, never strayed.

Not that she'd expected anything but full attention when
Sterling Costner found out she was back in town.

Though, silly ol' Mel had been hoping that she'd have more
time before she had this face-to-face.

Because, as much as she was hoping no one else would
catch wind of her arrival, she knew the gossip mill around
town was probably already aflame.

"I'm glad this wasn't destroyed," Mel said lamely once
she slid into the passenger seat, picking up her suitcase in the
process. She placed it on her lap.

She remembered leaving her apartment with it, but not
what she'd packed inside. At least now she could change out
of her hospital gown.

Sterling slid into his truck like a knife through butter.

The man could make anything look good.

"I didn't see your car, but Deputy Rossi said it looked like someone hit your back end," he said once the door was shut. "Whoever hit you probably got spooked and took off. We're looking for them, though, so don't worry."

Mel's stomach moved a little at that last part.

"Don't worry" in Sterling's voice used to be the soundtrack to her life. A comforting repetition that felt like it could fix everything.

She played with the zipper on her suitcase.

"I guess I'll deal with the technical stuff tomorrow. Not sure what my insurance is going to say about the whole situation. I suppose it depends on how many cases of amnesia they get."

Sterling shrugged. He was such a big man that even the most subtle movements drew attention.

"I'm sure you'll do fine with them," he said.

She decided talking about her past was as bad as talking about theirs, so she looked out the window and tried to pretend for a moment that nothing had changed.

That she hadn't married Rider Partridge.

That she hadn't waited so long to divorce him.

That she hadn't fallen in love with Sterling.

That she hadn't—

Mel sat up straighter.

She glanced at Sterling and found him already looking at her.

She smiled.

It wasn't returned.

Don't miss
Accidental Amnesia *by Tyler Anne Snell,*
available May 2022 wherever
Harlequin Intrigue books and ebooks are sold.

Harlequin.com